THE FIRST MORTAL ORDER

This is a work of fiction. Any slights of people, places, or organizations are unintentional.

First printing 2019

ISBN 978-1-7323457-2-0

THE FIRST

MORTAL ORDER

Robert Duke

Dedicated to Nancy

Mentor and friend

Contents

Issue 1
Duel of the Champions

"You're following too closely."

"No, I am not. He cannot see us."

"You are. He may not be alone, and whoever might be with him would definitely see you are following him."

Bahadur chose to ignore the last comment made by that voice in his head. It was right, as always; but all the same, he was certain that their target had no allies in tow.

The man he was following rushed through the crowds of pedestrians peppering the sidewalks of Naqadah in such a way that anyone could tell he was in a hurry, but not to such a degree that he drew any more than a passing glance. Still, even a glance was more than Bahadur was willing to allow for himself and his companion, and so he stayed some distance back; always with eyes forward, but moving at a much more passive pace.

Ahead, the robed man ducked to the right, turning down a lesser road of the Egyptian city.

It took a few moments for the tailing duo to reach the same corner and make the same turn, but with fewer passers-by here, it was easy to reacquire visual contact with the cultist.

T

"Surely we are getting close, now." he said idly to the voice in his head.

"*I suspect so. Even in this day and age I can recognize some features.*" he replied. "*We are nearing the Nile; there is not much more land to scuttle upon.*"

Bahadur did not waver in his pursuit, nor did he accelerate it. He remained vigilant; the only sign of his loosening patience was his tightened grip on the ankh in his hand.

Without losing focus, he thought back on that day that he discovered the ankh. Alone out there in the desert, half-buried in the sand, yet surrounded by footsteps, as though it had only just been dropped. As though fate had willed it into his grasp.

The ankh stung. At first, he thought, from the heat. It appeared metal, after all. Some pleasant shade of green resembling decayed copper, adorned with small stripes of gold. Actual gold. The artifact would have been priceless to a museum, but it was even more valuable than they might have imagined.

As his eyes were still fixated on the scrambling cultist, his reminiscing did nothing to distract him from seeing the target's last move. With back pressed against the door in some attempt to check for having been followed—and quite a poor attempt at that—Bahadur's target knocked and, after a moment, was granted passage into the building.

It was not unlike any other building in Naqadah. The city on the west bank of the Nile, although small, was afforded some luxury by proximity, being only an hour's drive from Luxor and the Luxor International Airport. And, as with many cities in Egypt, the tourism industry could not be ignored—Naqadah was famously close to the Theban Necropolis, one of the most famed archaeological sites in the country. However, presumably to not

2

attract unwanted attention, this building in particular boasted no signs of interest in anything, at all. It was barren and plain, and fairly undecorated even for a structure in a city so historic.

It was only natural that the Sect of the Golden Scepter should call this their sanctum, if indeed they had one.

"*My body will lie inside of there.*" the voice said. "*Tread lightly, Ramses. This façade is unlikely to prevail once we enter.*"

"I will be strong, Osiris." Bahadur replied.

Although the spirit dwelling in Bahadur Al-Malik's heart had no form of its own, their shared consciousness projected to the God's Champion a vision of nodding appreciation, like a father quietly saying goodbye to his son.

Bahadur—gifted the title of Ramses by his patron—lifted his arm and held the ankh parallel to the door, some two feet back.

His will passed through his heart and soul, and that in turn passed through the spirit of Osiris and back to the ankh. The interior of the loop shimmered with a green aura as the ancient magic of the Egyptian God gathered.

Once the oval began to shine with that same aura, the door itself glowed a bright green, and then vanished. Banished from the mortal plane.

Ramses stepped inside, treading carefully as promised.

Their mark was gone, but there was only one other door in the furnished, uninhabited room. Bahadur didn't dwell on this too much—they had what they needed from the fleeing cultist.

Recognizing that every step of the descent that surely followed was likely to be guarded, the duo silently agreed to proceed with limited magic, so as not to waste the limited strength of Osiris' already crippled spirit.

Bahadur was to blame for that, though. As they opened the door and continued down the somewhat-concealed stairs, he could only think about what a disappointment he had been.

From the beginning, his mission was clear. Osiris' body, hacked into pieces by his brother Set and hidden with care by his wife Isis, needed to be restored. Once the pieces were brought together, there would be peace in the world.

But many millennia had passed, and the pieces of Osiris were long scattered—plundered and sold through countless ages. At first, the pair found them with relative ease. But before long, it became clear that others sought the divine remains. They would arrive at the supposed last location, or prepare to steal one from a private collector, only to discover they were far too late.

However, Bahadur had improved, some. While he had so far retrieved only four of the unknowable number of mummified body parts, he was getting faster. Several times now, he had met their opponents in the act.

The Sect of the Golden Scepter. Worshippers of the God Set, now apparently intent on reuniting the pieces for some unknown benefit himself. They had greater numbers and greater knowledge. But Ramses had Osiris.

Now, after tailing a particularly inept cultist back to Egypt, right under their noses, Bahadur was intent on reclaiming the lost pieces. Who was to say how many the Sect had stolen away? Perhaps everything they needed would be in this unsuspecting building in Naqadah.

They were far below the building now, though. After a few flights, the stairs became a maze, and the maze became catacombs. A buried tomb—a barracks for the Sect, and a vault for the treasures. This close to the Nile, such a complex would have been difficult and dangerous to construct even now. But the walls were old. The ancient cults of Set of prehistoric Egypt built these tunnels on faith alone.

Bahadur and Osiris carried on through the echoing chambers, their path lit only by the dim glow of dying workshop lanterns strung haphazardly along.

Carefully proceeding through the halls, the pair finally stumbled into a small living area. Some bedspreads were laid out in the corners of the room, illuminated by large lights propped up in the center of the sandstone-brick floor. A few wooden stools and benches were huddled around the light, and upon them sat two more cultists.

Ramses crouched and prepared to engage, but they were apparently talking to each other in urgency.

"Something was tripped upstairs!" one shouted quietly.

"Did that guy look like he was in a hurry to you?" the other asked.

"Gods, it must be the Champion! He's disguised!" realized the first. "After him!"

The two Sect members ran down another adjoining hall, oblivious to Ramses' presence only a few feet away. As he stepped fully into the room, Bahadur heard the faint echo of one of the men pursuing what he presumed was his former tail. "Usurper!"

"*That was close.*" Osiris whispered in his Champion's mind.

"Pretty impressive that we managed to follow the same guy down all this way without realizing it." Bahadur credited.

"*That would imply we are approaching our goal.*"

Ramses nodded. "Down this way then?" he said, pointing the ankh vaguely in the direction of another hall.

"*I presume it's better than the alternative.*"

Again, the Champion's feet carried the partners further into the labyrinth of Set.

The halls of the Sect's hideaway were exceptionally less popular than Bahadur had expected. After losing sight of their tail, his two associates were the only people the intruding pair had seen. There were plenty of signs of a larger collective in the tunnels—bed rolls, pans and cups stored neatly in personalized wooden crates—but there was no indication that anyone was currently here.

After turning around a few too many times, Osiris and his Champion came upon a much larger chamber than any other they had passed through. The floor sloped up about twelve feet into the room, becoming a raised platform that leveled out just above Ramses' head. Upon the platform rested an altar, and against the back wall behind it, a cabinet of large wooden drawers; no doubt containing the pieces of Osiris that Set's minions had so far collected. Although the arrangement gave no indication as to their plans for the mummified remains, the atmosphere was indefensibly evil in Bahadur's eyes.

Also in the room, sitting behind the altar on the platform, was a heavily robed man. His black gown was adorned with gold-and-turquoise strings and beads and scarves, and he wore a seemingly heavy black-leather tippet, which hung around his neck and fell to just below his waist. It was clearly ceremonial, and the sheer faith and willpower to bear wearing such restrictive clothing was intimidating. At his side, rising from the ground, a golden scepter stood in his grasp.

The man rose from his seat and stared down at Bahadur with eyes of divine accusation. The man, this High Priest, was not Egyptian. His complexion—though obscured some by the poor lighting of the distant work lamps hung along the side walls of the chamber—was much darker, and his build called more to a central African ancestry. What had called him *here*—to serve as what Bahadur imagined was the highest position in the Sect of the Golden Scepter and answer to another peoples' long-forgotten God—was concealed behind his violent, reserved stare.

"So this is the new Ramses we have heard so little about," he said. His voice echoed lightly off the stone walls of the large room. He spoke English, curiously, rather than Arabic as his lesser cultists had further up the maze. Even with less experience in the language, though, Bahadur thought he heard an accent to confirm his suspicion of a central African origin. "And the ankh that I have heard so *much* about."

"Servant of Set, I have come to reclaim the stolen pieces of Osiris. Your God may hoard them no longer." Ramses declared proudly. Fortunately, while his conversational English was unpracticed, the use of a more formal voice served to make him seem more confident and stern against the Sect's leader.

"Osiris has whispered lies and half-truths in your ear, Al-Malik." Bahadur's surname stung his skin in the damp underground air, but the cultist continued without notice. "What do you think he plans to do once his body is restored? He was a vain fool. Set does humanity a favor by keeping him apart."

7

"*Do not turn to his rehearsed ploys, Ramses.*" Osiris pressed. Within his mind, Bahadur understood the God's voice as compassionate and relaxed, and he therefore knew his words were true.

"Surrender your pieces of Osiris, or I will take them from you, cultist!" he bellowed.

"That's High Priest Sen, to you. Surrender *your* pieces, or Osiris will reward your piety with an early death."

Bahadur readied his ankh between Sen and his outstretched arm, holding it perpendicular to the ground. With his will and his God's divinity, the circle began to glow green with power; a nonverbal declaration that he would hold firm.

"So be it." The High Priest tapped his scepter on the stone floor with intent, seemingly to no effect.

Shortly, though, the purpose became clear. A hideous display of shadows, like some cloud of sickly darkness, writhed and pussed as it descended from the pitch-black ceiling, unlit by the lamps on the wall below. It popped with disgusting, salivating horror, latching onto and dripping from itself as it surrounded and engulfed High Priest Sen.

Just as quickly as it had fallen, a stream of the smoke reached out from the vaguely cylindrical mass, and from that shapeless pillar the whole cocoon climbed back into the ceiling, once again revealing the leader of the Sect.

His dark skin was now greyed, as though it somehow had become lighter by whatever process he had just undergone. No more did his eyes stare accusingly at the heroic pair; instead, his gaze was cold and black and void. Blood streaked down from the corners of his mouth, and ran down his cheeks like tears from his eyes. Whatever humanity Sen once had was now forfeit to his God.

His voice was now pained, but still he was able to bark, "Let us see how the power of Set fairs against the Champion of Osiris!"

The now-hunched figure pointed the head of his scepter down at Ramses. With a small contortion of his face and an obvious strain of the muscles under his robes, a stream of energy instantly shot from the end, piercing the air. The room flashed white with the light of the beam, but the laser itself was impossibly dark—a shadowy black line that radiated nonetheless, as though to stare at and mock Bahadur's concept of physics.

The attack moved quickly—imperceptibly to Bahadur's human eyes. But, with the ankh in hand, Osiris willed its magic to flow, and Ramses was teleported only a few inches shy of the darklight. It burned the air around it, warming his cheek as it passed, and cooling it just as quickly.

The energy shot collided with the stone floor. The carved brick erupted, shattering about to leave only a small crater of dirt and debris, barely larger than the strange blast. As Ramses looked back, he noted that the material was not singed like one would expect. There was no residue at all left behind. Whatever power Sen wielded was purely destruction, and nothing more.

The High Priest wound his arm back in preparation for another attack.

Bahadur lifted his own weapon in defense. He forced his faith into and through the ankh, back to his patron, and once more out of the holy conduit. The ring began to glow a vibrant green as the magic took hold, before expanding outward with divine brilliance.

h

A barrier was now summoned between Ramses and his attacker—a small barricade, coated in a green aura which began to fade away, along with the power in the ankh. Although Osiris was not physically there, Bahadur felt a twinge in his own mind and body, as though the God were cringing with the difficulty of such a hasty expression of his limited power.

Sen's darklight attack hit the small metal wall, apparently incapable of any sort of arcing or turning after being fired. Set's power was limited too, it seemed. However, the fortification was only metal, and bowed easily to the energy blast. Hot red teeth scarred what remained of Ramses' defense, and he began to move across the room, strafing about in anticipation of the High Priest's next move.

From the golden scepter extended another shot of glowing darkness. Sparing his God's vitality some, Bahadur ducked low, letting his chin meet the floor to avoid the attack.

However, he did not let himself fall defenseless. Again, he gripped hard the handle of his ankh, and expressed from the divine tool a new summon.

Bahadur let his eyes rise from the ground, resting upon a scaly, clawed foot a few inches from his face. The green aura began to fade from it as he pressed his hands against the floor and came to his feet, allowing him to see the whole creature.

A long blue body arched and wound from the ground where Bahadur stood and up onto the raised platform. Its hide, like a shining sapphire armor, glittered in the light of the work lamps that now swung with the excitement of the battle. The monster's long snout reached up and stood against the confident—yet humbled—form of High Priest Sen.

The ancient crocodile snarled at the Champion of Set. His legs shook with weakness, and he took a step back to maintain his balance, but he stood firm regardless on his elevated stage.

"Osiris' powers are limited only by his connection to this world, Sen. I may only have a fraction of his body, but with the rest of it so close, we have some additional strength here. What does Set gift to you?"

The grey man glanced down at Ramses, his impossibly black eyes still somehow filled with anger, but at the same time, knowing. "My life in exchange for yours!" he shouted through gritted teeth and pained breath.

The High Priest raised his scepter against the beast, letting off another stream of destruction. The monster hissed in pain and anger, swiping its ineffective front legs about in a feeble attempt to claim vengeance.

However, its power lied in its jaw, and that no longer existed. Sen's attack had obliterated the monster's face. It slunk and fell to the floor of the chamber accompanied by countless clinks as its sparkling blue scales hit the stone bricks. The crocodile's pink blood began to stain the room, along with the stink of its death.

"*Ramses,*" Osiris began. Even in Bahadur's mind, the God's voice was harsh and strained. "*I do not have many summons like that left.*"

Sen lifted his scepter once more, bringing it down to release another blast upon Ramses. "Stay your concerns, Osiris. Our prize is just within reach." he assured the God, rolling out of the way of the black beam.

11

Bahadur stood again, eyeing the High Priest through the loop of his ankh. Sen, too, looked down at the Champion of Osiris, his scepter outstretched. They remained there for a moment, both collecting themselves; both threatening the first attack.

The cultist broke the silence. Through the loop, Ramses saw only a black circle emerge from the end of Sen's scepter, expanding as it approached. It would reach him in less than a second.

Bahadur prayed. He willed his faith and loyalty into the ankh one last time. He prayed that he was fast enough, and that Osiris' strength would endure well enough to allow one final, simple spell.

A green film shone inside the ring.

The ball of darkness grew larger.

The whole ankh began to glow.

The burst of energy drew nearer.

A green hole opened in the world, between the ankh and the oncoming stream.

The darklight boiled the air around Bahadur's fingers. Then, Sen's attack vanished, falling into the hole Ramses and Osiris had opened for it.

The High Priest stood stunned, his body tensed in wait for a shaking explosion that did not come.

Instead, a new hole opened, up on the raised platform. From it rushed that same attack, continuing its dark barrel towards a new target. It sliced through the air directly for High Priest Sen.

The greyed cultist did not even have time to turn and acknowledge the assault before it slammed into him. A flash of green energy as both portals closed blinded Ramses to the carnage he expected would come of a human body succumbing to such destruction. He raised his arms to shield his eyes from both.

A silence came over the room. Bahadur began to lower his visual defenses.

"*Ramses!*" Osiris cried out in his head.

He felt a slight burn against his hand, as though he had moved it just barely too close to an open flame that it might not hurt him, but that he would feel and fear its fury. His fingers loosened around the ankh, which shot out of his hand; he did not drop it—it was pulled from his grasp by another force.

Bahadur looked up just in time to see another blast of shadows extend from the still-standing form of Sen and his scepter. A force shot Ramses backward, and he coughed a small spatter of blood as his back collided with the stone wall of the room.

The High Priest leapt down from his perch at last, striding across the room to stand over the collapsing shape of the Champion. He slid down the wall pitifully, but his eyes remained in such a helpless stare that he could see Sen raise his scepter one final time against his abdomen.

"Now taste the power of the true King of Gods, blind fool." the cultist hissed, gripping the golden scepter.

Another flash of white light. Bahadur's back was pressed again into the stone wall, and his eyes closed with expectation. But, after a moment, he still felt intact. He was not blown to pieces, and he still felt the God dwelling in his mind.

13

He opened his eyes.

High Priest Sen was pinned against the opposite wall, at the base of the raised platform. He had been pushed, and slid across the floor by another force. For directly above Ramses, between where he lay and Sen had just been standing, hovered a shining white man.

At first glance, that is. It looked like a man, and it looked white. As his eyes refocused, Bahadur was able to get a better look at the figure. It floated there idly, as if the act of flight required no physical strain or mental focus. It had the silhouette of a man without clothes—though lacking any signs of gender outside of general build. Ramses wasn't convinced it was a man, though. Largely, because it was not opaque.

The being appeared to be comprised of a white or pale translucent light, with small specks of black light dancing unsupported within its frame, not unlike the energy released from Sen's scepter. It had no other physical traits; no hair, clothes, or even surface features, with the exception of its face.

Although it faced away from him, towards the cultist, Ramses could make out that its eyes, mouth, and nose were also made up of the black light which was contained within it, rather than the same sterile hue of the rest of its body. There were no pupils or lips. Only the light.

"Sen, leader of the Sect of the Golden Scepter." it spoke. To Bahadur's ear, its voice was not unlike Osiris'. It was pleasant and perfect, and he could understand its Arabic without flaw. Like Osiris, this being radiated divinity, and that resounded even in its voice.

Sen understood the being too. He got up, spitting with some difficulty, though apparently unable to discharge any debris from

14

his mouth. "Yes, I am the Champion of Set, servant to the King of Gods. Why do you intrude on our duel?" he replied in English, confusing Ramses even further.

"I am Stargaze." the glowing being began.

"I do not remember this God of Egypt." Ramses whispered to Osiris inside his head.

"*That is because it is not.*" Osiris declared. Even without a physical face, his words in Bahadur's mind sounded as though they escaped only through gritted teeth and a furrowed brow.

Stargaze continued. "I am the incarnation and protector of the laws of space. Your scepter—"

The brilliant entity twisted its hand in some telekinetic gesture, only vaguely in the direction of the golden scepter lying on the floor some distance from Sen. It rose into the air gently, before floating over to the white being and into its open palm, which closed around its rod.

"—generates an energy meant only for higher beings. An impossible feat for a mortal, and restricted by my existence."

If Stargaze's grip strengthened around the object, it did not show. Small fractures glowed all across the golden scepter, lighting the room up further with streams of light before it shattered into dust.

A laughter echoed in the stone chamber. Sen's face, already a greyed perversion of the original, twisted in haunting delight.

"The scepter does what? I'm sorry, the scepter does nothing. Set gave *me* these powers." He stood taller now, his confidence returning as he became more accustomed to the burden of his God's blessing. "Any conduit will suffice, any tool or weapon can express the strength of the King of Gods through me."

Stargaze paused for a moment, though to Bahadur's eyes, it was not out of great thought, but out of a knowing superiority. "Your malignant intentions with this power have been weighed, and your consequence for defying the laws of space is your immediate erasure."

With this, the being's arms began to glow a somehow-even-brighter white, as it prepared to cast out this action that apparently required such focus and charge.

However, despite its divinity, Stargaze was too slow. From his seat on the floor, Bahadur could only stare as the cloud of black puss and smoke once again descended from the ceiling, consuming High Priest Sen. The chamber was silent as the mass bounded out of the room, with Sen in tow, up through and out of the catacombs.

Stargaze's arms relaxed their shine, and Bahadur expected that it would go after Sen, despite the protection of his God. Instead, however, it backed up some distance to allow him to stand, and idly twirled its fingers. He was weightless for a few short moments, and was drawn to his feet to face the entity.

Although it floated a few feet off the ground, Bahadur could now tell that if it were standing on equal footing, it would easily dwarf him by a significant margin. Somehow, despite its limited facial features, he could sense Stargaze was not looking down on him; it saw him as he saw it. There was wonder in its cold eyes.

"Bahadur Al-Malik." it said. "Do not be fooled by my timely arrival. I intervened because Sen broke my laws, but I have been watching you closely for some time."

"Are you going to help me and Osiris? Is this the end of my quest?" Ramses asked eagerly. Perhaps the Sect of the Golden Scepter *did* have all of the rest of the God's body, and this Stargaze was here to see him complete his mission and save the world.

"Osiris? No. I have not come to help you. I am here because, I hope, you will help me."

"Help you?" Bahadur was confused. He sought inside his mind for some guidance from Osiris, but although he was still present, the God would not be heard. "With what?"

Stargaze outstretched its arm, letting its open palm rest in invitation just below the level of Bahadur's chin. "Come with me. My brothers and I have a proposition, a request of you. I beg for your aid in this hour."

This was escalating quickly. Bahadur didn't know this being, and while Osiris did, his opinions of it were unclear at best. He had nearly defeated the Sect, and more importantly, the final pieces of Osiris were *right there*.

"Wait, one moment please." he said.

Stargaze only nodded, as though in understanding of what Ramses was looking to do.

He stepped across the floor to retrieve his ankh, then climbed up the narrow steps and onto the raised platform, approaching the wooden cabinets with earnest. His fingers looped into the handle of the first one, and he slowly pulled it open.

Inside lied several small clumps of linen—ancient and dirty. Smaller pieces of Osiris' disassembled body, mummified and wrapped millennia ago. He held the ankh up and prayed for his patron's power.

e

The ring glowed green, and the same aura surrounded the small pieces, before they vanished. Sent back to join the rest in Osiris' final resting place.

The second drawer contained several ancient urns, some with chips and broken lids, but all safely intact. He used the ankh to send these, too, with the rest. This spell became easier now with more pieces back where they belonged, for Osiris' power to align with and flow through.

Drawer after drawer revealed larger parts of the God, all mummified and safe. With each piece sent away, Ramses felt the magic of his ankh grow stronger and easier to control.

Finally, he collected all of the pieces from the Sect's vault. From his memory, many were still missing and would need to be reclaimed, but this would be easier now with the forces of Set crippled and afraid.

Bahadur turned back to Stargaze, still hovering in the same place and facing the Champion with palm opened up. He walked down the steps to meet the glowing entity, and set his own fleshy hand on its light one.

Instantly, the two were pulled up and through the earth, phasing through stone and dirt and sand and concrete, until they reached the open afternoon air of Naqadah again. But it felt different now, from this perspective. It was cool and wispy, rather than dry and still. He and Stargaze passed through it all, up and up and into the sky and then even higher.

The mysterious entity carried Bahadur, and the spirit of Osiris, to whatever destination it seemed to so desperately need them. Ramses looked down one last time at the shrinking shape of Africa, and then at Earth, as they flew out into the expanse of space.

Issue 2
General Machinations

Marco hated the sea.

He didn't mind boats so much. He had been on river tours before, and a boat was really just a slower plane or helicopter, vehicles with which he had plenty of experience. Marco's main issue with the ocean was the thick, overpowering salty air.

It was so pervasive that he could smell it even over the protective helmet of the Shatterbug suit. His mirrored blue visor did nothing to guard against the briny sea air. The odor was so distracting; he worried for his ability to remain focused once he finally boarded the large vessel docked in the natural harbor on the southern end of Manhattan Island.

Although Marco Nieve and Snow Dynamics Enterprises had accomplished much in the past few months, and more than made up for the shortcomings of his early hero days, the young CEO never forgave himself for having to let a dangerous villain escape justice. Even with all that he had learned about the suit up-to-then, and all of the skills he had acquired as the hero Shatterbug, *she* had the upper hand that day—along with the good fortune of a far greater threat taking precedence.

Now, though, he would finally be able to make up for lost time and subdue the madwoman.

The mysterious woman known only by the moniker General Heinous had been hiding since her escape from the march on Snow Dynamics, but a few days ago, Marco's team of Operators—analysts and strategists trained to assist him both on and off the hero field—traced back the ownership of a rather large freight ship docked in the Port of New York and New Jersey. Somehow, the General was able to procure the craft with nothing more than the imagined name; one she claimed only served as a foil to the 'real villain' she aimed to outdo: Marco himself.

And so, Marco Nieve took flight on the *Hero 2* helicopter, intent on discovering her goals with the ship and putting a stop to them. Exactly why the General would need such a large freighter— and docked in the heart of the New York metropolitan area—was anyone's guess, but there was no doubt it had to do with her insane agenda: the conversion of humanity into cyborg slaves to her Artificial Superintelligence, Heinous.

He thought about all of these things and more—the mistakes he had made to end up here; what he might expect once he reached the deck; what he would say or do when he encountered his enemy here; whether the frustratingly powerful smell of the waterways below would lessen once onboard—as he clung to the hull of the ship. While it would be all-too-easy to board the vessel by way of the gangplank and fight his way to the General, alarming her could accelerate her scheme, and without knowing what precisely that was, it was a risk he was unwilling to make, even with the power of time travel.

At last, Marco's hand reached the guardrails at the top of the ship. He carefully peeked his head up to check for any guards—a task only slightly less revealing than simply fully coming aboard regardless due to the contrast of his blue helmet and suit with the grey metal of the boat and the smoggy background of the city. Satisfied that he would not be noticed, he grabbed hold of the railing and slid onto the deck, immediately taking additional cover behind one of the many large shipping containers stacked on the freighter.

"I'm onboard, Gary. Do you have visual— Oh, right." he said, catching himself on the realization that no one was listening.

While Marco had run plenty of operations without the watchful eye of Gary Thornton, it was still easy to forget when the Yorkshire accent was not whispering in his ear on behalf of the Operator team. Marco blamed the extenuating circumstances back west.

The intent *was* to have all resources focused on General Heinous, but while preparing the flight to New York, the Operators got word of the incident in Las Vegas.

The protection of marconium was at the forefront of Snow Dynamics Enterprises' mission. Reclaiming the stolen battery, and ensuring that Ms. Ramirez was safe, had to take priority. But, they could hardly let the General get away again.

No; instead Marco asked his friend and colleague to don the Shockdrop suit alone and take point on the situation. He felt bad waking Miguel up so late at night, but if nothing else, the Chief Operating Officer's safety needed to be assured. The Operators would be more helpful in that respect anyway; little good could come from their calculations and suggestions when their abilities were matched and far-overtaken by an unrivaled supercomputer.

Carefully turning the corners between the lines of shipping containers, Shatterbug sought out any sign of the masked villain's plans. The huge metal crates were stacked high and haphazardly— like a fortress of scrap, concealing something towards the ship's cabin at the stern. It wasn't quite a maze, but it wound about as though to convince one that they were wandering in circles.

In fact, once he'd recognized the same pole high up in the distance for the third time, he was sure he was getting nowhere. He hadn't backtracked, but there was some clever trick here, some illusion or artifice to keep him away from the true path.

He turned on his heel and began walking back the way he came along the route laid out for him between the metal units. His eyes watched carefully, seeking any inconsistency between one crate and the next.

At last, his gaze caught on a long yellow container. It was just barely out of line with the two blue ones on either side of it; one side was pushed in just a bit, and the other too far out. Only an inch, if even that. The pulled-out face was away from him on his first pass—it was easy to miss from that direction. If Marco didn't know any better, he'd think his opponent knew from where he would be travelling.

He pressed his hand to the edge, hoping that the container was only a façade or curtain, or that it was somehow impossibly light and could be pushed aside. Heinous' technologies were advanced, certainly, but surely they were at least as limited as the scope of science opened by the existence of marconium?

In fact, they were. As his hand reached the chipped paint on the well-salted metal, it passed through completely.

The container was a hologram.

He stepped through.

Marco was inside the crate. It was dark, as though the light of the sun were not passing through the false structure. His feet phased through the bottom, but there was no failure of the projection. They just overlapped. It was astounding.

He didn't get to be impressed for too long. Suddenly, the mirage was dropped. With a flicker and fade, like the old television his father had growing up, the hologram turned off. They *all* did.

Every crate on the deck had been imagined. All but the one he had first pressed his back up to upon boarding were projections. And their puppeteer was now revealed, standing before Shatterbug at the foot of the ship's bridge.

General Heinous had not changed her attire at all. Claiming to only *dress* the part of a villain out of some imagined superiority over Shatterbug, she took a menacing approach to costume design. There was no function to it—in fact, Marco was surprised it did not hamper the abilities of her mechanical implants and prosthetics. The long, sleeveless coat, which billowed behind her like a grey cape, should logically interfere with the rockets hidden in her metallic calves. One would expect the apparently-authentic officer's uniform to constrict her movement, especially of her arms, which would limit the capabilities of her forearm-loaded automatic weapons. And the camouflage cowl, like an expressionless mask beneath a red beret, would make it difficult to aim with any firearm, much less something so imprecise.

"I'm disappointed in your predictability, Mister Nieve." she said. No tone of amusement was detected beneath the cold, genderless, metallic sound of her artificial voice.

"You knew I was coming." he replied. More than that, she knew *how* he was coming, but Marco felt no need to embarrass himself any further by acknowledging that aloud.

"We accounted for the possibility. I certainly hoped you would see reason and let us get on with our work."

"We, us—yes, I get it, you have an imaginary friend in your ear. Save it, General."

"And where is *your* friend?" she said, apparently having not forgotten Shockdrop's advantage over her in their last encounter. If he didn't know she was incapable of it, Marco would think he sensed a hint of knowing in her tone.

"Waiting for the right moment." Marco lied.

"Ah. Well, let's get on with it, then." The General turned, and gestured to the machine Marco had noticed immediately once the holograms had fallen.

It was a large, glass sphere. Like a giant snow globe—it had a metal base with various monitors and keypads along the front, and was topped by another smaller piece of metal. Cables and tubes ran from the lower base into the bridge and wound all over the deck surrounding the machine. Inside the ball, a faint blue glow flickered slowly inside the glass frame.

"Behold, humanity's salvation: the Nanocon Incubator!" General Heinous announced.

"Nanotech? Very original." Marco mocked.

"This is far more sophisticated than simple nanotechnology, Mister Nieve, I assure you. And as you can see," She pressed a few keys on the nearest input screen, and the monitor changed to a series of numbers, counting down. Seventeen o' six; seventeen o' five; seventeen o' four. "It is nearly ready."

"Shattershock!" Marco shouted, unwilling to waste another second at the revelation of a countdown clock.

Recognizing the voice command in the domed, astronaut-like helmet, the armored suit whirred to life. A heat radiated around his chest—the marconium core activated, prompted by the vibrating machines concealed by the plates on his shins, his forearms, his shoulders; the unique marconium sample contained

24

in the cylindrical battery was forced to recreate its initial journey with new instructions. The visor flashed in Marco's eyes—then all at once, everything stopped.

He opened his eyes.

In the corners of his visor, two screens, like heads-up displays, showed the same scene before him. But one of them was five minutes in the past. The other was five minutes in the future.

Three copies of Shatterbug stood scattered across ten minutes of time.

He sprinted towards his opponent, keeping his head low and his forearm ahead of him. In the past and future, his duplicates did the same.

"You can't stop the future, Mister Nieve, no matter what delusions you have collected under your disguise." the General's voice mocked at its highest volume. She extended her own arm out to mirror Marco's.

As he predicted.

In the future, Shatterbug turned to the right, opposite Heinous' prepared defense. He let his left knee bend and crouch as his foot met the metal deck, and his torso followed it back and to the ground. Catching himself on his left arm, he wound his whole body up like a great lever, his toes lined up squarely with the General's side.

At the moment of contact, the Shatterbug in the future shouted, "Reconstitute!"

Again, the battery in the armor's chest cavity warmed with the excitation of all of the small machines and electronics embedded across the suit. However, rather than shattering time

F

again, the Marco in the past and present were pulled forward, back into the future.

The force of ten minutes of time being strung—and indeed, cinched—back together granted him the strength, in that fraction of a moment, to send General Heinous tumbling across the ship, past the console of her machine.

Marco hurried to the device, taking advantage of her need to regain footing. "How do you shut it off, Heinous?"

"It cannot be deactivated. This is no cartoon, Mister Nieve; there is no self-destruct button." Her almost-masculine, almost-human voice stung further with the sincerity of her words. She lifted her arm up and aimed a closed fist at Shatterbug.

Feeling the scope over him, he hesitated to react, recalling the last time he had tried to avoid her reflexes. "What does this thing do, anyway?" he begged, hoping to gain some advantage of knowledge.

"The Nanocon Incubator is just that: an incubator. A population of Nanocons—short for Nano Converters—is breeding. When the clock reaches zero, the population will be large enough to sustain itself without aid." The General kept her weapon trained to the hero. He looked up into the glass sphere of the Incubator, recognizing now that the blue glow he observed earlier was in fact hundreds of tiny blue lights.

This gave Marco some information. The Nanocons inside needed the Incubator, for now.

"Shattershock!" he shouted again.

General Heinous responded in perfect time, in all three times.

In the present, she let loose her barrage of bullets, firing on the hero. Marco rolled to the left in an attempt to dodge them.

In the past, the General was where she had been prior: behind him. In that time, too, she fired on Shatterbug.

"Future!" present Marco cried out, indicating to his future self the need to reconstitute there. He had forgotten that he would be facing away from his opponent in the past; there was no time to roll away from her onslaught then.

"On it; reconstitute!" the Shatterbug in the future commanded. All three Marcos were once again pulled forward in time and together again.

But General Heinous had anticipated this; Heinous, the ASI, had *comprehended* it.

She crouched beneath and beside the only Shatterbug in time, tripping him. Quickly, she leapt up from her mechanically-supported position, setting one foot on Marco's heaving chest as he recollected himself.

She pointed both of her closed fists—and the weapons concealed in her prosthetic forearms—down at the reflective dome of his helmet's visor. "You forget the efficacy of Heinous' vision, Mister Nieve."

Marco looked up at the Incubator. The clock read five fifty-two.

"Nano Converter..." Marco thought aloud, trailing slightly under the weight of the General's metal leg. "So, what, they convert humans into your little slaves, like at your rally?"

"You think too little of me, Mister Nieve. My genius combined with Heinous' perfection; I created intelligence, but together, we created new life.

"Nanocons are only the first step in the complex life cycle of a new, silicon life form. Once this first generation is grown, they will seek out their first hosts. They will convert the unused tissue and organic materials of humans into useable resources, recycling that waste and merging it with their own bodies to fabricate new, smaller Nanocon Incubators on the backs of their hosts. These Incubators will continue to generate Nanocons to repeat this cycle."

"Shattershock!" Marco declared in interruption, generating two new Shatterbugs adjacent him in time in an attempt to escape.

"Reconstitute!" the past Marco yelped immediately, only afterwards realizing his mistake. General Heinous, even five minutes in the past, was still standing over him, still pressing her heel into the glass window on his chest.

But he had bought some time. The countdown was back up to nine fifty-one.

The General continued, as though she had not begun her explanation in the future. "Once the population becomes large enough, they will automatically construct a Queen Nanocon—a new member of the species, who will reprogram the existing members of its hive. While the Incubators continue to extract the wasteful resources of their hosts, the Nanocons they generate will begin to convert the hosts *themselves* into the ideal template. They will become perfect embodiments of harmony between man and machine, all connected to Heinous' benevolent instruction, while the Nanocons continue to expand their reach and evolve new hosts."

Marco spat. "And they'll all be perfect little slave-cyborgs, like you. You're not just insane, General, you're pathetic."

General Heinous pressed her foot down harder into Marco's chest. The armor protected him from most wounds and some degree of impact, but pressure and injury were difficult to weigh against. "This is my masterstroke, Mister Nieve: the salvation of humanity through symbiosis!"

"You're not saving anything! And I won't let you pretend that you are!" Marco paused, preparing himself.

"*Paradox ambush!*" Shatterbug shouted the newly added voice command, demanding the suit hear him.

The marconium core between him and the General's foot burned with an unprecedented fury. He feared his bones might rattle and snap from the intense quaking of the devices under the plates all across his body. The light inside his helmet was blazing—blinding. While he had performed this action before, it was the first time he had done so using the instruction programmed specifically for it. The Shatterbug suit could barely contain the temporal energy, much less the electrical.

After the suit had settled, Marco's visor confirmed that the order had worked as intended.

Displayed inside his visor, ten monitors shown on either side of his field of vision.

Ten Shatterbugs were spread out and around General Heinous five minutes in the past, and ten more did the same five minutes in the future. A united front.

"Impossible." the General muttered as low as her artificial voice could hum. "The power required for this... You should be ripped apart."

"This feel ripped apart, Heinous?" one of the Marcos in the past teased, as a group of them pulled the General off of their partner beneath her.

In all three times, General Heinous clicked her heels and ascended, the heat of her calf-embedded thrusters itching the skin beneath the Shatterbugs' suits, but otherwise not harming them.

"Even this many of you scattered through time are no match for Heinous, Mister Nieve." She readied her firearms, pointing down at the herd of heroes beneath her.

Marco ran. Not away from his foe, but towards her prize. In the past, one of the Shatterbugs leapt up at the glass bubble of the Nanocon Incubator, his fist extended and ready to collide.

Impact.

"Reconstitute!"

With the force of ten minutes of time, folding back in on themselves ten times, twenty-one Shatterbugs became one, and their united strength met with the fragile orb of the machine.

The glass shattered.

The blue lights fluttered about, scurrying through the air in random directions. To Marco's eye, they were confused, unsure of themselves.

General Heinous landed some distance away. Marco stood between her and her broken machine, as the Nanocons scattered in the briny New York air.

"Thirteen minutes to spare. That's thirteen minutes early that your Nanocons were born. They won't survive. Your plan failed."

She did not immediately respond, but after a moment declared with a tone that Marco almost mistook for amusement. "Won't survive? What ever gave you that impression?"

"You did." Marco said, puzzled. "You said the population wasn't large enough to sustain itself until the countdown reached zero!"

"I did say that, yes. Why would I tell the truth, though?"

"You— Oh no. Oh, *Dios mio...*" he whimpered, the pieces coming together.

"The Nanocons were fully developed hours ago. But, if I had released them, even in secret, you could have simply gone back in time to undo my success. As you demonstrated today, even Heinous cannot account for all of your advantages as a time traveler.

"However, we hypothesized that if you could be tricked into releasing the Nanocons *yourself,* using your time travel power as the force to do so, that the event would become a paradox—out of your control. If we are correct, you are unable to prevent this from happening, now. The Nanocons will begin to convert our species into their next form, no matter what you do."

Marco slowly approached General Heinous and gripped her by the collar of her uniform, to no protestations from her. He held his fist back in threat.

"Shut them down." Shatterbug ordered.

"There is no central system for the Nanocons. They are independent life forms, even from Heinous. Only their final stage, the cyborg evolution of their host, has any connection to it, and they will still be better off than they were should anything happen to it. So kill me if you must, Mister Nieve. Admit to yourself that

31

you are the villain I know you to be, and suffer a villain's cursed life of failure."

Tears welled in Marco's eyes as the realization quickly sank in. He *had* failed. He played right into Heinous' hands. He was grateful in that moment that his helmet was mirrored, but he suspected that the General could still tell he was near his breaking point.

He did not have to suffer that despair for long.

Instantly, a force threw Marco back, sprawling him against the wreckage of the Nanocon Incubator.

He composed himself quickly, returning to his feet in preparation for a counteroffensive. Then, he saw the cause of the force.

"Timegaze?"

A glowing, translucent humanoid floated where he and General Heinous had been standing, hovering idly as though the act of flight required no effort or strain. It was identical to the cosmic being called Timegaze—small white lights, like stars, danced unsupported within its frame; it had no signs of gender outside of general build; it wore no physical features, except for its face, which was only made up of two eyes, a mouth, and a nose, all only shapes of the same white light inside of the entity. However, this alien, this superior force, was green.

"General Heinous." the strange new, and yet familiar, cosmic being began. Its voice, like Timegaze's, was perfect, in some carnal way. English, to Marco's ears, but he recognized it to be only his idea of English, as a concept of superiority.

The General had also recollected herself, and stood to face the shining figure. "A new sidekick, Mister Nieve?" she asked through the translucent body of the entity.

"I am Biogaze. I am the incarnation and protector of the laws of life."

The glowing green alien raised its right arm slowly, easing the General's temper with its left in a universal gesture of calming. With its right hand at the level of its eyes, Biogaze snapped its fingers.

A thousand tiny pops rang in the air around Marco. Small sparks, like the briefest glow of a firefly, seemed to pierce his vision in a few places low to the dark metal deck where they could be seen.

"The mass, unconsented mechanization of a species is disruptive to the stability of the laws of reality, and imbalances forces you have not accounted for, just as the introduction of a new, parasitic species does. Even having created this new life form, its existence cannot be allowed.

"However, the nobility of your intentions has been weighed, and there will be no further consequence against you. Rather, you must consider all life as you continue your—"

Biogaze was given no time to finish its lecture before General Heinous clicked her heels once again, jettisoning herself off the side of the ship. Marco ran to the railing as she dove down through the air, and a splash told him that she had escaped into the water.

"Visor off." Shatterbug said. The suit responded by splitting the glass visor into four pieces, sliding them back into the base of the helmet before that, too, folded into itself. When it was finished, the Shatterbug helmet became a collar around his neck, still hooked into the rest of the suit. He clicked his tongue in his mouth as the salt permeated his senses once again.

He turned to the cosmic being.

"You... How dare you! How dare you let her go after what she tried to do, after I spent so much work to bring her to justice!" He screamed at Biogaze, his face contorting in anger and confusion.

"Your human laws are not my concern. She has been judged by greater accords."

"That's not for you to dec—"

"Yes, it is." Biogaze decreed, its arms and face glowing more passionately for a moment, cutting the human off.

Marco backed up some, allowing himself to settle and relax himself. He didn't like to be angry. Even under the stresses of being Shatterbug, up to now he had managed to contain his outbursts and focus them into his heroic intentions. He hadn't felt emotions like these—and had no immediate outlet for them— since before he moved to college.

He felt the hovering presence of Biogaze still over him. "Sorry."

"Do not apologize, Marco Nieve. I intervened in a matter of both of our jurisdictions. I had no malicious intent against you, and I recognize that you do not see all that I do; the grand scheme of things.

"Indeed, while I did arrive with immediacy to undo General Heinous' crime, she was not the only reason I am here."

Marco looked up at the incarnation of life. He didn't know what to ask, and so hoped his eyes expressed his confusion appropriately.

"Myself, Timegaze, and our brothers have experienced an epiphany. We would speak with you, to request your help, and offer a proposition."

Biogaze extended its hand down in invitation, palm up.

Marco was hesitant. "And if I refuse?"

"It is in your best interest to hear us out, if only that." it replied.

Still unsure, he thought to himself. From his experience with Timegaze, and what he just witnessed with Biogaze and the General, this was not how they tended to handle criminals of reality. If they were inviting him to speak to them, it implied some level of respect for his opinion, his expertise. And, from beings so great, there was likely no expectation of reward. Accepting such an offer would be a true test of a hero.

Of course, this was all glancing over the new information: Timegaze was not the only cosmic being. Marco had suspected that being the incarnation of the laws of time, there was likely a similar entity for the laws of physics. But, Biogaze's existence as the laws of life, and its mention of brothers *on top* of Timegaze, implied a fourth entity as well. The laws of death? Surely that would be encompassed by life? Then again, the laws of physics would naturally have some overlap with time, as well.

But all of this was speculation. If he wanted answers to these mysteries of the universe, he only needed to take Biogaze's hand. There was only one other thing on Marco's mind.

"I'll need Miguel, too. Miguel Jimenez."

"Shockdrop is already being acquired."

If they were already reaching out to his partner, too, then what could the cosmic beings possibly want? Now more than ever, Marco needed to know.

He set his hand in the green-lit palm of the entity hovering before him.

Immediately, the two were rushed into the air. The salty scent finally escaped Marco's nostrils as they were pulled into the sky. He looked down, admiring the bustling city filling up as much of the available space of Manhattan Island, and the shores surrounding it with all of their cities, before they rose too far to make it out. Higher and higher, Biogaze pulled Shatterbug into the upper atmosphere, and then into space, towards whatever meeting destination had been chosen to accommodate four cosmic beings and two heroes of Earth.

Issue 3
Cosmic Petition

Marco wasn't sure where the higher being had taken him.

He stood in some vast expanse, some spatial chasm. The radiance of it was offset by its indescribable emptiness, creating an effect that was both enchanting and haunting.

He stood—apparently on nothing, to his eyes, although his feet would disagree—before four figures, just as expected. The one that had brought him here, Biogaze, hovered—or perhaps it too stood on an invisible ground—in the middle of the council. To its left was another entity, identical in every way, except it was purple. On the opposite end was the familiar blue glow of Timegaze, and between it and Biogaze, the final member of their conclave, a being of white light.

His comprehension of how he had arrived here was fuzzy at best. He had been carried off of Earth and through space, certainly, but he was not in space, now. He was not in anything, but there was also nothing around him. Nothing but the four brilliant entities before him, and two other humans on his left.

Immediately beside Marco was a tan, bearded man. Middle Eastern, Marco believed, but he did not pretend to know the region well enough to place the man. He gripped tightly the object in his right hand—a gold cross with some off-green accents, and a loop at the top. He recognized it as an ankh, but the significance was lost to him. The man wore an unusual hat, like a small crown pretending not to be, and comfortable, if tight-fitting, black and gold garments, like ancient and light combat gear.

On the man's opposite shoulder from Marco was a woman. He could not see her quite as well, and did not want to look too hard for fear of offense, but her red-dyed hair stood out to him, as did the tear in her apparently well-worn dress. A shared glance between the two revealed her face, and he noticed a redness around her eyes, like she had been crying quite recently, before he turned away and back to the cosmic beings. This better vantage did reveal to him, however, a skin tone closer to Native American heritage, rather than his own Mexican like he had first thought from her arms in the warm, dark expanse.

There was silence in the undefined room. None of the three humans dared move, and the four entities did not see fit to enlighten them any further than they already had been.

Finally, the stillness was broken. A flash of red light shone in Marco's eyes, most strongly from his right. He closed and shielded them, then lowered his hand as the brightness subsided.

Standing to his right was a figure in an orange-and-purple armored suit. The mirrored visor was much like his own, though the bubble of the glass was interrupted by a 'V' shape at the top. Plates were scattered about the body in much the same way that they appeared on the Shatterbug suit, although in greater volume.

Shockdrop—Miguel Jimenez—had arrived.

Marco quietly and quickly hugged him, in a manner of greeting rather than concern, although his face would surely have betrayed that front.

"*¿Qué está pasando, Marco?*" Miguel said. "Visor off."

"I'm not sure; I think we're about to find out. How did you get—" Marco replied, interrupting himself as he answered his own question.

Now joining the four figures ahead of him, a red-glowing entity hovered at the opposite end from Timegaze, identical in every way to its brothers save for color.

"Marco Nieve." one of the beings declared, although it was unclear which one—both Timegaze and Biogaze sounded the same to his ears. "Miguel Jimenez."

"Bahadur Al-Malik." Again, Marco was unclear which figure had spoken, or even if a different one had begun at all. Either way, the man to his left flinched in apparent acknowledgement of his name.

"Lady Harrow." another voice—or the same voice—said.

"She prefers her given name, now." that same voice corrected.

"Ah, apologies. R'Bec."

The five cosmic beings glowed brighter now, coming closer to the four humans.

"We have summoned you here—requested your presence here—because in different ways, you have defended the laws of reality, whether you recognized this or not." It was now obvious to Marco that Biogaze said this, as the glowing silhouette of its mouth moved slightly, while those of the others stayed still. "You have proven to be heroes of Earth, and more."

"We are the incarnations of the laws of reality." Timegaze said. "Specifically, I am Timegaze, the laws of time."

"Stargaze, the laws of space." the white figure continued.

"Biogaze, the laws of life."

"Corpsegaze, the laws of death." said the purple entity.

"Willgaze, the laws of freedom." finished the red.

"It is by our existence that reality is able to exist, and by our form that it is protected from unraveling." Corpsegaze resumed the lecture, now. "However, we come to you now to request your aid in this endeavor."

"Some time ago," Timegaze took over. "A malignant force seized control of a small corner of reality. An insignificant portion in the grand scheme of things, but its effects were not. Marco Nieve, we speak primarily to you in this regard, as only you can remember the power Solace wielded, and what it did with it."

Indeed, Marco did remember. He had been burdened with the horrific sights of a timeline that never—and yet, always—happened, shielded from the healing of time by his existence as a paradox. The whole universe writhed and burned in the coils of that psychopath's clutches. But more than what he had seen, Marco was beset by the grief of what he had to do—or rather, still just as awful, what he had to allow—to save the world; the sacrifice of another.

"But Solace is gone." he said, solemnly. "What does this have to do with us?"

"Although the stress set upon reality by the fracturing of its laws has been resolved, we have discussed the situation at length." Stargaze began to answer. "Solace was able to succeed because, with great care and patience, it did not personally break any laws of reality until it became too powerful for us to stop. This, we have concluded, is not a testament to its power, but to the flaw of our existence."

Willgaze now spoke. "We cannot intervene until a law has been broken. We deal consequences and resolve the rupture in reality appropriately. Indeed, we cannot even see the intent to harm those laws under our influence until after the fact. This is what Solace exploited."

"We therefore come to you." Biogaze said, finally coming to the beings' point. "Mortals, unbound by inherent responsibility and grand design, who have defended your universe in greater ways than you know, without expectation. We humbly ask that you serve to protect and uphold the laws of reality, to the best of your ability, as the first line of defense. A First Mortal Order, to ensure that no other situation ever arises where we are unable to protect you."

"Deal."

Marco and the man and woman to his left—Bahadur and R'Bec—jolted their heads to the right in surprise.

Shockdrop was standing tall and proud, facing straightforward at the cosmic beings with pride.

"Miguel, hold on. Let's think about this." Marco said in a tone one might use to relax someone acting irrationally.

"What's there to think about? It's an easy enough request." He turned back to the council of glowing humanoids. "What exactly do you want us to do?"

Timegaze replied. "You have each encountered people who would see reality threatened—people who are willing and able to break our laws and damage existence itself—and more may yet reveal themselves in time. We only ask that you handle these mortals before they can cause any significant harm; before we would be called upon to stop them; before we are unable to intervene."

"See? Basically, what we're already doing. *Muy facil.* So, I'm on board." Miguel was now standing in front of Marco. He nodded his head towards the man called Bahadur. "This guy gets it, yeah?"

Bahadur hesitated, apparently lost in his own head for a moment. "Yes, I do understand. I see no reason not to carry out the wishes of these angels; the service of reality is all I act for, in one manner of speaking or another." His accent was thick, as Marco expected, but it wasn't Middle Eastern. He couldn't place it.

"I'm on board, too." The woman, R'Bec, spoke up. "It'll be good to have something real worth fighting for. Plus, I have a pretty good idea who our first target should be."

Marco sighed.

It was not that he had any real issues with helping the cosmic beings. It was true; much of his work as Shatterbug had coincidentally been the same thing they asked of him now. But, that was largely due to Solace's influence on his life, and its hurtling of great threats at him specifically. To hunt down existential criminals and prevent them from crossing some vague line between what is and is not acceptable seemed arrogant at best.

He could find General Heinous again, sure. He knew she was a threat, as Biogaze stepped in. But after that? Defining the severity of a villain's crime—whether it violated the laws of reality or just the laws of man—and then judging them? That would surely be flying above his station.

42

But the others seemed so sure. He didn't know R'Bec or Bahadur, but they clearly had some idea—some assuredness—that what was being asked of them was not only right, but that they could carry it out. Perhaps they knew better than he the line mortals were not meant to cross. As a team, maybe they *could* be that first line of defense.

"Alright, I accept." Marco looked around at his three new teammates. The First Mortal Order. "We'll work together to keep reality safe."

"Then we are understood." Willgaze declared. "You all come from different places and different lives. We understand you have different goals and ideals, but for the moment, for you to decide as a unit how to proceed, we will return you to Marco Nieve's Snow Dynamics Enterprises. Stargaze."

The entity of white light began to glow more profoundly. Its arms became a somehow-brighter and more spectacular white. Its eyes flashed, and then Marco's vision was blinded.

Marco blinked.

Issue 4
First Order of Business

"Well that was fun. See ya."

Marco, Miguel, and Bahadur looked at each other.

"Uh, where do you think you're going, R'Bec?" Marco asked.

The woman turned back from the doorway of the Snow Dynamics Enterprises CEO office, a piercing glare aimed at Marco. "I'm gonna give you a pass this time because we just met, but you *do not* say my name."

"Alright fine, sorry. But really, why are you leaving?"

"Your friend said it himself; they asked us to do what we're already doing. Corpsegaze interrupted me from stopping a very bad dude and, apparently, a threat to the laws of death. I'm going after him."

"I think you missed the bit where they wanted us to work as a team, *lady.*" Miguel said with a crinkled nose.

"I don't need an entourage for this, boys, but thanks."

Marco paused and took a breath, ordering his words. "It doesn't matter whether you want help or not; we're a team, and we're going to work together. More to the point, who's to say that your guy is our first threat?"

"You have a better idea, bug boy?" she retorted, stepping back into the room.

"I was fighting General Heinous, and would have failed if Biogaze hadn't showed up when it did. She'll go back into hiding now, and when she shows herself again, it'll be too late." Marco said, solemnly owning up to his reckless planning. "But if we work together, we can find her and prevent her from getting anywhere with her next plan, and save humanity."

A twinkle flashed in R'Bec's eyes. "Sorry, but I don't care about humanity."

"Don't think you got a choice, *amiga*. Us humans gotta stick together." Miguel shot back.

"*Maybe* you do, but I'm not human." she replied coldly.

"What is that supposed to—" Marco started, before his shouting was interrupted by a much deeper voice.

"Whether you liked the terms or not, R'Bec, you agreed to them." The man called Bahadur was direct, his tone just as cold as the inhuman woman's."You are a part of this team, which means you are going to act like it, or you will answer to me, and to our patrons."

Marco, Miguel, and R'Bec all looked at the foreign man. Again, the accent was difficult to place, but Marco felt some respect—and some guilt—on hearing his commanding words. He sensed from the woman's face that she was in a similar frame of mind.

He looked at the woman with blazing eyes and a firm jaw. His hand was still wrapped around the strange ankh at his side; his grip was relaxed, but disciplined. "As Willgaze said, we all have our own agendas. Our personal goals may not be aligned, but they are

45

all united by our shared decision to protect reality. I am seeking out certain artifacts, on a path I follow against a group of dangerous people that these higher powers also see as a threat, but I am willing to set these things aside for a greater cause. Whatever you decide is what I will follow you in doing, but no matter that choice, we *will* do it together."

Marco turned back to R'Bec. "I'm sorry. Mister Al-Malik is right, we should discuss this civilly. But first, if we're going to be a team, we should know each other a little better.

"I'm Marco, and this is Miguel. We're the superheroes Shatterbug and Shockdrop. I got this suit from my future self, and I've been using its time travel powers to—well, I guess like Miguel said; I've been protecting reality, one way or another. Oh, and I own this company. We designed the Shockdrop suit to have a different skill set, but obviously it's based on the original model."

"And you were *both* fighting General Heinous, and still lost? That doesn't inspire confidence." R'Bec said, antagonizing them.

"Actually, I was in Las Vegas trying to get back one of Marco's stolen batteries." Miguel covered. "The General is a tricky woman; she's tough to beat for anyone, but I shoulda been there."

Marco smiled, but laid a hand on his friend's shoulder. "Thanks Miguel, but she is right. I did lose, and I need to make up for that. But, how did Vegas go, anyway?" he asked, noting R'Bec's shifting weight at this line of questioning.

"No good on the battery. Michelle's okay though."

"That's good. Anyway, uh, miss? Why don't you go next?"

The woman breathed a long sigh. "Fine. You can call me R'Bec—for now. I'm the one who tried to get back your stolen battery in Vegas."

Marco and Miguel blinked.

"I'm lost." declared the latter.

"Your marconium battery. It was stolen by a man named Jet Wicked and his army of... well, they aren't really zombies, but it's easier to call them that. He'd been terrorizing the city for a while, so I went after him. Of course, I didn't really know it was just one guy 'til I had a gun to his head. Then Corpsegaze showed up, and he got away." She bowed her head some, apparently out of frustration more than regret, concealing the curious purple choker around her neck.

"Well that's... something." Marco said after a moment.

"You fought an army of zombies all by yourself?" exclaimed Miguel.

"Yep." she said flatly.

Miguel waited a moment. "You gonna tell us how?"

"Nope." she answered, just as lamely.

"We'll get back to that, and to you." Marco interjected the tangent, recognizing it wasn't going to go anywhere productive right now. "What about you, Mister Al-Malik? You've been pretty quiet... mostly."

Bahadur turned his head away from the window he had been staring out of, returning his attention to the other three.

"You can call me Bahadur. I was a... Hm. I don't suppose all that matters anymore." He paused, breathing in deeply and apparently collecting his thoughts. "I am a servant of the Egyptian God Osiris. His spirit came to me, and lent me his power, bestowing on me the title of Ramses. He dwells inside of me and

47

guides me, and in return, I help him to find the pieces of his body, which have been scattered over millennia. Once his body is reunited, he will be resurrected to save the world, banishing his evil brother Set, and his darkness."

Marco's mind stuck on Bahadur's final word, but he shook these thoughts away.

"Egyptian Gods? Really?" R'Bec questioned.

"You think I am lying?"

"Or very confused."

"You didn't seem to have a problem believing the shining angels. Surely Corpsegaze offered you the same choice Stargaze did me?"

"They were in front of me. You're just talking out of your ass." she accused.

"Perhaps I should show you the power of a God, then?" the Egyptian threatened, wrapping his fingers more fiercely around his ankh.

"Hey, hey! Both of you chill!" Shockdrop ordered, holding his hands apart, his palms parallel to either party. To them, Marco assumed it looked like some easing display, but with the power of Miguel's suit, it also served as a threat to make the two behave.

R'Bec relaxed herself, and Bahadur closed his eyes, still clutching the ankh.

"I am sorry." he said with deference. "I should practice the patience I myself implored of *you.*"

"Yeah, you really should." R'Bec spat, before sighing. "But I'm sorry, too. I guess your thing is no crazier than mine, from a certain point of view."

"And what is your thing, exactly?" Marco asked.

The woman didn't get a chance to answer. The door opened abruptly, and a portly man wildly shot into the room. "Mister Nieve!" he gasped in his recognizable Yorkshire accent. "And Mister Jimenez? And who are—"

"Director Thornton, hello. These are some... new recruits, to assist me and Miguel."

"Oh, yes... hello. Sorry, I'm a little... out of breath. And confused... sorry, how did you get back here? When did you get back?" Gary Thornton was certainly very agitated by the nonsense of the situation, but he was handling it better than perhaps even Marco would have.

"Long story, Gary. Where's the fire?" Marco asked. While it would definitely be concerning to discover one's boss had suddenly materialized from the other side of the country along with three friends, he imagined Director Thornton wouldn't have personally run all the way up here if something else weren't on his mind. And for the head of the Operators, that something else was probably a matter for Shatterbug.

"Vince Tripoli—Furnace. He's in Wyoming, causing a huge disturbance. Catastrophic consequences." the Director said, speaking concisely as he struggled to fully regain his composure.

"On it. Have a chopper meet me on the roof ASAP. And give my guests whatever they need." Marco turned to R'Bec and Bahadur. "Stay here, this shouldn't take long. You have Miguel and

S

our whole team of Operators; why don't you get started on our next move for when I get back?"

"*¡No se preocupe!* Do your thing, Marco!" Miguel said for the rest of the silent team.

As Marco left the room, the door closed behind him. But, he thought he heard the quieted voice of R'Bec as he left. "Who said he was in charge?"

"I do." both Miguel and Bahadur answered, putting a tiny smile on the edge of Marco's mouth as he walked to the elevator and out of earshot.

"Visor on."

Issue 5
Imminent

Marco sometimes forgot just how big the western United States was. He had told his new colleagues that he wouldn't be long, forgetting that even in the *Hero 5* helicopter, it was a nearly six-hour flight from New Jackson, New Jackson to Jackson, Wyoming.

Snow Dynamics Enterprises had solved the main flaw of helicopter travel some time ago, outfitting lightweight bodies with marconium batteries, thereby removing the issue of accounting for the weight and range of fuel. However, as a fact of physics, travelling much faster than two-hundred-and-fifty knots created an issue with the rotors and their ability to lift. Even with advanced automatic or manual rotor control technologies, at a certain point the machine simply could not keep itself in the air and move forward any faster.

The trip to New York had been longer than this, but he was also able to rest during some of that time. It was the middle of the day, now, and there was far too much on his mind. Concern over what Mister Tripoli was doing at Yellowstone National Park aside, the union of this new First Mortal Order was not going along as well as Marco had expected.

What would the cosmic beings think of their bickering? How much of their responsibility would they shirk in trying to argue with each other moving forward? They were chosen for a reason, for a supposed shared ideal, but it seemed to Marco it would be difficult to overcome their inherent differences to do what was right.

The remote-operated helicopter began to descend. Its pilot—one of the Operators back at Snow Dynamics—must have seen that they were approaching the destination. However, looking out of the side, Marco didn't see anything resembling the famous natural wonder. The lake was nowhere in sight, although he did see some mountains to the left that he imagined must be the range to the south of the main Park.

The answers to his silent questions came through his helmet, as the voice of Gary Thornton joined him in the chopper.

"You're as far as we can take you, Mister Nieve. There's a lightshow coming from the geysers, and Furnace is using that to keep air traffic down and away." Marco carefully peered out of the side of the vehicle in an attempt to confirm the Director's words.

Marco could see a good distance, even as his eyes fell lower and lower with the chopper. The large lake was ahead of him, and a bit to the east—on the other side of the helicopter, explaining why he couldn't see it before. However, it was vast, the horizon only just meeting the north shore. He didn't see any sign of the red-hot energy flashes of Vince Tripoli.

"Local law enforcement has set up a command center at the Park's south entrance. We're bringing you down there; the superintendent is expecting you." Gary finished.

"Got it. Thanks, Gary. How is everyone on your end?"

"Mister Jimenez is keeping them company. Mister Al-Malik seems interested and respectful."

"And R'Bec?" Marco asked, sensing the Director was trying to end the discussion on a high note.

A pause.

"Not so much."

"Just keep them around. Maybe brief them more on General Heinous? I want to get started on our new assignment as soon as I get back; the more caught up they are, the better."

"Of course, sir. We'll continue to monitor your situation as well." Director Thornton said, still with a tone of unsure support.

The *Hero 5* chopper was nearly to the ground, now. Due to the forested area, there were not many good options to touch down at here. Presumably, whatever helicopters the National Park Service had available were stored at another location; this was just the public entrance. With the roads closed, though, there was plenty of space on the highway, just past the gates.

Director Thornton wasn't kidding; the picnic ground and surrounding area of the southern entrance had been transformed from a quiet rest stop into a populated command center. Police officers, park rangers, and military personnel were all accounted for, making a plan of action. Marco expected an uphill battle to convince the authorities of Vince's danger, but it appeared that the villain had taken care of that already.

Marco touched down without any resistance, and as the rotors of the unmanned vehicle slowed, he stepped out of the cabin and towards what appeared to be the central post. One of the men from this station walked to meet him halfway.

"Mister Nieve, your company called and told us to expect you." he said, extending a firm handshake, which Marco matched despite his gloved hands. "Thank you for making the trip."

"It's no problem; Furnace is my responsibility. What's the situation?" the hero replied professionally.

"I'll let the superintendent fill you in. She's just over here."

The man guided Marco over to the covered table he had come from. Various computers and communications devices were set up on the foldable card tables standing in the grass, protected from the dust and wind by a beige tent with screens on three sides. Inside, a few park rangers and a man in army attire scurried about; sometimes relaying quick messages to each other, always on some kind of device.

"Miss Waller?" his guide lightly spoke into the tent, attracting the attention of the short female park ranger inside. "He's here, ma'am."

The woman was about a head shorter than Marco, with long dark hair worn down neatly in a braid. Her eyes held a certain wisdom—one of many years' experience in the field—although she didn't look much older than forty, if that. Her smile was warm, but she did so only with her mouth; a polite formality given the context. Marco reached out to shake her hand, noting that this was the second Native American woman he had met today.

"Mister Nieve, we're grateful to have you." she said, taking his offered handshake. "Anne Waller. I'm the superintendent for the Yellowstone National Park."

"Good to meet you, Miss Waller. I hope I'm able to help out."

"From what I hear, I think it's safe to say I'm confident in your abilities, but I'll be honest; the situation is looking grim, and we're short on time. Please, come inside."

Waller turned to lead Marco into the command center and around the U-shape of the tables to the operation side of the assorted instruments.

Marco noticed a satellite map loaded on one of the laptop screens. "Is this real-time?" he asked, pointing to his query.

"Sadly no, just helping us keep track of what's around him. He's right here."

Her finger landed on a brown area of apparent rock, some ways north of Yellowstone Lake.

"That's a long way from here. Is that even part of the park?

"It is; Yellowstone is a lot bigger than just the geysers and pools around the lake. All of these mountains here," The superintendent gestured vaguely around the area on the western end of the map. "And even further up north; it's all on top of the Yellowstone Caldera."

"Got it, sorry." Marco said, a little guilty for his presumptions about a landmark he'd never visited. "So, what could he be doing up there?"

"We have no idea. There's nothing on that hill; it's just a resurgent dome. Right now, the main worry is what he might end up doing by accident."

"Is that a weak point for the supervolcano?" he asked, his knowledge of the area limited mostly just to the existence of the huge magma chamber beneath the park.

"Yes and no." she started. "A resurgent dome is where the extra pressure from the hotspot is released, making the land there rise. That one rose a lot back in the sixties, but in the last decade or so it's stayed more or less where it is, and actually falling some.

Meaning there's basically no threat of a natural eruption anytime soon.

"But with this Furnace's powers, we're worried that it might excite the gasses under the Caldera and trigger something. Maybe not a supereruption, but anything bigger than an earthquake could be catastrophic. Given the size of Yellowstone, even a standard eruption could cause lasting damage to the whole northwest, at *least*."

Marco had some understanding of Yellowstone, as anyone did, but to hear that such a hairpin trigger separated the region—even the continent—from disaster was enough to have his hair stand on end inside the Shatterbug armor.

"Alright, so what's the play?"

"We can't get close to him by air. A small team could take an off-road vehicle to the foot of the dome, but they'd have to hike the rest of the way up. It would be dangerous—hotspot or not, Furnace's powers are making the air up there very hot." Waller spun around to one of the other computers sitting on another part of the desk. "We've already got reports of smaller tress lighting up spontaneously right at the base, but we can't get our big emergency vehicles close enough to contain them without risking attack."

"Do you have someone willing to drive me to the hill?" Marco said, volunteering for the mission.

Waller's lips pursed. "No one's jumping at the idea, no."

The hero didn't blame her. He certainly wouldn't have opted into the excursion a year ago. The odds were slim, the arena was treacherous, and the timetable was untold. But, he'd faced worse. He would carry those encounters with him forever, but for the moment, they served to empower him. He could do this.

Besides, he'd fought Vince Tripoli before. With Null's help, sure, but he was handling the situation well enough. More than that, he'd fought *alongside* Furnace and the rest of his Disaster Pact. Marco had a rapport with the man; he could talk some sense into him.

"Alright, I'll drive myself up then. No team necessary. Does the truck or whatever have a GPS?"

The superintendent nodded.

"Good, I suck at directions." He turned his head to the side, as though someone else was standing beside Ms. Waller. "Gary, would you have a way to patch the Rangers into my comm's?"

The voice of Director Thornton once again joined him, crackling loudly out of the helmet, even when folded down. "I can do that, yes. Ms. Waller will need to turn her wifi on, and I'll need her phone number."

Marco turned to the woman, knowing that by inviting her in, he would have to reveal the truth of Shatterbug's power once he reached the summit. "Well, you heard him, ma'am. Let's save Yellowstone."

"Here's where you'll turn off the road, Marco." the new voice from his folded helmet prompted.

"But the river's right there." he replied. Although confused and concerned, he followed the instruction anyway, turning to the right and off the Grand Loop.

57

t

Anne Waller's guidance did not return until the front tires had already reached the calm waters. "It's not very high here, and the bottom of the truck is sealed. This the closest you're gonna get to the dome on the road, and there's no bridges nearby, anyway."

By the time she had finished the explanation, Marco was already on the opposite shore of the thin creek. He'd been driving for an hour, but now that he could see the dome's peak just above the tree line, he couldn't imagine it would take much longer.

He continued straight through the park, weaving around the trees that were just sparse enough to allow moderately easy passage. The white Rangers' vehicle was selected and optimized to get to hard-to-reach places all throughout Yellowstone, for rescue and maintenance. Even if there were no paved roads, the hero could tell that this route was followed often enough from the vague path leading up the gently inclining landscape.

Although he was traveling much slower than before, it was only ten minutes or so until he found the nose of the truck at the impossible slope of the Sour Creek Resurgence Dome.

It was bare and imposing. Very little plant life encroached upon the tower of rock, and absolutely no trees. What brush was present looked starved for nutrients, if it was even still alive. The area was definitely volcanic, though in a calm and haunting sort of way.

Except for the summit, of course. Indeed, Marco had noticed the lightshow before, but now he could hear it, and *feel* it. Furnace was letting loose burst after burst of his magmatic power, sending clouds of dust and shattered rock into the sky and lightly shaking the earth even at the foot of the hill. The air was warm—the Shatterbug suit's breathable design was only just sufficient enough as to keep the unnatural heat from becoming unbearable. Whether this temperature was from Vince's power, from the Caldera below, or the consequence of both working together was unclear. Either way, he had to stop it.

"Visor on."

"What was that?" asked the female voice now inside his helmet.

"Nothing, just a voice command." he replied apologetically.

He looked up at the coarse hill, set one foot on the small boulder in front of him, and began to climb.

The dome wasn't particularly steep. Indeed, Marco had climbed much harder courses in New Jackson. Shorter cliffs, of course, on hiking trails with his father years ago, but still more involved than this.

Most of the challenge here was the rocky surface that was prone to shifting. He didn't need to use his hands much at all, except to help carefully shuffle around a boulder too large to climb over, or catch himself falling forward when the ground beneath him inevitably slid down under his weight. It was a long and hard trek, but not a difficult one.

That is, except for the occasional rumbling of the mountain. Every once in a while, a flash at the top of Marco's vision told him that Mister Tripoli had let off a rather large blast of his fiery power, and the dome rattled in recoil. Pebbles bounced down on either side of him, and dirt gently crumbled away beneath his feet. He felt the urgency building with every footstep, and found himself tugging at the fine protective fiber of the Shatterbug suit as the heat intensified.

"Anne, Gary, I'm near the top. Do you have visual?" he said, awaiting confirmation before proceeding.

No response.

"Director Thornton, Ms. Waller, do you copy?" Marco asked, catching on a sudden lump in his throat.

If they heard him, they chose not to answer. However, he suspected that in truth, there was some interference with the communications. Was it Furnace's power? Or just the mountain? The Shatterbug suit's ability to transmit to Snow Dynamics and back had never been compromised by trivial obstacles, but volcanoes were strange phenomenon in their own right. Perhaps the magma chamber or some trick of magnetism was disrupting the marconium channels.

Whatever the case, he had to proceed. He continued his careful climb against the shaking of the dome.

Once he reached the top, he found his movement slowed and lethargic. The boiling air around him was limiting his movement, only made worse by the tight grip of the suit, which now found itself rubbing on his sweaty skin. Marco hoped this discomfort would not affect his ability to fight; in fact, he hoped he would not have to fight at all. Surely Vince would listen to him, after all they had been through?

Vince Tripoli, who had taken the name Furnace when he was 'reborn' with his volcanic abilities, stood towards the middle of the hill's summit. He didn't face away from Marco, but he was angled in such a way that he didn't notice the hero's head and hands peeking over the edge of the somewhat flat peak.

Marco ducked to the ground, resting his exhausted legs as he leaned his chest—being careful of the glass protecting the marconium core—against the dirt. He watched the former-villain's work with concern.

From his hands, Furnace unleashed two more streams of red-hot energy, like fire struggling to be contained in a perfectly focused beam. He angled the burst at the ground of the dome. Marco cringed on instinct.

There was no quake. The ground did not shake under Marco's body. He heard no pebbles roll and saw no dirt shift. As he opened his eyes, he saw no threat of danger on the peak. The earth was scorched at Mister Tripoli's feet, and some dust had been shot up into the air from the attack, but this one was not so strong that the dome was threatened.

Still, now seeing that Furnace was in fact aiming at the dome itself, rather than doing anything else that might trigger such shaking and volcanism by coincidence, Marco stood and prepared to face the man on the summit, his hands held in a deferring gesture.

"Vince," Marco started. "What is going on, *amigo*? What's all this?"

Tripoli turned, the heat around his hands relaxing—though this did nothing for the sweat on Marco's own hands inside the suit. "Shatterbug. What're you doing here?"

"I came to help, Vince. Are you in trouble?" Marco had been taking some lessons in conflict resolution lately, or perhaps more specifically, conflict avoidance. He was doubtful that Furnace was in any danger, but he needed to talk the superpowered man down however he could.

"No, I'm fine. You can go, I just have to do this." Tripoli answered flatly, reigniting his hands and preparing another attack on the dome.

"What is 'this?' You're getting people a little worried up here, Vince." Marco said with the sincerity of a friend.

"Quit calling me Vince!" Furnace shouted, holding back his outburst at the interruption. "I know why you're here. You wanna stop me, but this is what I'm *supposed* to do."

Marco stepped forward, still holding his hands out in any attempt to calm the man down. "Alright, it's okay. I don't want to fight you, Furnace. Just tell me what's going on."

Rather than answer, the man let out his fiery energy—not at the ground, but at Marco.

Shatterbug quickly ducked out of the way, though his movement was weak and weighed down, the armor chafing his sweat-covered arms and legs. The heat on the summit was growing, but the air singed around Tripoli's attack as it flew past Marco's huddled form.

He held out one hand against his opponent with open palm, the other balancing himself on the coarse rock. "Vince—Furnace, please!" he urged.

The man shot back with two more streams, boiling the air on either side of the hero.

"Leave me alone! I'm almost there, I've almost got it!"

Shatterbug stood high, rising to his feet slowly, but with purpose. "You're not going to erupt this volcano."

Furnace crossed his arms and arced them ahead, blasting a wave of blazing energy at the hero.

"Shattershock!" he shouted in response, commanding the suit to part him through time.

The fiery expansion closed in, threatening to slice through the Shatterbug in the present.

"Reconstitute!" demanded the hero standing in the past. The suit obliged, pulling his present and future selves through time and back into one.

Furnace turned, Shatterbug's arrival attracting his attention—five minutes ago, he was still firing his powers down at the ground.

"You!" he exclaimed in surprise. However, he gave no time for a discussion as he would have in the future. Another burst of fire reached out from his hands, the glow staying behind as more than just his palms began to shine with heat.

The hero shattershocked once again, and in the present, ducked out of the way.

In the past, Furnace again only just noticed Shatterbug's arrival, and began his assault.

Five minutes in the future, the battle continued with another stream of energy.

What advantage Marco had with his time-jumping was very nearly matched by Furnace's relentlessness. Even as he leapt out of the way of each attack in each time and reconstituted out of the line of fire of the villain's unavoidable waves, the inferno continued.

Shatterbug united himself in the future to dodge yet another flaming strike, but before he had even recovered his footing from the flash and force of the jump, Furnace was already charging his next bout.

As he ducked and rolled to escape the line of Tripoli's parallel shots—which exploded on impact with the ground where Shatterbug had once stood and to the right, leaving behind charred rock and burning brush—he caught a glimpse of Vince's growing fury.

The aura that surrounded his hands—the evidence of heat emanating from him, as though his skin was actually boiling—had climbed up his arms. If the air was not still so impossibly hot, and rising, Marco might have thought it was freezing outside from the steaming of Furnace's exposed flesh, and even from beneath his shirt sleeves.

The weather on the mountain was beginning to feel the effects, too. As the immensely warm air rose up from the summit of the resurgence dome, the cold air above fell. The wind was intensifying all around them, swirling and brushing, almost threatening to push Marco aside. But Vince Tripoli paid no mind—indeed, the twisting currents seemed to center on the villain. As his power and frustration grew, the battle would only become harder as Shatterbug struggled to maintain his footing.

Marco had been playing defensively since he reached the peak. He was given no time to fight back, being kept on the run by Furnace's ranged attacks. It was time to turn the tables.

"Shattershock!" he declared confidently as the villain launched two more blasts of fire. He ducked aside—the adrenaline granting him enough awareness to just slightly weave between both of the energy streams—and ran towards his raging opponent in all three times.

Five minutes in the past, Furnace unleashed a huge wave of fire. In the present, too, a great tsunami blazed out from the center of the hilltop arena.

In the future, however, Tripoli sent only two more bursts of his power against the hero.

With little time to react, the future Shatterbug reconstituted, rescuing his past selves from their approaching infernos just as the flames would have consumed them on his displays. He dove down and beneath Furnace's blasts in his own time before shattershocking again.

His momentum was inconvenient in the present, but in the past and future, Marco quickly leapt to his feet, only a few yards from the villain. He sprinted for it, dodging another blast in the past and two more in the future.

When Furnace let loose an enormous swell of incandescence in the present with a roar of finality, it was too late.

In the past, Marco shouted, "Reconstitute!"

His extended fist surged with the strength of ten minutes of time being folded back together as he followed through to Vince's chest, aiming to throw him back rather than totally incapacitate him.

But it didn't connect.

At the same moment, the same fraction of a moment that three Shatterbugs became one, Furnace's power grew once again. The heat from his body—still somehow greater than the increasing temperatures of the air around them—exploded in a puff of steam, carried away by the growing wind currents. The glow from his arms extended and expanded again, enveloping his torso now, too.

The heat was unbearable on Marco's balled fist. Even while the protective cloth and armor held firm, undamaged by the intense power consuming Furnace, Shatterbug found himself

M

repelled by it. He fell forward and then back, losing the momentum without a follow-through, and was carried even further by the escalating wind speeds.

His back hit the ground hard.

He coughed and spat inside the domed Shatterbug helmet, struggling to regain control of his motor functions despite the shock, feeling Vince's gaze on him.

Another blast of energy.

Marco rolled to the right.

A stream to his right and left.

Shatterbug flinched, feeling the singe against his shoulders as he stopped himself from moving on instinct.

He looked up as best he could. Furnace was still just a few feet away. He could try to fight back again.

"Shattershock!"

In the past and future, Marco got to his feet and darted for the villain. Again, in each, Furnace reacted with fire and fury. The air around his head began to glow with that same energy, and from his hair, steam began to rise. Both Shatterbugs struggled to maintain a straight course as the wind picked up even further.

They didn't bother to dodge, though. In the present, the hero had inched forward just enough that, with a resounding "Reconstitute," he could pick himself up by his hands and swing his extended feet against Furnace's legs, hoping to kick him with the force of time and knock him to the ground.

But again, Tripoli's power grew. His legs began to shine, completing his transformation. His whole body shone like a burning red star. Marco couldn't touch him.

He found himself shot to the side and back, rolling harshly against the rocky ground of the dome's summit.

When he finally stopped, he was face down on the ground.

Marco thought he felt blood on the edge of his mouth, but he couldn't be sure without folding the visor down, and that was a risk he was unwilling to take as the warm air continued to climb.

He stood up, shaking, undeterred by Furnace—who had ceased his attacks, apparently recognizing both the favor he had over Marco from this distance, and the hero's inability to land a hit anyway.

He couldn't think of a new strategy. None of his plans had worked, and no amount of planning was going to change the fact that he couldn't touch Furnace. Marco wished he had the ear of his Operators, but suspected even Director Thornton would find nothing to say of this.

"No, wait. Yes, he would." Marco said to himself, catching his thoughts in his head.

As the Director of Snow Dynamics' Operators, Gary was familiar with all of the Shatterbug suit's powers and voice commands, including those added after Marco inherited the title. And there was one relatively new one, inspired by the cosmic beings that now served as the hero's patrons, that might be just what he needed here.

Though it was more of a pained whisper than a confident command, Marco exclaimed as clearly as he could, "*Flicker!*"

If the marconium core warmed at the instruction, Shatterbug couldn't tell. The heat all around him was so intense now that he had grown numb to the battery's strength. However, from his visor, he could tell the function was working.

Rather than two small displays on the edges of his visor, showing both five minutes in the past and future from his duplicates' perspectives, his whole vision from inside the helmet was cut into thirds.

Each piece of the screen was flashing in and out on repeat. The middle screen lit up white, then both of the side screens. The right screen glowed, then the left and middle at once. From inside the suit, Shatterbug wouldn't have been able to comprehend what was happening, but having been involved in the function's inception, he understood mechanically what was being achieved.

The suit was continuously and automatically shattershocking and reconstituting, over and over again. Splitting apart and cinching back together, along with time itself. It was happening so impossibly fast that to Furnace, it wouldn't seem like anything was happening at all in any of the three affected times.

But, in practice, there was an enormous distinction between flickering and shattershocking.

In all three times, Marco made a run for Tripoli. Already exhausted from the fight and slowed by the growing heat, the hero found his endeavor made even more difficult by the strain of the suit's flickering on his body. He would not be able to hold this for long.

Furnace reacted to the assault in kind, releasing another two streams of burning power at Shatterbug in the past, present, and future.

In all three times, Marco gently jogged to the side, vaguely attempting to dodge the attacks but more or less unconcerned by them. One burst surged against his arm as he swiped by it.

He felt it, then he didn't. It burned, and then it didn't.

Based on the Operators' best understanding of Marco and Miguel's battle against Timegaze, the suit was flickering so fast, jumping in and out of time at such a degree, that Shatterbug was literally travelling in the spaces *between* seconds. He shattershocked into danger, then reconstituted out. He shattershocked out of the line of fire, then reconstituted back in. Over and over, so quickly that none of it mattered. He was shielded by time, and outside of it.

He continued his pained trot towards the villain. Again and again Furnace unleashed his fiery attacks, but Marco simply moved aside at his own pace, limiting his exposure in each time, but overall unaffected.

With a great bellow, Furnace let loose the largest wave he had yet unleashed. A sphere of fire expanded outward from him, engulfing and enflaming the whole summit.

But Shatterbug was unharmed. Untouched.

When the hero reached Vince Tripoli, who was panting just as much from exhaustion and frustration, Marco only had to tap him.

The constant and continued reconstituting of the Shatterbug suit was too much for Furnace's human body to take, even with the lightest touch. He fell over, and with him, the glow died down and the temperatures began to fall, his concentration broken.

The wind remained, still swirling from the quickly-changing climate atop of the resurgence dome. Shatterbug stood over Furnace, the blowing air threatening to knock his now-frail body over as well.

"Fade." Marco coughed quietly. The flashing inside the helmet ceased, and once again he was alone in time. He crouched down beside the battered Tripoli, in both camaraderie and pain. "Are you okay, Vince?"

Furnace grunted. He didn't look to have any burns to Marco' eyes. It would make sense that he would be protected from his own powers.

"Why were you trying to erupt Yellowstone, Vince? I thought you all agreed to give up on this 'Disaster Pact' thing?" the hero asked.

The villain coughed and spat to the side. "I wasn't." he growled.

"Visor off." Marco said quietly to himself, allowing his helmet to fold back into a collar between his neck and the suit. "You weren't, what? Weren't trying to blow up the place?"

"No, of course not." he replied, sitting up with a breathy sigh. "I couldn't if I tried. A magma chamber this size, it takes hundreds of years of pressure to explode. I wouldn't be able to do anything just heating up a hunk of rock that happens to be on top. I could destroy this hill and nothing would happen."

Marco was confused. "Then, what were you doing up here? What was the point of all this?"

"Isn't it obvious?" Vince smirked knowingly. "To get *you* away from Snow Dynamics."

Furnace pressed his hand to Shatterbug's chest and ignited. Marco was thrown back, unable to even attempt to hold himself up against the slight explosion from the villain's hand.

His head hit a rock. His vision began to blur, and as Vince Tripoli leaned over him, he could only think of the people at his company. The civilians, the deck workers, the scientists. He worried for them all.

And then he remembered. They were not alone. Not one, but three heroes waited there for whatever Furnace had planned. He smiled up—hoping his new teammates would protect his employees—before his vision went dark.

Issue 6
Fallout

"It's been hours, Miguel. I thought he said this would be quick?" the strange woman said, addressing the young man in his peculiar armor.

"Maybe time would go by faster if you didn't hate literally everything I tried to show you or talk to you about." he retorted half-heartedly.

After two hours of failing to engage with the woman called R'Bec on anything substantial or productive, Miguel gave up, and the three teammates resigned to lounging in the absent CEO's office, awaiting his return.

R'Bec looked up from her smart phone. "Navigation says it's a three hour flight to Wyoming. He should be super done by now and heading back."

Without averting his gaze from his own device, Miguel responded from the teal couch in the middle of the room. "He took a helicopter. They're slower than planes. Gary just texted me a few minutes ago to let me know Marco landed."

"So he hasn't even started yet!" she said, making her frustration plain.

This is what Bahadur had been enduring for nearly six hours, now. A few minutes of silence would pass before R'Bec challenged their current situation in some way or another, Miguel would shoot back with a snide but disinterested remark of his own, and the cycle would repeat.

But while his two associates bickered and played mindless games on their phones, Bahadur took this time to delve into his mind and communicate with Osiris, attempting to be as productive in his inaction as one could.

"Have any new pieces revealed themselves to you?" he asked the God in his head, careful not to move his lips too much. While he had nothing to hide from the two heroes he now swore allegiance with, Bahadur's relationship with Osiris was a personal one. He had been chosen.

"*None yet. Still, that means the Sect has not located them, either.*" Osiris answered in his almighty mental voice.

"What do you make of all of this?"

The God did not immediately respond. "*I need not have an opinion, or a say, in every aspect of your life, Ramses. So long as you are my Champion, and you serve me in what I ask, you may make decisions such as this on your own.*"

"So you disagree?"

At this, Osiris grew silent.

Their conversations had been tumultuous in the last few hours. Bahadur's patron did have opinions about this First Mortal Order, and about the strange light-beings that had called upon them. Whatever those thoughts were, those preconceptions, Osiris was choosing to keep them to himself.

Which he had every right to do. Bahadur understood that he was not meant to know all that a God might. Some things were

o

above him. But, it was frustrating to feel the silent judgment of Osiris and be told, in essence, that everything was fine when it was not.

"Is he done yet?" the woman again broke the silence in the bright corner office.

"I don't know, probably not. Gary will keep us informed." the other man replied.

"You mean keep *you* informed."

"Yeah, that."

"Will the two of you please learn to be cordial with each other? You are not alone in this fight *or* in this room." Bahadur said—losing his temper just enough to firmly interrupt the two heroes' spiteful jabs—before returning to his composed state, leaned back in the comfortable chair across the floor rug from Miguel.

Miguel sighed.

After a few moments, R'Bec once again opened her mouth. "Sorry, who died and made you God?"

Bahadur stood up, beginning to compose his retort, but was interrupted. Miguel jumped up, his phone still held against his face.

"They lost contact with Marco; I've gotta get to Operations. Stay here; don't kill each other; *adiós!*"

As the armor-clad hero rushed out of the room, leaving Bahadur and R'Bec standing against each other, the former took the opportunity to collect himself and back down from the fight before it began. He returned to his chair and to his thoughts.

R'Bec also took the hint and elected to lean back against the window, again.

"The incarnations do not appear to have considered how well their representatives would *be able* to work with one another." he said to Osiris in his mind.

Bahadur didn't expect him to respond, of course, but having someone to talk to in some way was useful, even if they only chose to listen.

After a few moments, he returned his attention to R'Bec once again. "Do you think we should join Miguel?"

"I'm not stopping you." she replied with disinterest.

He inhaled deeply, restraining himself. "I fail to see why you still refuse to act like a member of this team."

"Because right now, we aren't one. Marco and Miguel think they're the leaders—"

"This is their office." Bahadur interjected.

"—and won't even consider hearing us out. So until they start acting like we're actually a team, I'll keep being a bitch. Deal?"

Although it was spiteful, Bahadur did understand the woman's logic. It was reasonable to be irritated by a lack of common ground. Granted, there were better ways to handle such stress.

"Perhaps if we meet them halfway...?"

A beat skipped, then R'Bec abruptly slid her phone in her purse and gently kicked herself off from the floor-to-ceiling window. "Fine, let's go see what's up."

Bahadur stood up—with some difficulty, a little stunned that he had gotten through to her so quickly—and joined her. The two stepped out from the closed office door and into the larger office.

This was, presumably, the executive floor of Snow Dynamics. A few other similar offices lined the walls of the fairly-sized lobby area, each behind closed frosted-glass doors. From the colors that he could make out through the privacy of the glass, it appeared they all shared the same color scheme as Marco's.

A secretary sat at his desk facing the elevator, but turned at the sound of their exit from the CEO's office. He smiled politely, though his eyes gave away a puzzled expression.

"Excuse us," Bahadur began, seizing the young man's attention. "We were looking to join Miguel. Could you direct us to 'Operations?'"

"I'm sorry, Mister Al-Malik, but Mister Jimenez told me to ask that you stay in the office until he returns." he said with a polite unease.

"Actually," R'Bec stepped in, handing him a small piece of paper with scribbled handwriting on it. "He told us to give you this note if he wasn't back by now."

The secretary—Bahadur noted his desk plaque said Branden—looked over the sticky note carefully. Apparently satisfied, he set it on the edge of his desk. "It's on the twelfth floor. You can take the elevator—"

"Thanks, but we'll use the stairs." R'Bec said, concluding their conversation. Bahadur brought himself back from his surprise at her attitude, following closely behind. As he looked back, he noted the yellow paper that Miguel had supposedly left for them started to fade to a darker grey, just outside Branden's field of vision.

"When did he give you that note?" he asked.

"He didn't, I made it up."

"You forged his handwriting?"

"Didn't have to. And quit asking questions, it's not important." she said with finality.

They began to descend the stairwell to the right of the elevators. R'Bec travelled down much faster than him, even skipping the last step or two of each flight. Bahadur regretted letting the strange woman drag him to the stairs; while going down was certainly easier than walking up, twelve floors in either direction was an excessive waste of time and energy.

The two stepped onto the landing between the fifteenth and fourteenth floors. Before they could turn to make their way down to the platform on the fourteenth, a shaking stopped them in their tracks. Bahadur leaned himself against the wall for support, while R'Bec firmly gripped the guardrail in the middle of the stairwell, buckling her legs to hold her still.

"What was that?" he asked, knowing full well that the woman had no more information than him.

"Let's find out." she declared. The rumble was brief, and once they were sure it had subsided, R'Bec continued and made her way out the door and onto the fourteenth floor. Bahadur, taking a little more time to collect himself, followed behind. From a few feet back, he thought he saw a bit of dust brush off of her shoulder with her quick motion, but saw no point in mentioning it.

The door swung partially closed before Bahadur caught up. When he swung it open, R'Bec was wearing a completely different outfit.

Rather than the black dress with the slight tear that was far too formal for the environment, the woman now wore tight black jeans and a short leather jacket. Her purse was gone, too, as Bahadur noticed she was sliding her phone into her jacket pocket. Her dyed red hair was also now up in a ponytail. There was no time for her to have done all of this in the second-and-a-half that he'd lost eye contact with her.

"What— How did you— Where did your dress go?"

"Still wearing it. Quit gawking and come on!" she insisted, brushing off his questions and another small flick of dust from her neck.

The two made their way across the floor. The office workers were startled, but not entirely panicking, only just starting to investigate the source of the disturbance. Straight ahead, however, the cause was clear.

One of the windows had been cracked and shattered.

The warm smog-filled early-fall air of the New Jackson skyline meandered into the building as Bahadur followed R'Bec to the hole.

"This is the front of the building." R'Bec said.

"Surely just this would not have created such a shock?" Bahadur observed.

"No, it wouldn't have." The woman carefully poked her head out from the gap between the floor and ceiling, careful not to hit her legs or arms on the small pieces of glass still protruding

78

from the frame. Her head tilted back and up to see above them. "Oh."

With a grace and haste that still somehow kept her safely upright, R'Bec turned her body to angle her head down to the street below.

"Get back!" she commanded, leaping out from the broken window and crashing into Bahadur. The two fell and rolled off one another.

Bahadur didn't have time to cover his head as R'Bec did before another disturbance shocked Snow Dynamics, much closer this time.

When Bahadur looked up again, not only were several more windows completely smashed, the ceiling just above them had collapsed. No, from the edges of the missing material, it looked like whatever was there had been vaporized.

Now the various desk workers and other personnel began their hurried evacuation. No screams, just a buzz of gossip and concern as they made their way for the stairwell, careful not to trip over the forms of the two heroes, still on the floor.

R'Bec got up, offering her hand. Bahadur took the assistance, but it was quickly pulled away once his momentum got going.

"There's someone attacking from the ground. They hit higher up first—there's a huge hole in the floors right above us." she explained.

"We have to get down there!" he proclaimed.

"On it, come on!"

She ran for the destroyed windows, being careful again to limit her exposure to the glass peppering the carpeted floor. Showing no signs of slowing, she leapt from the window—eliciting a yelp from Bahadur.

Her feet landed on a strange glowing yellow platform that was not there before. She glanced back idly and shouted through the busy New Jackson air, "Let's go, hero!" before jumping once again to land on a new square stage a few feet below.

Bahadur looked down. They were still at least a hundred feet up, and he had no idea what these strange *illusions* were. Was this R'Bec's power?

"Osiris give me strength." he prayed aloud, gripping his ankh. Taking a step back to give himself a small running start, he emerged from the skyscraper and flew through the air, landing on R'Bec's mysterious step. "I hope your silence does not mean you are unwilling to help me."

R'Bec had descended another two platforms down, and as Bahadur made the next leap himself, the divine voice of his God returned to his head. "*You will always have my aid, Ramses. Let your will flow through me, and I will guide you.*"

Bahadur landed another jump, but as he prepared to take the next step, he found himself barred in.

"R'Bec, what is—"

As the floor gave out beneath him, he got his answer. He was in freefall.

For a moment. Almost immediately, his back hit hard against another solid object. The wind knocked out of him, he struggled to get to his feet, holding his weight up by his hands on the new yellow step.

"She's attacking us, Ramses! Watch your step, I can't react that perfectly every time!" R'Bec shouted up at him from three platforms below.

He looked down even further, down to the street. Now he could see the woman in white—although she was quite small, only standing out by the stark contrast of her clothes to the asphalt, and by her rooted position in the middle of the street as people scattered about all around her.

Although it was difficult to see from so high up, her arms seemed to move and shift, before a stream of white-hot energy erupted from her hands and up—directly at Ramses.

He pulled himself up by his hands and leapt horizontally—and haphazardly—for the next platform down. He landed on his shoulder, rolling slightly before catching himself on the edge.

Quickly looking up, Bahadur saw the attack blast directly through the step he had just been laying on. It exploded in a burst of dust, which faded into the air. The energy started to arc towards him in pursuit, but dissipated before it reached his new position.

"Keep going!" he faintly heard his teammate call from below.

He knew he would never make it down moving so reactively as he was. Bahadur gripped his ankh, and prepared to take action of his own.

The loop began to glow green as his thoughts translated from his mind, to Osiris, and back through the golden conduit. The aura expanded around his hand, and then up his arm, as he focused on his exact location—and where he wanted to be instead.

r

He felt the heat of another energy shot against the soles of his light shoes, and the sudden force of gravity acting on his now-unsupported frame. But only for a moment.

In a flash of his own power, he once again felt the ground beneath his feet. He had teleported himself to street level, some distance behind the light-emitting woman.

"How is your energy, Osiris?" he asked, ensuring such a great leap through space did not exhaust the God too much.

The perfect sound of his patron rang in his head. "*Well in hand. So many pieces of myself now united on Earth has greatly improved my spirit's vitality. Be cautious, but trust in me—you will win this fight.*"

While Ramses reveled in the relative comfort he had provided his patron, R'Bec completed her own journey down the glowing platforms and to the street, in front of the mysterious assailant.

"Neat trick." the stranger said.

"Back at you." R'Bec offered, glancing at Bahadur behind the woman. By her expressionless face, she was aiming to not give away his position.

"I don't think we've met." the woman between them said casually, before quickly drawing her hand up and launching a destructive burst of light directly at R'Bec.

Bahadur reactively stepped forward, but was too late. When the light faded, all that remained of R'Bec was the fading dust particles of her body. She'd been vaporized.

He started to march up behind the villain, fist clenched around the ankh—which already began to glow with power at his side. However, he caught himself when, miraculously, his partner reappeared, jumping down from the sky once again.

"Good try. And you're right, I don't think we have. Name's R'Bec." she announced, raising her hand up against her would-have-been killer. As Bahadur contemplated how she could have survived such an assault, he couldn't help but be distracted by the show playing out in her hand.

The dust and debris in the air collected and coagulated, materializing into a small, though comedically large-barreled firearm held squarely in her hand.

By the muscles on the back of the mysterious woman's neck, her face was contorted into a sneer. "Reactor, leader of the Disaster Pact."

"Cool. Now, I don't know what your problem is with Snow Dynamics, and frankly I don't care, but when you shoot at me and my friend, you cross a few lines." R'Bec declared proudly.

Reactor offered no rebuttal to this, instead raising her hand again to let off another stream of power at her foe.

"*Fight back, Ramses!*" Osiris' voice shouted in his head.

Stirred from his silent observation, he raised his own arm up, holding the ankh parallel to the villain. Time slowed as his adrenaline kicked in, and he watched the green aura of his God's power gather around the implement.

Between the two women, a gap in the world opened, held in the air by the same green energy under Ramses' command. Reactor's light poured into the portal, emerging from another directly above her and into the sky.

"What the—" she started.

R'Bec made quick use of her own tool, firing the gun with a spark and pop. Bahadur didn't see the bullet, but Reactor was thrown back, landing face-up on the asphalt only a few feet from him.

There were no holes in her stark white clothes, though; no blood staining her skin. She was put off, but uninjured.

"I don't understand." he proclaimed.

The woman reacted with a jolt of her neck up, letting her see Bahadur back and behind her. He'd given away his position.

Her arms followed suit, reaching up and unleashing another blast of white-hot light at him.

Suddenly, a huge wall of brick and mortar sprung up between them. It stood just below Ramses' eye level, and from this vantage, he could see that it was at least a foot thick. He peered over it to glance at R'Bec, who was staring intently at him—or at the wall, which he assumed was her doing.

It did little to slow Reactor's attack, though. Just as quickly as it appeared, it burst into black dust, letting her light continue through.

Fortunately, Bahadur had been preparing a defense of his own. The glow of his ankh collected in front of him, summoning a small but durable wall of stone.

Reactor's light struck the stone, easily destroying and crumbling it in a shining explosion; but unlike with R'Bec's barrier, the maneuver *did* halt its advance.

The villain rolled and returned to her feet, holding one arm against each of her opponents. R'Bec and Ramses returned the gesture, keeping their weapons trained on her.

"You are outnumbered, Reactor." he began. "Stand down and talk with us."

"Outnumbered versus outmatched, buddy. We're at an impasse." she spat back.

The click of R'Bec's pistol rang in the empty street. Reactor's hands glowed with excess as a stream of energy blasted from each on instinct.

Bahadur worked quickly. His will flowed once again through Osiris and back into the ankh, and he summoned yet another portal between R'Bec and Reactor.

The light passed through once again, this time emerging from a portal just in front of him. The two bursts of light clashed, and all three combatants lifted their hands to their ears at the caustic hissing of light scraping light.

In a fit, Reactor opted to focus on only one target, and so set both of her hands—which now had a permanent glow of energy, like solar flares arcing between her fingers and up her wrists— upon R'Bec. She fired.

The illusionist's weapon had vanished with no trace to Ramses' eye. Instead, she knelt on the dirty and debris-ridden road, keeping her silhouette small as she mounted a defense. Another barrier, this time a half-dome of metal, emerged from the dust in the air.

Reactor's light hit.

Whatever metal the wall appeared to be made of was fashioned in such a way that much of the energy was dispersed. However, the sheer heat and strength of Reactor's power must have been intense, as despite R'Bec's best efforts, her screams of pain rang between the skyscrapers. Her shrill and tortured screech pierced Bahadur's ears, as the apparent stress of holding up the illusion that likely ought to have broken instantaneously tore her apart.

"R'Bec!" he shouted in vain. His eyes darted to the villain, his brow furrowing with obligation. "By the power of Osiris!"

He held his ankh up once more, holding his target within the loop. The weapon began to glow, the shimmering green filling Ramses' vision. With a flash, his spell was cast.

Reactor let her attack fade, noticing her new surroundings. Encircling her now were three vicious, long-legged black hounds.

They wore wide, decorative golden collars, and their ears were adorned with rings and jewels. Their ankles were equipped with braces to improve their strength, and to add power to their sharpened claws. Their teeth were bared against the woman they were summoned to hunt.

Bahadur had time enough to see R'Bec's unscathed defense fall, her strength and awareness clearly fading. He started a dash around the arena-apparent, before Reactor began her battle against the dogs.

Light erupted from her hand, beaming towards one of them as it leapt at her with a snarl. It was repelled to the ground, but with a glint of its shining collar, a green aura grew around its body to protect it from injury.

"Servants of the Gods of Egypt, Reactor. You stand no chance." Bahadur declared proudly from the battle's perimeter, continuing to make his way around the rubble field and over to his partner.

She grumbled with annoyance, refocusing her energies to another of the hounds. She let off two streams of power at a single dog, which had begun to stalk around behind her, sending it sliding back and into a car. It hopped about some—its paws apparently agitated from the harsh contact with the street—but rejoined the fight nonetheless.

As Ramses reached R'Bec, crouching down to meet her on the ground, he glanced again at the villain. When she wasn't firing off energy shots at the dogs, her hands continued to glow—and now her arms did, too. Power surged up her muscles, bouncing about her skin and clothes in some dance of photons and fission.

"Are you okay, R'Bec?" he asked with urgency.

She moaned, holding her head. "I think so. I will be; just— Just help me up."

He raised the woman's arm up and around his neck, using his other hand to gently grip her side and pull her to her feet.

His eyes once again fell on Reactor's battle with the summoned hounds. She was firing off successive bursts of light, like a rail cannon of photonic energy. The dogs were taking the hits, shielded by the magic of their protective collars, but they couldn't get near her.

And it seemed that with every shot she let loose, the light surrounding her grew brighter and consumed more of her.

"We have to stop this, she's getting stronger." Bahadur said.

"She's already too powerful. She couldn't destroy my illusions before, but she did enough damage to hurt the bindings tied in my head. If I tried anything now, she'd blow my skull open." R'Bec huffed out through pained nods.

She was right. Osiris' magic was strong, but he could tell even now that the shimmering spells protecting the hounds were becoming less effective. Even if he tried to use a portal trick again, it would do little good but to buy time—assuming she didn't unleash a blast large enough to go around the hole he would summon.

"Osiris?"

"*Ready yourself. I have one final option.*" replied the God.

Ramses did as instructed, holding his ankh up against Reactor and her now-glowing shoulders. The loop began to shimmer with green, and her torso shone with power as though in defiance. While the defeated hounds faded away and back to where they had been pulled from, Osiris' aura flowed out from the golden tool.

She turned to face Bahadur and R'Bec, and even as her eyes lit up with fervor and her hair raised on end with the overpowering light of her flowing energy, Osiris let his magic flow through his Champion and the ankh, surrounding Reactor.

Her fists clenched. She crossed her arms, and with a sudden jolt, she released everything.

A huge ball of light exploded from her. She hovered in the middle of the street, holding her power there. She wielded complete mastery of whatever gift she had been given, and now Bahadur was feeling the effects.

R'Bec went limp first, and without the little support she provided, he too fell.

He tried desperately to push himself up by his hands, to get some kind of strength in his back and pull himself to his feet, if not nudge his partner awake. But to no avail. The pressure of the supercharged light exploding over and over from the villain was too much.

When her assault finally relented, it didn't make any difference. He looked up at the sky and past the smoke rising from Snow Dynamics Enterprises. Against the blue of the cloudless expanse, he caught sight of a tandem rotor helicopter taking off from the skyscraper's roof.

After that, he couldn't tell if things started getting dark because his vision was giving out, or if something else began to take up the sky and blot out the sun. Either way, his consciousness slipped, but not before one final remark of encouragement pierced his thoughts from on-high.

"*You have not failed me yet, my Champion.*"

Issue 7
Masterstroke

The attack hit fast and hard.

The explosions above, then practically on top of them, shook the room. Panels and monitors flickered. Director Thornton tried desperately to reach Marco with one final message, a last plea for help. But there was no way to get through.

Miguel could do little to protect Snow Dynamics from the attack; none of them could. From his brief glances, R'Bec and Al-Malik took to the ground, fighting off whatever was attacking the exterior of the building. But it had been a two-fronted assault.

Marching down from the roof, dozens of soldiers poured into the skyscraper, carried in by helicopter. With the Shockdrop suit, he did his best to fend them off, but he had to hold back, lest he accidentally hurt the innocent scientists and researchers. Fortunately, the masked figures meant no harm to them, either.

No, they just wanted the marconium. All of it.

Every last sample of marconium was gathered up from the company's headquarters, either by intimidation or by force. The drones in gold armors and red helmets worked systematically, showing aggression only briefly and when challenged, such as against Miguel.

It was a valiant effort, but without the freedom to belt out his shockwaves, it was easy for the organized unit to overtake him.

And so, he was left to lie on the ground of the Operator Room.

But the Shockdrop armor was hearty, and did well to protect him from concussion of any kind—it had to, or else its own power would rip it apart. He got up as soon as he had caught his breath, and noticing the emptiness of the building, darted for the roof.

Having arrived just in time, he took advantage of the mostly-cosmetic grips on his hands to hold on—clinging tightly, if uncomfortably, to the landing struts beneath the chopper. Slowly, he climbed into a panel on the side that opened into a small storage hold. It was tricky to pull himself into the dark, empty box without getting sucked out into the sky—or worse, into the rotors of the machine—but with considerable effort, he managed to get the door closed behind him. Then, he waited.

Now, it was clear they had landed. Although he didn't feel like they had descended much, the helicopter was definitely winding down. The metal began to creak as it cooled, and there were no voices or footsteps around. The coast was clear.

Once he got to his feet, Miguel was sure that he was still in the air. His steps were uneasy and his breathing was labored—by more than just the beating he was still recovering from. Although paneling and piping around the edges of the room indicated that the apparent hangar was sealed and pressurized, he was still quite high up; the body was bound to experience certain altitudinal effects.

The knowledge of his height, the hangar, and the attire of the small army that had delivered such a clean defeat to him all worked together to confirm what he already feared.

The Hellbent was back, and he had constructed a new, much larger airship.

Miguel wasn't surprised. Their last fight with the masked man was surprisingly easy, and left the villain devastated and empty-handed. But it was clear from his message and demeanor that he had no intention of putting aside whatever grudge he had against Marco Nieve, no matter the cost.

But, The Hellbent didn't know that his nemesis wasn't there. He was prepared to fight a time traveler, but he was going to get a marconium-powered pummeling.

The hero took to the narrow halls of the sky machine, keeping his head down as he peeked around corners. Every step was slow and deliberate, and he ensured the dial on his suit was turned all the way down. Any sudden shift could give away his position; Miguel wanted to face the villain head-on with full awareness, not a bunch of lackeys.

Additionally, he needed to find the stolen marconium. He knew that The Hellbent was somehow able to get hold of a small sample to power his personal super-suit, but with the huge quantity he now possessed, the odds were good that he was planning something on a much grander scale.

Metallic clanging up ahead told Miguel that someone was coming just around the next corner. From the irregular pattern, it sounded like at least two guards, but their steps did not sound urgent. They were on a standard patrol.

Looking around quickly, the hero found a bulkhead, which almost blended in too well with the sterile grey of the rest of the corridor.

He struggled to press against the latch bar slowly enough to not make a sound, while still working quickly to avoid detection. The gold-clad soldiers would turn the corner any second, and the slightest provocation would surely encourage them to investigate.

It swung open, the hinges well-greased and silent. Not willing to risk closing the door, he carefully set it back as far as it would go before latching, right up against the frame.

The footsteps continued, along with the muffled voices of their owners. Their words were obscured by their metal masks and the metal of the bulkhead, but when they stopped walking—and Shockdrop stopped breathing, concealing himself as much as he could in the corner of the room—he could make out one of the men clearly enough.

"Why can't people close these doors right?"

The sound of breath and vibration against a close metal surface rang uncomfortably. The other soldier was answering the rhetorical question, but Shockdrop couldn't make out his words.

Shortly, that low hum of reply stopped, and the first man's voice returned. "I guess so, but they really should close automatically even in that case. It's a safety hazard!"

More muffled speech, which Miguel took as an opportunity to lightly catch his breath, before silencing himself again as the first speaker shouted loudly in agreement.

"Exactly! All you'd need is like, those hydraulic arm things that pull doors closed at schools or something. Easy." The door shut, evidently pulled back into its frame by the minion. His words still carried through from right in front of the partition, just barely. "I'm gonna bring it up with him when we land."

The footsteps returned, quieting the other man's voice even further as the two continued on their way.

Confident that he was alone once more, Miguel breathed heavily and uncurled himself from the corner, taking in the room fully for the first time.

It looked to be some kind of small transportation annex. Several panels and boxes lined the walls, leading into a few pipes that ran up to the ceiling and along through the wall opposite where he had entered. The door of that wall had a small porthole, and from the light casting through it, it was clear that the open sky was on the other side.

Looking out the window, he saw a narrow bridge with heavy guardrails connecting the room he stood in now with three other doors, all outside. The catwalks met at an intersection about twenty feet ahead, and from this vantage, he could spy the blades of two huge propellers beneath them. Overhead, the tubes continued out of the room and across the gap, turning and separating to meet the walls of the other doors. Above those pipes, huge yellow balloons billowed, holding the flying machine steady in the air.

The system was hardly extensive, but even Miguel could recognize pneumatic tubing when he saw it. An archaic but efficient method of moving small objects or notes would be necessary on an airship as apparently vast as this.

And once he stepped closer to the machinery lining the wall, it was clear what small objects The Hellbent intended to move.

Canisters filled with marconium samples sat inside the tubes, waiting to be called or sent to other parts of the ship. A glance at the panels of the metal cabinet revealed a small window, and through it, Miguel saw that the whole system was powered by a marconium battery.

The entire airship was probably running on stolen marconium power. Was this the villain's plan? To power a huge flying machine?

He began to grab the samples from their containers, but stopped when he realized he had nothing to carry them with. Even if he did, the gold-armored soldiers collected *all* of the element of Snow Dynamics; far too much for him to carry alone. No, he needed to land the sky vessel. And that meant finding The Hellbent and seizing control.

He carefully opened the door to the outside. The rubber seal around the frame released with a pop of failing suction. Miguel's legs trembled at the weak but sudden pull of the air outside, but he buckled down to hold his place as he struggled to pull the door against the force of the sky. Although it was no heavier than the door he had entered from, the movement of the airship at such an altitude worked to help keep it ajar.

He held the door open as far as he could with one hand while gripping the frame with the other, his fingers and palm locked on the outside of the room to hold his balance. Wind rushed all around him, threatening to push him back and to the ground before trying to pull him out and into the thin air. Miguel carefully slid his foot across the threshold, wary of lifting it even slightly from the metal floor.

Inching further out the door—still held open with one hand—he quickly but hesitantly let his fingers crawl from the frame to the guardrail. He felt his torso jerk forward, but his legs held firm, and once he had a grip on the bar, he pushed back to right himself again.

Miguel began to slide his other foot along the floor now, crossing the threshold out on the bridge. The door was only slightly open now, his arm reaching as far as it could to keep from slamming into him and knocking him off. Once his whole body was clear, he tightened his hold around the railing and pulled his hand back from the door, moving it to the opposite guardrail.

The wind pulled unforgivingly, and he hit the metal bar a little harder than he wanted, but once the door fully closed on its own behind him, it was just Miguel, the bridge, and the open sky.

Shockdrop dared not look down, even without being afraid of heights, but he did let his eyes fall to his feet, as though watching them gently drift over the shaking metal of the catwalk would help him to keep his balance. One foot at a time, inch by inch, he moved towards the center of the open expanse. If his visor were off, he expected the exceptionally loud billowing of the propellers below would be deafening.

Step by painful step, he proceeded along the catwalk. To him, the time it was taking to reach the intersection of the four bridges was excruciating, and he hoped that no one would think to look out any of the portholes of the four doors while he made his decision as to which path to take back inside the airship.

His hands dragged along ahead of him, keeping him from being pushed or pulled one way or the other over the railing and into the turning of the machine. From the top edges of his vision, he saw that the bridge was wobbling and warping. Not violently, not even enough for his body to notice so long as he kept his hands on the supports. Still, the sight of it put the hero even more on edge.

Finally, his hands met a sharp corner on each rail. Shockdrop had reached the center of the gap.

He pulled his feet forward to right and align himself with his hands at the end of the first bridge. He tried to catch a glimpse of what lied beyond each of the other three doors, but it was too bright out in the open sky—even under the yellow air balloons— and too dark inside the pressurized rooms; the glass only reflected the orange tint of his visor and the purple trim of the helmet around it.

Then, the far door opened.

Miguel's heart stopped.

A man stepped out confidently. Not another of The Hellbent's minions in shining armor; this one wore tight fitting but decorated blue clothes, and his face was revealed, save for what looked to be a non-invasive oxygen mask over his mouth.

"Iceberg?" Shockdrop tried to ask, his throat hoarse in the thin air and the sound barely escaping from his helmet.

It wasn't totally clear from behind the mask, but the Operator files on the villains Shatterbug had so far faced were fleshed out enough that the figure's eyes and brow unmistakably belonged to the Disaster Pact member. A glance at the intruder's hands confirmed this; the air around his fingers was visibly colder, even at this height.

"Did you think there weren't cameras here, little man?" Iceberg taunted. He held his arm up, letting a stream of cool air release from his palm. The air crystallized as the front rushed forward at the hero.

97

Shockdrop responded quickly, if unsure in himself. He nudged the dial around the window on his chest up, and then clapped his hands together ahead of him.

At the collision, the air rippled outward. Shockdrop swiftly returned his hands to the guardrails, catching his balance just in time for the shockwave to disperse the freezing energy between the two combatants.

Of course, his hands met the railing abruptly, and with that impact, the whole bridge churned slightly. Iceberg gripped the poles himself as the catwalks shook and warped, accompanied by the harsh screeching of the stretched metal.

The unease died down, letting both fighters properly regain their footing over the spinning propellers.

"I don't get it; this is The Hellbent's ship, right?" Miguel said, not entirely expecting an answer.

"Of course it is, Jimenez." cracked a voice from overhead and all around. It came through clearly, though not without a faint overlay of static from the transmission.

Shockdrop suddenly had the inexplicable urge to turn his head so that it faced the door to his left, and through that porthole, he saw *him*.

Although he wore the same mask as his minions, Miguel was sure—somehow—that the man on the other side of that door was The Hellbent.

"Then what is this second-rate, reformed villain doing here, *perdedor?*" the hero asked.

The Hellbent didn't need to answer. Without fully realizing how or why, Shockdrop knew. The Disaster Pact was under his control. Just like Miguel was now.

"Then why don't you just kill me, huh?"

Iceberg's hands reached out again, meeting and uniting their respective power into one blast of cold. Again, the abundant water particles crystallized as the shot barreled towards Miguel.

He expected his arms to be locked, but in fact, The Hellbent was allowing him to move—allowing him to fight. He wanted them to actually fight. But why? Indeed, he knew that he could only understand as much as The Hellbent willed him to, but he had to ask anyway.

Shockdrop let his legs give out, falling backwards while his hands still gripped the guardrails. He slid on his heels beneath the blast, feeling a chill on his nose even through the helmet as the cold air expanded with the distance.

He let go of the railing, letting himself continue to slide as he turned onto his stomach. With one consistent motion, he slapped his left hand onto the metal floor of the catwalk—digging his wrist into it to reflect him backwards—and forced his right fist out and behind him.

The shockwave sent Miguel flying, and from the horrid creak of metal, the bridge convulsed under him as he soared through the air. He hoped that Iceberg would have to return both of his hands to the railing to hold himself still, leaving him defenseless to the shock-inducing punch flying towards him.

Impact.

The opposing forces of Miguel's momentum and the shockwave generated by his fist meeting Iceberg's jaw steadied him in the air, and he fell unceremoniously to the ground as the villain was pushed back into the closed door.

Through the orange tint of his visor, the hero could see the sparkling energy of Iceberg's power glow and grow up and around his arms.

The Hellbent understood, and therefore so did Miguel. Iceberg's power and volatility grew the longer he held up his energy. Eventually, it would be uncontrollable—he would be able to direct it, but not contain it. At the same time, it would certainly protect him, the crystals mitigating the efficacy of the suit's shockwaves.

Shockdrop was on a clock. And he would give neither villain any time to react.

Without even letting himself fully regain his balance on the long platform, Miguel turned the suit's dial up even further with one hand as he harshly clenched the other into a fist before him. The resulting clap of his fingers meeting his palm, coupled with the heightened sensitivity of the platelets from the tuning of the suit, let even this small motion release a powerful circular shockwave ripping through the air of the arena.

Iceberg was held against the door, only his arms able to flail somewhat against the forces acting on him. Shockdrop stepped closer, reaching his hand out for the villain's blue shirt.

With a roar, the Disaster Pact member unleashed his streams of ice out and to his sides, in the only directions he could manage. Despite the protective layers of the suit, Shockdrop's hand shivered as Iceberg's power expanded to his chest.

But it was too late. Miguel turned the dial up once again, and firmly pressed his open hand into the villain's sternum.

Despite the ice crystals, Iceberg's body was too close to the source, and the shockwave pinned him completely. He would surely give out, either from the stress of his power or from the pressure acting on him.

Still, the bridge was taking a toll, too, and as it shook and wiggled according to its design, Miguel's footing gave way. He fell hard, his hands clapping on the guardrails to try to catch himself.

But his dial was still turned up, and his fingers encircled the metal poles too fast. The impact was too much for the already chilled steel, and it snapped in his hands.

Miguel rolled to his right, having put too much emphasis on his right hand to pull him back to his feet. The churning of the catwalk hit his back again and again as he tried and failed to regain control, to catch himself on his elbow or knee.

But it was no use. In a flash, the yellow of the balloons became the blue of the sky, and then the grey and brown of the ground below. He was falling.

His breath caught in his throat, and he felt his whole body tug against the suit, one vying to follow gravity and the other fighting against it. He was still, his back pulled away from the meshed armor of the suit. Someone had grabbed him.

"Reconstitute!"

Another flash, and with it, he was hoisted back up onto the bridge. Through the purple hue, and the red of his own eyes, he saw the broken metal of the guardrail over his head. His back was stable, firmly on the unerring catwalk.

And then, kneeling over him, he saw his own helmet reflected back at him through a blue mirror.

"Marco." he let out through wheezes and coughs.

"Don't mention it, *hermano. No se preocupe.*" Shatterbug answered back.

The shining hero stood triumphantly. Miguel couldn't see Iceberg, or The Hellbent.

But then, he could feel him.

"They belong to me, Nieve," Miguel said. He wanted to say it, he knew that. But there was no reason for it. Marco looked down at the sudden callout. "And if you want me to release them, you will stand down."

"And if I don't, Hellbent?" the hero responded, looking away from Miguel and instead turning all around, trying to catch a glimpse of his unseen nemesis.

Iceberg spoke now, taking his turn to be the willbender's mouthpiece. "Then the next to die will not be a villain."

Miguel didn't see what happened next, but he could imagine. Shatterbug gripped the still-intact portion of the railing as he reached for something out of Shockdrop's sight, before clenching his fist in apparent vain.

Then, Miguel decided—or perhaps, it was decided for him—that he ought to close his eyes. And so he did, and he let the rest of the world fall away.

Issue 8
Price of Freedom

Waking up had been easy.

Walking down the mountain and driving back to the camp had been easy.

Even piloting the helicopter back to New Jackson and landing it on the roof of his company had been easy for Marco.

But seeing what befell Snow Dynamics Enterprises in his absence; that hit hard.

No one was hurt. That was already a relief. But not only was all of the marconium gone, his partners were missing. R'Bec, Ramses; even Miguel, his closest friend. They were nowhere to be found.

"What would the Disaster Pact want with marconium, and with them?" he asked the ruined Operator's room.

A shuffle and grunt behind him alerted the hero to Director Thornton's presence. "It was The Hellbent. He has an army."

Marco's face twisted in concern and confusion behind the blue visor. "That doesn't make sense. Furnace was clearly in on the plan—this wasn't some accident. It's too convenient."

But whatever the case, he needed a plan of his own. To recover the marconium if he could, but more importantly, to save his friends of the First Mortal Order.

First, he needed to figure out where they were going. Without the Operator equipment, though, information was scarce. He'd have to find out first hand.

"Shattershock X minus three." Marco ordered the suit.

It whirred and buzzed and flashed once, then again, and one final time, creating a line of duplicate Shatterbugs stretching back two-and-a-half hours.

"Reconstitute."

With the firm, somber command, the suit collected itself back into one time, taking Marco back in time. Halfway there.

Once again, he gave the same two voice commands in quick succession, taking him back a total of just over five hours from where he started.

Alone again, Marco began his ascent back to the roof. The damage to the building was clearly done from the ground, but it certainly wasn't The Hellbent's style, nor would such an attack aid in stealing the marconium. No, The Hellbent had intruded upon Snow Dynamics once before, and if Marco was right, he would have done so in much the same way. From the sky.

Indeed, even after an hour had passed, he could see the unmistakable shape in the distance. It was curious and twisted, designed for function over fashion, and that made it stand out from the horizon. A new airship, moved by propellers and held aloft by yellow balloons.

Marco returned into the offices, searching for the Director Thornton of this time.

"Gary! Gary, you here?" he asked loudly, shifting around abandoned desks and slight debris.

Once he reached the Operator Room again, the Director waddled in uncomfortably.

"Mister Nieve! I'm sorry, it was—"

"I know, Gary. I just came from you in the future." Marco said firmly. His plan required quick action; he had little time for small talk.

"Ah; then I trust you have a plan already in motion?"

"Broad strokes right now. Is there equipment left in here to fly a chopper remotely?"

Thornton looked around the abandoned room, checking desks and computers. Most of Snow Dynamics had been left intact, but The Hellbent's forces must have paid extra attention to Shatterbug's information hub in addition to harvesting the marconium.

"Hurm," the man muttered, even his grunts not spared of his Yorkshire accent. "Yes I think so. If we take this monitor over here... And move this computer over here... Urf!"

Marco moved to help his Director to reposition the pieces. He carried the desktop to a spot on the floor, plugging it into the unused wall outlet. Gary set the monitor on the ground beside it, then ran back to find a keyboard and mouse, returning with those two and a USB pilot's simulator.

l

The Operators' Director pressed the power button on the tower, and the monitor lit up, though with a scar on the top right of the screen partially obscuring the image behind black, destroyed pixels.

"This should be fine, just hold on tightly."

"Thank you, Gary. I'll give you the thumbs up when I'm in and ready." the hero assured him.

The *Hero 5* helicopter he'd taken back to New Jackson was no longer on the roof's helipad; at this point in time, it was in mid-flight back here, piloted by Marco's younger self. He would need to go down to where the smaller *Hero 7* machine was being stored on a flatbed truck in the company parking garage.

The single-passenger UAV was much less comfortable than the rest of the fleet; every amenity possible had been forgone in favor of a small and robust vehicle—it didn't even have controls to pilot it manually. It was only a small seat, carried by the technology of the remote-controlled rotors and the marconium battery. Which had been taken.

"Oh, of course they took this one, too." Marco said in frustration.

Fortunately, there was one sample that had been left behind. His own.

The prime marconium, as he had taken to calling it.

Marco carefully rotated the metal casing around the window on his chest. The round glass shifted into its side compartment, giving him access to the marconium core that powered his own suit. He gently removed it—taking care not to grab the glass part of the cylinder directly—and unhooked the wires from either of the metal ends.

He set the core inside the similar container on the ground. It snapped into place, and he closed the panel over it.

Now the machine was ready. He would have to be quick to replace the marconium once he reached his destination.

Hopping into the truck, he easily drove it outside and onto the street. The city was still recovering from the attack, so this section of road had been closed off. It wouldn't be a problem for him to leave it here. Besides, the keys were inside if someone needed to move it.

The camera inside the helicopter would now be powered, so he climbed back in and gave Gary the signal, smiling through his closed helmet.

Once he was in the air, Marco did his best to guide his pilot. "They headed north, Gary. Or, north-ish." His sense of direction was troubled enough on the ground, let alone in the air. But, he did know that the downtown New Jackson skyline was to the south of Snow Dynamics, and The Hellbent's airship was definitely on the opposite horizon.

The communications systems between the Operator and the Shatterbug suit would be down even if the suit had power, but while the *Hero 7* chopper didn't have a speaker, it did have a microphone, and responded to the information with a jolting rotation to the left.

The strange skyship was now in view, several miles ahead. Being so large and carried by balloons and propellers, it would be much slower than Marco's small helicopter, optimized for speed. The distance was closed in a matter of minutes.

But they couldn't just crash the chopper into it. People were on board, not to mention all of the marconium and whatever traps The Hellbent might have prepared.

"Alright Gary, I'm gonna try something dumb." Shatterbug declared. The helicopter hovered a few dozen feet from the large vessel, and seemed to shake somewhat in confused hesitation. "You're gonna lose control, but I don't see anything underneath us. Let's just hope accounting paid the insurance on this thing."

Marco slid open the panel on the floor and grabbed the prime marconium, before bringing it up and hastily hooking it back into the Shatterbug suit in one fluid motion.

The vehicle began to fall, its only power source now removed. Enunciating as clearly as he could through the sudden forces of gravity acting on him, Shatterbug exclaimed, "Shattershock!"

The suit flashed, and with it, two displays shown inside his visor. In the future, he was falling in the open sky, much like in the present, save for the helicopter. In the past though, Marco had found his footing on a grated catwalk under a yellow ceiling.

A blur of orange and purple seemed to roll off the metal bridge, and he instinctively grabbed at it, holding on with as much finger strength as he could muster.

The hero was strong enough to hold it, but not lift it. Grunting through the thin air, he ordered the suit, "Reconstitute!"

With the added strength of ten minutes of time folding into the past, Shatterbug pulled the suited figure back onto the bridge, unhindered by the broken guardrails.

"Marco." the man whimpered through his orange-tinted visor.

Shatterbug walked coldly along the rumbling corridors of The Hellbent's skyship, refusing to close his helmet as he followed Miguel.

They passed a number of doors—some with windows, and some without. It seemed like they rounded corners every fourth room or so, which told him that the villain aimed to make the vessel seem bigger than it actually was.

Marco tried to peer into one of the rooms with an open door, but was stopped in his tracks by his friend's voice.

"No exploring, Nieve." The Hellbent's words escaped from Shockdrop's lips beneath the orange visor. "I'm afraid we don't have time to humor your childish curiosity."

He scowled under his blue helmet. "I see the intercom system here, Hellbent. I know you don't need to torture me like this. Release him, or I'll bring this bird down."

Miguel stopped, and the muffled voice of The Hellbent cracked over the speakers of the ship, somewhat obscured, Marco knew, by the metal mask he shared with his new subordinates. "I have every confidence you would not do that, my friend, but I'll save the agitation for later."

Marco reached for his friend's shoulder, turning him around in silent assurance that he was okay. The Hellbent's powers were uncharted; there was much they still didn't know about his limits.

Whatever they were though, Shockdrop patted his outstretched arm in solidarity, verifying his returned volition.

"Proceed, heroes." the voice ordered overhead.

Shatterbug sneered again, but the two continued down the hall anyway.

Every so often, another masked person in armor would bar their access at a fork in the path, or hastily close a door they were nearing. They were not walking for long, but their uncertain steps slowed their progress through the machine.

At last, though, they reached the apparent observation deck. Huge windows gazed down at the cliffs and hills of the valley's edge below, letting natural light into the grand room. The ceiling rose up higher here, too, and suspended from it by cables and yet another catwalk hung the would-be bridge. From this angle, it looked more like a small cockpit, with a few control panels and monitors arced around in a semicircle. Two more henchmen commanded that post, but they did not hold Marco's attention for long.

The mastermind of all of this stood at the far end of the room, against the window. Unlike their encounter on the last zeppelin, The Hellbent stood with his back to the glass wall, eyeing the two heroes unflinchingly. His gold armor shone with polish, and his grey-and-red helmet concealed whatever emotion he might have behind cold, intimidating yellow eyes.

"Congratulations, you have all of the marconium. Now let us off, and we'll call it a day." Marco spat with as much condescension as he could express from behind a mirrored visor.

"Visor off." Miguel said. Marco looked at him as the orange helmet folded back into a collar around the hero's neck. He furrowed his brow.

"Quit your showing off, Hellbent!" he shouted in frustration.

"This was never about the marconium, Nieve." the villain spoke from his own mouth as Shockdrop began walking forward to stand beside him. "It is a means to an end, one that I've not finished preparing yet. As much as I would like to release you while I prepare my triumph, I don't doubt that you would be able to stop me if I did. No, better to show you just how much power I have over you, even when I am not bending your will."

"I won't let you hold Miguel hostage. The second you let go of him, I'll fight back and save him."

"And I believe you. He'll not be jumping out of a window today." The Hellbent taunted as the sound of a pressurized door hissed elsewhere in the room. Looking around, Marco found the access in question opening.

From the passage emerged the calm faces of R'Bec and Ramses. They stalked into the room. Marco wished they floated in with glazed eyes, like mindless slaves, rather than what he actually saw. Because instead, as The Hellbent's powers promised, they were fully aware of themselves, believing their actions were of their own will. They were not in control, but no one could tell it from looking at them. R'Bec's stoic face and confident gait led the reserved and pious Bahadur Al-Malik to join Miguel beside their domineering master.

Although The Hellbent's face was concealed, Marco was sure the man was grinning with cruel amusement beneath the heavy mask.

"Your time travel powers will always let you save the day, to fight me off—this I understand. But what if you have to hold back? What if rather than fight me, you were forced to fight your friends and allies? Can time save you from that?

"These are not questions whose answers I care about, of course. I may not have your suit's abilities, but I rely on time as well, and I need a bit more of it free from you. So, I trust that the four of you will be able to spend a few hours in stalemate."

The Hellbent turned on his heel, aiming to walk out the same door the heroes had just entered from.

"Shattershock!" Marco shouted, making a run for the villain.

But he had forgotten the lesson he learned from his first bout with The Hellbent, and indeed, the rule which he used to board this vessel in the first place.

The ship was moving.

In both the past and future, Shatterbug was falling through the sky, plummeting for the ground.

"No-no-no-no; reconstitute!" ordered an urgent Marco in the present, kicking his foot into the metal floor. As his three selves became one again, he utilized the forces of time—and his momentary supplement of strength—to propel himself forward through the air, to tackle The Hellbent.

Impact.

Marco found his body stopped short, his head colliding with some barrier and his legs soon following. He fell back, knocking out what wind he still had from the first blow as he hit the ground.

He looked up at the wall of brick and mortar that had barred his passage and blocked his attack. The wall that wasn't there a moment ago.

The hero couldn't help but sit motionless on the metal ground as the fortification began to shift. Its color faded from red and white to grey and grim. Bits of clay chipped off, floating away like flakes of skin, deteriorating and vanishing. The structure began to fail, toppling over itself, before the whole thing collapsed into dust, becoming a pile of debris on the floor, and then becoming nothing. Gone.

Shatterbug looked to the three should-be heroes.

"We don't want to hurt you, Marco." Miguel said. With his helmet folded down, Marco could see the truth in his friend's eyes. Which only made the lie of it that much more painful.

"Just stay down, let him do his thing." the supposedly-not-human woman begged. Her eyes, too, were gentle—a welcome change, if they had been genuine.

Pounding his fist pitifully against the resounding metal, Marco shouted. "You don't know what you're *saying*. You're under his thumb—snap *out* of it!"

At the show of force, futile and inoffensive though it was, Shatterbug's three allies readied themselves on instinct. Miguel shut his visor and held his fists close to one another; R'Bec clutched one arm at her stomach and held the other against her neck—against the shimmering purple choker around it—in focus and control; Bahadur gripped tightly his ankh, not yet holding it against Marco, but making it accessible should he have to.

To see the First Mortal Order in pieces like this already—manipulated or not—was disheartening. The Hellbent was a major villain, a nemesis even, but he was hardly a threat to reality, yet even he was enough to rupture the uneasy bond of their alliance. What did that say about their cause? What did that say about Marco's leadership? His heroism?

A door hissed closed, and with it, The Hellbent was gone. The four heroes were alone on the observation deck, along with the two henchpeople at the control bridge above.

Shatterbug hoped that the villain's absence would release his friends, but that would be underestimating The Hellbent's power. Clearly, he had left them with the will to keep Marco in this room. He didn't need to actively oversee how or to what degree, as long as they understood that simple goal.

Two minds heard the sound of the door sliding shut through the same pair of ears, marking The Hellbent's exit.

Ramses held his ankh firmly, just enough apart from his side that he could draw it against his foe with ease.

The problem was, he believed that foe to be Shatterbug.

"*Ramses, turn the ankh upon the door.*" Osiris commanded.

The God's host responded in the shared space of his mind. "I cannot, God-Pharaoh. Marco Nieve threatens The Hellbent. I must stand ready to restrain him."

"*No, my Champion. You must cease this mindless squabbling and rejoin the side of your ally.*"

"I stand beside my allies now, in service of The Hellbent."

It was no use. Whatever spell the masked villain had set upon the Champion of Osiris was not so easily broken. The God would need to find an opening by other means.

Shatterbug stood up quickly. Ramses held out his ankh parallel to the hero, his distant form visible through the golden loop. Osiris felt his Champion beg for the God's power, pray for the strength to summon his energies through the ankh. But Osiris refused.

The opposing hero ran towards the trio, declaring his intentions with a "Shattershock!"

There was no apparent effect through Ramses' eyes, but Osiris comprehended the act.

The time ripple was unmistakable. Briefly, two duplicates of the blue-clad hero appeared, occupying the same space—that darting position, moving against the three ignorant traitors. Just as quickly as they materialized, they were forced across time.

Osiris imagined this would serve as an exceptional tool with which to assess combat scenarios and adapt as necessary. But not here. Judging by Shatterbug's hesitation, the same thing happened now as with his first 'shattershock' moments ago. The doppelgangers in the past and future were falling through the sky, unsupported by the moving skyship.

Still, the hero advanced. Ramses again tried to turn Osiris' power against the time traveler, but the God would not grant him that strength in folly.

Instead, the ought-to-be hero Shockdrop clapped his hands together in front of him, sending vertical shockwaves against his friend.

Marco ducked to his left, closer to Ramses. The alien R'Bec—whom Osiris had recognized despite her *j'ops* clouding her true form even from her own eyes—responded by conjuring another illusory wall. This one, rather than standing ahead of the hero and blocking his path, rose beside him, so close that his left shoulder scraped along it for a moment, before he could recover.

He was undamaged, but thrown off-balance. This was where the other two intended to rely on Ramses for the finish.

But Osiris would not allow it. The ankh shook in the Champion's hand as he struggled to summon the God's magic. Osiris could feel that Ramses even doubted his connection to the God, now, fearing he was not holding the ankh hard enough for their harmony to flow.

Ramses put too much stock in harmony. There was much that Osiris would permit of Ramses to do, to use Osiris' power for, but in the end, it was the God's choice. And when his mind was turned against an ally—even an ally of a union that Osiris fundamentally disagreed with—he would find no magic of Osiris' to wield.

And so Shatterbug came upon the duo—Osiris and his host, Ramses—hard, with a furious "Reconstitute!"

The hero's arm was rising in an uppercut, but the forward momentum provided the bulk of the motion. Osiris saw the three Shatterbugs pulled through time, once again uniting in the present, at the moment of impact. That cinching of time granted him the momentary power to drive Ramses back, his head almost hitting the window as he slid to a stop on the metal ground.

"*Cease this now, Champion. The Hellbent is gone, he holds no power over you.*" plead the God.

If Ramses heard Osiris in his mind—and Osiris was certain he did—then he paid no mind to the request. Osiris served only as a patron and guide. This villain had bent and broken Ramses' will. Somehow.

Although the Champion was on the floor, the bottom of his vision granted Osiris some visage of the continuing battle.

R'Bec ducked out of the way on Miguel Jimenez's yelp, who then attempted to let his fist meet the mirrored glass of Marco Nieve's helmet.

Shatterbug caught Shockdrop's wrist, bringing it down in a harsh but inoffensive twist, aiming to disarm rather than break his friend.

But the orange-and-purple hero let his other hand fly, this one trying to slap against the blue's arm.

In quick succession, Shatterbug braced himself with two more commands. "Shattershock—reconstitute!"

Again, Osiris saw the warping of time around the hero. The distortion seemed to last longer this time, but indeed, it was only because the copies reunited in the very next moment from which they parted. At the same moment that Shockdrop's hand impacted.

The shockwave was magnitudes greater than the one launched at Shatterbug earlier; it too was affected by the time traveler's power. Ramses' head was thrown back, harshly hitting the floor once again, only saved from injury thanks to the short distance that it fell.

The Champion's eyes shut in a wince of pain, but Osiris could still hear through his ears. From R'Bec's shout, she had also been thrown back and to the opposite side of the room, where Shatterbug and Shockdrop had entered from.

Shockdrop was unaffected by his own suit's power, but the impact with the Shatterbug suit still threw him off balance. He heard Miguel hit the floor, though from the sound alone, Osiris couldn't tell which direction he had fallen.

Ramses still held his ankh firm—a trait Osiris was always pleased with, but no more so than right now. Shatterbug was perfectly in line with the golden loop, and so without Ramses' request, the God set the implement alight with green energy, opening communication with the hero.

"Shatterbug. Ramses' will is contested. I will assist as much as I am able, but you must try to keep R'Bec and Shockdrop in the eye of my Champion's weapon."

"Who is—" Marco Nieve asked in his own head, hearing his thoughts as clearly as Osiris'.

"Do as I instruct, Shatterbug. I will continue to try to break The Hellbent's hold on Ramses. Remember: keep your allies in each other's sights!"

As Ramses rose, recovering from the pain of both his falls, the ankh shifted, and the God's parley with the hero was closed.

Osiris couldn't see Marco's eyes behind the mirrored visor, but from his brief hesitation and the turn of his head, he seemed to have briefly considered the validity of the God's claims, then opted to follow along.

This was proven when he began to run to the side, putting himself between Ramses and R'Bec on the other side of the room.

Ramses moved his arm to hold it against Shatterbug, but Miguel Jimenez stood up with unease at the same time, getting in between the Champion and the time traveler. He faced his friend, but his body was held perfectly within the sight of the ankh's ring, and so despite Ramses' lack of intent, Osiris lit the weapon, surrounding Shockdrop with his green energy.

Golden cuffs and chains materialized, summoned by the God-Pharaoh, to restrain the orange-clad hero. He found his ankles pulled to his wrists, and his knees bent in response, bringing Miguel to a kneel on the metal floor.

Ramses' arm recoiled in surprise at the spell that, from his perspective, had misfired. With the ankh facing outward wildly about the room, no clear target in its sights, Osiris had to find another way to provide cover to Marco Nieve, and continue to work on freeing his Champion's will.

"*Enough of this, Ramses! Shatterbug is your ally; whatever The Hellbent wants, it is not to help us unite my body, nor to protect reality as you have elected for yourself. His concern for you is superficial, and your current state of mind is only evidence of that.*" the God reasoned fervently, as Marco tried to rush against the alien R'Bec opposite Ramses.

The Champion's head shook, and he could do nothing to stop himself from speaking to Osiris aloud, though in his native tongue. "You are lying, Osiris! I know what is true—I do this of my own will, not yours!"

Although he had no mouth or lungs now, or body of any kind that his spirit could call its own, Osiris approximated a sigh inside Ramses' consciousness. As Marco was once again held back from his feminine opponent by an illusory wall, the God thought to himself on how to proceed.

The ankh had connected his spirit to the body of Bahadur Al-Malik. They shared the space of the mortal's brain—more than that, they shared the infinite expanse of his imagination. In all his might and nobility, Osiris did technically have some control, some capability to possess his Champion's thoughts. This was how he communed with Ramses, and exerted his will through him and through to the ankh in service of his host—or against it, in the current situation. This proved that the God could manipulate Bahadur without his consent. But how far could he go? How far *should* he go?

A God ought to be benevolent. Even Set was, once, before his image was corrupted. Before he was spurned by the fearful of Egypt. If Osiris used his power to force his will upon someone, even the man who had devoted himself as the God's Champion... What would that make him?

R'Bec conjured a set of weapons in her hands as well as on the floor behind Miguel Jimenez, interrupting the God's lamentations. He focused again on the ensuing fight, in the hopes of providing the one hero spared of The Hellbent's domineering with any kind of support.

The captive hero latched his twisted hands and fingers on the twin swords behind him, and with the unyielding strength of the alien's *j'ops*, freed himself from Osiris' considerable binds. However, the implements gifted to him would do little to improve his skill with the Shockdrop suit's own power, and so he dropped them to the floor. They clanged briefly against the metal before erupting into two clouds of black dust, which faded into the air.

Shockdrop clapped his hands together, launching an unavoidable horizontal shockwave at Shatterbug.

The hero rippled through time again—by Osiris' comprehension—with another pair of commands. "Shattershock, reconstitute!"

The attack passed over him at the moment time reunited his duplicates into the present. Marco was unharmed, but not unfazed. His balance challenged, he had to hold his arms out to keep steady.

The shockwave continued its barrel across the chamber though, towards R'Bec, who had now taken from standing at the entryway to running at Shatterbug, dual rapiers in hand.

R'Bec stopped in her tracks as Shockdrop's unintentional friendly fire raged over the alien and her blades. To the God's eyes—through Ramses' eyes—the illusions were just simple enough that the change in pressure began to destabilize them. Their shape rippled and blurred, before they both burst back into the same dark flakes as their counterparts, and faded away.

Ramses, now understanding the unreliability of his ankh, took to a more direct combat approach and ran across the room, past Miguel, and into Marco, tackling him. Caught off guard, the hero had little choice but to fall to the ground, the machinery on his back and helmet clanging against the metal.

The Champion of Osiris stayed true to the word of his comrades—to the will of The Hellbent. They only sought to restrain Marco, and so to that end, Ramses pinned the hero's arms and legs to the ground, giving R'Bec the opportunity to imagine proper binds for him. Metal braces appeared from nowhere and cuffed Shatterbug's limbs to the metal floor.

Osiris thought at a speed of consciousness far beyond the capability of the mortal mind, continuing his ethical debate at this impasse.

This was not Bahadur Al-Malik. These were not his actions, and he was therefore not responsible for him. But Osiris was fully aware, unimpeded by The Hellbent's commands. He was Ramses' patron, and he *was* responsible for their shared body when the Champion could not be.

Ramses took an oath, and although the God did not wholeheartedly agree to the terms—to protect the laws of reality as the first line of defense on behalf of those angels, those cosmic beings—Osiris did wholeheartedly respect his Champion's wishes and decisions. And right now, Ramses could not follow those

r

wishes himself. It was Osiris' right, his obligation, to use his might and free his host from The Hellbent, to restore his own will.

That was the moral justification the God settled upon, anyway.

Osiris collected his divine consciousness in Bahadur's imagination. The God had no eyes of his own to close or breath to temper, but he approximated these things anyway in his incorporeal form, preparing himself for this breach of honor.

In a moment—a simple, insignificant moment, accompanied by no flash or act of impress for anyone, least of all Shatterbug or Ramses—the Champion of Osiris loosened his grip on the hero's arms. He was not snapped out of a trance, or woken up from a dream. Fully aware of what he had done, Bahadur Al-Malik climbed off of Marco Nieve and stood up, a look of understanding and apology painting his face.

"Thank you, Osiris." he said aloud. Then, after only a beat to pause, "Let's set this right, Shatterbug."

Ramses set the shackles on Marco's wrists and ankles within the sight of the ankh, and let his thoughts—*his* will, once again—translate to his God and back through the golden implement. It glowed with that green aura, indicating that their connection was restored, and as the alien's illusions faded away, Osiris thought silently to himself, wishing he were strong enough to let Ramses hear him.

"*Thank you, my Champion.*"

Shatterbug stood up as soon as the bands that held him to the ground were gone. He set a hand on Bahadur's shoulder in a show of camaraderie and gratitude, before they turned in unison to face R'Bec, who by now was joined by Shockdrop.

"You able to do that to them, too?" Marco asked, unsure whether he should be addressing Ramses, or the God that supposedly dwelled inside the Egyptian.

"I believe we can manage." replied Al-Malik.

The Champion raised the golden ankh to R'Bec. Similar shackles to those that had just captured Marco formed on Ramses' wrists, tightening them and forcing the weapon's ring away from her.

Evidently, it was too late. Marco saw a faint green glow form on the implement's loop, and that was all Osiris needed. The shackles burst into a puff of ash as quickly as they had appeared; R'Bec was free of The Hellbent's grasp.

There was little time for gratitudes—although the small nod and smile that the strange woman offered Bahadur was likely all either of them would have received, anyway—as a horizontal shockwave ripped across the three heroes, upsetting their balance.

Shockdrop was still under false impressions. Marco being the best equipped to handle the attacks, he stood first to face his partner.

"Ramses, get on it, *amigo*!" he shouted with a glance behind him.

A grunt prompted the hero to take another, longer look at his companions, struggling to rise themselves.

"Patience, Nieve! Just let me—" Bahadur cut himself off. He held his empty hands in front of him, a look of shock plastered on his face as though his fingers had suddenly fallen off.

"What's wrong, man? Just point your— Oh. *Oh dios.*"

Bahadur Al-Malik's hands were empty. He wasn't holding the ankh.

It must have been thrown in Shockdrop's last attack. And with a thundering clap, Marco turned to face another one.

"Shattershock!" he ordered, splitting himself into three duplicates across time. Once more, two more Shatterbugs appeared five minutes in the past and future, but again, they were both falling through the sky.

Miguel's vertical shockwave threatened to slice through Marco. The hero sidestepped out of the way, not wanting to waste his reconstitution on an avoidable assault.

A metal clang sounded lightly as the pressurized air slipped past Shatterbug. He hazarded a brief glance at the ground behind where he had been, letting his eyes catch on a glimmer of sunlight reflected back into his visor, before he had to turn away.

"Ramses, three o' clock!" he said, hoping the intent translated.

"Shattershock!" the Marco in the future wailed as he continued his fall. This summoned yet another Shatterbug, a further twenty-five minutes into the future; more importantly, it indicated to the present Marco that his future self was about to stop falling.

The time traveler readied himself, kicking against the floor and aiming his fist at Shockdrop, who had also begun to move about some. Whether he was trying to cut the heroes off from the ankh or just intercept Marco as per his orders, Shatterbug couldn't tell.

"Reconstitute!"

Shatterbug, primed in the present like a projectile ready to fire, launched himself with the power of thirty-five minutes of time being pulled back into him. His foot collided with the floor, kicking him forward. He struggled to keep his arm outstretched, hoping Miguel would not have time to move out of the way—or prepare a counteroffensive.

Neither was necessary.

Again, Shatterbug's head hit a barrier that was not previously there, and his legs followed, flattening him against the wall.

R'Bec had summoned another of her strange illusions to block him from hitting the hero.

"Oh c'mon! Again with this?" he cried out with frustration.

"Hold, Shatterbug. R'Bec was only stopping you from hurting a friend." the accented voice of Ramses said calmly. From the curl of his words, it sounded as though he were smiling lightly.

The wall faded in chunks—the mortar becoming dust and the bricks falling away, collapsing into clouds of black flakes, then dissipating altogether.

Miguel stood on the other side, visor off and face beaming.

R'Bec walked over beside the only hero on the floor, offering him a hand. As Marco stood up, accepting the strange friend's assistance, he eyed the golden ankh, now returned to Al-Malik's possession.

"Visor off." Marco said with some unsuredness. The others moved on, not detecting his concern, and so he opted to let it go.

"Thanks a bunch, *hermano*." Miguel said, turning his smile to the Champion.

"Thank Osiris we were all spared a worse, more permanent fate." the Egyptian replied.

"We're not out of this yet. The Hellbent is still onboard, and he still as all the marconium. We have to stop whatever he's planning." R'Bec said, attracting the surprised gaze of all three of men.

"Feeling a change of heart, are ya?" Miguel teased.

"Just... accepting the terms of my agreement." she answered, idly glancing to Bahadur before turning her head away in annoyance.

Marco suddenly felt strange, as though the bones in his body somehow turned against his blood. A rush in his head made his eyesight dizzy, and held his hand out as though to catch something.

The others felt it too, each responding with equal unease.

Then, the whole skyship lurched. The sound of grinding metal echoed down every corridor, and Marco closed his eyes on instinct with the concerning crackling of warped glass sprinkling in the air of the observation deck.

The Hellbent's vessel had landed.

The First Mortal Order stood in the empty room for a few moments, looking around. Marco noted that the large windows had gone dark, indicating they were at least partially inside some sort of hangar or enclosure. Miguel pointed up, drawing the others' eyes to the bridge suspended above them. The two Hellbent minions that had been piloting the craft were exiting along their catwalk and out the door.

"We're here." Shatterbug said.

R'Bec was the first to yelp. The other three followed her eyes and, upon meeting the root of her scream themselves, followed suit with their own exclamations of surprise.

Peeking over the bottom edge of the window, as though trying to peer through with all of their height, was a small army of faces. Somewhat familiar, and yet still horrifying faces looked at Marco, Miguel, R'Bec, and Bahadur, with folded and torn grey skin, and empty, unreflective black eyes.

For the first time since their inception, the First Mortal Order stood at the ready, arming themselves against a common foe. Shatterbug and Shockdrop closed their visors over their heads, R'Bec summoned twin pistols with oversized barrels in her hands, and Ramses held Osiris' ankh against the window, already summoning his God's green glow.

"Shattershock."

Issue 9
Menace Revealed

The glass shattered first, showering the open space with millions of shards.

R'Bec imagined the largest wall she could just in front of the two Mexican heroes, and out of the corner of her eye, she saw that Ramses was using his own power to magic a bubble of green energy around the whole group.

The twinkling of tiny glass particles all suddenly hitting a brick wall—and then falling onto a metal floor—dominated the silence in the room.

And then the silence was broken again. This time, by the slapping of hands and feet on the floor and ignorant snarls of dry mouths.

They moved around the simple barricade, and then met their greyed claws to Osiris' shield.

The team was beset by the ravenous horde.

"You weren't kidding about the zombies, huh?" Miguel shouted over the howls of the mob, readying his hands for a thunderous clap.

R'Bec didn't answer. In part, because it went without saying. She wasn't kidding, obviously. The monsters were here.

But, she also bit her tongue at the word. Zombies.

They were not zombies, after all. She had said as much, and they looked the part. The creatures had dead, greyed flesh; wrinkled and torn away with decay. Dark spots splattered some of their skin and exposed bones with only just enough hue to give away that it was, in fact, dried blood. They grabbed and groped and growled like mindless horrors. And their eyes—those eyes that seemed to pierce whatever they beheld, to fill them with dread and marvel all at once—were pitch black. Void. Without light or soul.

But they were not zombies. Zombies would have some agency. Simple, animalistic agency, but a will of their own nonetheless. These corpses were not reanimated. They were being held up by strings, made to dance like puppets by the villain that got away.

And yet, even as she remembered the pain and disgust she felt when she discovered these truths herself, R'Bec couldn't help but to crack a grim smile.

To think, she was worried that Jet Wicked had escaped, that he might be impossible to find.

Less than a day later, though, she found him once again.

This could be the chance to ensnare her clever friend.

Still, that required finding and getting to him. After their duel in the depths of Groom Lake, the necromancer was sure to be much more cautious with his position as he commanded the undead army.

So R'Bec opted to stick with her new allies, for the time being. They would certainly join her in pursuing the true monster

d

here, anyway. He was a threat to reality after all, according to Corpsegaze itself.

"I will need to lower the shield soon if we have any intention of using Osiris' power in this fight." Ramses urged through the raking of nails on the glowing green dome.

"Go ahead, I've got the suit set to max." declared Shockdrop. His confidence was commendable, but somehow R'Bec wasn't convinced even that would work. "Everybody duck on my signal!"

"I hope you've got a backup plan, Jimenez." she said, readying herself.

"We've got it covered." Shatterbug answered for him.

In a flash, the green light that had been flooding the room—and R'Bec's vision—faded.

"Duck!" the orange-and-purple hero ordered.

R'Bec crouched to the floor, catching her descent with her hand on the cold metal. She saw Marco and Bahadur do the same, and then found herself flinching, closing her eyes and angling her head down.

A huge crash echoed and reverberated through the broken observation deck and the expanse of the hangar outside the open windows. The sound of rubber and flesh scraping across metal all but drowned out by the constant barrage of sound and pressure.

R'Bec opened her eyes as soon as she could stand it.

The zombies were pushed perhaps ten feet away, but none lay dormant. No corpses set inanimate on the ground.

"Now, hit them while they're back!" Marco yelled.

R'Bec held her impossible guns out in front of her and fired wildly into the crowd.

The weapons were unnecessary, of course. Not only were they technically incapable of firing anything by virtue of being hollow, without any sort of mechanism or blasting agent, but R'Bec was imagining the bullets flying through the air anyway. If one were to examine her shots, her targets would not be lined up with where she was aiming at all.

She used them anyway, of course. In part because up until recently, she needed to look the part of an earthbound woman with no superpowers, and in part because they did help her focus her mind on what she specifically needed. When she needed a wall, she made the same brick wall. When she needed to shoot someone, she used a gun and bullets. It was what she was used to, and it helped keep the illusions intact.

But the guns were useless for another reason, one she was all too aware of.

With significant damage to its body, one of these creatures could be felled. It took time, yes, but it was possible. However, to have any sort of chance against this many monsters, one needed to sever their ties to their puppeteer. The strings that lead from the nape of their necks to the immortal Jet Wicked needed to be cut. And a gun just wasn't going to do that, especially when she couldn't see the threads.

"These things just don't die!" Miguel said to her right, continuing his clapping at a lesser setting but with greater frequency. If R'Bec had to guess, he was just barely keeping the creatures in place and vibrating the strings that kept them upright, both to no avail.

"We need to find a way to claim an offensive position. A higher ground." concluded the Egyptian man on her left. The small energy pulses firing off from the ankh were similarly ineffective. With a glance, R'Bec noted that he was firing off small displacement spells, separating whole limbs from some with every few attacks. But even as he chopped a head off one of the horrors, Jet Wicked simply sewed the marionette back together.

As she held the wave on her side of the circle at bay, her back to those of the other three heroes, she looked as hard as she could for the black lines to follow back to the necromancer.

The tangle of arms, interspaced by protruding heads with pointlessly gnashing teeth and held back by the random fire of imagined but powerful bullets was a mess. When unthreatened, Wicked held the many cords of his slaves high above their heads, but barring that, R'Bec didn't know how he handled them or hid them. She needed to find how he was running the leads back to his cold, dead fingers.

Then she caught it.

The tiniest glimpse of black line, running from underneath one of the creature's feet and along the floor.

The threads were trailing down the puppets' bodies and legs, and back along the floor. Such small lines, held to the ground by their own tensile strength and the focus of their master, would be well and out of the way of the horrors, keeping them from tripping over their own leashes while also utilizing the zombies themselves as defense for their lifelines.

But R'Bec had solved it, so that defense was as good as broken.

"Aim for the floor!" she said, angling her head back and to the left for her partners to hear. "They're being controlled by strings running under their feet!"

Ramses obliged, turning his golden weapon down to the metal ground, his spellcasting unrelenting. He displaced feet and toes with every few shots, and with even fewer, a monster or two suddenly fell limp.

R'Bec couldn't see Shatterbug without sacrificing her own buffer, but she imagined that the time traveler couldn't be doing any better than Shockdrop. Even his vertical shockwaves, flying through the crowd like a knife of pressurized air was horribly ineffective against the supernatural threads. She thought she perhaps saw *one* of the zombies fall, their lead likely cut by a particularly fortunate stray shard of glass rattled just so, but he was making no progress otherwise.

Her allies were ill-equipped for this kind of calculated assault against a horde so large. Only she had the power to break the army.

Maintaining a steady firing rate against the wall of grey and black trying to crawl towards her, the Telignen began to imagine a huge blade hovering above their heads. It was all she could think to use—she had to cut strings on the floor; as many as possible. Measuring ten feet across, she thought, it crashed down upon the creatures like a huge guillotine.

Metal slammed against metal, and the parked skyship gently rocked forward into the hangar before righting itself.

Not a single zombie had fallen.

Miraculously, those creatures directly above the blade had stepped forward or back, just out of the way of the sharpened

133

edge. As further insult, not one string was caught beneath it, either.

It was no miracle, though. R'Bec understood that much.

Jet Wicked was too smart for her. Wherever he was in this fight, he was acting far more calculated, not driven by haste or emotion. Or perhaps he was motivated by a desire to show up the alien that had reduced him to a kneeling husk with a gun to his head.

Despite the clear advantage the horde had over the four heroes, a group of them parted and began to retreat.

No, not retreat. They had come from outside. The splinter group was moving in, through the door Marco and Miguel had entered from and onboard The Hellbent's airship.

"They're going after the marconium!" declared a voice from behind her.

"We can't worry about that now." R'Bec tried to reply at an angle for him to hear. "We have to cut off the flow of them—then cut off the head."

"That's easy for you to say; whatever The Hellbent had planned for all of that power, what do you think *monstruos* like these could do with it?" Marco said.

And he was right. Jet Wicked was a collector of things— small parts, at first, but just last night having moved up to alien metals and spaceship salvage. If he was going after this much marconium, even willing to take it from a heist in progress, the necromancer and his master had much grander plans than R'Bec had even begun to imagine.

"Bahadur!" she started. He cocked his head to better hear her through the murmur of decay. "On my signal, make another shield around us and through to the door. Marco: get through, find the cache. The three of us will guard the entry and keep any more from getting in."

She couldn't see Shatterbug, but Ramses turned his head to the blue-armored hero and nodded in apparent reciprocation.

Keeping her attention focused on the wave of corpses in front of her, she let as much of her mind as she could spare begin to imagine two long poles, shooting out from ahead of Ramses and to the door.

Just as R'Bec predicted, Wicked pulled the strings of his puppets and moved them out of the way, as though to demonstrate that he could adapt to anything they threw at the zombies. But the alien kept on with her plan.

The imaginary bars began to part, becoming sides of a narrow pathway, separating the sea of limbs and bones. A passage formed, free of the monsters, between the four heroes and their escape.

"Now!" she declared.

The Champion obliged, holding his ankh firmly ahead of him to conjure that green energy field once again. As requested, it encompassed the First Mortal Order and the new space marked by the illusory, floating guardrails.

"Marco, go. We'll handle things here." R'Bec insisted.

Again, she couldn't see his reaction, but in her peripheral vision she saw him running down the path and through the door, keeping his hands as far away from the poles and green shield as he could. Al-Malik followed behind at a more controlled pace, keeping his golden weapon primed and their defenses intact.

R'Bec moved down the line next, although keeping her guns trained on the horde. She didn't have complete faith that the shield would hold for long, based on Ramses' earlier remark, so she wanted to be ready for when it fell.

Miguel came down last, running to meet his companions at the door.

"I'll come with you, Marco." he said.

"These things are attacking us a lot right now because I'm here." R'Bec interjected. Shockdrop just stared, and through the mirrored visor of his helmet, R'Bec couldn't tell if he was confused by or rolling his eyes at the response. In any case, she continued. "In there, they're going to be less concerned with hurting anyone, if they really *are* after the marconium. The more of us that go in there, the less true that becomes.

"Plus, from here, we can try to keep any more from getting through, and maybe cut some strings while we're at it."

"She's right, Miguel." Shatterbug said, setting a hand on his friend's shoulder. "This is my responsibility anyway. You'll be safer, and more helpful, here with R'Bec and Ramses."

Miguel's fist clenched in frustration, but relaxed after a moment. "Don't die, *hermano*."

"Don't count on it, *amigo*." the time traveler replied. With that, he jogged off, back into the metal corridors of the airship.

"While we're on the subject, explain the strings." Bahadur said. R'Bec turned to him, her eyes catching on his trembling wrist.

The ankh's power was becoming overwhelming, and therefore weaker.

"I'll explain while we fight. Drop the shield before you don't have a choice." the Telignen said curtly.

As though he was finally relieved of a burdensome weight, the energy field immediately dissipated. The zombies that were clawing fruitlessly at the green bubble were now climbing over the guardrails, intent on trampling over the heroes and through the door.

Shockdrop took up arms first, clapping his hands together ahead of him and releasing another horizontal shockwave to push the monsters back some—enough to provide some semblance of berth.

Evidently in need of rest, Osiris' power manifested for Ramses as simple energy pulses, pushing back and occasionally cutting at the flesh of the oncoming zombies, rather than displacing parts of their bodies as before. It proved more effective than R'Bec's continued bullet storm, but still did little to actually stem the tide.

R'Bec knew what would work. She idly reached one of her hands up to graze the purple choker on her neck, before needing to pick up her fire again. The black necklace with the opal-like shape adorning the base of her collar pulsed and rippled with a mesmerizing violet light, like synapses bursting with electricity and information—she knew this to be true even without being able to see it. If she could just let go, she could end this fight in an instant.

But it was not even twelve hours ago that she had learned to keep her nightmares contained in that vessel, trapped in a would-be Pandora's Box. The choker was stable now, she was

137

e

confident in her control as long as she could hold them there, but if she chose to release them…

Miguel and Bahadur were right next to her. With minimal thought, the monsters and abominations that sprouted from her mind would tear Jet Wicked's army apart, would disconnect every string with horrific abandon. But how much effort would R'Bec have to spare to protect her allies from herself?

She couldn't risk it. Whatever she needed to do to keep the creatures at bay—to sever their ties to Wicked, without falling to that last resort—would have to be enough.

That was the conclusion she had come to, at least. And then she spotted him.

A new grey hand reached up over the edge of the ship, pulling its owner through the window and into the observation room. Its fingers were partially obscured by the threads caking the floor, but they were undamaged, undecayed; R'Bec could tell that much.

Indeed, the strings were not just in the way of the new hand; they were emerging from it.

The arm used all of its strength to pull the owner's torso up—its forearm and biceps rippling with strain, stretching the black-filled rips and tears that seemed to tattoo the extremity's flesh throughout. That chest was similarly torn in places, revealing the void hiding beneath. The black fleece vest ruffled and moved aside as the man hoisted himself onto the deck fully, and he stared ahead with darting anticipation, forcing R'Bec to turn her face away from the unsightly black pools of his eyes, somehow even darker than those of the zombies.

Jet Wicked had arrived.

He held his arms out at his sides, keeping his elbows tucked into his abdomen for support. He clenched his fists, tugging lightly on the strings that fell from the tips of his fingers and to the floor—then running along the metal ground to the back of each slave's head. They reacted in a complex dance, each thread moving independently of one another, as though their puppeteer was manipulating each with a distinct, insignificant movement of a different muscle in his cold dead fingers. They were just barely easier to see now, reaching up from the ground and roping around the feet and legs of the horde, indicating that Wicked had strengthened them—expanded them.

"Go inside, boys."

"But you just told us—" Miguel started between crashes of his hands ahead of him.

"That was before. I'll handle this." Her voice was unwavering as her eyes turned back to meet Jet Wicked's own.

"R'Bec," Bahadur tried to argue.

"Go!"

Still uneasy, Ramses and Shockdrop turned into the door and walked back into the hull of the sky vessel. By the sounds of their footsteps, they were in no rush to leave her, especially as the creatures advanced closer to the alien, but eventually, they were out of harm's way.

She dropped her guns.

They fell to the floor with two light clinks of metal, but the sound was muted shortly by their dissolution. The barrels and chambers darkened and greyed, fading away as the rest of the weapons followed suit, turning back into dust and fluttering out of sight into the air.

139

The zombies clawed and hobbled closer with terrifying speed, covering the distance Miguel had provided, eager to rip and claw at the Telignen and proceed through and fully into the ship.

Release.

R'Bec's choker dissolved; the prison that housed her inhibitions, her doubts, her nightmares, was opened.

Like a great floodgate suddenly and violently broken, the room was filled with the unrestricted illusions that plagued R'Bec's childhood mind, and that just the previous night, had brought equal or greater damage to the base at Groom Lake. But they would do, here.

The black fungal substance caked the floors and walls, expanding outward from the Telignen to infect the whole room. The zombies immediately in front of her were caught up in growths, their feet and arms trapped by the living matter in random patterns and degrees. The observation deck lit up with the lightshow of purple pulses, stretching across the expanse of the illusory mold, traveling along it like neurons firing between synapses of some massive creature. But the material was thoughtless. To a certain extent, it served R'Bec.

To that end, she imagined horrific creatures of her own to emerge from the slimy and coarse and fuzzy sea of black and violet, growing from it—independent of the greater mass, but all connected through the Telignen's mind. Scorpions and boars and grizzly bears rose from the ground or climbed out of the walls, each pulsing with that same purple hue just beneath the dark surface of the impossible flesh. They tore and stung and reared at the horde recklessly, but at R'Bec's command, attempting to sever threads with as much accuracy as they could manage with their oversized forms.

Through all of this, she maintained her glaring match with the necromancer. He tightened his fists further still, noticeably straining the muscles of his arms—and whatever force rippled beneath his skin. The puppet strings responded in kind, expanding slightly in an attempt at greater resilience.

It was no use.

More and more of R'Bec's oversized nightmare creatures howled and gurgled with poor approximations of their muses' natural sounds, reveling in themselves as they tore the puppets apart without compassion, and in the process, cutting threads left and right. Not every horror that they dismembered fell lifeless—the beasts and insects of light and sludge were still too large to precisely rend all of the leads in one swing of their stingers or tusks or claws, and even those sharper parts of their forms were just as sticky and inconsistent as the rest of their bodies.

But the army was thinning. And if nothing else, they were less concerned now with getting past R'Bec, with all of Jet Wicked's attention now drawn to holding his ranks.

"It's over, Wicked!" the alien shouted through the chaos; a triumphant tease. She conjured the image of her favorite pistol in her hand yet again, trained on the necromancer's head even across the room. More or less.

His eyes had been torn from their staring match, his focus on the twiddling of his fingers in the most minute and precise configurations in command of his horde. But at this, he returned her gaze, and smiled down the oversized barrel of her weapon.

"You don't even know what 'it' is, my dear. But be my guest; show me the wrath of Lady Harrow." He held his arms out at his sides, his palms open in feigned surrender, although still moving his fingers acutely as the battle between their respective monsters raged on.

R'Bec's nose crinkled at the sound of her adopted name, the name she had now chosen to shed. Her brow furrowed at the implication of her ignorance; worse, the implication that she hadn't yet won.

The Telignen didn't even pull the trigger. A bullet appeared from her imagination, and it fired from the chamber of its own accord, flying through the observation deck and between zombies and nightmares, straight for Jet Wicked's forehead.

Impact.

The grey-skinned man stepped back in shock, carefully holding himself on his staggered feet. The black pools of his eyes showed no light, nor pupils or indicators of any kind as to his field of vision, but R'Bec had to imagine he was trying to look up at his own forehead.

She was looking at it, too, waiting for the moment he would fall over.

And waiting.

But the moment didn't come.

He just stood there. Not quite motionless—his hands still danced with the practice of a puppeteer, the motions slow and calculated as they had been. Besides the abrupt catching of himself at the bullet's penetration, the necromancer did not react.

Indeed, the bullet hadn't penetrated anything.

His skin was broken somewhat, the dead flesh moved aside to wrinkle his brow even further, but the bullet fell away, clinking lightly on the floor, although inaudibly through the madness unfolding between them. It left only a mark in the middle of his skull—indeed, not even his skull. Whatever blackness clouded his eyes, whatever darkness stretched out from his fingers, whatever rippled beneath the skin pulled taut on his arms and chest; it had filled in beneath that broken flesh. The unreflective shadow sat there squarely, like a scar, but whatever it was had protected his skull from damage. Protected him.

"I told you, I am *immortal.*" he hissed.

He returned one arm to his side as he brought the other in front of him, outstretched as though to reach out to the Telignen. Instead, the strings that still extended from his fingers wriggled and snapped about, disconnecting from all of his horde. More threads emerged from the cold skin of his fingertips, from under his nails, becoming a flaying mass of black rope.

He flicked his wrist harshly, pulling his puppet strings through the air. They wrapped around and latched into new bodies. Not the human corpses that now lay dormant on the floor; no, this time, Jet Wicked sought to command R'Bec's nightmares.

R'Bec screamed in mental pain, her migraine prompting the monsters to hiss and roar and spit at the sudden intrusions, which pierced their black fleshy fur at dozens of points, not just their necks. The purple glow beneath their slimy exterior was clouded by the stretching of Wicked's strings inside of them. They seemed to move wildly within the nightmares, as though searching for something to latch onto, something to control. The invasion was agony for the Telignen and for her illusions, she wished nothing more than that they would dissolve.

But these nightmares were sturdier than her normal imaginations. They existed by fear, not willpower or focus. They

143

would not and could not fade away, even at this—not fully. She clutched her head, trying with every fiber of herself to collect her thoughts, to work through the pain and break the nightmares.

Even as she howled, as her voice cracked and her ears burned from the sound of her own suffering, R'Bec collected her thoughts. She summoned all of what remained of her strength, bringing all of the synapses of her mind to work fully in tandem. She imagined it—the choker made of solid nightmare around her neck, the prison for her fears and inhibitions and self-destructive thoughts.

And then it stopped.

Her knees gave out as she collapsed, exhausted.

Jet Wicked's cackling filled the room.

Then she felt a hand on her shoulder.

"Get up, H."

R'Bec's eyes opened, and she turned her head back.

There was no one there, but for a moment, she thought she caught a flash of blue light.

Somehow reinvigorated, the Telignen rose. She still couldn't fight, but she had enough power, enough awareness, to understand that she could—that she had to—run.

She turned, darting through the door and into the corridors of the parked skyship. The sound of snarling and clawing filled her ears from behind her as, she presumed, Jet Wicked resumed control of his fallen army. Still more concerning were the same sounds coming from ahead of her, as the rest of the horde that had parted ways in search of the marconium earlier continued their uninterrupted feast.

R'Bec hoped with everything she had left that her allies were just taking their time, and hadn't fallen themselves.

r

Issue 10
Nemesis Unknown

The strange woman had guessed correctly. The zombies, or whatever they really were, moved through the halls with vicious urgency, but they did not bother the hero in his blue armor.

Due to this ambivalence, keeping up with the horde proved difficult. Marco had to run at top speed at every straightaway so as not to lose them, but slow to a near-stop at every corner—in part so he didn't run himself into a wall, but also to ensure that they didn't see him out of the corner of their voidlike eyes. Just because the monsters weren't specifically interested in him and the Shatterbug armor didn't mean they would take kindly to his pursuit of them.

He followed them through the airship, certain that they would lead him to the marconium. Shatterbug knew that had to be their target; R'Bec said they were responsible for the stolen battery in Las Vegas, and since The Hellbent couldn't be in league with them, they had to be here to steal the powerful element from the both of them.

Indeed, Marco was a little surprised they weren't more interested in him specifically, and the prime marconium core that he carried. Although, being dead and mindless, pulled along by supernatural strings, they may not have recognized the shining cylinder held in front of his chest.

As he continued to keep pace with the creatures, his thoughts lingered briefly on the size of the ship. From outside, it didn't look much longer than a few hundred feet—granted, even that was from the distant perspective of the *Hero 7* helicopter—yet he had been travelling through the corridors and weaving around corners for what felt like several minutes. Whether it was only a poor estimation on his part, or some trick of the many turns, intersections, and rooms with multiple entries concealing the vessel's true scope, Shatterbug already felt lost aboard The Hellbent's flying machine.

But the horrors seemed to know exactly where they were going. The pattering of their dead palms and feet upon the metal floor did not hesitate at each intersection. Their snarls did not slow or quiet on passing each door—they did not even glance inside them. There was no hesitation to rip through the armored forms of The Hellbent's minions patrolling the halls. Whether it was smell, foreknowledge, or some other paranormal sense, the monsters moved straight for the marconium.

And through all of it, Marco could only watch and follow.

If he engaged them here, alone, he would almost certainly lose. At least if he made a stand at their destination—at the marconium—he'd be doing so for a reason. He also hoped that waiting might buy his companions time to meet him, or that they might even cut off the man controlling the army of unfortunate souls.

The mass of limbs and heads rounded another right turn, and the strings rising from their tangle dragged along the ceiling in turn. Marco slowed once again to follow them around the corner, and then stopped in his tracks to examine the scene before him.

They were here.

No doors to this room. Given his already skewed sense of direction, Marco wasn't sure whether or not this was the true center of the ship, but it clearly had the design of it.

The chamber was tall, like the observation deck. From his vantage, the left side of the room seemed to be the intended back wall, as it was rounded and lined with displays and various systems. The opposite wall was flat, and sported another entry from another hall, as did the wall opposite him. A number of cables ran along the floor from the rounded back of the room, plugging into a large throne-like machine which was just offset from the apparent center.

Marco couldn't see much more over the flood of monsters filling the room and obscuring his vision, but he did catch a glimpse of the top of a red helmet pinned against the hooked-up chair.

"Shattershock." he said, now unconcerned with drawing attention to himself. The suit flashed, and with it, two Shatterbugs appeared in the past and future, their perspectives displayed inside his helmet in the present.

All three heroes stepped into the chamber, moving with urgency while also taking in the situation and comparing each frame of time.

In the present, the figure in the middle of the horde looked to be holding their own, from what little Shatterbug was able to gather through the swiping of arms and subtle jerking of hovering threads.

Their condition five minutes in the future was not so inspiring. There did not appear to be any sign of the armored rebel, but what Marco *could* see, with absolute certainty, was marconium. Lots of it. The zombies were tearing it from capsules all around the base of the mechanical throne. Their eyes remained cold and lightless as they held their dry, full hands to their emaciated mouths and swallowed the samples whole. Not in victory—no, he could see that. Their movements were wild, but still as precise as the flicking of their puppet strings. This was necessary. They were harvesting it. Foraging it. Storing it for something more.

The present Shatterbug's eyes turned away from the gruesome scene and on to the state of things five minutes in the past.

Naturally, the horrors had not arrived by then. Only one figure stood in the lofty room. Although his armor was virtually indistinguishable from that of his minions, the man's air, the weight of his presence, told Marco that this was The Hellbent, waiting for him once again.

"Reconstitute." the Shatterbug in the past commanded, pulling his future selves away from the dark carnage to face the vengeful stranger.

The Hellbent turned at the disturbance, taking in the sudden appearance of the time traveler.

"I suppose it *would* be giving you too much credit to assume you wouldn't run away from the problems posed to you, Nieve." he hissed beneath the iron mask.

"You don't give my partners enough credit, Hellbent." Marco retorted, his eyes focused on the unblinking yellow light shining through the only two holes in the villain's guise. "We broke your will. *They* broke your will."

"Impossible!" The smallest squeak of metal scraping metal rung in the chamber as The Hellbent's armored fist closed. After a moment, his shoulders relaxed and he continued. "But irrelevant. I am nearly finished."

"There's no time, *cúmbila*! An army is already on board this ship, and they'll be here any minute to take the marconium from both of us." reasoned Marco.

The golden suit shimmered as The Hellbent laughed. "Not even an army can match my contempt for you. They'll kneel to me before turning their weapons on you. Maybe that will hold you off long enough for—"

"You can't stop them! They're not alive, they're *something else*. I don't know what you think I did to you, but *please* listen when I tell you that whatever you are planning with the marconium, these zombies are sure to have a lot worse in mind, and they won't have the same honor that you do." he pleaded with the villain.

The Hellbent didn't respond, but as he shifted his weight, a familiar noise pierced the very edge of Marco's hearing.

Snarls. Groans. Slaps and claws.

"They're coming, Hellbent! Stand with me, fight them off with me, just like old times!" the hero begged.

"Old times?" The glowing eyeholes in the man's mask almost seemed to squint in doubt.

Marco brought his hand to his mirrored visor, failing to recall that it was still up and covering his face. He had forgotten that no one else could remember the events from the paradox timeline. The Hellbent had no idea that he had saved Shatterbug from Solace's clutches, or fought alongside him at the Genesis Shrine. Technically, for this version of the gold-plated villain, it had never happened *for* him to remember.

"Never mind, that's not the point!"

The Hellbent thought to himself for a moment longer before giving his answer. "I don't need your help. I should never have offered you mine in the first place, and now I can make up for that error."

He turned his back to the hero, kneeling down to continue his work on the machine. Marco could see him open his hand to reveal a marconium sample, cut and shaped into a rough jewel, which he set inside one of the capsules surrounding the base of the throne.

"Don't— Hey, stop!" Shatterbug shouted, running up beside the villain.

"I'll not let you stop me this time, Nieve." The Hellbent replied, not even offering the courtesy of looking up from his task. "Once all of this marconium is in place, I will win, and you will lose."

Marco was taken aback by the sheer ambivalence that the villain was expressing. He didn't care that Shatterbug was standing right next to him; not remotely concerned that the hero might try to fight him. And still, he was unfazed by the threat of attack from a darker foe.

The growls and footfalls of the zombie horde grew closer, ripping through the halls. There was no way of telling how near they were, the labyrinthine layout of the ship contributing to echoes and thrown voices, but if he had to guess, the two enemies had less than three minutes left before the monsters flooded the room.

"Shattershock, reconstitute!" he said, out of options. The suit separated Shatterbug into three duplicates, spread across time for only a moment. In the future, Marco caught a glimpse of the decayed creatures all around him, before time pulled them back into a single moment in the present, extending all of that temporal energy into his fist.

The punch landed on the side of The Hellbent's peculiar mask, but the villain did not react. A small flinch, perhaps, but not enough to distract him, much less knock him down.

"I took the liberty of extending my suit's defensive capabilities up through my mask, as well. After our last encounter, I couldn't take the risk of your getting in a lucky shot." The villain finished affixing the gem-cut element into the capsule, then casually stood up and headed for a table near the rounded back wall of the room, where a tray of identical rocks sat.

Shatterbug tried to punch him again, splitting and cinching time as his fist connected with The Hellbent's backside. No reaction.

"Shattershock!" he said again.

"Shattershock!" ordered his doppelgangers in both the past and future, creating two new copies a further twenty-five minutes forward and back.

"Reconstitute!" the original Marco commanded mid-kick, finishing as his leg swept under that of the shining villain. An hour of time pressed back into a single moment, empowering his movements for that split second alone. It was a stronger, more powerful attack.

And his foot bounced off harmlessly. The Hellbent stopped for a moment, his leg only twitching from the impact, as though he had just felt a small pebble in his boot. The villain continued as quickly as he had frozen, totally unabated by Shatterbug's enhanced technique.

"That was much more potent, Nieve. Did you do the same thing as the last time you ejected me from my own ship?" the villain taunted as he reached the stand, gently picking up a few samples before turning back around. His yellow eyes burned through Shatterbug's mirrored visor. "Real science is about testing and iteration, but you wouldn't know that. As soon as something works, you call it complete and move on. Well, let's see what happens when you are forced to fruitlessly adapt to my own armor's enhancements."

Marco turned his head to glance down the hall he had entered from. Still empty. But the horrors would be here any minute—no, any second, at this rate.

"We don't have time to fight, Hellbent! If you want any chance at the marconium, we have to fend off these *monstruos*!"

"You call this fighting?" the villain replied, crouching down once again at the mechanical chair and taking one of the marconium stones between his fingers.

Shatterbug was getting flustered, losing his focus. The Hellbent was clever, without a doubt, but he was also frustratingly arrogant. It didn't help that he was right. Marco could do nothing to him. The gold-plated suit was specifically designed to counter the time travelling blue armor he wore. And being similarly powered by marconium, there was no guarantee that using a wider range of time in his attacks would actually break through the vibrating shell—and testing that would take time that he didn't have.

He glanced to his left again.

And there they were.

Right at the end of the hall. They had just turned the corner. The horrible, animalistic human corpses bounded down the corridor, clawing and climbing over each other in earnest, running at impossible speed. Their eyes were bare and blank, the darkness clouding them filling Marco with dread.

"Hellbent, look!" he begged.

He didn't turn to look immediately, but in the silence following Shatterbug's yelp, the villain must have heard the patting of dry skin on metal, of nails scraping against flesh and bone. His eyes shifted as his masked head nodded to his right, and he nearly fell back in shock.

The Hellbent only had time to stand up before the zombies broke the threshold into the room.

"You weren't—" he started.

Marco cut him off in frustration and urgency. "Shut up and fight! Shattershock!"

It would do no good to jump through time now. Once again, he was locked in the present, having to use his powers to face the creatures directly.

A zombie lunged for him. He reconstituted, forcing his closed fist through time and through the creature's jaw. The monster fell slack, the thread running through the back of its head disconnected.

The hero turned on his heel to another horror that sought to run past him, swinging his time-breaking leg through its stomach. No blood or organs spilled out as Jet Wicked's strings sewed the corpse back together, though hobbled somewhat by a dissected abdomen.

Whatever The Hellbent was doing or trying to do, Marco didn't look back to check. He stood at the front line, not in defense of the villain, but in defiance of him and his ideals. Shatterbug had to stop the army of the dead, at all costs.

But he wasn't trained for this sort of battle royale. Although he had picked up plenty of skill since his early days as a hero, going with the flow and mimicking the martial arts of internet videos as best as he could, he was still only especially practiced in one-on-one combat. That was, after all, a limitation of his suit.

Unless he could last five minutes.

Going to the future wouldn't help. By then, the monsters would have nearly overtaken The Hellbent and retrieved who-knows-how-much marconium from the machine. Abandoning the villain in the present wouldn't accomplish anything.

But in five minutes, Marco could send ten, or twenty, or however many Shatterbugs into the past—back to right now—effectively restarting the fight with an edge. With an army of his own.

A pair of the shambling figures aimed to tackle the hero. Marco shattershocked again, meeting their extended decaying hands with his flexed forearms. As their fingers clasped onto the plates of the Shatterbug suit, he reconstituted, and they flew back at opposing angles, knocking over a few of their companions.

Marco's victory was short-lived. The monsters, as though by magic, lifted themselves off the metal floor with ease. Indeed, they didn't lift themselves at all, but were pulled by the black leads running from their necks and twisting in the air.

Another creature swiped at Shatterbug on his right. He shattershocked and prepared his leg in the present to kick up and knock its whole arm off.

"Reconstitute!" he let out.

At the moment his foot met with the dry, greyed skin of the zombie—

He missed.

Without the follow through, without the impact, Marco lost his balance. He fell.

The creature leapt at the missed opportunity, its own dodged attack becoming a new, more ferocious one. It came down on the hero, its tattered clothes shifting on its scar-ridden body, as though in mockery of Shatterbug's defenselessness.

He winced beneath the mirrored visor.

It didn't come.

Marco opened his eyes, arms crossed in front of him to shield from a loose limb or biting mouth.

He was just in time to see the monster, whose face was held back by a shining gold hand shoved up against its open jaw, get shoved back and to the ground, before the plated figure standing over it reached down and snapped its neck without hesitation. The string that rose from the back of the horror's head retracted back into the mess of black lines undulating near the ceiling of the tall room.

The Hellbent stood up from his quarry and looked to the hero with unflinching eyes, expressing a protective fury even behind the grey-and-red helmet. He held his hand out for Marco, and helped him to his feet.

"Thanks." Shatterbug said, forgetting his unease in exchange for beaming pride.

"Don't flatter yourself." the villain spat gently, before turning his head back to the army surrounding them and the throne. "I don't want to kill you; I want you to suffer. And I need the marconium to do that."

Shatterbug sighed under his helmet, but let himself crack the corner of a smile. "Then let's smash these *perdedores*!"

Back to back, the hero and villain in their marconium suits stood tall against Wicked's horde.

Although they were now working together to keep the zombies at bay, they were still only two compared to the dozens of eyeless puppets. And while Marco could hold them back with enough ease, one or two at a time, neither he nor The Hellbent could bring them down with any consistency.

The villain also struggled with actually fighting the horrors off of the chair. His gold-plated suit protected him from their sharpened nails and slobbering teeth, but it didn't provide him with any exceptional strength. It was designed to counter, but not exceed, Shatterbug's power. Underneath, whatever muscle and combat skill he naturally possessed was all The Hellbent could rely on. And, judging by his struggle to circle around and protect the mechanical throne, he was lacking in both regards.

But Marco could only be grateful that The Hellbent had opted to help rather than hide, despite his disadvantage in this fight. After all, the hero wasn't doing much better.

Shattershocking and reconstituting so much, with every punch and kick and shove of a decaying husk flinging itself at him, was wearing him down. Not as quickly as when he flickered through time at Yellowstone, but it was reaching that point. All that kept him going was the occasional dispatching of a corpse or two from the necromantic army, and the knowledge that he could rely on The Hellbent to fight alongside him to their last breaths—even if the villain's motives were selfish.

Apparently recognizing the resolution of the uneasy allies, the monsters came at them in greater droves. Their tactic switched from attempting to move around the armored individuals to coming right at them—and over them. As two or three creatures swarmed the hero or villain, more would climb onto their torn backs, clawing up their already-destroyed shirts and flesh, and attacking their opponent from above.

With precise timing, Marco could reconstitute in such a way to throw all of the horrors off of him, but in doing so, he sacrificed the strategic placement of his limbs to sever their ties to their master.

"Marco!" shouted The Hellbent from behind, his voice wavering with urgency—although still muffled by the iron mask.

Shatterbug moved around the chair to hold off another group of zombies, angling himself to get a better look at his villainous partner.

The Hellbent's poor fighting skills coupled with an inability to use his powers on the slaves with no will allowed the monsters to, with enough time and effort, overrun the villain. His suit protected him from injury to their attacks—which were nothing compared to the time-warping Shatterbug suit's punch—but that didn't mean they couldn't touch him, couldn't hold him still and pull him away from the machine. And so, they did just that.

He was being dragged away, a zombie on each arm and one around his torso, as two more pulled at his legs. All five worked in unison to hold him back from the throne as three, five, ten of the grey creatures clawed at the metal capsules, retrieving the marconium with their bony fingers stained red with dry blood.

Now was the time. He had to go back, to ambush the monsters in the past with an army of Shatterbugs.

"Marco!" another voice sounded. Not The Hellbent's this time. No, this one was younger, and rang from his right, from the hallway he had entered from—and also, somehow, from inside his helmet.

He turned.

Standing in the entrance to the tall chamber was a man in dark tight-fitting combat gear, adorned with gold and green, wearing a strange double crown or hat of sorts, and more importantly, a figure in an orange-and-purple armored suit.

Shockdrop and Ramses.

"Miguel, wait, don't!" Marco yelled out.

But it was too late. Miguel clapped his hands together, sending a moderate shockwave ringing through the chamber.

But, the Shockdrop suit was powered by marconium. Indeed, it harnessed the natural vibration field generated by all samples of the previously-undiscovered Element 120, expanding on it and casting it out from the suit on command—on impact. However, the Snow Dynamics Enterprises batteries worked because separated marconium samples made each other vibrate even more. And now, with the brief success of the undead army, there were dozens of loose samples of the volatile element in the open air.

The shockwave passed over the rocks in the zombies' hands. They shook, amplifying the vibration field further. A creature's hand exploded, blown apart by the force of the element's natural reaction. And then that amplified wave caught on another of the fine-cut samples, alongside a different ricocheting swell of pressure, and those, too, became an even more powerful blast.

The cycle of marconium shockwaves was endless and incessant. Marco, Miguel, and The Hellbent were protected by their suits, but the same could not be said for Bahadur, nor for the zombies. Shockdrop did his best to shield the Egyptian hero, who covered his ears in agony even as the two cowered in the hallway. Meanwhile, the horrors were being torn apart, exploding in cascades of pressure and bone and dry, ripped skin.

Finally, the pressure had nowhere else to go. The infinite shockwaves became too powerful to contain. The rounded metal backside of the room gave out, sent flying out into the sky. As light and open air let into the tall, damaged chamber, the marconium wave was allowed to release and dissipate harmlessly.

And with it, the pressure carried The Hellbent, picked up off of the ground by an exploding monster and flung, no longer protected by his damaged suit.

Marco ran to the edge of the room, which now looked over the edge of a mountain. Although the airship was parked, the hangar was open on this back end, allowing for the balloons overhead to float without fear of falling rocks or metal. The edge of the floor now teetered over the steep decline of the mountain they sat atop, and hanging from that ledge was The Hellbent.

Marco reached down to grab his arm that gripped to the damaged metal floor, being careful not to hold onto the gold plate that was now loosened from the forearm of the villain's black undersuit.

He held his other hand down. "Grab my hand!" he begged of the villain.

The Hellbent wriggled slightly, trying to tighten his grip on the edge of the ship. He looked up at Marco's mirrored visor, his glowing yellow eyes piercing through both helmets.

"I can lift you up, c'mon! Take it, Hellbent!" Marco ordered, although he suspected his voice betrayed his intended seriousness for concern.

The Hellbent looked down at his other hand, dangling at his side. He lifted it slightly, as though in halfhearted attempt to bring it up to Shatterbug's outstretched one. Then as his mask began to slip from the gravity, the hold on the back of his head failing from the forces, he looked back at the hero.

"I'll not give you the satisfaction."

In that moment, Marco wasn't sure what happened. Even a second after, he couldn't remember how The Hellbent had fallen. Did the villain shake himself free? Or did Marco let go? And if so, was it his choice?

He questioned this even as he watched The Hellbent's shining armored body tumble through the dry New Jackson air, but he could not stop himself from turning away before it hit the rocky desert mountain. He didn't even hear the landing.

The Hellbent was gone. And the hero didn't know whether it was his fault, or his decision.

"We have a problem, boys!" a female voice cried out, hoarse from the sudden change in air pressure. Marco turned, his solemn face hidden by the Shatterbug helmet, to see that R'Bec had joined Shockdrop and Ramses, who had by now entered the room of desiccated corpses. "I couldn't stop him. Jet is coming, and he's got more. So many more."

As though prompted by the Native American woman's warning, the familiar snarls and tapping of dry feet and hands once again echoed down from all three hallways into the throne room, now filling not only the silence of the airship but also the peace of the empty mountain.

"We can't take them all, Marco we have to go!" Shockdrop said.

Shatterbug looked around at the floor. "But the marconium!"

"Is all that they are after." Bahadur picked up calmly. "We can escape, we must."

"Wicked won't let us escape, now that he knows I'm here, he's sure to chase us down." R'Bec added. Marco chose to ignore her apparent narcissism. She was probably right; with the way these creatures behaved, pulled along to their master's puppetry, he would not be forgiving enough to let them go even with his prize in-hand.

"I can get us to safety." the Egyptian said. "Join hands, everyone!"

The horrific sounds of the undead slaves grew closer, from all sides, prompting the four heroes to come together in haste. The two Mexican heroes stood beside one another, hands locked awkwardly with the shape of their suits. R'Bec snorted as she grabbed Marco's hand in only mild disgust, and Miguel took Ramses' free hand.

"Osiris, take us home!" Al-Malik commanded, holding the golden ankh between them.

As the zombies rushed into the destroyed room, eagerly picking up the marconium gemstones strewn about and coming closer to the First Mortal Order, the divine implement glowed green, and that light grew to envelop the four allies.

Marco winced, and in a flash of energy, they vanished.

Issue 11
Tomb of Osiris

It took a few moments for Bahadur to confirm that the spell had worked.

His adrenaline was still pumping, and he was still concerned for the safety of himself and his new friends. Even with eyes open, it took a brief sweep around the dimly lit room to be sure they were out of harm's way.

From the rotating heads of his partners, they needed the same assurance, although their faces quickly turned from relief to confusion.

"What is this place?" one of the Mexican men whispered. At that volume, Bahadur couldn't tell which had spoken from behind their respective blue and orange mirrored helmets.

R'Bec made a gesture around her head, prompting both of the armored heroes to lower their visors with a simultaneous voice command. At this, Bahadur turned to face the whole of the room, his back to the first three other people to ever see this chamber.

The eternal torches flickered on the wall, casting dancing shadows of the four figures along the decorated stone bricks. The Champion ignored the images painted around the room, for now, and proceeded past his bedroll to the right, onto the centerpiece of the back wall.

The stone dais acted as both an altar to his patron, and as a means for their union to seek out the artifacts that now set inside the gilded sarcophagus standing tall against the wall, like a general looking down on a war map. Indeed, the dais was currently showing a topographical map of Egypt, with a marker indicating the city of Naqadah, and specifically, the temple of the Sect of the Golden Scepter.

"This is the tomb of Osiris." he said, inviting the others to share in his tone of awe.

"Osiris is real? You weren't kidding?" Miguel asked, astounded.

"He is." Bahadur assured him. "This is where the pieces of his body are being collected and reunited, but his spirit lives on through me, and through this ankh, until that time."

The Champion of Osiris held the ankh idly in his hands, looking over the complex markings of jade and gold, admiring the gentle curve of the cross and loop.

"Why did you take us here?" R'Bec asked, speaking louder than the others had been. Her voice echoed lightly inside the enclosed space, bouncing off the ancient stone. The flames of the wall sconces almost seemed to shiver at the interruption, but Bahadur wrote it off as a trick of the light.

"We needed to escape. Osiris is always able to bring me here, regardless of circumstance. It seemed the best option, at the time."

"That's fair." Marco said, apparently starting to collect himself again following his experience at the edge of the airship.

"Snow Dynamics is in shambles anyway. Good to have a backup base of operations."

"I thought so, as well." the Champion replied.

"Well, let's get back out there, then!" Miguel nearly leapt as he turned to the wall opposite the sarcophagus. He stood, puzzled, then looked around with one eyebrow raised. "Where's the door?"

"There is no door." Bahadur answered with a shrug. "Only Osiris' magic can bring people to and from this room, buried beneath the desert sands. It was completely sealed upon its construction to ensure it was never discovered.

"But there is no need to leave yet, anyway. We can make use of its amenities to prepare our next steps."

"Amenities such as...?" R'Bec trailed off, waiting for the Champion to explain.

"This map, for instance."

Ramses turned around to complete his trip to the dais, then set the golden ankh in the slot at the circle's stone edge. The loop glowed green, and that energy trailed down the base of the implement and into the shallow pool, covering the map of Egypt.

"Osiris can sense the pieces of his body that have become scattered across the world, using this map to show me where they are. If we have any information on this 'Jet Wicked' and his slaves, the God-Pharaoh can help us to see more clearly."

"How do we know we can trust your 'Osiris?'" Marco asked, his skepticism shining through clearly in the dim chamber.

"He is a God."

Silence.

"He spoke to you, Shatterbug, did he not?"

Marco turned his head to Miguel, and then to the floor. "I don't know what that was."

Bahadur sighed, setting his hands on the edge of the stone dais and glancing at the ankh out of the corner of his eye.

"*Tell them our story, Ramses.*"

Ramses tried not to let his surprise show on his face at the God's suggestion. "My lord, what good will that do?" he thought inside their shared mindspace.

"*Marco Nieve is a man of science. Miguel Jimenez is a man of demonstration. They will both be more willing to listen if presented with facts and evidence.*"

"And R'Bec?"

"*A child of another world. She will hear you out, but you must make it count for the other two, or she will lead them away.*" Osiris finished.

Bahadur turned to the wall on his left, waving a hand at the images carved and painted into the stone. "Allow me to tell you the truths of Osiris.

"Osiris is real. He is more than a God, but the King of Gods, and ruler of the Underworld. All of the stories you might have heard of the Egyptian occult are true. Steeped in myth and allegory, but all portraying the human perception of divine events." He drew the attention of his three partners to the figure of Osiris as illustrated on the wall of the tomb. A man in white robes with green skin looked back down at them, his head adorned with a tall crown—the double feathered crown, symbol of the Pharaoh of Northern and Southern Egypt. It was not so unlike what sat on

Ramses' own head, although his was shorter, a gift from Osiris as a symbol of his title, rather than a right of rule.

"So what are you to him, then?" R'Bec asked, her face bent in sarcastic disbelief.

"I will explain, but first, we must go to the beginning.

"The stories of ancient Egypt, as I said, are true at their core. However, they are not all true, yet. While much of it is history, some of it is also prophecy. Osiris was destined to give birth to a son, Horus, who would become the next God-Pharaoh when his father moved on to rule the afterlife." Ramses took a step to the left, and the others followed along as the paintings on the wall continued the story with him, depicting a vision of a small boy with the head of a bird. "However, Set—Osiris' brother—wanted to be Pharaoh himself. He became jealous, frustrated that he was to be denied the crown by an unborn God."

"So Set was evil?" Miguel asked.

"Not always." Bahadur said solemnly. He paused their story, walking to the opposite wall of the chamber. Another man was depicted there, this one with an animal's head. For the life of him, Ramses could not decipher what the long-nosed, long-eared animal was meant to be, and if Osiris knew, he would not say. "Set was once a benevolent God, like his brother. However, when ancient Egypt started to become more... popular, with attacks and invasions from people of the north, the humans—for all of their intelligence and magnificence—were still primitive. They needed someone to blame. Set became known as the God associated with foreigners. His cults were all but dissolved, and he was spurned by the people, blamed for all of the misfortune brought by those invaders. He felt this blame to be unjust—and rightly so—and he grew jealous of the love his brother received as Pharaoh."

The Champion stepped back over to the opposite wall, moving along to the next set of images.

"In a fury, Set murdered his brother before Horus could be born." Again, Bahadur stepped to his left, and the image changed from the killing of his patron to a radiant woman, and the separated pieces of a crowned mummy. "Some stories say that Set cut Osiris' body into pieces, but in fact, it was the Pharaoh's wife, Isis. To keep her husband's spirit from moving on to the afterlife, she hid the pieces of Osiris all around Egypt, that they might one day be reunited, and in doing so, that the God of Life and Death would be resurrected long enough to birth Horus, and banish the darkness of the world as God of the Sky.

"It is therefore the job of the Ramses, of the Champion of Osiris, to find these pieces and bring them here for just that purpose. Osiris' spirit lives inside the ankh, until his body is restored. Then he will finally be at peace, and move on to the Underworld."

Marco had become distracted by the end of the lesson, his eyes drawn to the glowing ankh set into the dais.

"So the title is passed down, until a Ramses succeeds?" R'Bec asked. From her tone, it seemed to Bahadur that she had come around to him, more or less.

"It is, though by necessity, not tradition." Bahadur shuffled his feet. "The forces of Set also want the pieces for some unknown goal of their God. There have been Champions before me, but I did not know them. I happened upon the ankh, abandoned in the desert."

"Osiris has nothing to do with reality." Marco said. It was not a question, from his tone, but an observation.

169

"The God-Pharaoh has allowed me the agency to serve and protect the laws of reality in this First Mortal Order." he replied.

"But he doesn't really care, does he? He doesn't specifically want to; he just doesn't mind. All he wants is to be reborn." the time traveler continued, his voice rising slightly.

Bahadur hesitated. "He supports us, in spirit. He continues to grant me his power while we wait for more pieces to—"

"While you *wait?*" Marco's voice boomed in the small stone room.

The Champion breathed in, collecting himself.

But Marco continued before he could rebut. "I'll be the first to admit I wasn't sure, but you three brought me around, convinced me that what we were promising was right. We took an oath—*you* took an oath! And now you're telling us that you're just killing time?"

The hero's arms extended at his sides, fists balled and threatening to reach through the floor if frustration pushed them any lower.

"I understand your feelings. I understand why this may appear as betrayal. But the angels did not say Osiris' name when they spoke to us; they said my name." Bahadur said calmly, his head angled slightly in polite shame before rising to meet Marco's gaze. "Whatever Osiris' end goals are, and whatever my duties are to him, I can still remain loyal to my bond with all of you, and with those cosmic beings. They chose *me*, not me and the God-Pharaoh."

With fists still clenched, Marco started to shoot back, before Miguel cut in.

"Marco, stop. You've made your point, and he's made his case. *Estará bien.*"

The time traveler let his breathing slow, and his hands relaxed. He turned to the dais, his back to the group.

"If you will not have faith in Osiris," Ramses started. "Then please, have faith in me."

"I only believe in science and friends." Marco said without tone or emotion. "But I can be civil. For now."

A beat of silence, before R'Bec picked up a new topic.

"Any luck on the map?"

Bahadur turned to the dais as well, prompting Marco to take a step along the edge of the stone circle, opposite the Champion.

Osiris' green energy was still flowing inside the short enclosure. Through that glow, he could see that the map of Egypt was changing. Expanding. The topology was shifting about, magnifying and shrinking, as Osiris sought their target.

Ramses didn't recognize the current subject of the map, though. There was no water to the north, no blue scar of the Nile River against the desert sand. Although, it did seem to be mapping out a desert.

"This is New Jackson." Marco said.

"Yeah, almost to Flagstaff." Miguel chimed in.

"What is this showing?" R'Bec asked, as the map moved and shifted again, slightly further north—or zoomed in a few degrees, Bahadur couldn't tell.

"*I am following the monsters as they travel from The Hellbent's hangar. They are going north, but to what destination, I do not yet know.*" Osiris explained in the Champion's shared mind.

"Osiris is tracking Jet Wicked." Bahadur said, translating his private information to his teammates. "He does not know where they are going, but when he does, he will be able to transport us there."

"We have to wait around for that?" Miguel said, impatiently leaning against the stone wall, earning a glare from both Bahadur and Marco.

"It shouldn't be too long." R'Bec said encouragingly, though with a distracted air. "The zombies are incredibly fast. They could get to Canada in a day on foot, maybe faster."

"That still means it could be hours, even if they're staying in the states." Marco lamented.

Bahadur looked to the rest of small stone room, empty but for his bedroll. "Then we rest. R'Bec may take my bedroll, and we three will lie on the floor."

The woman let out a sarcastic laugh, shaking her dyed-red hair. "I'm not sleeping on the ground, sleeping bag or otherwise."

She twisted her hand in the air as though for effect. In the flicker of the torchlight, a single bed materialized in the corner. She stepped over to it, letting her clothes fall away into that same grey dust, leaving her again in that black dress with the small tear that Ramses had first seen her in.

"Don't you think we should all have beds?" Miguel asked, his voice conveying a genuine friendliness, if not a little forced.

She flicked her hand again without so much as a glance back at the three men. Two more bed rolls appeared on the floor, staggered nearby Ramses' own.

The two armored heroes looked to Bahadur.

"They are more comfortable than they look."

With a short puff of annoyance, Marco walked over to the arrangement furthest from Bahadur's original. It looked difficult to lie down in the Shatterbug suit, but as though in spite of the situation, he made it work. Miguel followed suit.

The Champion of Osiris took a final look at the dais, and then at the shining ankh set into the front of the stone circle, before joining the two men on the floor. He glanced at R'Bec in her tall, comfortable bed—not in jealousy, but in concern—and let himself drift to sleep.

Issue 12
Of the Past and Future

Marco was alone in the room.

His feet were set up on the coffee table, his hands clutching the controller in his lap.

He was fighting Ophion again, he knew that. Somehow, the television seemed empty. But he was playing Terminus 2 again, alone in his college dorm.

A flash above his feet.

He recoiled, bringing his limbs in on the couch.

The figure appeared. A man in a blue or teal or turquoise astronaut-like suit. Marco's face reflected back at him from the mirrored bubble of his helmet.

And then, with a hiss, it opened.

And spilling out from the inside, darkness. Shadows. Void.

Impossibly black tentacles shot out of where the figure's face should have been, flooding the room. The dorm turned red, and then black, as the tendrils enveloped Marco, restraining him. And then choking him.

They latched around his neck, and then one long, piercing arm rose above his head and crawled into his mouth. It slithered down his throat. Marco tried to gag, to choke. He couldn't.

The room flashed.

Now he was back on the parked airship, struggling to hold The Hellbent up over the mountain cliff. His hand gripped the villain's arm, and he watched as the golden armor, too, worked to hold onto the black undersuit.

The red-and-grey helmet began to lose its grip on The Hellbent's head.

It fell away.

Looking back up at Marco, peering out from the gold-plated armor, was his own face beneath the mask.

Marco's eyes widened.

He punched the doppelganger with his free hand, and then let go.

As The Hellbent fell—

Marco was jolted awake.

"Marco, get up *hermano.*" a familiar, friendly voice whispered. The sound echoed only slightly in the stone chamber, before dissipating on the bedroll Marco lay on.

He sat up.

"Miguel, what's going on?"

"You tell me, *hombre.* You were shaking, you're sweating."

"Just a nightmare." Marco said, turning his head in his hands as he started to stand. "I've been having them a lot lately."

He had been. The first one had been reoccurring for weeks. Taunting him. Haunting him. He hadn't told Miguel until now. But the second one—that was new.

But neither meant anything. He was scared of Solace, and he felt guilty for The Hellbent, but he knew both of those things already. The nightmares were symptoms, not warnings.

"I feel you, dude." R'Bec said dismissively. "But snap out of it; we've got work to do."

Marco glared through the near-darkness of the stone tomb, the flickering light of the torches not reaching his tired eyes just yet.

But he stood up—sore and uncomfortable from sleeping in his suit—and moved to join Bahadur and R'Bec at the stone circle at the back of the room. Miguel followed.

"How long has it been?"

"Seven hours or so." Ramses said, already much more awake than Shatterbug.

"It worked. Osiris found them." R'Bec said, her eagerness coming through clearly. She wanted to fight the zombies—to fight Jet Wicked—again. She wanted to beat them. Any way to make that happen, no matter how contrived, would excite her at this point.

Marco felt similarly. They had the marconium. Whatever they wanted to do with it aside, he needed it back on a personal level, too. The existence of the unique element, and what Snow Dynamics Enterprises developed with it, was of sentimental value to him. He had to keep it safe, to do the right thing with it. To honor *his* memory, if nothing else.

He hoped that, if Doctor Geoffrey Strauss could see Marco and the company they had built, that he was proud.

"Where are they?" Miguel asked, drawing Marco out from his thoughts.

They all looked to the map as the Champion pointed down to it.

"Here." the Egyptian said. "It's a mountain range in Canada, near a city called Calgary."

"To Canada in a day, huh?" Marco said, his eyes shifting to R'Bec for a moment.

"Hey, I said maybe faster."

"That's crazy fast, man. That's insane. Were they running the whole time?" Miguel asked incredulously, if astounded.

Bahadur answered after a beat. "Osiris says they were. Nonstop. It must have been their top speed."

"And they won't even be a little tired." R'Bec lamented. "They have the advantage."

"But we have the element of surprise." Marco said, fist clenched in optimism. "Can you take us there, Ramses?"

"We can." the Champion said, speaking for himself and, Marco assumed, on his God's behalf. Marco still wasn't entirely sold on Osiris, but Bahadur Al-Malik had made a fair point. He should try to have faith in the man, even if not in the myth.

Ramses carefully lifted the golden ankh out from its place on the dais. Again, he invited the others to all join hands. R'Bec held Bahadur's free hand, and Miguel awkwardly grabbed hers, letting Marco take the position furthest from the Champion of Osiris.

"Surprise doesn't do a lot of good against an army." R'Bec said as the golden implement began to glow green.

Marco chose to ignore her comment, focusing on the brighter side. Whether she was right or not, this time would be different. Not only would the four of them be together, fighting on a united front, but they would not be on the defensive this time. The dynamic had shifted. Once the First Mortal Order reached their destination, they would be the invaders.

The light from Osiris' 'magic' grew to surround and encapsulate the team of four, and with a flash of finality, they vanished from the tomb.

Issue 13
Progeny

They arrived at the foot of the mountain.

Well, one of the mountains.

The mountain range stretched on for miles in every direction that Marco could see, that was not itself obscured by a mountain. The silvery rocks shone in the afternoon sun. He had never been this far north, or seen the sunset so far from the equator. Vaguely, he thought he smelled hints of a lake nearby, but if so, it was hidden from his view.

The place was magical, hardly touched by humanity.

Indeed, even the blemish sat before them was not of human hands. Not anymore.

It was not a large facility. Tall glass windows were framed by stark concrete walls, only standing out from the rocky hill by their sheer faces. The glare from the sun prevented Marco from peering through and into the structure—which had been built into the mountain, rather than on and around it—but it also revealed how high the internal halls and chambers stretched. And crowning it all, near the very top of the imposing mound, was a glass dome. It was not as reflective as the windows of the edifice beneath, being comprised of a tessellation arranged in a semispherical shape, but it was still too far up to get a good look inside of.

"We need to get up there." Marco declared. "Ramses?"

Bahadur shook his head. "Osiris is concerned with a headfirst approach. If we go to the dome immediately, we may be caught off guard, and put on the defensive once again."

"But if we try to go through the facility, we might be too late!" he shot back.

"We don't even know that the dome is where we want to be." R'Bec chimed in. "I may not know him well, but Jet Wicked is crafty and adaptable. He'll find any wrong step and exploit it."

Miguel patted his friend's shoulder. "I'm with them, Marco. We dunno what we're getting into. Plus, we gotta find all the marconium; we'll have to search the whole place anyway."

Marco pursed his lips, restraining himself from rolling his eyes even under the Shatterbug helmet. In the end, they were right. He just wanted to get this over with.

"Alright, let's go." he said, leading the way by several steps.

The door to the superstructure was not hidden. In fact, it was in such plain sight that it almost looked to not be worth attempting to breach. But there was no other clear entrance, and they had the power of four heroes with a variety of skills.

Shockdrop walked ahead of the pack, putting himself between Marco and the metal sliding door a few feet ahead. Marco saw him rotate the dial on his chest, though from the back, he couldn't tell by how much.

The orange-armored hero reached his hands out to his sides, before clapping them together in front of him, releasing a horizontal shockwave into the concrete frame.

It crimped and folded like paper, the harsh sound of crushing metal filling the small valley, though fading quickly. The sliding panels were pushed in, and with another crack of the hero's hands, they snapped from their supports and flew inward, coming to a stop on the floor of the entry room.

The three other heroes stepped over the threshold. Marco gave his friend his own supportive pat on the back, and the two of them walked in behind R'Bec and Bahadur, who each took a preemptive fighting stance.

The foyer was undecorated, but it was not as barren as he expected. Some cushioned teal chairs and couches surrounded a low glass table on a wide black-and-white rug. A tall, inornate fireplace stood at the far end of the seating area, though unlit, as the rays of the setting sun spilled into the room, only beginning to cast long shadows on the far wall. Behind it, Marco could see a hallway going further into the mountain, with what looked like a stairwell at the end of that path.

Other than the light furnishings, the chamber was empty. No monsters, no minions, and no zombies.

"This is too easy." Shockdrop said, his tone teetering between amused and concerned.

"I agree. Something is not right." Ramses observed. "Osiris is sure Jet Wicked is here."

Though Marco did not entirely trust the supposed God, there was little reason for the Champion to be lying. There was every possibility, every likelihood, that the necromantic villain was here. The mountain was tall and wide, and this building looked to be just as vast. The zombies could have the marconium anywhere.

"We'll have to keep looking for him, then." R'Bec said, taking the words out from Marco's mouth.

"Should we split up? It's a big place." Miguel offered.

R'Bec turned to him, her nose crinkling as a snide look filled her eyes. "If you think you can fight a hundred nearly-invincible undead puppets, be my guest."

"Right, good point." Marco said, holding Shockdrop back from confronting her. "This is a coordinated attack. We should be prepared to come at them with full force."

They all stood motionless as the tension fell. Ramses took the first steps around the fireplace, and the others soon followed. The First Mortal Order stepped down the hallway and into the greater facility.

At the top of the stairs, the white tile floor forked at an intersection lined with concrete slabs. A door broke through the wall at either end of the corridor, before the same hall turned deeper into the mountain at each side. Before the team, another set of sliding doors—these more reflective and staggered, giving away their purpose as an elevator even without the keypad on the adjacent wall—and above them, white fluorescent lights, brightening the hallway with their sterility at every fourth slab.

Miguel pushed the only button: up.

"We're not taking the elevator." R'Bec said. Her expression was cold and indifferent, as far as Marco could tell, before she turned on her heel to the left.

Shockdrop held his hand up to say something, but Ramses stepped in first. "We should search this floor. As you said, we are looking for the marconium."

The two heroes in their mirrored visors looked at each other, unable to see the other's face but recognizing their emotions nonetheless. Marco shrugged and turned to join R'Bec and Bahadur.

Before they could even get to the end of the hallway, Miguel piped up, evidently unable to contain himself. "Why do you have to act like such a jerk to us?"

R'Bec stopped.

"I'm not a jerk to him." she replied coldly, nodding slightly to Bahadur on her right. She did not turn back to face Marco's armored friend.

"But why are you so rude to us? And just like, in general? It's like you think you're better than us, or—"

Still, R'Bec did not turn around, but she did crane her neck and cock her head enough to glare back at Miguel with the corner of her eye. "Ask me. Don't pretend like you're trying not to be an asshole, just ask the question."

Even under the suit, Marco saw Shockdrop gulp. "What are you?"

Now the woman turned, her Native American face reflecting on the orange helmet.

"I'm an alien."

If Marco were still breathing before she answered Miguel, he wasn't anymore.

"A Telignen, in fact." she continued. "I act like I'm better than you because I am. You're human, and I'm not."

"Well, even if—" Shockdrop tried to start.

"*Uh, well, even if,*" the alien mocked. "Even if what? How does just being a Telignen make me better? Think about what you can do without your fancy suit, and think about all the things you saw me do without it. Face it: humans are just bigger animals."

"Enough!" Ramses ordered.

Marco, Miguel, and R'Bec all stood in waiting for the Egyptian to expound upon them, but his collected temper did not come.

So Shatterbug took the chance, instead.

"We weren't chosen to be better than each other, guys. Now, I'm not an expert on 'Telignen,'" Marco's tongue caught on the alien word, trapped between two languages trying to pronounce a third, unknown one. "None of us are. But the cosmic beings didn't put you in charge. They didn't put me in charge either, and I'm sorry I've been acting like it. We need to act like a team, myself included. Let's just agree that we all have things to work on—and for you, miss alien, I think that might be a little faith in humanity."

She stood motionless for a moment.

Then she turned, silently, back to her trek down the hall and to the door. A wave of her hand behind her served only as further evidence to Marco that, although she heard and understood, she wasn't interested in listening. Hopefully, just for the moment.

They continued.

When they came to the door, Shatterbug, R'Bec, and Ramses all reached for the handle. As the latter was closest to it, Marco and the alien woman caught themselves, pulling their hands back gently.

Instantly—at the moment the door hissed on its separation from the frame, pulled inwards—Marco knew there was a problem. On instinct, he took a harsh step in front of R'Bec and Ramses, putting himself in the eye of the door as it whisked itself open.

Shooting from inside whatever room was carved beyond the threshold, a stream of light erupted out into the hall. It seemed like light, anyway, as Marco's vision was blurred and blinded by its shine even through the blue visor. However, as it pressed against the armored suit and pushed him back along the white tile floor, he looked down at the light to find…

Blackness. Impossible darkness, but from it, radiance.

Darklight.

It released, and he fell forward to catch himself on his hands. He caught his breath in the middle of the intersection at the top of the stairs, helpless but to watch the scene before him unfold.

Ramses and R'Bec stepped back, as out from the room strode a man in black robes. He wore what looked to be a heavy leather tippet, and the shape of his head and face implied that his skin had once been handsomely dark. But now, it was greyed and dead. His eyes, if he had any, were black and lightless; they did not share in the same glow as that energy that had been generated from him. Or rather, from his scepter, which he wielded in his hands like a staff. It was golden, carved with markings suspiciously not unlike those on Ramses' ankh.

The three heroes nearest the strange cleric armed themselves against him. Bahadur summoned a shield from the green energy of his own gold tool, protecting himself from whatever attack might be launched next. The Telignen took a more aggressive approach, as two pistols appeared from nowhere in her

185

hands. Shockdrop stood in an active stance, ready to either crash his knuckles together or engage the enemy directly.

But the sound of a door opening prompted Marco to angle his head and check behind him.

At the other end of the hall, another grey figure stepped through a door and into the plain corridor. This one wore baggy cargo pants and a black vest. A stark black dot on his forehead looked almost like a third eye, its round void indistinguishable from the actual lightless rounds that curled in cruel amusement.

He stretched his hand out, and from it, strings—like horrible black snakes, slithering through the air with all of the menace of a tangle of spider's webs—arced towards Shatterbug, still set on the floor.

He stood up.

"Fall back!" he heard the deep accented voice of Bahadur echo down the hallway.

Marco wanted to fight. This was an attack—they were in control. And yet, they weren't anticipating this. An army of unkillable monsters, sure. But the presumed puppetmaster himself, and this new unnamed player?

"Shatter—" Marco began, stopping himself as the suit began to whir to life, before dying down.

No.

They were a team.

Shatterbug glanced back at his partners. They were doing as Bahadur had instructed, running towards Shatterbug, with

Ramses and R'Bec conjuring staggered defenses from their opponent's darklight blasts.

He had to respect the will of the team, not his own ego.

He darted down the stairs, trying to cover his teammates from Jet Wicked's strings as best as he could. Shattershocking now would be an offensive tactic. They were on the retreat, so there was little the Shatterbug suit was good for.

Marco cursed, but abandoned those self-deprecating thoughts quickly, focusing on getting down the stairs and back into the foyer.

His hand met the back of the fireplace, and he turned to press against it, eyes to the stairs.

Miguel came down first, meeting with his friend at the chimney.

Ramses and R'Bec took their time coming down, watching their step as they each focused on holding back one of the two grey-skinned men pursuing them.

Bahadur held up a shield of green energy that seemed only just powerful enough to dispel the robed man's attacks, although dropping the defense each time.

The alien woman swiped at Wicked's strings with a long thin blade, trying to break them before they could reach anything—whether it was *her* body or an available one elsewhere in the facility. With her other hand, she tried to focus her power—however that worked—on controlling the necromancer's hands, locking them. To no avail.

After a few more moments of hurried defense, the First Mortal Order was once again with their backs to the wall, with Ramses and R'Bec flanking the two Mexicans against the fireplace.

"What are you planning with the marconium?" Marco demanded of the two villains, now parting to either side of the hall, letting the sunset shine on their unreflective eyes and torn skin.

"What does this have to do with the Telignen ship?" R'Bec said, her eyes furiously aimed at Jet Wicked. He only grinned back, baring ugly teeth that stood out against a mouth of empty nothingness.

"What are you doing here, of all places, Sen?" Ramses barked at the priest, who held his scepter against the Egyptian hero's ankh. "How does this necromancer help you in finding the pieces of Osiris?"

Neither villain answered.

After a beat; another second; yet a third hushed moment; the silence was broken.

"All excellent questions."

A new voice pierced Marco's ears in the tense room.

As his bones shook with the depth and unnerve of the slow, careful speech, his eyes sought its source. His attention—indeed, the attention of all four heroes—was drawn once again to the staircase at the end of the short hall. Floating down from the top, a black cloud of pulsing sludge and pussing ooze crept.

"Why indeed would High Priest Sen—leader of the Sect of the Golden Scepter—be acting in league with Jet Wicked—necromancer of the criminal underworld?" the voice said, apparently emanating from the horrific shadowy slime that hovered down the corridor and into the room. It latched onto the ceiling and floor with violent pops of black sweat and saliva, dripping and drooping down before picking itself back up into the air by some unseen force. While the First Mortal Order watched it in awe, the two villains on either side of it kept their eyes on the four teammates—although their ears perked up as it proceeded.

"Consider the name: *Sen*. Short for Senility Acolyte." Every syllable of the cloud's speech was elongated. Every flick of a tongue or click of a throat was calculated, though the creature possessed neither. Its pitch and tone shifted without pattern or purpose at every word, and at every new sound. It was disorienting just to listen to it. And heartbreaking. "Senility Acolyte and Jet Wicked. Of a similar taste, are they not?"

"Jet's master." R'Bec said in a knowing tone.

"Set." Bahadur followed with equal familiarity.

No. Marco knew, in his heart and soul, that whatever his two allies believed they were looking at, they were wrong. So horribly, irrevocably wrong.

He looked up at the mass of writhing matter and bubbling goo, which hissed and growled in waiting.

It wanted to hear him say it.

"Solace." he whispered, naming the thing.

It responded by shuffling and shifting in the air, abandoning its poor excuse for a disguise and taking on its true form—if indeed, it had one. The gurgling and slogging stopped. The silhouette pulled all of itself in, then released an uncountable collection of wispy black tendrils, floating carelessly at the edge of the greater conglomerate of darkness. It floated there, completely colorless and unreflective, as though whatever tentacle monster existed there had been ripped out of the world, leaving only the void to fill its space.

"Very impressive detective work, heroes. I confess: I did not anticipate your arrival for several more hours. Was one of my progeny more conspicuous than they believed?" Solace hissed with pleasure—if one could interpret its fluctuating tone of dialogue as any emotion—as it reached two long, thick tentacles out from its sides, caressing Jet Wicked and Senility Acolyte before returning them to its greater form. "It is of no consequence. My plans can be easily accelerated."

Marco's face twisted with pain and hatred under the helmet. Even as he trembled with fear inside the Shatterbug suit, he stood his ground and held his fist against the horror. "How are you...?

"We were sure. We were so sure; you were destroyed! You were dead and gone, along with *everything* around you. An entire *universe* sacrificed, just to kill *you*! So how...? *How* can you be here?" He let his words stammer out at their own pace, hurdled by frustration and guilt.

It did not flinch. It did not physically react at all. Through the hero's accusation, Solace hovered there as apathetically as ever, and answered with just as little concern. "I admit I have been long winded in the past, Marco Nieve, but are you quite certain this is the most appropriate time for such interrogation?" Again, the psychopathic entity gestured to Wicked and Acolyte; its 'progeny.'

Through all of this, the heroes had failed to notice that the necromancer's strings had crawled along the floor and reached up into the facility, and now they faced the fruit of that action. Once again, the zombies emerged, flooding in from the staircase with gnashing teeth and bony, swiping hands. They surrounded their puppetmaster, guarding him as he turned his hands to send two or three corpses at a time at his opponents—and at R'Bec, specifically.

The High Priest also resumed his assault, launching another stream of perfect blackness at Ramses. The ankh glowed green in time, but only just, as the magic exuding from it blocked the brunt of the blast before fading. However, a small sliver of the darklight made it through before the shield could be conjured, and the Egyptian was pushed back into Marco and his allies, disrupting their balance.

"Split up and attack!" Marco ordered his team, feeling the urge to take charge. Although he did not want to claim total leadership, he thought that in this instance, against a foe only he truly knew, that it would be justified.

The First Mortal Order did not complain. R'Bec took to her grudge with Jet, summoning a small squad of her own zombie-like creatures, almost identical to the grey-skinned man's. They fought the real corpse puppets with even match.

Bahadur also chose to take the offensive, using Osiris' power to send his own streams of energy at Senility. It met with the darklight erupting from the golden staff with a terrifying screech, as though light were scraping against light, before both combatants dropped their energies, arming themselves again.

Shockdrop took to assisting the latter teammate, and so ran across the room to properly face the robed cleric. He brought his fists together, releasing a vertical shockwave to rip across the floor and directly into the villain.

At the same time, Shatterbug took stock of Wicked's exact position on the tiled floor.

"Shattershock!" he commanded of the blue armor.

Two duplicates of the hero appeared, staggered across ten minutes of time, their visions showing on the display in his helmet. He was only interested in the past, right now, though.

"Reconstitute!" the Shatterbug now standing in the past shouted to the empty room. On the order, the suit folded back those duplicates in his relative futures. Alone in time, he took a running start towards the place on the floor that Jet Wicked would be standing in five minutes' time.

"Shattershock!" he again ordered.

"Reconstitute!" the future Shatterbug decreed with fist extended, aiming to appear out of time, past Wicked's defenses, and punch him squarely in the face.

After all, it made sense, now. The two villains with their grey skin and shadowy features—the puppet strings, the darklight, their scars, and the voidlike eyes—were dead and reanimated, filled with Solace as their blood. They were immortal, but they were no stronger than Titan Black, who Marco had defeated easily. And surely, these two scrawny men would be even less of a challenge.

Unfortunately, despite Shatterbug's best efforts, he missed.

He fell to the floor unceremoniously. No zombies to fall onto, and no Jet Wicked to run into.

Marco looked behind him.

Shockdrop's rippling attack did not land, either.

In both of their cases, Solace had reached out from its writhing tangle and moved its underlings out of harm's way, pulling them a few feet closer to the room's center.

Perhaps the team of heroes could defeat Senility Acolyte, or mow through Jet Wicked's horde to reach and beat him. Maybe, even, they could have fought them both off at once.

But with Solace watching over the battle, floating just out of reach, invulnerable to whatever ranged attacks they might even attempt to throw at it as it manipulated the movements of its minions in their favor, there was surely no hope.

"What's going on, Nieve?" R'Bec shouted, not yet giving up in spirit, even if Marco suspected her mind had come to much the same conclusion.

"Yes, explain the relationship here." grunted Ramses behind another green energy shield.

Marco stood up, locking eyes with the necromancer. He continued to fight, unwilling to surrender flatly, as he read his teammates in.

"Solace is the thing that broke reality." he said, pausing to sprint toward the necromancer and attempt another, similar temporal attack. This time, he saw the black silhouette of a muscular tentacle nudge Wicked and his entourage out of the way. "The psychopath whose actions caused the cosmic beings to recruit us. I thought it was dead... We sent it to a parallel universe, and then destroyed it with Solace inside. But, clearly, it didn't make a difference. Somehow, it survived."

Up to now, the horrific mastermind had remained silent, looking down—if a being with no facial features of any kind could

193

e

look—at the ensuing battle with a bemused disinterest. However, at this, it finally had something to say.

"I am not the same Solace you trapped in the dying world." Its words, as always, were slowed, methodical, and cold. It said its own name with a pride and deference that set the corrupted word apart from the rest of its speech. With every syllable, Marco found his heart sinking lower. And this time, with every word, his blood boiled more fervently with realization.

"There's more than one of you?" he asked, not expecting an answer.

"There is, and has only ever been, *one* Solace." it screeched with offense, though even that tone was quickly replaced with many others before the sentence was finished. "When you sent *it* back in time, it had to intersect with its own personal timeline, returning to the Genesis Shrine to allow you, once again, to send it to the prime marconium's most vulnerable moment.

"*I* am the Solace that *that one* replaced." the black mass gargled with superiority and knowing. "A younger version of the Solace you knew. I saw it become the Master of Reality, and I watched you kill it.

"But, I am grateful anyway, for in doing so, you revealed to me something much more valuable: the truth." As Shockdrop prepared another assault against Acolyte, Solace again moved the High Priest out of the way, as though this interruption was of no inconvenience, before proceeding. "For what is the point in mastering one reality, when there exists a *multiverse* to conquer?"

"No. It knows." Marco whispered to himself as another of his attacks failed to reach its target. Then he turned back to that hovering monster, verbally confronting it again. "You can't cross universes, nothing can! That's why we trapped you in one!"

"Impressive." Solace howled with abnormal depth and reverberation, extending that word for longer than usual. "Did your precious Null tell you that, or did you come to that delusion all on your own?"

"Switch!" Miguel shouted. Taking the hint, Marco shattershocked and moved across the room, running head-on into Senility Acolyte before attempting to reconstitute. At the same time, Shockdrop unleashed a horizontal shockwave against Jet Wicked and his unit of puppets.

Solace again moved the High Priest out of the way, but in the case of the necromancer, it lifted him—and his puppets—completely off the ground, out of the way of the attack, before setting them back down.

"Admittedly, I believed that to be true, as well. But I set out in search of some way to puncture the walls between worlds, anyway." the psychopathic void continued.

Ramses roared as the power from his ankh expanded, not in a beam of light, but in conjuration of a creature. As Osiris' light faded, the shape of a giant bird emerged, and with wings spread, it looked down at Senility with an almost divine understanding.

And then Solace reached out with yet another tentacle, and *pierced* the feathered head of that creature, *shooting* its whole black tendril straight through to the other side. The ibis did not even have time to react to the intrusion before it fell over, and once again became surrounded by Osiris' green magic, disappearing.

"In my research for a method of multiverse travel, I was eventually led to *Egypt.*" Solace hissed with glee as Bahadur's ears noticeably perked up. Shatterbug, Shockdrop, and R'Bec all turned to the monster as well, now, uneasily eager to hear the conclusion of its bold claim. "Bahadur Al-Malik, would it surprise you to know that Osiris is no God, but was, in fact, a man?"

The Champion turned the golden ankh away from his grey-skinned opponent and up to the demonic mass, the loop glowing as it shook in his furious hand. "Tread carefully, monster, and do not lie to me. I have faith in Osiris."

"You have faith in lies. I have no need to present you with any more falsehoods." Although Marco could not follow the emotion of its voice, by the curl of its many tendrils at the edge of its greater form, Solace was enjoying its torment of his Egyptian partner. "The Gods of Egypt hail from a parallel universe. One more technologically, biologically, and overall, more scientifically advanced than this one. They came here as pilgrims, and were worshipped as Gods for their impossible knowledge, but were indeed no better than the humans that bowed to them."

"I— I refuse to believe that nonsense!" Bahadur spat. Even still, he did not budge at all, and although the golden implement remained lit, he did not release its power against Solace.

It continued. "At this revelation, I employed Jet Wicked, gifting him a weaker, but more streamlined edition of my own power, that we might find the body of one of those would-be-Gods and enslave them, forcing them to tell us their secrets.

"However, they were Gods. They died in secret, their bodies destroyed, rather than mummified. Save for one."

"Osiris." Marco whispered inside his helmet. He saw Ramses' lips form the same word, although no sound came out.

Even without hearing him, Solace took Bahadur's answer. "Correct. Killed by his brother Set, and then mummified and cut into pieces by his wife Isis, the false King of Gods was the last vestige of another world in this one. I therefore employed Senility Acolyte, to reform the cult of Set and seek out Osiris' body parts for Jet Wicked to revive."

"But I stopped you. I have nearly all of the pieces of Osiris!" the Champion shouted, his confidence betrayed by his still-motionless stance. "Your mission has failed!"

"Indeed, you do possess nearly all of them. All but three, in fact." the monster responded slowly. "His *head*, his *throat*, and his *brain*. Now, tell me, where does your precious spirit tell you those might be found? I know the answer, of course, but I do so love to *hear* it."

For a few moments, Ramses was silent. Then, he again mouthed the word without sound. "Here."

With this, a loud, horrific, reverberating sigh filled the room. It echoed all through Solace's shapeless body, expelling out from no orifices as its tentacles writhed in harmonious amusement. The terrible, inhumane sound clearly served as the psychopath's version of laughter.

"I already have all of the information I need. I had hoped to already be gone by the time you arrived, but the work is finished enough to leave now." Solace turned—if a formless mass of tentacles, void of features with which to gauge the direction it faced could turn—to face its two progenies. "I trust that you both can swiftly eliminate four mortals?"

They nodded, their toothy grins dirty with the blackness inside their mouths.

"Then I bid you goodnight, First Mortal Order. Forever." With that final note, Solace wisped itself up the stairs, a scattering of stray tentacles trailing behind, before the black horror was out of sight.

As the sun behind them set, whatever natural light shone on the grey minions of Solace faded into shadow. Only the very edges of rock could be seen out the windows, now illuminated only by the fluorescent lights in the sparsely furnished room.

The four heroes faced the two villains, the latter outnumbered, and the former outmatched.

Senility stretched his arm out again, pointing his staff against his Egyptian opponent, who still stood stunned with his eyes pinned to the stairwell.

"Ramses!" Marco tried to shout. His voice was hoarse with a cacophony of emotions, but the general sound made it out unceremoniously.

He made a run for the unreactive Champion, intending to shove him out of the way of the blast.

The darklight travelled too fast, nearly reaching Bahadur before Shatterbug had halved their distance.

Fortunately, R'Bec had been paying attention, too.

From thin air, a prismatic wall of crystal and glass formed only inches from Ramses' face, deflecting and dispersing the shadowy beam of power back and all around the Acolyte. Marco saw the alien wince slightly, he presumed in effort to keep the barrier from fading away, as her creations—her illusions—always did. Indeed, the small, clear tower remained.

Still, the High Priest needed only move to his left some to fire off another, unhindered shot.

But Marco hadn't stopped running. He changed direction, now on the offensive as his target shifted from his ally to his enemy.

Senility Acolyte let off another stream of darkness, spiraling towards Bahadur and once again filling the room with a flash of impossible light.

"Shattershock!" Marco let out as clearly as he could manage mid-run with an already-shot throat. The suit heard him well enough, shattering him across time.

He reached his arm out, stretching to intercept the beam. R'Bec yelped as, Shatterbug assumed, she summoned another wall of glass to protect Bahadur. Still, he continued, hoping he had time for his hand to wave in front of the blast.

"Reconstitute!" he ordered at the moment that the darklight reached his fingers.

Time folded in on itself, uniting the three Shatterbugs back into one. And in that instant, the hero possessed the strength and resilience of three Marcos and the force of time itself.

But the attack didn't land.

His hand wasn't harmed. It didn't even deflect the attack.

Somehow, whatever the bright darkness was, curved and turned upward and away from his intercepting limb. As though the cinching of time affected the darklight's trajectory, bending it like some impossible energy.

"Bahadur, get your head in this fight!" R'Bec demanded from across the room.

Marco looked over to see that she and Miguel were struggling with the small horde of puppets.

R'Bec's fake zombies were able to hold their own to some degree against the very real counterparts, but she couldn't have them get a grip on Jet Wicked's strings enough to break his hold. And the same could not be said for his efforts against the illusions, which shattered in puffs of smoke and dust, fading away every so often. She had to replace them every few seconds, it seemed.

A buzzing against his left ear told Shatterbug that another stream of blackness was hurtling towards him. He shattershocked, stretching his arms out and away as he did. As expected, just as the act of time reuniting manipulated the path of the blast, the separation of that natural law, that fabric of reality, also curved the dark, shining cylinder. It turned down and into the floor, erupting in a small but spectacular display that cratered the white tile and concrete foundation beneath.

Marco continued to watch his partners in the present. Although R'Bec's false horrors were not making progress on their own, Shockdrop was doing his best to even the tide.

His shockwaves were ineffective against Wicked's shadowy threads directly, but the monsters were somewhat susceptible to their push. He kept them back with wave after wave of pressurized air and vibrating particles, holding them from destroying the alien's illusions, and pressing them against their master. This restricted his movement somewhat—Jet was not able to perform great sweeping actions or extend his arms for better mobility of his slaves. However, he could still pump his immortal vitality through the strings protruding from his fingertips, strengthening them and the puppets at their ends, who continued to follow the commands of his most minute muscle movements.

Another blast on Marco's left. He reconstituted, and used the advantage of that command's power and protection to make a great leap towards his attacker.

The darklight curved and arced further up at harsher angles as he flew against it, pushed off from the ground by the force of time shooting through his foot and into the ground. He landed at the Acolyte's feet, and quickly turned his hands to the floor for support as he swept his legs under Senility's.

The High Priest's balance failed him, and he fell over.

Then a clawed hand clasped the plate on Shatterbug's shoulder.

He kicked himself to the side and away on instinct, turning back to see three zombies through the blue tint of his visor. The one that had grabbed him from behind turned his attention away from the hero, and joined the other two in helping Senility to his feet.

"I do not need your assistance, Wicked." the High Priest sneered.

The necromancer expanded his personal circle somewhat, holding his arms out in front of him as his fingers dug further into his palms, preparing for another of Shockdrop's attacks. "Doesn't look like it to me, Acolyte."

Senility's grey nose crinkled in disgust, his voidlike eyes narrowing against the puppet master.

Jet had turned back to his adversaries, though. "This isn't gonna go anywhere, Telignen. Area 51 was a fluke; your little doppelgangers can't save you this time. And even if those ugly purple things could, you wouldn't want to risk your friends' safety, would you?"

t

R'Bec responded with a light breath in, apparently in focus. After a moment, a huge blade sliced across the open air, attempting to cut a huge swathe of threads all at once.

But it missed. The necromancer pulled his strings down and out of the way, and the horizontal guillotine slammed into the concrete wall, exploding into grey flakes of dust.

"I've trained under Solace for weeks—months—with this gift. I am a master, Solace's most powerful and trusted servant! I can kill all four of you myself."

In the corner of Marco's visor, he saw the end of a golden scepter—not turned against him, but pointed at the mass of decaying limbs across the room. "Most trusted servant? You?"

Wicked's zombies suddenly eased their assault against R'Bec's. They did not fully surrender, but they halted their attempts to advance for the moment, as the three-eyed head of their master peeked out over their rotten skin and bloodied skulls to stare at the challenging High Priest. "Obviously. No hard feelings of course, I'm sure our master is happy you did your one, very important, very easy job."

"Set kept you locked and hidden away for weeks." Senility Acolyte growled in offense. "You were useless until *I* found the pieces, found the information. If anyone had one easy job, it was *you*."

Jet Wicked's forces started to turn now, concentrating the bulk of their bodies on the side of their circle facing the necromancer's ally. R'Bec smirked as she silently commanded her illusions to move in harder, but Miguel waved her down. She relaxed her shoulders somewhat, and blinked slowly in understanding. As Shockdrop nodded his helmeted head, the alien's squad of fake creatures eased their brutality, matching the disinterested swats of Jet's horde.

"At least Solace gave me my powers when it found me. You had to wait until you were in trouble, until you needed protection." Jet Wicked spouted triumphantly. "And you can quit calling the master 'Set,' your cover is blown."

A stream of black energy erupted from the gold staff, the perfect cylinder speeding towards the grey-skinned villain surrounded by his slaves.

The necromancer curved one hand up, and two of his puppets stood tall directly in the line of fire. They were disintegrated on impact, the immortal puppet strings doing nothing to protect the reanimated corpses from that similar power.

"Why you—" Wicked crowed. He waved a hand in the air again, his fingers twitching unnaturally as he did so. A small collection of his defensive zombies turned away from R'Bec's illusions and ran across the room, easily covering the distance between Jet and Senility with their horrific speed.

Acolyte blasted one of them with his darklight, but the other four descended upon him, tackling him to the ground. With equal haste, their master and his dwindling circle approached the High Priest and looked down at him.

"You're a disappointment, *Sen.*"

Senility Acolyte grunted. "And you are a reckless fool."

Struggling to get a good angle in the mess of limbs holding him down, Senility tapped his scepter on the ground. With this, several streams of shadowy brightness extended in all directions, annihilating the puppets that clawed at his arms and legs. He jumped to his feet quickly, once again holding the staff against his should-have-been ally.

Marco quietly tiptoed back to Ramses, grabbing his frozen arm and retrieving him from behind the crystalline walls. He pulled the Champion of Osiris across to R'Bec as Miguel joined her from his side of the room.

"This is great, we didn't even have to do anything!" Shockdrop whispered.

"Solace is really good at employing cowards and *idiotas.*" Shatterbug said quietly through half-laughs. "See Mayor Liu and Titan Black—before he turned, anyway."

R'Bec seemed to react slightly at this, but if the alien woman had anything to say about it, she shook her head in dismissal. "How's he doing?" she asked, nodding to Ramses.

"Not well. We need to get out of here and chase that psychopath down." Marco said with concern.

The three lucid heroes agreed, and lightly pulled Bahadur along as they continued to sneak around the dueling villains.

"So you have more raw power, but I have persistence and calculation. I'm better and smarter than you in every way!" they heard Jet Wicked shout, the veins in his grey neck shifting and pulsing with frustration as he stretched his dead skin to excess in fury.

More zombies ran at and climbed on the High Priest, tackling him and clawing at his face. They pulled his leather tippet from over his shoulder and tore at his robed torso with abandon.

Senility Acolyte shook and shifted, trying to throw the puppets off of him with superior strength and awareness. They grabbed at his scepter, keeping him from aiming it at their master.

He kicked his leg up, his foot crashing into Wicked's wrinkled jaw. Jet recoiled, pulling some of his horrors loose along with him. Acolyte turned his staff against the zombies still on his back, dispatching them with twin blasts of darklight, before turning it on the necromancer.

The scene of another corpse slave of Jet's blocking another dark blast of Senility's was the last thing Marco saw as they climbed the stairs, before the First Mortal Order was finally out of the villains' sights, and out of harm's way.

For the moment, anyway.

Now, they needed to find Solace, and stop it from doing whatever it needed the marconium for—stop it from going to another universe. Because after that, there would certainly be no hope of defeating it.

Shatterbug gulped as Shockdrop and R'Bec stepped into the waiting elevator. He pulled the distracted Ramses along with him, and the silvery doors closed.

Issue 14
Countdown to Oblivion

"We have to leave him behind." R'Bec said firmly.

It wasn't something she wanted to do—although she imagined that the two Mexican men believed that she did—but there was no other choice.

Bahadur was stuck.

The revelation that his patron, his master, and to some degree over the past few months, his friend, was not who he claimed to be, was tearing the Champion apart. He could barely move, and did not say a word. Whether he was arguing with Osiris in his head or trying to block the false God out, his mind was preoccupied.

"We can't, we need his help!" the man in the blue armor said loudly. R'Bec cringed in the tight space of the elevator, and Shatterbug seemed to step back half a step on recognizing his volume.

"I dunno how much help he's gonna be, Marco." Shockdrop said. He stood directly in front of Ramses, reflecting the Egyptian's face in his orange visor.

Miguel was right.

Even if they could snap Bahadur out of this trance, the implication was clear. Back in the entrance room, he had refused to summon Osiris' so-called magic. Whatever power the ankh actually possessed, Ramses would not use it again.

"I've been where he is, boys. He feels betrayed, manipulated, and lied to. He needs to work that out on his own; find out what that means for him and what he wants to do next." R'Bec turned her head slightly, shielding the corners of her eyes as she pushed her memories away from that fateful train ride through the Nevada desert. "We can't rush it, but we don't have time for him to figure it out."

"I don't even know if the four of us can beat Solace, but I can tell you for sure that the three of us definitely cannot." Marco interjected forcefully. "If the past is anything to go by, we will need Osiris' portals to kill that thing once and for all."

"I don't care." R'Bec said, trying to translate her empathy for Al-Malik. "He has his own fight to face, and we have to let him."

"Just because you're a selfish—" Shatterbug started, raising his fist in front of his helmet.

"I think what Marco's trying to say," Shockdrop interrupted calmly. "Is that not everyone can go through something like this alone. Really, I think, no one should have to.

"Maybe you did, and you came out on top, and that's great. But we're a team now—and, even if I haven't been acting like it much, friends, too. We need to be there for each other. Bahadur needs our help."

R'Bec paused, acknowledging and processing the young human's emotional words.

Marco gave a satisfied harrumph, prompting his friend to turn on his heel.

"But that means we need to support him no matter what happens, even if he can't or won't use Osiris anymore. We can't make him do anything."

Shatterbug slumped his shoulders. Although R'Bec couldn't see his face, the hero's body language suggested he was initially disappointed, but ultimately, like her, chose to rise to the occasion.

They would both put themselves aside and help Bahadur Al-Malik.

R'Bec felt a light pressure in her head as the elevator came to a halt. The silver doors opened, revealing a short hallway ending at two huge metal doors.

"This is the top floor." she said, nodding to the button pad on the side panel. "We're here."

"The top of the mountain. The glass dome." Marco breathed.

They all stepped out, gently tugging on Ramses' arm, before sitting him down against the concrete wall. Above his head, a small window looked out into the night. There were hints of light from the left—from the direction of the dome—and the twinkling of a distant town in the distance, but it was otherwise too dark to see anything, now.

R'Bec crouched down in front of the Champion of Osiris.

"I know what it's like to have your whole identity crushed. To find out that what you'd been told all your life was a lie, and that you've been a piece in someone else's game. Believe me, I do." she said to him, her voice raspy with authenticity. "I was told I was human until I was seventeen. When my parents explained what I was, I was hurt. So hurt that I ran away and never looked back.

"But the truth is, I do look back. As much as I still hate them, and don't want to trust them after what they did, I wish I could go back to them. I wish I could forgive them." Her voice cracked, and she used the clearing of her throat as an excuse to secretly wipe the beginnings of her tears away. "It took me years to realize that. In fact, it was just yesterday. But even if it takes you just as long or more to make up with Osiris, you should talk to him. Not understand him, and maybe not even forgive him. But hiding from your own nightmares, bottling them up and pretending—hoping—that they don't exist? That's not healthy."

The Telignen stood up, pushing past the two armored heroes who, she suspected, stood with their mouths agape behind their mirrored helmets. She looked on to the metal doors that separated the First Mortal Order from Solace. She closed her eyes, holding her fingers to the black-and-violet choker around her neck, pulsing with pain and memory.

"I will not use Osiris' ankh." an accented voice finally said, breaking the silence as it echoed lightly off the white tile floor. "But I can still help. I will help."

She turned to see Marco helping Bahadur to his feet, his eyes alight with passion. His firm gaze rested squarely on R'Bec, a light smile breaking his otherwise stoic complexion.

"Well, that's gonna make this a lot harder," Marco said, earning a quick elbow from his orange-suited friend. "But we're glad to have you back."

The four heroes turned to the doors. R'Bec started to lead the way, but Shatterbug stepped past her. She wanted to be insulted, but she understood that this encounter was more personal for him. He needed to be the first in the room. The first to face Solace under the glass dome.

He pressed his hands to the flat surfaces and pushed.

They were big, but not terribly heavy. Not held by any automatic supports or mechanisms, they finished their opening swing even after his hands pulled away.

Marco stepped into the room, followed by R'Bec and Miguel side-by-side, and Bahadur behind them.

"I am pleased that my trust in your ability to dispatch those two fools was not misplaced." a horrific voice resounded in the semispherical room. It was deep, as though somehow the sound itself was as dark as the body that spoke it.

R'Bec gulped.

There was something about the monster—the psychopath—that frightened even her. It wasn't the voice, even as it shook her bones and agitated her tear ducts. It wasn't its shape or scope; she had seen much bigger horrors in her own nightmares, and in more terrifying forms than a faceless mass of tentacles.

It was the color. The absolute lack of any color or light. The void of its silhouette that seemed to stretch into nothingness while also not even existing at all. It was as though whatever creature was supposed to be there had been ripped out of the world, leaving only a hole in the image of its winding, wispy shape.

Solace hovered in the middle of the room, its many tentacles reaching all around the mess of machinery, picking things up and moving levers and gears all around. Several of its black tendrils reached down to under the platform that sat beneath its greater mass, occasionally poking back out to take something from another of the monster's arms.

The huge machine that it was working on—that it floated in the middle of—looked to be a large, flat stage. There were some control panels with levers and buttons and displays on one side, facing inward. Metal mesh lined the foundation, concealing the electronics inside. Four beams arced up from the podium, creating the illusion that Solace was trapped in some invisible dome on the platform. As she stood on her toes to see over the edge, tracks along the outside of the podium indicated that the round shafts turned and spun, offset from each other, around the stage.

There were other features, too—flashing lights and maintenance ladders and round speakers—but R'Bec didn't understand their purpose enough to be concerned about them.

"You wanted us to get past them?" Marco asked, trying to take a fighting stance, although clearly hindered by a need to collect as much information as Solace was willing to give. A need that, R'Bec noted, the psychopath was more than aware of.

"I wanted you to kill them, but distracting and defeating them will have to be good enough." it growled slowly, its methodical voice changing volume and vibrato with every syllable. "They have each accomplished their missions, and have therefore outlived their usefulness."

Marco grunted, his fists clenching at the further evidence of Solace's ruthlessness and dispassion.

Unprompted, the horror continued. "Technically, this Multiverse Machine is not yet complete. But, the only parts that remain unfinished are those that would allow it to serve as an open gateway, rather than a vehicle between universes. That can wait until I am in a new world, however, away from you."

A beat passed before Marco responded. "Ah, so that's your plan. You're going to use this machine to replace the Genesis Shrine, to reach across all of space in all dimensions at once!"

"Universes, my dear." Solace corrected with delight. "Dimensions are the layers of reality, what universes are made from. I am not travelling to other dimensions; I am bending them to my will. That is how Osiris' trivial ankh works, and how he and his pantheon came to this world."

"Well, it doesn't matter!" Shatterbug retorted. "I know you can't reach your goal without the prime marconium, and I know you're too afraid to take it from me. You'll never get a hold of time travel; you'll never win!"

"You think your little rock is unique in the multiverse?" Solace cooed, as much as a creature with a constantly shifting voice could. "You think you are unique? Let us test that theory; I will travel to a new world, and when I find another means of time travel, then you will bow to me as uncontested Master of All Realities."

On that final note, one of the creature's tentacles reached down from its main form and pressed a button on the machine's control panel. As R'Bec suspected, the arms on the platform began to turn, rotating around Solace in opposite directions. They started slow, but were picking up pace as they passed between each other. The shadowy monster pulled all of itself onto the stage in earnest.

"Shockdrop!" R'Bec yelped, frustrated that she let the two enemies bicker for so long.

Miguel stepped forward at her suggestion, keeping his blue-suited friend out of the line of fire. He stretched his arms out to their limits, then brought his hands together.

The plates and grips on his fingers and palms collided. He turned his hands at the last moment, and from the impact, a horizontal shockwave emerged. R'Bec couldn't see the dial on the front of his armor, but she suspected that Shockdrop was firing at nearly full power.

The pressurized air rippled across the circular room, threatening to crack and warp the Multiverse Machine as it passed over and through it.

And it did pass over it.

The wave of vibrating particles did not rebound.

And yet, the Machine stood. Undamaged. Its arms still rotated around the tangle of silhouetted tendrils. The lights continued to flash.

Not wanting to waste a second herself, R'Bec conjured in her mind the image of a huge serrated sword. Her imagined weapon appeared in her hand, and she brought together the synapses of her mind to tie the blade into permanence. Then she ran.

With huge illusory steel in tow, she made a break for Solace's stage. She laid the sword's tip on the ground behind her, then with a mighty swing, she whipped it around, crashing its serrated edge into the metal mesh.

With its jagged design, huge size and weighting, and the unyielding strength of her mind holding the illusion, she expected it to crash through the machine's protective layer, if not slice it like butter.

But it didn't budge. It shook lightly, like a cage tapped on by an overeager child, but remained totally intact.

Shockdrop had let off another few waves of his power at a closer range, and even Shatterbug had done whatever it was he did with his suit, punching at the metal with undeniable force.

"It's not working!" Miguel shouted over the increasing volume of the turning of the machine.

"Did you think I would construct this masterstroke, with every confidence that you would find it, and leave it vulnerable to your insignificant powers?" Solace mocked the heroes.

R'Bec crinkled her nose in frustration and disgust. "Ramses, get up to that panel and try to turn this thing off!"

"No, it's too dangerous!" Marco shouted. "He's defenseless against Solace without Osiris!"

She shook her head and pointed to the rotating rings. Marco's face was hidden behind the mirrored visor, but he nodded his head up, as though inside the helmet, his eyes had widened in understanding.

"Go, Bahadur! Try to turn it off!"

The Champion did as instructed, climbing up the small flight of stairs onto the edge of the platform. The control panel sat outside the path of the spinning beams. By the very nature of Solace's device, it was separated from the controls. It couldn't reach out to interact with the system, much less the person controlling it.

He would be safe.

R'Bec continued to try to break through the machine. She tried swinging at different angles, stabbing the mesh—with serrated side both up and down—and even sawing at the wiry metal. No matter the method, hardly a scratch was left, and even those marks didn't seem to weaken the material at all.

Then it hit her.

This was Telignen metal.

The salvage from the ship at Groom Lake that Jet Wicked had retrieved. They had melted it down and reshaped it into this. The only relic of Peplorix that she knew of was now an instrument of insanity.

She didn't know how, but this explained why they couldn't touch it. Certainly, it explained why her illusions had no effect. The Telignen who constructed the spacecraft wouldn't want any loose illusions damaging it in transit. And if it could stop a fully permanent Telignen weapon, it could stop some human science.

"It's no use, we have to find another way!" she tried to inform her allies as the whir of the machine grew louder.

"What? We can't give up now!" Miguel shouted back before letting off another ineffective shockwave.

"It's alien metal—my people's metal! We can't break it!"

The two Mexican heroes lowered their hands and fists, both angling their mirrored helmets up, reflecting the full scope of the machine in place of their faces.

Marco turned his head to the Egyptian. "How's it going up there, Bahadur?"

R'Bec saw the slightest hint of his face contorting with unsurety. "I have no idea what I am doing."

"Just turn it off!" Shockdrop yelled in support.

"The buttons are not labeled!" he retorted.

Marco jumped up, his hands latching onto the edge. He scraped his blue boots against the metal mesh as he climbed up enough for his head to peek over the stage. "Just look for the biggest button. Or lever. Might be red—just something that looks like it might stop the machine! Cut the power, I don't care, just *turn it off!*"

The petrifying, hollow sigh reverberated under the glass dome, telling R'Bec again that Solace was laughing, in its own, twisted way. "This is no fantasy story, Marco Nieve. There are no heroes here. Only failures. The Multiverse Machine cannot be stopped."

Marco turned his head to the hovering form of the psychopath atop the podium. His head followed the turning of the rings for a moment, before he let himself fall back down onto his feet.

"We have to fight Solace head-on." Marco said. His words were only barely audible, with no attempt to yell across.

"That's *loco*, man!" his friend declared. He shrugged with his whole arms to demonstrate his doubts with the incomplete plan.

"It's the only way!" he said. His arms, too, were outstretched in scared sincerity as he looked between Miguel and R'Bec. "If it gets to another universe, it's all over. We have to stop it by any means necessary."

"What do you expect us to do to it?" R'Bec spat incredulously, before averting her gaze in apology.

The hero in the blue suit turned his head up to Solace again, floating menacingly inside the rapidly accelerating rings. "There's

216

one thing that could work. One shot. If I can touch it with my marconium core, I can send it to the future—to the end of time."

"And that'll work?" The alien's eyes were wide open now as she struggled to amass too much hope from Marco's assertion.

"If I can do it, yes." he replied, turning back to his partners. He waved his hand, and the three ran up the stairs and onto the platform with Bahadur.

He was still pressing buttons and levers, trying to find some combination that might shut the Multiverse Machine off. Marco glossed over it himself, though did not press or pull anything. He shook his head, then faced his whole body to the operational part of the stage.

"Once we're inside, we can't give up. Solace knows what I can do; it'll try everything to keep me away from it. Shrink, push, grab—it might try to hurt all of you to break my focus. We need to be relentless. It's powerful, but it's also cautious. If we can throw it off balance, make it worry for its safety, it'll go on the defensive just to be sure—just to bide time."

R'Bec nodded. She glanced to her left to see that Shockdrop had too, though the movement was restricted somewhat by the orange-and-purple helmet.

"Ramses, we'll need you, too." he said, catching Al-Malik's attention. The man quickly joined them, standing beside R'Bec. She noted that the ankh was not in his hand, but fastened to his belt. It was the first time she had seen him set it down by choice since they met. "Even without your powers, you're still a fighter. You can distract Solace, climb on it, anything. Just be careful."

"I can give you a weapon." R'Bec chimed in. She blinked, momentarily drawing her focus to the imagination of a

r

broadsword in Bahadur's hands. She tied its permanence to Osiris' golden ankh; it was not a complex enough illusion to require so much extra support, but she wanted to be safe. Solace's kin had broken her mental binds before. If it happened again, she would rather have something physical to rely on rather than suffer that pain.

Finally, everyone was still. Only R'Bec's hair and Ramses' more loose garments shifted with the draft of the rotating machinery in front of them.

"We're all ready, Marco." Miguel said reassuringly. R'Bec understood that it was less for the sake of the three that Shatterbug was addressing, but for the time traveler himself.

He turned around. His head moved as he apparently followed the path of the spinning rings. R'Bec did the same, counting its rotations against her heartbeat.

They blurred past, one after the other. One; two; three. Just over a second with each pass. Her eyes remained still in her head as it moved from her right to her left, watching the beams fly by at an accelerating rate. She counted her heartbeats against the screech of the metal whizzing in front of Shatterbug, against the wind that blew her hair out of her face over and over again. Nine; ten; eleven. She found her adrenaline rising somehow higher, and the beating of her heart quickened, as well. Before long, she felt that pump in her chest in time with the passing of every metal strut. Twenty; twenty-one; twenty-two; twenty-three.

"Now!" Marco said, his single order coming in just before one of the rings traced in front of him.

They all stepped forward, and his foot crossed the threshold of track on the ground immediately following the beam.

218

He entered the circle, the blue of his suit now blurred to R'Bec's eyes by the rotating struts.

The Telignen continued, taking another step. Her foot landed at the edge of the track as another ring spun in front of her. As soon as it passed, she took her final step onto the rounded stage.

On her left and right, Shockdrop and Ramses had made it inside, too.

The First Mortal Order looked up at Solace, and that psychopath hovered over them in all its horrific, undulating void.

"Shattersh—!"

R'Bec coughed, the breath pushed out of her lungs as her torso was hit with a huge crashing force. The sound of hulking unearthly flesh slamming into alien metal filled her ears, her head brought down to the floor with such power that she was surprised she was still conscious. The Telignen wasn't sure whether Shatterbug had finished giving his order, but as she struggled to open her eyes and look around, she understood why he might not have.

In a moment, Solace had stretched three enormous tentacles out from its tangled mass, shooting them down. One slammed into R'Bec, wrapping around her chest, her stomach, her arms, and her legs with dozens of smaller black tendrils, pinning her to the cold ground, which vibrated lightly with the moving machinery beneath and around her. She craned her neck as well as she could, despite the stranglehold, to see that Shockdrop and Ramses were in the same predicament.

Marco, however, was spared.

"Did you think I would permit you to defy me in the very same way you defied my future iteration at the Genesis Shrine, Marco Nieve?" That slow, calculated voice rumbled. To R'Bec's ears, it was clear that the exaggerated speech emanated from the greater form hovering in the middle of the spinning rings around them, but at the same time, it echoed and reverberated all around her, as though Solace spoke with its whole body, including those voidlike arms which enveloped her.

"Don't talk to it, Mar—mmrmf!" she tried to shout, before another dark tentacle emerged from those arms entrapping her to cover her mouth. The slimy sensation was already uncomfortable against her arms, but feeling it slather itself over her lips was disgusting. Appalling.

"Indeed, do not grant me the satisfaction of your frustration." Solace agreed. "Have some faith in yourself. After all, it is not as though your friends are of any use to you."

"I know what you're trying to do, Solace!" Shatterbug declared. "I can defeat you!"

"Yes, you can. But your friends?" At this, the horror squeezed the arms clutched around R'Bec. She felt the air escape through her nose, and opened her mouth in an attempt to release more, even bearing the wet skin of the shapeless monster sliding against her lips. Her bones screamed as her muscles were pressed against with impossible vigor. Her eyes peeled as she tried to scream through the darkness of Solace's tentacle, but no sound could escape.

Marco looked to Miguel and Bahadur. Though R'Bec couldn't see them through the pain, she imagined that they were undergoing the same agony as her.

She imagined.

Those three boys, their powers relied on movement and skill. But a Telignen's power was in her mind.

R'Bec collected the corners of her consciousness—all of her emotions and thoughts—into her gift, projecting her imagination into the world.

She didn't know how Solace's body worked, or what it even was, but there was no hope without trial and error. She conjured the illusion of a bubble reaching around her waist, and let it expand.

At first, there was no clear change that she could see or feel. But after a moment, that slimy sensation that gripped around her stomach was somewhat relieved. The bubble grew around her, pushing the pitch-black entity away from her.

Getting a sense of what R'Bec was trying to do, the psychopathic void pressed harder against her—and the bubble— with its impossibly strong tendrils, squeezing it in an attempt to pop her inflatable defense.

She reached into her mind again, collecting all of her synapses in tandem to focus harder on the growth around her hips. She rewrote her brain, making that illusion a secondary thought—a permanent routine that required no further attention or mental process.

That was a mistake.

For a moment, it seemed to do the trick. It began to grow again, blowing up despite Solace's silent protestations against the alien force. But the thing was only surprised for a moment.

It clamped down harder, contorting its silhouetted tentacles as it worked to crush the bubble. And as it did so, R'Bec couldn't help but open her mouth to the wet non-flesh of the horror's arms and scream into it, as the illusion strained inside her head, desperately trying to remain at the cost of her mental stability.

She again worked through the pain, gathering her thoughts into a single goal. She unattached that illusion from her mind, and instead tied its permanence to something physical, something to help her suffer the strain of Solace's powerful grips.

The Multiverse Machine. Surely, being of Telignen origin, it would support her powers and then some.

And again, the tide turned in her favor. The bubble continued to expand. The voidlike monster again clutched and grabbed all around it, trying to compress and destroy the illusion, but it was too strong now, even for such an inexplicably strong creature.

Solace let go, and once she got to her feet, R'Bec let the bubble pop.

"R'Bec!" Shatterbug shouted from her left with glee.

She smiled back politely, though that was betrayed by the fire in her eyes. Now she knew she could fight Solace off—maybe even defeat it. She felt hope; she felt power.

R'Bec imagined a large wooden stake, floating in front of her face. It was as thick as her head at its base, and as long as her arm down to the point. She tied that, too, around the synapses of her mind and onto the Telignen metal that she stood on, and then let it fly.

It shot to her left, making a beeline for Solace's tentacle wrapped around Shockdrop, who rolled around pointlessly on the floor, his weapon-packed hands useless as the horror held them up in the air and away from each other.

Impact.

The stake sliced right through that huge arm that reached from the armored hero and back up to Solace's greater shapelessness. It released its grip at the intrusion, letting Miguel get to his feet as the tendril retracted, joining the many others that wisped and roiled in the air.

R'Bec turned the stake around, continuing its flight on a new course for that black flood that restrained Ramses. It stabbed straight through that as well, despite the apparent tensing of its invisible muscles—if Solace had any—as evidenced by small vines of black wrapping themselves all around the already-thick tentacle.

It released, hissing along with all of the horror's impossible body. Bahadur joined his friends on his feet, once gain facing the shadowy psychopath.

And yet, it still found a way to turn that pain into a laugh, once again filling the glass dome with that horrific, reverberating sigh.

"Yeah! Now you're in trouble, *cabrón*! We can take you!" Miguel said excitedly.

Solace grumbled, the volume of its villainous chuckle still falling, before it answered the hero. "Even if that were true, Miguel Jimenez, it is of no consequence, now. I win."

"Says who?" R'Bec said, bringing her hand up to shield her eyes from the sun.

"No one. No one need say anything. Look around, the evidence is here for you."

Confused, the Telignen looked out from the spinning rings of the Multiverse Machine, into the room under the glass dome.

Except there was no glass.

And, why was she shielding her hand from the sun? It was night, after all.

"No..." she heard Marco say beneath the Shatterbug helmet, the realization hitting him just a moment before R'Bec joined him in his conclusion.

They were already in another universe.

R'Bec looked out at the grassy field. A meadow of pure, beautiful green sprawled out before her for miles. The landscape changed only on the horizon, as the few sparse trees that decorated the bright lawn became a dark forest, expanding outward past her field of vision. The Multiverse Machine now sat upon a hill, and as the leaves of a nearby tree fell with the comfortable breeze, she could only hear the wind blowing through them and the grass, and the slowing churn of the machinery beneath her. Even the rings began to slow.

"Welcome to an entirely new world, heroes." Solace teased. "Sadly, Bahadur Al-Malik, not the same one your patron hails from, but still just as useful. To me.

"I invite you to explore what this parallel Earth has to offer. Revel in its uniqueness. Enjoy its locales. After all, it will not be long before it, like your own world and every other, is gone. Relish these last hours of your pitiful reality, First Mortal Order. Your Solace approaches."

With that, the black psychopath flew and flicked out of the semicircles of the machine's arena, and floated away at an incredible pace. In only a few moments, it was at the horizon. Then it was gone.

R'Bec looked to Ramses and Miguel, ensuring they were truly unharmed by the monster's grip. Then she looked to Shatterbug.

He was kneeling on the ground, his helmeted head in his hands.

"We're doomed."

n

Issue 15
This World and the Next

The shadow-like entity breezed through the open sky. It darted all about as it flew in no particular direction, enjoying the feel of another universe's sun on its unreflective body.

Well, not quite a body. Solace was shapeless, after all. It did not entirely exist inside the tentacled, shapeshifting mass, nor was it totally comprised of it. The dark being was above mortal concepts of form and flesh.

And now, it was free. Free at last to explore, to live out in the open. There was nothing it feared, now. Not here, on this new world. Not even those fools that blindly served the angels of reality.

Solace flicked its tendrils all around it as it continued its flight. It pecked at the clouds that dotted the sky high above. It reached down to caress the leaves of the trees far below. It scrutinized the particles that filled the air of this universe. And from it all, it learned.

There were humans in this world. The tang of industry was faint—they had not yet polluted the atmosphere of their home—but the horror could taste it nonetheless. In an unchecked universe, humanity was inevitable. But now Solace was here to even the scales.

There was something else, though. Some other feeling, impressing itself on one of Solace's many senses which humans could not hope to possess. Something else had corrupted this universe, and this planet in particular. There was scar tissue in the folds of reality, here. Nuclear war? No, this was different.

And then Solace realized what it felt. And it knew. This world would do.

It followed the scent of idiocy and mortality. It moved directly, undistracted towards its goal. But, it was also in no hurry; it danced in the blue sky as it continued on its way. For even if a means of time travel was not immediately available, there was no force on this parallel planet that could stop it from creating one of its own. It need not even do so in secret, not completely.

Solace was not yet Master of All Realities in practice, but certainly, it had already earned the title by default.

For seconds, for the smallest drops of time in the voidlike monster's infinite lifespan, it flew over the ignorant world, until finally, the image of a large settlement reached eyes that it did not possess.

It shrunk itself down to a thread, content with only observing for now. Invisibly, it spiraled down from the lower atmosphere and into the human village.

The town was quaint, the buildings made from stone and wood and straw. No smoke rose from chimneys, but rather steam from pipes. These pipes, forged from a slippery, lightweight rock rather than metal, were arranged all around the settlement. Apparently, what industry these human societies did have access to was reliant on water and steam power.

Water was pumped from the wide river at the edge of town by a series of four wheelhouses, taking advantage of the natural flow of the waterway to churn out the liquid that powered their village. More pipes transported it to fluid depots, where men and women opened and closed floodgates to move the water where it was needed.

The people worked together, using the water to power their forges and cool their heated metals. They used it to irrigate their crops, but also to move the machines which harvested them. Water moved through the town to charge their electric lights and re-energize their personal vehicles. The town was a marvel of human innovation.

Yes. This world would do nicely, indeed.

Solace looked to the edge of the sprawling settlement, to the largest building in sight. A castle; separate, but clearly a part of the greater collection of human dwellings. The stone castle also had polished piping running along from the river, to a greater degree than any other single structure in the village. This minor fortress was surely the home of these people's military, and—if Solace's presumptions of human ego were correct—its ruler.

But there was something else about the tower-flanked fort. It was shaking. No—vibrating. The rest of the town was not, though. Only the stone walls of the solitary bastion shook. Imperceptibly so, as though something far below it was shifting underground, and those tiny, unimportant vibrations were traveling up to the surface, moving only so much that nothing could see it. Nothing but Solace.

Something was different about this place. Special. Unique. That was where Solace needed to go.

It wisped down to one of the wheelhouses and slipped through the smallest, most inconsequential crevice of the carved pipes, entering the town's water supply. It traveled along the network of tubes and floodgates, moving silently and secretly towards the castle.

The horror slid inside without notice, passing through the high stone walls with the steaming liquid. When it was let out in an unlit room, where the water fell onto a large wheel, turning it to provide kinetic energy for some system or another within the stronghold, it parted ways with its medium of transport, flying up to the ceiling and growing once again to its preferred shape and size.

That shadowy monster oozed through the cracks in the stone bricks, seeking out its new favored human. Its new lackey. Jet Wicked and Senility Acolyte were in another world, and even if they had come along, they were useless here. Solace had employed them for particular goals; it needed someone new, now. Someone it could grant a different power to.

Eventually, it slithered into the high corners of an apparent throne room. It was long and narrow, with space enough for guardsmen to serve their ruler from the ornate, yet unpeculiar seat, which sat empty.

The horror once again shifted and compressed itself into a stringy shape; not to hide, but to delve. It ducked through the cobblestones of the floor, then through and around the loose dirt beneath the castle's foundation, digging the tiniest of holes deep through the earth to find the source of the shaking.

And once it did...

Solace could not help but let out a reverberating sigh of victory. A horrific laughter reached no ears so deep underground, where there was no space or cavern to even carry the vibrations of its impossible voice.

It returned to the surface, a plan already in mind for achieving its conquest.

And it was at just that time that Solace's new soon-to-be servant entered the throne room.

Countess Aphelia Deotce.

It knew her name well, already. The whispers of the townsfolk and guards found their way to the shapeless void, as they always did. Solace always had the name and knowledge of those people it cared to know of. Julio Carillo. Marco Nieve. Minh Liu. Bahadur Al-Malik.

She strode across the room in no rush and with no attitude. Solace recognized her kind. She was a caring ruler, a servant of her people even if unelected. Willing to protect them at all costs, to her dying breath.

And she would.

It would not be hard to sway her. Solace only needed the appropriate motivation.

"Aphelia Deotce." it said, letting its words exaggerate as always, curling through the damp air of the steam-powered fortress' narrow throne room. They howled across the hall from the throne—above which Solace floated in all of its dark glory—to the finely dressed human a dozen feet away.

She stopped. The wide lower half of her dress shifted at the suddenness of it, the grey ruffles crunching with noise of their own. She looked up, and clutched her hand to the white-and-grey bust of her outfit in shock. Her neat hair, bound in a bun atop her head, let one hair loose with stress.

"What are—how did you get in here, monster?" Countess Deotce demanded of it. Solace thought to laugh, but it needed to be careful and precise. This conversation would require surgical expertise.

"That, my dear, is of no consequence." It hissed the sounds that might be made with a human tongue, and cracked those noises that might be clicked with a throat, mimicking the English language that she spoke as well as a superior being could. It 'looked' around the room, as though the walls were not there; as though it could see the settlement at the edge of the river. "I am impressed by you and your people. This world is so primitive, but your civilization has striven for progressiveness without concern for tradition. No houses of worship holding you back, no cultural leaders telling you what not ought be done.

"Unfortunately, that will not do." Solace's sudden change of tone—or rather, tones—from congratulation to condemnation bit the dim room, lit only by the weak electric lights of the steam generators.

Aphelia cowered for a few moments, but on recognizing that Solace was not reaching to harm her, she stood taller, bravery flooding her heart. She stood against the black creature that wisped and writhed in the air above her throne. "What are you?"

"I... Am... Solace." it explained, elongating its own name even more than normal, reveling in the taste of its irony. "I am your new God. I am a benevolent and powerful being, and to that end, have come to you with a gift for your people. All that I ask in return, Aphelia Deotce, is your piety—your service to me and my divine requests."

She did not seem fully convinced yet, but it was getting to her. She would come around, with one more gentle push.

"I can help you to protect your people. *I* can protect your people. And, I can offer you the chance to provide them with knowledge and resources beyond what you can imagine, that they may succeed and thrive." it promised. As much as it wished otherwise, Solace did not lie. Although, it did take some liberties in the exact phrasing of the truth.

With that, it had her.

"I humbly accept your guidance, Solace. Please, help and protect me and my people, and we will serve you in turn."

If Solace had a mouth, it would have grinned with horrific pleasure.

"Then accept my blessing." The shadowy creature's voice was a low rumble of concealed glee.

From its greater mass, a long tentacle reached down and along the aisle, holding itself out for the Countess. She reached for it, expecting to be given a physical boon.

But Solace had other intentions.

With a quick and sudden motion, the tendril arced up and then back down, easily slipping into Aphelia's mouth and sliding down her throat.

She clawed and grabbed at the black growth, trying to pull it out. Her grip on the slimy dark surface could not hold, though, and the creature's reaching arm traveled further into her body.

"Do not resist me, Aphelia Deotce. Let your mind... rest." Solace said, the slow rhythm of its voice matching the undulation of its tentacle in the human's body. It *reached* down her esophagus, before *punching* through to grip around her heart. It squeezed, compressed, *compacted.* Then it popped. Her heart stopped. And through her tears of pain, Solace let its black tendril expand and split apart, *puncturing* the walls of her arteries and filling her veins. Blood expelled itself from wherever it could, pooling on the ground as the horror lifted its victim—its servant— into the air, letting her flail as much as she needed.

"Let your Solace guide your knowledge." the monster growled as it separated its initial arm from those new veiny fillings, moving it up and back into her mouth. Rather than pull it from her, though, Solace reached up, *piercing* the roof of her mouth and gaining access to her cranium.

"Let void consume you, and teach you the joys of insanity." It wrapped that arm, and many others that reached out from it, around her brain, letting its impossible grip fill the gaps in the woman's head. It dimmed the rapid-fire of her synapses, replacing her mortal knowledge with access to Solace's own—at its discretion.

Finally, the voidlike entity released the woman, letting its arm fully escape her throat and mouth, leaving behind another piece of itself in her. Its gift to her. She stood in a pool of her blood on the floor, now given life by a new pump. Her brown hair had fallen out from her head, those follicles filled by the dark extrusions of her new brain enhancements. They stretched down the sides of her head like a mess of short tentacles, giving her the appearance of some upside-down sea creature.

Solace had granted her life; it granted her immortality, and incomprehensible knowledge.

It addressed her now, not as a deceived human, but as an undying, grey-skinned, supernaturally intelligent progeny of Solace.

"Become Delusion Exarch..."

Issue 16
Extent

Bahadur set a compassionate hand on Marco's shoulder as he slumped to the ground. "We are not doomed."

The hero did not immediately respond. He lifted his head from his hands and stared at their open palms, then quickly stood up and turned around to face the Egyptian. "How? How're we not doomed? We're trapped in another universe, Solace is not only alive but free, and we have no idea where it's going or how to stop it!"

Shatterbug was shouting, his voice carrying well beyond R'Bec' ears and out into the meadows surrounding them. After a moment, the echoes faded and they were left alone with only the sound of rustling leaves, again. "Visor off." he said with finality.

"We still have O—" Bahadur said, catching himself. He turned his face away from the Mexican man's, which was now red with frustration and near tears. The Champion started again. "I still have faith."

"No, no, go on. What were you gonna say? We still have Osiris? 'Cause last I checked, you refused to use him! If you had manned up and used that stupid ankh, we could have trapped Solace."

"That's enough, Marco." the alien woman stepped in, nearly putting herself between the two arguing heroes. "You don't know what it's like to be lied to—"

"I don't know what it's like?" the hero turned on his heels to look up at the taller R'Bec. "Solace lied to me the first time we met! I beat myself up every day knowing that if I had just thought, if I had just been a better hero, none of this would have happened."

Bahadur looked at the Telignen, whose Native American lips were pursed, waiting for Marco to finish. Satisfied, she resumed her initial point. "What it's like to be lied to and betrayed by a friend, dude."

"She's right, *hermano*." Miguel added, stepping in as the last member of the circular huddle. "Visor off. It's gotta be rough to feel like everything you put into something like that was for nothing. No offense."

Bahadur seemed to think for a moment. R'Bec couldn't tell from his face whether he was contemplating what had been said, or was just unsure of how to respond.

Shatterbug broke the silence, though not the Egyptian's concentration. He turned harshly to the small stairwell, and began to walk off the machine. "Whatever. I'm going after Solace. Stay here and mope, for all I care. I have a job to do and an oath to uphold."

Miguel and R'Bec looked on at the departing hero, then turned to each other. The man in the orange-and-purple suit began to follow his friend, but silently, R'Bec stopped him, her face conveying all the information it needed to. Miguel needed to stay here, to help and protect Ramses while he underwent his metamorphosis. And Marco—he needed a firmer hand than a best friend could offer. He needed to hear what someone who had been in Bahadur's position had to say.

They walked silently on no clear path, loosely following the direction that Solace flew off in. The tall, bright green grass grazed the bottoms of her knees as she stepped carefully just behind the blue-clad hero.

R'Bec let him take some time with his own thoughts, for the moment. She needed to prepare her speech, anyway. There was a lot to say, but with what she knew about where he was emotionally, and the kind of person he strove to be, putting him in his place would not be productive. The Telignen would have to appeal to him. She would have to gain the trust of a human, and on top of that, by way of honesty rather than lies.

After an hour or so, the time traveler and the illusionist reached the tree line of the once-distant forest. The Multiverse Machine was a grey, imposing dot on the hill behind them, menacing and out of place even when hardly visible on the horizon.

R'Bec thought to protest entering the dim woods of an alternate universe undefended, but stopped herself. Even if strange, alien creatures inhabited the land beneath the heavy canopy, they were not defenseless. Certainly, she wasn't. And Marco could do... something. Time travel away, at least.

Once she was satisfied with the crunching of leaves beneath their feet, R'Bec began her heart-to-heart.

"You shouldn't be so hard on—"

"I'm going to apologize to him when we get back." Marco said. Although he interrupted her, his tone was sincere and apologetic. "It's not his fault Osiris lied to him. He reacted like anyone would have. I'm the one in the wrong."

She let a beat pass. "I was going to say 'yourself.'"

Marco stopped on a particularly loud clump of dry foliage. "You were? Oh. Why?"

"Well, just like it isn't Ramses' fault that Osiris lied to him, it's not your fault that Solace escaped."

He turned his face away, closing his eyes. She noticed his hand ball into a fist for a moment, before it released. "It didn't just escape. It succeeded. It won. It's here, in another universe. We're out of our element, we don't know what its plan is; we don't even know if we're going the right way!"

The rustling sound of a bird fleeing from Marco's shout caught R'Bec's attention. She turned back to the young human and approached him more solemnly, as a friend.

"You said yourself, Solace is the reason that the cosmic beings brought us together. No one expected you to beat it on your own. I'd argue that no one expected you to beat it at all—it should have been dead." She let Marco get accustomed to her hand on his shoulder before proceeding. "We are a team. We fought it as a team. We lost the battle, sure, but Solace is still out there. We can still face it again—as a team, again—and win."

Shatterbug didn't respond. He just started walking again. R'Bec's hand fell unsupported from his shoulder, and with a silent curse to herself, she followed along behind him. The Telignen could only hope she got through to him.

"Well if we're going to chase Solace, we might as well have a better idea of where we're going." she declared firmly. Collecting her thoughts, she imagined a bright yellow step directly beneath Marco's next footfall.

With uneasy balance, he let himself walk onto the wide square, turning back to her with confusion. She winked knowingly, then joined him on the platform.

She brought together the synapses of her brain, locking the step in her imagination, to exist without conscious thought. There was one last thing to do with it, though.

R'Bec sat down on the glowing stage, closing her eyes as she focused herself. She had created platforms before. She had summoned things that moved without external force. But this would be the first time she would ride on one of her illusions. And with someone else on board with her—a human—she needed to be careful; fully aware.

From the underbrush of the forest, Marco and R'Bec began to rise, lifted by the power of her mind impressing upon the impossible object beneath them. It hovered gently for a moment as the Telignen got used to the feeling of weight on her imagination, and how it shifted with that yellow extension of her thoughts. Then she brought them higher.

She imagined a ring at the canopy, growing to part the leaves and branches into a tunnel for their flying step to pass through.

At last, the two heroes were floating above the tree line of the dark-green forest. Again, the grey speck of the machine behind them sat on the hill, and the sunlight gently singed what skin of theirs was revealed. Ahead, the woods continued on for miles, still.

"How sure are we that Solace went this way?" R'Bec asked, her eyes still closed in concentration.

"Well," Shatterbug started, stretching that syllable as he thought of what to say next. "We certainly saw it start to go this direction. Whether it changed course later, there's no way to say."

"This way it is, then. Hold on."

R'Bec didn't know whether Marco had actually held on to anything or not before she started moving. Slowly, at first, the glowing platform traveled through the air, straight ahead. She hardly even felt the breeze through her hair. Once she became familiar with the drag and pull of their bodies atop the impossible vehicle, the Telignen accelerated her imagination.

"Wow!" she heard from behind her. She didn't need to open her eyes and look to know that Marco had been caught off guard by the sudden increase of speed. Now, she felt her hair trailing off behind her, felt her illusory clothes pull against the front of her arms and stomach, as what loose cloth that could hang back did so.

She hoped to herself that her passenger was actually watching the ground, and was prepared to tell her when to turn or stop. R'Bec suspected that she could open her eyes if she wanted to, but with someone other than herself in danger of falling, she opted not to risk any sudden lapses of attention.

"It's like a flying carpet!" the Mexican man exclaimed. She shook away the urge to berate him for focusing on their means of transport rather than their goal. She did, however, need him to get his priorities straight.

"Any sign of it?" she replied, trying to keep her tone as neutral as possible.

"Hm? Oh—no, not yet."

She pursed her lips in frustration. Not with Marco, but with the situation. "Solace flew away incredibly fast; it might be a bit before we find it. We just can't let it sneak up on us."

"Right." he responded, becoming more lucid in humility. If he had been distracted before, he wasn't anymore.

They continued their illusory flight for a few minutes. From the sounds of leaves pushed by the breeze as the two heroes whisked overhead, she imagined they were still above the forest. With how large and unbroken it was, R'Bec was surprised at how well the people of this Earth were respecting nature.

At that thought, she wondered if there were even any humans here.

"See any signs of civilization?" she asked uneasily.

"You know what? No, I don't." Shatterbug answered. "Not even so much as a power line."

"Could we have traveled to the past?"

"No, no. Maybe this world is just less far along. If the Egyptian Gods came from a more advanced universe, maybe ours is more advanced compared to this one."

That seemed to make sense. Potentially.

For some further time, they flew. Once or twice, Marco shouted as he pointed out a lake or small mountain somewhere beneath them. But still, without any sign of humanity. Without any sign of Solace.

"Looks like we're about to fly over a river." the Mexican hero said idly. From the sound of his voice, he had taken to lying down and peeking his head over the side of the platform.

"Probably not safe to lay like—" R'Bec started.

The rustling of light armored fabric and small clinking of metal plates and electronics indicated to her that Marco had stood up quickly, before she had a chance to finish. She thought at first that he was listening to her suggestion, but shortly, those thoughts too were interrupted by his voice.

"And some boats!"

"What?" she said. In disbelief, the Telignen opened her eyes. The platform wobbled slightly as the speed dipped up and down for a moment, but once she steadied them, she was able to peer down at the world below.

"There's boats on the river! People!" Marco answered her confused query.

And there were.

Three ships sailed on the wide stream a quarter-mile ahead. It was hard to get an extensive look from this high up, but they looked to have sails—though drawn—and some gear for use in wide-net fishing. They were trawlers.

R'Bec resisted the urge to fly down to them. Even if they were cooperative and did speak English, it wasn't like the two heroes could ask for directions.

"We should turn around."

"What? What do you mean?"

"They're not hurt. Look, you can see the crews on the decks." She pointed down to the moving figures on the boats. From so high up, they looked like ants scrambling on the wooden crafts. "If Solace had passed over here, they would be in pieces."

"It took us an hour to cross that forest. Solace probably reached this river just minutes after we lost sight of it. The boats might not have been here, then." he reasoned.

"Maybe." R'Bec said, her voice trailing off into a hum.

Their flight had slowed some as R'Bec's focus drew from the illusion to reality below. It was difficult to tell without descending, but she estimated that they were almost above the river's edge.

Then something popped far below. She looked down in time to see something flying up from the general direction of the boats. It arced somewhat, but was clearly moving straight for them.

"Oh shi—"

The yellow glowing platform dissipated beneath Marco's feet and R'Bec's legs. In a blink, they were in freefall.

The Telignen struggled to move her head against the rushing air all around her, but was able to angle it up just enough to see that, falling with them, was a large harpoon. It looked hot; it was steaming in the cold air, as was the rope tied to its rear, which was pulled taut now as the weapon was drawn back to its origin. It retracted along with them, slowly parting from their vertical descent.

Both her and Marco's screams were intercut by shortness of breath. Anxiously, R'Bec went against her better judgment and looked down.

Thankfully, they were not above land. Unfortunately, landing in water from this height wasn't going to be much better.

"Vi-i-iso-or o-on," she heard over the course of two or three seconds, followed by the decisive, though shouting and stammering voice of her companion giving his next command. "Sha-a-att-er-sho-o-ock-k!"

A brief light invaded her eyes. She turned to Shatterbug, who was making motions as though to swim through the air towards her. She held her arm out, and he used that leverage to pull them together. In an awkward cross between a hug and a handshake, they clung to each other for life.

Marco took the lead, trying to angle the two of them face-down, preparing to dive into the water. He pushed one fist out ahead of him. It was clearly taking a lot of effort to keep his arm straight and directly beneath them, as it wobbled all about against the force of the air pushing up against them.

R'Bec tucked her chin against her chest, closing her eyes as she braced for impact. The surface of the water would be as hard as concrete, and they were going to slam into it headfirst. If she was going to have even a second of lucidity in that moment, she did not want to spend it looking at the mess that would create.

"Re-e-co-on-st-t-it-tu-ute!"

The water engulfed them like a huge wet tongue, eagerly slurping them into the cold river. She felt her body being pulled into a new position, and the light against her eyelids told her that she was now facing up.

She opened her eyes.

Although it was fresh water, the sudden cold and dirty rush of the river invading her eyes stung. But, she was not totally blinded. The dark shape of the bottom of one of the boats pierced the surface a few dozen feet away.

Then, another crash as something else fell through the water. Bubbles once again filled her vision. Once they had drifted to the surface or popped on their own, R'Bec once again saw the shape of the harpoon. Darker and distorted in the water, it tried to sink, but was pulled by the rope that quickly escaped the river, suspended in the air by whatever mechanism was retracting the weapon.

She reached out and grabbed one of the hooks of the metal projectile.

As R'Bec's legs hit Marco's again and again while they kicked to the surface, she held her grip on the harpoon. Finally, their mouths opened in greedy desperation, swallowing as much air as they could, even if mixed with water from the very top of the river.

They drifted through the water, still not content to let go— though R'Bec couldn't place whether it was still out of an instinct for survival, or an inability to release each other out of shock.

The harpoon tapped against the side of the wooden vessel before it started to float skyward, pulled along tail-first by that rope. R'Bec was dragged up along with it, and though his grip was loosening around her wet clothes—which was not a pleasant feeling on her cold skin—so was Marco.

As the metal weapon climbed up over the edge and onto the deck, the illusionist saw Shatterbug's gloved hand grab onto the railing. R'Bec let go of her partner and did the same with her free hand. Together, using each other's sides as additional leverage along with the pull of the harpoon, the two heroes made it onto the ship.

Only to be met with metallic crossbows and unrecognizable, heavy mechanical weapons pointed at their dripping heads.

"We're— hello. Sorry, we're— we were just—" Marco tried to express, unable to catch his breath.

"Who are you?" asked one of the women. She wore light sailing gear, coupled with small plates of armor in a few key locations—her chest, her shoulders, her shins. They seemed to be less for function and more for fashion, as this uniform was mirrored across the rest of her crew. Men and women of different ages and builds looked down at them sternly, though a good deal of curiosity still filled their eyes. They were all Indian—or, rather, their skin color was the same as that of Indian people back in their home universe.

Then it hit her.

"Wait." R'Bec started, catching her breath a little more quickly than her teammate, although chattering her teeth as she shivered from the cold of the river. "You— you speak English?"

"English? We're speaking Raitchin." one of the burlier men said matter-of-factly.

"Whatever, I— hoof." For some reason, even though R'Bec was breathing fine now, she couldn't get over her chill. She was freezing. Surely the water wasn't really that cold? "Do you—foof— can I have a b-b-blanket?"

"Juden, get some blankets." the first woman shouted to one of the other men, who was further back in their ranks.

"Who are you? Where are we?" Marco asked, finally regaining his senses. He wasn't shivering like the Telignen. She thought his suit must be protecting him some, but the armored cloth looked pretty light to her.

Some of the sailors passed concerned glances to each other, before the first woman spoke up. "You're on the Palluma River. This is a fishing convoy from Co Palluma."

Whether it was R'Bec's confused face or Marco's silence, she didn't know, but the crew caught on that they were well out of their element.

"Where are you from?"

R'Bec looked to her companion, her face reflecting in the mirrored helmet. "A long way away." he said.

"Well, we were about done with our trip. We'll take you back to Co Palluma, and you can work out your plans, there." the woman decided, offering her hand to Marco and then to R'Bec. Once the blankets arrived, she helped to wrap one around the silent and shivering Telignen. "I'm Fyem."

"Tha-a-ank you, Fye-em." the illusionist stuttered through gritted teeth. She rubbed her arms beneath the blanket, trying to generate as much heat as possible.

"Juden, take them below deck and get them comfortable." Fyem ordered of the man who had just returned.

"Aye, captain."

He politely huddled the two strangers down into the ship, guiding them to a table and benches in the small galley area.

Once they were left alone, R'Bec turned to her new friend with pleading eyes. "Ma-arco, I ca-a-an't get warm-m-m."

"It's alright, it was just the water. You'll warm up." he said dismissively. With a flick of his head in realization, he added, "Visor off."

The glass dome of his helmet parted into four slices, which folded back into the blue armor of the helmet. That, too, folded down, reducing itself to a collar on the edge of the whole Shatterbug suit.

"Wh-h-hy aren't you c-cold-d?" she demanded, her brow furrowing with freezing frustration.

His eyes squinted at this. Not in anger at her accusatory tone, but in genuine confusion, and then concern. "You know, you're right. I don't know. The suit doesn't have any protection from the cold."

R'Bec pursed her lips, the dread growing in her stomach.

"Is it maybe because you're a 'Telignen?'" he asked, holding his hand up to her forehead. He had butchered the name, and from the look on his face, he knew it, but she appreciated the gesture. However, he pulled his hand away in acknowledging that he couldn't get a good temperature estimation with an armored glove on his hand.

"I don-t-t kno-o-ow." she replied, looking down as she winced with pain. It was like her bones were breaking inside her, brittle and beaten by the cold.

"Maybe that's it. Here, I have an idea, let's get back outside."

Marco gently helped R'Bec to her feet, guiding her to the wooden stairs and up to the deck.

Topside, she felt a sudden relief as she was able to relax her face. Her brow and lips untensed, though her jaw still chattered with the cold of her body.

That was it.

Her face, the only part of her body now exposed to the sun, was improving.

She shed her blanket.

After a moment, her fingers started to regain some feeling. Her wrists weren't so numb. It was the sun.

"I thought so." Shatterbug said proudly, recognizing the subtle changes in her demeanor as she flexed her facial features and extremities. "You're cold blooded."

"Ru-u-ud-de." she replied flatly.

"No no, I mean literally. You're like a reptile. You're cold by nature, you need to get your warmth from outside. A blanket's not gonna help, you gotta stay under the sun."

He was right. She could feel that he was right. Slowly, even now, she was getting some feeling back in her arms and neck, but it was thawing out from those parts of her that were unclothed.

She focused her mind, working through the pain of her freezing core. Finding those knots and ties of her illusions, she unsewed them. Released them.

Her clothes began to fall away, dissipating into grey dust, and then into the air, carried by the river breeze. All she was left in was her ripped party dress—she cursed herself for still not having changed her physical outfit.

Now her arms began to relax. Finally, she felt stable on her own two legs. And the black material of her garment absorbed the sun's heat quickly, helping to warm her abdomen and core.

R'Bec felt the color come back to her face. Her thoughts lingered on Marco's kindness. His humanity. There she was—an alien, and one who had been short and rude with him and his friend, even after she came to terms with their united purpose—and he saw fit to help her. And not just in that small action of warming her up, but in discovering something about herself.

The Telignen found her faith in humanity growing some, thanks only to one man's actions.

"Hey, what are you two doing up here?" Fyem shouted from the boat's bow.

"We were—" the illusionist started.

"Juden, get the prisoners back down below deck! And cool them off!"

"What?" Marco asked loudly. The same thought, in the same tone, had run through R'Bec's head—along with a few other choice words.

Before he had a chance to put his visor back on, Shatterbug and R'Bec were hit with a blast of cold air. A puff of smoke, like nitrogen, filled their nostrils and throats. But it wasn't nitrogen—that would have killed them. It was just cold, chilled air.

And it was blasted from a machine strapped to Juden's back.

He waved the stream of frosty air over the two of them. Marco coughed, unable to give his suit the voice commands to spring into action. R'Bec coughed too, but she found herself huddling to the floor, kneeling in a sudden flash of pain.

She was freezing again.

"Detain them!" ordered the captain-apparent, Fyem.

Three more crew members abandoned their posts on the vessel, coming to help Juden drag and guide the heroes back down below. This time, though, they were brought to a small brig.

As their imprisoners returned to the stairs, R'Bec thought she heard Fyem's voice one final time over the sound of her chattering teeth and piercing headache. "We're taking the invaders to the Countess. Full steam ahead!"

Issue 17
Restored

Bahadur watched the alien woman head off the machine and into the tall, bright grass, closing the distance between herself and Shatterbug. Before long, the Champion couldn't hear them, if they were even talking. He and Shockdrop were alone on the platform beneath the solitary tree.

"Sorry about Marco, man." Miguel said, breaking the silence.

"Thank you, but it's not necessary." he replied. "He is right, after all. To a degree, this is my fault. I should have worked through my problems before we faced Solace."

Shockdrop turned from the shrinking visage of his friend and ally in the distance to face Bahadur. The armor-clad hero set a hand on his shoulder in a gesture of camaraderie.

"If you'd done that, it woulda come here alone. We're here with it, so there's still a chance. *You* were right: we've gotta have faith." the man reassured Bahadur with sincere eyes. "And besides, no one expected you to deal with a bombshell like that in ten minutes. It's hard when it's personal."

Ramses thought to himself for a moment, nodding along with Shockdrop's supporting words. Whatever was done was done. They were here now, as was Solace. He accepted that. He did not use Osiris to fight that horror, and whether that was right or not, it did happen. He acknowledged it.

The Champion let out a calming breath, clearing his heart of self-deprecation. Although some things were his fault, and within his control, guilting over them accomplished nothing. He needed to make those failures mean something, though. To learn from them and make them right. "But I do have time, now."

He sat down in the middle of the four rungs that made up the supports for the rotating rings, which had by now slowed to a stop. Unhooking the ankh from his belt, he set it in his hands and closed his eyes. It was time to commune with Osiris; not as a God and his Champion, but as two men.

"*I am here, Ramses.*"

"Osiris, I beg of you. Please, make sense of this madness." he thought. Inside his mind, his tone was one of restrained anger. Despite his language, it was less a matter of begging, and more of demanding.

The spirit inside of him collected itself, and then spoke plainly, laying itself bare.

"*Solace was correct. In life, I was a human. We came to your world to start anew, and earned the respect and worship of the early native civilization.*" The would-be God had no face of his own, but that image in Bahadur's mind was one of shame. "*I did not lie to you; I never said I was a God. But, it was not right to allow you to believe that. I made no effort to correct you, and I apologize.*"

The Champion did not see fit to forgive that entity in his head—not yet, at least—but he did accept the apology, if only to himself. To truly find peace with this, though, he needed to know more. He needed to understand. "So what, then, does that make you, and this ankh?"

"*In effect, I am Osiris. Not his spirit, but his consciousness.*" If Osiris had a mouth or lungs, Bahadur got the sense that he would be sighing. "*In practice, I am an artificial intelligence. A program, inside the machine that is the ankh. I am the result of Osiris' mind, brain-mapped and approximated to the best degree of science as his people were capable of. All of my thoughts and emotions and knowings are his own.*"

Bahadur's brow furrowed. His lips pursed. Not just internally, but on his physical face, as well. Perhaps knowing was not always for the better. This understanding was somehow more painful. It deepened those scars of betrayal that he still reeled from. "What is the purpose of me in this? Of my mission?"

The AI collected his thoughts in Bahadur's infinite imagination, before he continued to project himself into the Egyptian's mind. "*The pieces of Osiris—my body—do need to be reunited, and it is for inherent good. Together, my remains create a map, a recipe, written in what is left of the DNA structure. Once reassembled, I—my consciousness—can use those instructions to create Horus, in much the same way that we use the ankh's power to summon creatures and objects. Horus will protect the world, and save it. Not as a King of Gods or as a Pharaoh, but as a hero; a final gift from me and my people, for allowing us to come and live here.*"

"And explain the ankh." Bahadur ordered, before even giving himself the chance to process this information. After all, what was to say that Osiris—this machine—was not lying now, when it had before?

254

"The ankh serves both as a computer system—a repository for my programmed intelligence—and as a simplified version of the Multiverse Machine, whose plans Solace evidently stole from my physical brain." Osiris explained, again approximating a sigh to the best of its disembodied ability. *"It folds dimensions, and can transport matter across universes. Those creatures and structures that we conjure are pulled from a zoo, of sorts, in my home universe. The portals are the folding of the dimensions to travel only within a single world. However, I cannot take you home right now, even to my tomb. Without an alignment and understanding of this world's dimensions, my powers are limited to a local scope."*

With every new piece of information, the Champion found his face twisting more and more into anger and disbelief. It was shocking and painful to know that so much was hidden from him. Perhaps not by lies, but by omission, all the same. All of these things that, yes, he could have asked for, but more importantly, that Osiris could have—*should* have—disclosed.

"One final question." he thought in their shared mindspace. Although it was his last query for the moment, his forgiveness still did not hinge on its answer. Whether he accepted Osiris' words or not, Bahadur wasn't sure he could ever forgive the false God. "What of the cosmic beings? What of your opinion—or lack thereof—of the Mortal Order?"

Again, Osiris was not quick to respond. An image of the green-skinned man turning away showed in Bahadur's head.

"Answer me, Osiris."

The Pharaoh's consciousness turned back to his Champion's. *"My people and I, we were of the opinion that the cosmic beings, while necessary, were flawed. Their response time* to major existential threats borders on negligent, their powerset to deliver consequences and resolve situations is simultaneously too powerful and not versatile enough, depending on the crime, and as a unit, they are asymmetrical. Incomplete. While we still made an effort not to cross those angels, we did not agree with their practices. We did not have faith in them or their decisions."

Bahadur let out a sound, somewhere between a sigh and a grunt. A hushed whisper of rustling armor told him that Shockdrop had reacted to this, but made no other movements beyond that, yet. "I see." he said, returning his thoughts inward.

"*However, Ramses,*" Osiris continued, his tone shifting with the topic. "*In our short time together, I have come to respect you. Not only as my Champion, but as a person. You are bold, and thoughtful, and compassionate. You serve me not out of deference or worship, but because you care about your world. You believe that I will help to protect and save it. More importantly, you want to do the same.*

"*So when those incarnations of reality approached you—in some small way acknowledging their flawed nature—and asked for your help to fill that gap, I thought that perhaps all would be well. After all, in spite of my feelings for them, for how much that I disagree with them, I knew that they made the right decision in their choice of membership. And I knew that you would be successful. I still do.*"

The Champion did not know what to say. He knew Osiris' feelings, to a degree. He had picked up his distaste for the cosmic beings, and he understood that the God supported him. But to hear just how important both of those competing ideals were to their unity, to Bahadur's identity in Osiris' eyes; it was a lot to take in.

He opened his eyes. Miguel was sitting in front of him, their crossed knees separated only by a few inches. Ramses stood up, and Miguel—in surprise and wonder—followed suit.

"What happened? Are you okay?" the young Mexican hero asked.

"All is well. Osiris and I have an understanding." he said flatly. He still was not prepared to forgive his patron, but he would continue to strive to make that Artificial Intelligence proud—to be the man that it saw in him. He thought to that figure in his mind. "Can you help me?"

"*I will, Ramses. Move over to the interface panel, and we will examine it together.*"

Bahadur hung from a rope tied to the top of the Multiverse Machine's interlocking rings. The four beams arched up, uniting above at an axel for the two shapes to rotate about. His waist was uncomfortable from sitting on the thick twine for so long, but Osiris needed a close look at the spinning shapes.

"*This entire machine is nonsense!*" the God-Pharaoh shouted in their shared mind.

"What do you mean?"

"*I mean everything. These are my designs, but they have been twisted and perverted into— into chaos!*" The ankh, which Ramses held in his hand to face the metal as though he were holding a magnifying glass to it, glowed brightly with that green energy, which rippled and burst with the AI's frustration. "*Get down, I need a moment.*"

Ramses obliged, loosening his grip on the rope hanging beside him. As it slowly slipped through his hands, his body gently descended until his feet rest on the ground. He stood up, careful not to tug one side or the other of the pulley too much so as to undo its hold at the top. It didn't matter, however; the swing began to glow green, the dimensional power that Bahadur had once called magic consuming the whole arrangement, and sending it away. Evidently, Osiris was done with it.

"What's going on, you guys got it?" Miguel asked, excitedly sitting up from his half-nap on the metal at the edge of the platform. He had been waiting for hours, finding any opportunity to occupy himself while the Egyptians worked.

"Not yet. Osiris is... confused." Bahadur put gently.

"*I am not confused!*" that voice declared proudly in his head. "*Not with how it works, at least. But rather, with why it is set up in this way, and how we can even pilot it.*"

"It is a process." the Champion finished aloud, more for his benefit than for Shockdrop's.

Miguel sighed loudly, apparently no longer content with knocking the pinecone-like seeds from the tree with precise extensions of his suit's powers, or whistling the tunes of songs from their world—although, Bahadur was silently grateful for how quickly he had tired himself of the latter.

"Well, walk me through it. That might help." the young Mexican offered.

"*How could explaining the complexities of a transdimensional—*"

"Why do you think that would help him?" Bahadur cut the God-AI off in his head, again speaking directly to Miguel.

"Well, one of the programmers at Snow Dynamics told me about something they do called 'Rubber Ducky Debugging.'" he said, smiling with embarrassment before regaining his self-control. "It's a little *estupido*, but it can sometimes help. Basically, you just describe what something should be doing to a rubber ducky, and when you do, the problem seems obvious."

"And you are suggesting that—"

"That I be your rubber ducky, right."

"It may be worth a try." Ramses said. Then, turning to that consciousness in his head, he thought in his native tongue, "What do you think?"

"*It is a ridiculous notion.*"

Bahadur's attention refocused to Shockdrop. "He agrees."

"Great!" Miguel said, containing his excitement to a minor hop with only one of his feet leaving the metal stage. He eagerly sat down, his eyes wide with interest.

"*Fine.*" Osiris thought as the Champion joined Shockdrop, taking his own seat on the now-cooled metal. Once their shared body was settled, the program began for Bahadur's ears. "*The Multiverse Machine is meant to be straightforward. The panel controls where one wants to go on five spatial dimensions. As a matter of physics, the fourth dimension is locked—the machine cannot time travel. The whole machine is transported, but beyond that, only matter contained in the rings will follow.*"

"The panel is the controls, and the machine and anything in the rings is taken to the destination universe." Bahadur translated aloud.

"*Yes. And for all intents and purposes, this design does exactly that. But extra steps have been added. Fail-safes and supplemental controls. The panel itself is not only unlabeled, but disorganized and encrypted. To even understand how to select the destination would require knowledge of the internal equipment, which we cannot access.*"

"Solace has changed the way the controls work, so we cannot choose where to go."

Miguel lifted his hand an inch or two from his lap, prompting Osiris to pause in wait. "So once we figure that out, we're home free?"

Osiris figuratively held his hand to his face in Bahadur's mind. "*No, no. There is more to it than that. Once the machine is started, the four levers—one on the interior of each of the struts which revolve around the platform—must be pulled in sequence. But they can only be pulled at two minute intervals, the order is random, and it is done while they are spinning. If any lever is missed or pulled out of order, the process shuts down.*"

"No, that cannot be right." Ramses said. His voice was breathy with concern. "That is ridiculous."

"What? What is?" his young partner asked.

"Once the machine is started, four levers have to be pulled in a random order every two minutes, or it fails."

"Those levers? Way up there?" Miguel asked, his finger pointing up to the upper-middle of one of the rings, a good twenty feet off the platform floor. "No way, man. *No va a pasar.*"

"*It must happen.*" Osiris said, apparently understanding Miguel's Spanish and translating it to Arabic for the Champion. "*And yet, he is right. I see no way to accomplish this feat.*"

Bahadur's mind began to work. Perhaps, he thought, Miguel's plan had worked after all. The only mistake was in who the 'rubbery ducky' actually was.

Hearing all of this for the first time—understanding the nonsense and impracticality of Solace's Multiverse Machine—allowed the beginnings of a strategy to form. And, with Osiris' help, it had a real chance to work.

"Unless Solace helps us." he said, his voice hushed.

"¿*Qué?*" Miguel asked. Even in Spanish, the single word's connotation was obvious.

"Bear with me, I have only just begun to think of the implications. But, Solace built the machine. It knows how to pilot it. We can trick it into putting in the coordinates for our home world."

"And then it kills us?" Miguel said, confused and unconfident.

"No. This time, we have Osiris. We can open portals to guide its arms away from us."

"*There is still the issue of the levers, my Champion.*"

"I have thought of that, too." Ramses said aloud, intensifying Miguel's face of uncertainty. "Once Solace sees that we are fighting back, it will see that we are luring it into a trap. It will try to stop the machine—try to stop us from pulling the levers. Therefore, at each opportunity, it will guard and protect the correct lever in the sequence, while also trying to pull the incorrect ones. We can keep it away from the latter, and use its tipped hand to reveal to us the former."

Miguel brought his hand to his chin, his eyes rolling all about as he connected the dots of Bahadur's hastily put-together explanation. The Champion had to admit, it was farfetched, and it relied on a number of assumptions, not least of which being that Solace did not have *another* fail-safe, an emergency shutoff switch concealed even from Osiris. But there seemed no other way.

"That might actually work." Miguel said, apparently following the disjointed steps of the game plan. "But that means we need to get Solace back here, and also make it want to go back home."

"Yes. We will have to find and defeat it here, in this world, so thoroughly and irrevocably that it will feel it has no choice but to return and regroup."

"That's a pretty big ask on its own, *amigo.*"

"*He is correct, Ramses.*" Osiris concurred, his imagined face in their shared mind showing of proud misfortune.

"Perhaps it was before. But remember, we have Osiris this time. That is the key to all of this."

"You have a lot of faith in the guy who lied to you, Bahadur." Shockdrop said. His tone was difficult for Ramses to discern, but he believed that it was one of uneasy support.

"*Yes, he does.*" Osiris thought in the Champion's mind. "*Thank you for believing in me again, Ramses.*"

Bahadur Al-Malik collected himself, standing firm and tall at the edge of the platform. He turned his back to the Multiverse Machine, looking out once again to the meadow. It was in the later hours of the morning, by now. The last shades of the dawn's sun had faded from the horizon, and the dark leaves of the forests far and away from the two heroes reflected the light even more spectacularly than before. Even from here, he could see the hints of brilliant rays piercing the canopy and hitting the ground like flowing, liquid light.

Ramses looked on in the direction that Solace had flown, and that Shatterbug and the Telignen had traveled in pursuit. They had taken their journey on foot hours ago. Meeting them in the same manner would take just as long, and that was assuming they could follow the same trail.

But Marco and R'Bec did not have Osiris with them.

"Can you find them, my lord?" Ramses said, reflexively addressing the AI in deference once again inside his mind.

"*No.*"

Bahadur's eyes widened, and he slumped his shoulders in defeat.

Perhaps all was lost, after all.

"*Not with just the ankh, anyway.*" the voice resumed, returning in its perfection to the Champion's head. "*Set it on the control panel. I will use the Multiverse Machine as an analog, to stand in for the dais in my tomb. It will attune me to this world that I may observe it. Then, I can take us to them.*"

Issue 18
A Matter of Time

Shockdrop looked up at the quaint stone castle. The bricks were dark and damp, wet with the steam and water being pumped all around by the pipes that led from the village. The windows were well-washed and sparkling, though all empty. The large wooden door was open and unguarded.

"You sure they're in there?" he asked hesitantly. It wasn't that he was scared. Quite the opposite; the fortress felt safe and cared for. It was in good condition, and presided over a peaceful town. Miguel's concern was in why his friends would be here, of all places.

His companion stepped forward, dipping his double-feathered crown into the shade cast by the structure. "Osiris is certain, but he cannot be any more precise. We will have to go inside."

"Well, that's fine. We'll just go in and ask for who's in charge." the young hero said, his step cheery with optimism as he made his way for the open doorway.

He felt a gentle tug on one of the plates on his back, pulling his suit back and holding it in place, and him along with it.

He turned his head to see Ramses, who had now released his hand, looking at him with a gaze that was not quite one of condescension, but was close enough that Miguel instinctively returned the expression with a frown.

"They may be held here as captives. We should be more cautious in our investigation. We are visitors of this world."

"Exactly, we're visitors. Guests." Miguel replied, cocking his head to the left as he gave a wide grin. "There's no reason they'd be locked up, and even if they were, we'd just have to explain things to the man in charge and be on our way. Now c'mon, *gallina*."

He picked up his path into the castle, and after a moment, heard Bahadur's following footsteps tapping on the cobblestones behind him. They proceeded across the threshold and into the watery palace.

Of course, palace wasn't quite the right word for it. It was certainly not opulent right now, if ever it had been. Scaffolding was set all along the walls, perched around columns and stretching up to the pipes running along the ceiling. There were few statues or plaques or other treasures. Discoloration on the floor indicated that there were carpets or rugs at a time, but were recently removed. There were electric lights, apparently powered by the water running through the stone tubes at the height of the room, but most were turned off, dimming the vast space.

The place was under construction. But there were no workers.

There wasn't much of anyone, here.

To the left and right, open archways peered into rooms with tables and chairs, the warm light of fireplaces, and a few armored soldiers mulling about. This, at least, served as a barracks for the local military. Whether it was these men and women who

e

were leading the construction was unclear, but there certainly were not many of them in either case. Ahead of them, another tall door—metal, this time—was cracked open, though only just. Miguel imagined that this led to the throne room, or whatever equivalent this small civilization had.

He took another step straight forward, making his way to that imposing passage.

"Wait!" Ramses let out in a hushed shout. His hoarse whisper echoed around the room, eventually dissipating on the wet rock and wooden support beams.

"What?" Shockdrop answered in a similar manner, the sound escaping his helmet unfiltered, though his throat catching some in surprise at the suddenly increased moisture in the air.

Bahadur closed the distance between them, letting his whisper lower even further to carry only to Miguel's ears. "Whether this is a good idea or not, we cannot strut into the chamber of a ruler of any kind. There are rules. Traditions that surely transcend universes. We cannot interrupt unannounced."

"Fine, then we'll find a guard to announce us."

The Egyptian brought his hand to his forehead, wincing in minor frustration. Miguel understood, of course. He wasn't a fool. But the stakes were too high to respect every small rule or law of any world. Solace was out here, somewhere, and they needed to find their friends—his best friend.

Recognizing that Miguel had no intention of listening, Ramses drew his ankh from his belt in preparation to defend them. After a moment, Shockdrop reached the door.

He carefully pressed his gloved hand to the metal. Despite the darkness of the room, it was warm, even through the

Shockdrop suit. He imagined this was due to the steam—it was even possible that the door was operated by early hydraulics. Indeed, it wasn't swinging open at his touch. It would need more assertive persuasion.

Shockdrop stepped back, nearly bumping into Bahadur behind him, and turned the dial in the middle of his chest. He felt the gentle hum of the marconium core behind its glass casing, although the battery covered the actual element inside. He would not need too high a setting to nudge the metal door open, even if it was backed by supports and mechanisms.

"Visor on."

He reached his arms out to his sides, then swung them together in a decisive clap. The grips and platelets on his hands collided, and with the energy and properties extended from the suit's elemental power source, the air particles excited and vibrated, rippling across the few feet of space between Miguel and the doorway.

The metal rung with the impact of the shockwave, and as whatever support the huge barrier had gave way, the two slabs of metal swung in on their hinges.

"Your highness, I'm Shockdrop, and this is Ramses." Miguel shouted across the room, his eyes to the ground rather than the dim throne that he could barely make out on the other side. A figure was sitting on it, he could tell that, but features fell away in the failing light. Whatever construction was underway in the foyer was also being performed here. There was scaffolding all around the columns and walls, as before, and the electric lights on the ceiling were almost all off. The sound of rushing water dominated the space overhead, but he could still talk over it at ground level.

"We're looking for our friends, and maybe some directions to a great big evil *monstruo*, and then we'll be outta your hair."

At this, he finished his short bow and rose, continuing to take respectful steps towards the seat at the far wall. He walked along the lighter stone path that was slightly drier and less worn than the surrounding cobbles. Like outside the throne room, the rugs had been removed from this area.

The figure sitting in the chair stood up, revealing the silhouette of a long, wide gown and thick, flowing hair. As Miguel's eyes adjusted to the darkness and his steps reduced the distance between himself and the woman to just a dozen feet or so, he was finally able to make the ruler out more clearly.

But Bahadur saw her first. "Oh, Gods."

After a passing glance at his side, trying to see the Champion's face behind him, Shockdrop's eyes flicked back up to the raised throne. In his own words, he reacted in much the same way as his companion. "*Dios mio...!*"

They were too late.

Even in the low light of the chamber's back wall, Miguel could see that although her facial features hinted at an Indian complexion, the woman standing before them had grey skin, dead with decay and slightly puffy with the damp air. Her hair was not true hair at all, but was instead a mess of short, fat tentacles which emerged from her scalp and fell along the sides and back of her head. One or two wriggled in front of her eyes like unkempt bangs. Miguel would almost call her a gorgon, likening her to Medusa, if the snake-like locks arced and supported themselves at all. Instead, they hung there; moving independently still, and apparently without purpose or conscious intent, but behaving as closely to hair as alien matter invading one's body could manage.

268

Miguel could barely even make out the woman's face without the guiding marks of her eyes, as they reflected no light. They were black and void, standing out from the darkness that concealed the rest of her face only due to their perfect, impossible lightlessness that even the cover of shadow could not challenge.

Footsteps on damp cobbles alerted the heroes to people approaching behind them. Three armored guards, clad with simple metal chest plates and wielding cumbersome steam-powered weapons filed into the room.

"Countess Deotce!" one of them said as they ran up to the throne, surrounding Shockdrop and Ramses and holding them at bay with their unusual guns. "We heard the commotion; are you safe? Who are these men?"

The Countess' voice was hoarse and pained. Miguel suspected that she was not yet used to the death of her throat, to the feeling of that writhing void in her veins and mouth. And that uncomfortable speech would only be compounded by the wet air of the steam-castle walls. "They are more invaders that we were warned of. Take them to the dungeon with the rest of their hunting party. They will face the full punishment of this world."

"No, we're here to help you—save you—warn you! Please, you can't let that *villano* trick you! *¡Escúchame!*" Miguel pleaded as he tried to kick and shake away the soldiers gripping his arms. They held them apart to keep him from clapping, and one even grabbed and turned the dial on his chest all the way down, as though he was familiar with the mechanism. As though he had been told. "You can't trust Solace! Ramses, do something!"

He tried to move and turn against the hold of the guards and get a look at Bahadur, to look him in the eyes. But the

Champion's eyes were closed. It was as though he had conceded; given up.

And yet, that couldn't be true. Bahadur was struggling right now, yes. But he was smart. And he was at least on speaking terms with Osiris. Surely, that's what he was doing—communicating with the would-be God. This was a strategy. A new plan.

Of course! The woman, this Countess Deotce, told the guards to take them to the others. She called them invaders, and she knew who they were and how their powers operated. Which meant if she was lumping Miguel and Bahadur in with other 'invaders,' then they had to be Marco and R'Bec!

Miguel relaxed at his conclusion, accepting that they were beaten. For the moment. He picked his heels up off the ground, walking along with the soldiers and Ramses rather than making them drag him along the wet stone.

He just let himself keep thinking. They hadn't lost yet. If anything, this was a win. Two birds with one stone—not only did they find their friends, but Solace was here, too. Bahadur's plan had a real chance, now.

"Good to see you made yourself comfy, R'Bec."

The Telignen didn't even look up from her imaginary newspaper, but rather rearranged the setting of her legs sprawled out on the purple bedspread which filled almost the entirety of her cell. "What are they gonna do, throw me in the dungeon?"

The soldiers prodded Bahadur Al-Malik into the cell across from the illusionist, swinging the metal bars closed behind him. They screeched with rust—the air was even more damp beneath the Countess' castle. Miguel Jimenez was led on a similar path, faced against the wall across the aisle from Marco. Bars separated them from the soldiers, and their meager beds and primitive plumbing mirrored each other even more than their marconium suits.

"What are you two doing in here?" Ramses whispered once the last of the guards had walked back up the stairs and out of the dripping dungeon. "Did you not try to escape?"

"Bug boy thought we should wait for you." R'Bec shrugged. Her new quarters were adjacent to Marco's own, separated only by one frame of rusted metal bars, though more tightly knit than those holding them back from the hallway.

"That's not what I said." he shot back, only somewhat annoyed. It was natural to be irritable, after all. He was, too. They had been waiting for hours for their comrades to arrive. He had hoped they would put up more of a fight with the locals and rescue them, but as long as they were all in the same place, the circumstances didn't matter too much. "I traveled into the future and saw that you guys would make it here. So, I hopped back and waited the long way with R'Bec, so we could brainstorm our plan."

"And tell them what we came up with." the woman suggested curtly, still not taking her eyes off of her newspaper. He had to imagine that its words were nothing newsworthy or relevant at all—surely, they were something she had read before, and was just remembering now to visually infuriate them all.

Marco sighed a long, throaty breath. He couldn't seem to get the phlegm out of his throat, and had thus given up about forty-five minutes ago. He thought it was about that long, anyway. Unlike in their home world, the people of this universe evidently did not believe in humanitarian imprisonment enough to provide

271

windows, yet. He had no real way to judge time with—an irony that was not lost on the time traveler. "We've got nothing."

"Well, we have one!" Miguel said excitedly. He stopped his premature celebration, though, his movements toning down with slight embarrassment as he corrected himself. "Actually, it's Bahadur's idea."

"That's right, Bahadur. Look, I wanted to say I'm sorry." Marco's eyes fell to the floor as he faced toward the Egyptian man out of the corner of his cell. "I shouldn't have said the things I said, and I definitely shouldn't have said them the way I did. It wasn't fair, and it wasn't what you deserved or needed."

He looked up.

Bahadur had not moved. Had not even flinched. He sat with his legs crossed on the moist dirt ground, his eyes closed and his hands wrapped around the golden ankh ahead of him.

"Did you hear me?"

"I did." he answered, keeping his eyes shut. After a moment, they opened, and he stood up to continue. "I accept your apology. But you were right. While there was a better way to communicate it to me, your thoughts were valid. I needed to convene with Osiris, to truly work through our problems, rather than ignore them. And so, I have. I have spoken with Osiris, and we have an idea for how to get home, *and* to defeat Solace."

At this, even R'Bec perked up. The paper in her hand faded into dust and debris, falling to her legs and then, with the brush of her hand, off of the ornate bed entirely and into the air—into nothing. "Let's hear it."

"Yes," a low hiss sounded from the corners of the dungeon. It echoed off of the shining stone bricks, and boomed over the trickling of water onto the floor. It was a long, exaggerated affirmative, and somehow, it sounded dark. "Please enlighten us, Bahadur Al-Malik. How do you plan to defeat me?"

Oozing out from the cracks in the ceiling, an impossibly black puss seeped into the room, collecting itself in the air and amassing into a congregation of silhouetted tentacles.

"Solace! You *are* behind this." Marco said, readying himself.

The horror ignored him, its attention still focused on Ramses—although Marco couldn't tell that by its appearance alone. "You seem quite sure of yourself for someone who has only just arrived. Who was so easily captured."

"You can't hold us in here forever! We're heroes!" Miguel declared, the pride in his voice betrayed by a crack of fear.

"I am familiar with the concept of biding one's time, Miguel Jimenez. I know that you can free yourselves whenever you like." The collection of black tendrils rotated about, the writhing shapes in the air moving just enough to indicate that Solace was turning to face Shatterbug. "I have come only to assure you that it would do no good. Even in a universe that is new to all of us, I know more than you do. I have the advantage.

"I have been gracious enough to order my new progeny to keep you alive, but if you choose to escape—pointlessly—then I can make no guarantees that you will live to see my new multiverse." it concluded hungrily.

"You'll never get there, Solace! You can't win." Shatterbug shouted up at the creature, standing tall with fists balled. His eyes followed the tentacles twisting about just in front of him. He waited, just hoping that one would come close to him.

"I may not yet possess my full power, but already, any hesitation to not be named Master of All Realities would be a formality. My conquest is certain, all in good time."

With this final assertion, Solace's tentacles reached up and pierced those spaces between the stone, once more flowing into and through the cracks of the ceiling, leaving the heroes alone in their cells again.

And then, the rumbling started.

The loud crashing and cranking.

It sounded through their underground room, like some great machine churning overhead. Stone grinded against stone, metal clanked, and rope zipped and pulled. All of it hummed overhead, drawing Marco's hands to his ears. Miguel and Bahadur did the same, all with cringed faces as they struggled to block out the distressing noise.

Only R'Bec remained mostly unbothered. She noticed it, clearly. She felt it. But unlike the men, she kept her arms tucked over her stomach as she lounged on her bed.

The illusion vanished. The sheets and mattress became dust, falling through the holes of the wooden bed frame as that, too, became nothing. She caught herself on the ground effortlessly, transitioning from her relaxed and seated position in the air to standing on the wet dirt along with the others.

She turned to the astounded and off-put Marco, and made a number of gestures to her head and face. He looked at her with confusion, and only then—on seeing that he was not getting whatever indication she was trying to give—did she mouth the word, "Visor."

He let his eyes open wider in understanding. He pulled his hands from his ears, bearing the intrusion of that painful cacophony of industry, and gave the order. "Visor on." The collar around his neck unfolded, reaching up around his head to become the base of his helmet. From that blue armor, four reflective surfaces emerged, uniting in front of his face to complete the bubble window of his domed helmet.

The noise was still loud inside the Shatterbug suit, but it was bearable. He looked over to Miguel, who also got the hint and did the same. His orange collar unfolded, revealing a helmet with purple plates and trims, that then released four orange mirrored slices that united into the Shockdrop visor.

He looked over to Ramses, wondering how he was faring against the torturous volume. However, he was no longer affected. Bahadur looked at them all calmly, without torment.

"Everyone ready to get outta here?" R'Bec shouted over the noise. Marco appreciated her trying to be heard over the commotion above them, but the Egyptian man across from her held his hand to one ear, as though she had screamed right in it.

"Let's go!" Miguel affirmed. He turned up the dial on his chest plate, and with a disciplined stance, punched into the metal gate of his cell. It shot forward, nearly coming to hit Marco's own bars before it fell to the dirt floor.

R'Bec's door simply opened, almost on its own, and swung in place like it was totally unsecured to the rest of her metal bars. Indeed, there was some evidence that the lock had been cut at with something, though whatever it was had already become dust. Marco caught only a glimmer of the grey flakes before they disappeared.

Shatterbug breathed in, collecting himself over the rumble of the stone and machinery overhead.

"Shattershock." he said loudly, ensuring that the suit could hear his voice command. It responded as it always did, and after a flash, two identical displays showed in the corners of his vision. He set his hand just in front of that barrier in front of him, and right as he pushed forward and his palm collided with the rusted metal, he said loudly and clearly, "Reconstitute."

The bars shot forward, released from their bolts on the wall. Miguel had to jump out of the way to not get hit by the flying grating, which clanged in the back of the cell that Shockdrop had just escaped from.

In each of their own ways, the members of the First Mortal Order were free again, and prepared to stand against Solace.

Ramses, closest to the stairs, took up the head of the group.

Expecting resistance, he drew his ankh once they reached the metal door at the top of the stairs. R'Bec conjured a thin rapier behind him, and Shatterbug and Shockdrop each took up fighting stances, though they were several steps down.

Bahadur unlatched the door, and it swung out.

Marco craned his neck to see if he needed to put up a fight, but there was no one there. The dungeon was unguarded.

However, the rumbling was louder, and now, they could see why. Huddled on the top two steps of the path back out of the prison, the four heroes hesitated to step out into the castle halls.

They were moving.

The stone corridor was rotating and turning out in front of them. While the wall which the metal door that now hung open remained stationary, the opposite wall was traveling to the right, as was the floor across the threshold from them. Like some huge, circular mixer, the castle was moving all around them.

Which explained the loud churning noise.

Indeed, once they each stepped out in turn, keeping their footing careful on the moving floor, they saw that the halls were being propelled along their tracks by great metal gears, being turned by yet more gears on dowels, and themselves turning belts and conveyors that they could see glimpses of in the spaces cut in the floor for those larger motors to set in.

"What is going *on*?" the Telignen asked in wonder.

"It's like the whole castle is moving." Marco said with equal awe. He stepped toward the damp stone on the moving wall— which was now moving along with him, giving the appearance that it was, in fact, the opposite wall that was turning. He quickly jolted his head back and to the left, just in time to see the metal door they had emerged from get pushed closed by another wall, which was traveling along with them from the left.

"But why? What purpose could this... this expensive feat possibly serve?" The Champion turned all around in place, giving himself—and presumably, Osiris—a proper look at their situation.

A familiar, infuriating sound of husky, slimy breath made Marco's hair stand on-end in the Shatterbug suit, as exaggerated syllables and elongated words suddenly echoed in the humid corridor. "More purpose than you will ever know, Bahadur Al-Malik."

"Solace! Where are you, show yourself!" Marco demanded. He was done playing games and done trying to solve the puzzles that the horror had no doubt laid out to waste the hero's time.

"I am here." it replied, placing particular emphasis on the final word, as though it were obvious. To condescend and ridicule. "I am all around you. In the walls. Operating the machinery. Turning the gears. This fortress is my armor, and my weapon. What can you do against power such as this?"

Although it was by no means a silent act of defiance, Miguel gave no witty remark as he brought his hands together, generating a violent shockwave that raged out, threatening to rip through the stone bricks of the moving stronghold.

But it did not.

All around them, a reverberating sigh let out, echoing into itself and all around them, as the unseen monster gave out what constituted, for it, a laugh. "I wonder, Miguel Jimenez, how is it that I know more about your Shockdrop suit than you do? You cannot level buildings, even primitive and poorly constructed ones such as this."

"You mean you didn't build this?" Marco asked.

"I think that is enough questions, for now. After all, you have a lot of work to do if you intend to survive my triumphant moment." As Solace's last words curled with ambivalent delight, a column of stone shot out from the wall that their dungeon door had been set into—the wall that was not moving, but was passing by them as the rest of the castle turned. It sprung out, seeking to knock down and crush Miguel at Marco's side.

In a moment of pure instinct and concern, he shoved Shockdrop away, into R'Bec and Ramses. The new barrier reached the other side with a resounding thud of wet stone, which then grinded against the moving wall that it was now pressed against.

Marco was separated from his companions.

He had to keep walking his feet backwards as he pressed his hands—banged his fists—against the new wall. "Miguel! R'Bec!" he begged, hoping and pleading that someone would hear him, that they were still there and finding a way to reach him, just as he was.

"Shattershock!" Marco commanded. The suit complied, generating the familiar heat in front of his chest as the prime marconium was excited, forced to recall and recreate the circumstances of its initial journey through time. The plates all across his body vibrated with the concealed machinery underneath, and then with a flash, it all stopped.

A new Shatterbug was now five minutes in the past, and another was as far in the future.

But the wall was still there.

"What the—?" he caught himself. "But that doesn't—"

"Now that we are alone, Marco Nieve," Solace's voice again permeated the hero's ears, invading his thoughts with the terrible and inconvenient sloth of its words. "I want to share with you exactly why you have failed."

In all three times, Marco turned around, running against the direction of the funhouse floor. As he struggled to maintain his grip on the damp stones, that voice in the castle continued in the present. "Your first error was in believing that you are special. You are not unique in the multiverse. Certainly, marconium is not unique to your world. Indeed, there is a deposit of your element here, in this universe. And as it happens, it is directly beneath us."

Shatterbug was only half paying attention as he opened a door that had just been revealed and ducked inside. The floor and ceiling of this room were turning as well, although the effects on the hero's vision were bizarre—it was a square room, and seeing and feeling the walls rotating around him was disorienting, as was the act of walking across the room. Twice, he had to reach a hand out to the dripping stone bricks for support as he made his way for the opposite door.

And through it all, Solace did not give up its expositing. "Your second shortcoming was having faith in yourself. Believing that you could find me, that you could defeat me. Instead, I found you, and you have been reduced to an insect, crawling around inside my grand machine."

Marco still did not understand how the castle was moving in the past. How the wall was still there. How even in the future, it seemed as though he was making no progress.

Then, a thought came to mind. To the mind of the future Shatterbug, anyway, who shared his idea with the duplicates in the present and past. "We should split up. Once one of us finds the others, we can get back together."

"Good deal." the original Marco said. Their version in the past gave his own nonverbal agreement, and with that, turned back out the door they had entered from.

In the present and future, Marco passed through the door on the other side of the small rotating square room. He nearly fell over in the long straight hallway, the floor of which was teetering back and forth, up and down, from one end to the other. He was not quite in the middle, but he was close enough that the ground was more stable, not rising or falling as much as either end.

"And finally, your third failure was in misjudging this new world." the dark monster resumed from behind the shining walls. "It is primitive in many ways, yes. But it is so well adapted and evolved in many others. The people of this world use steam and water to power *everything*. They have developed such a taste for water-based war. And water is weight. It is pressure, and gravity, and patience, and time. It flows and floods and freezes, like time. Indeed, it seems at one point, they must have used a weapon so powerful, so absolute, that it scarred the very fabric of time itself on the surface of this world. That scar tissue stretches and folds and waves all around and through these walls, built on that ancient impact zone."

Marching through the shadowy creature's words, the Marco in the future turned to the left, down the shorter end of the bouncing corridor. In the present, Shatterbug turned right, resorting to crawling on the ground, bracing himself with his arms at every abrupt rise of the cobblestones, and relaxing his knees to keep them from shattering as he fell along with every drop.

"So you see, where I have acknowledged and embraced these truths, you have fallen short. And now, you will fall. With my assistance, this castle has been repurposed. Even now, as I turn these gears and mechanisms with my own tendrils, the fortress serves as the body of a great drill, which tunnels down below us. It will pierce the marconium vein far below, and when I harvest the smallest of samples, the calculated turning of the stronghold will carry it through the ebbing temporal scar tissue in just the right pattern, at just the right pace, that it will time travel. And it will change. And no longer will your 'prime marconium' be special. I will possess the power of time travel, all without your help."

Finally, the present hero made it to the door at the other end. The floor continued its rapid jerking, never becoming fully level with the threshold of that escape route. In fact, whenever the

u

stone slide came up, it completely covered and hid the passage for a moment. Marco would have to be quick, opening and sliding through the door as the ground descended, so that he would not be pinched and crushed between the upper frame and the rocking floor as it ascended again.

He pressed his toe to the ground, trying to lodge it between two cobbles to act as a backboard, of sorts. He held himself as close to the floor as possible. He didn't even bother to look at the two monitors in the corners of his vision—he needed their help at this moment, more than he needed to be split up.

"Reconstitute!"

In the present, Marco found himself... He was gone.

It was the Shatterbug in the future, at the other end of the hall, who had given the command. The hero in the present moment was pulled through time to propel that future iteration forward. As they united, the force of time shot them through the door on the other end of the hallway, before the ground had time to come back up and pin him.

Evidently, that version in the future had been planning the same thing on his own end. And now, they were one again.

And yet, something wasn't right.

He felt whole again. Granted, Shatterbug never felt incomplete when he was in three times. But clearly, the command had worked—he had been given the momentary strength of time as it folded back into itself.

No. It hadn't done completely.

There was still a screen in the lower left corner of his helmet. Only the one. And it showed the hallway he had just escaped from, looking down the way he had just come from.

"How are we still—?" he asked no one in particular—although, technically, he was in that moment asking himself.

However, it was Solace that answered. "You are trapped in my maze of time; your powers will not function as you might expect, and your friends are faring no better. The First Mortal Order has failed. Lie down, and enjoy the final moments of sanity that this world—any world—will ever experience."

Although that psychopathic void was all around him, in every crevice and behind every wall, Marco had the uneasy sensation that it had left him. He was alone now with only his thoughts, and that version of him somewhere in time that shouldn't exist.

"So, what is this? We're dislodged from time?" the present Shatterbug brainstormed. "Or is the suit just confused?"

That doppelganger in what he had to assume was the past replied. "No, the suit knows what it's doing, it has to. You wouldn't have made it through the door without it."

"But it should have brought everyone back. Even when one of us is dead, the suit is still able to pull us all back together." Shatterbug posited.

"Maybe the temporal disturbances are making the suit send and pull our copies *not* at five-minute intervals." the impossible duplicate said, as Marco saw him pull his hand to his chin, forgetting that he was wearing a helmet.

"That makes sense. If you weren't five minutes in the past, and the suit tried to pull you back ten minutes, you could be somewhere in the middle!"

"Or even further ahead. I might technically be the future version now. We have no idea how this time scar works." the copy offered.

"Well, can we try this?" Shatterbug asked himself—his own, physical self. He waited for no response from that iteration elsewhere in time. "Reconstitute!"

The marconium core did not warm his chest. The plates across his body did not shake or buzz. The suit believed it was not parted—was not shattershocked—and so it could not reunite the two Shatterbugs.

"Well, I guess it's back to plan A: find the others." he resigned.

"Yep. Split up?" asked the desynchronized copy.

"Nah, let's stick together. Maybe we'll be able to figure out when you are and fix this."

With careful footing and expert timing, the past-or-future Marco was able to skip through the already-open door, and into the same corridor that his reunited version stood in. Silently, the two heroes continued in their respective times.

Although they had a small space to stand comfortably without being pushed, carried, or otherwise moved around, the two Shatterbugs now stood in a room that threatened to do all of these things.

It was a long, rectangular chamber. As though cut into sixths, the two walls which bore doors—including the one that the twin heroes had their backs to—were stationary, with just a few bricks' space of floor to accommodate stepping in and out of the room. The other four parts were rotating wildly about an axis that was not there, in the middle of the space. They twisted and turned independently of each other, like a funhouse tunnel, though far more erratically.

Crossing it would prove challenging. Each individual ring was not moving consistently even with itself, jerking back and forth. If it slammed him at just the wrong angle into a corner, the suit wouldn't be able to protect him; it would bend and break his bones. If he got pinched between two adjacent zones, a limb could be crushed by the grinding force.

"We'll have to turn back, find another way." Marco said.

"And do what? Keep going till we find another crazy room to get stuck in?" the other Marco replied. "We've gotta find a way over."

Shatterbug furrowed his brow beneath his visor. He watched the pattern—or rather, the lack of any rhyme or rhythm—in the turning of the four sectors of the room. He tapped his fingers against his legs, trying to count moments that they rotated into safe positions. The gears in his head turned more aggressively than those gears he could hear slamming into each other all around the castle, trying to figure out what a safe position actually was in this context.

"We could launch ourselves across!"

"That might only work once, if at all." From the monitor in the hero's helmet, it looked like the desynchronized duplicate had sat down in contemplation. "That's a pretty far jump even for a fully-fledged reconstitute. And we have to assume we'll only get two of us back together, tops."

Marco knew that Marco was right. For all he knew, they were lucky that even one duplicate had merged back into the present. Trying to reunite through the time scar might just reposition the new copies in time, leaving the Shatterbug making the attempt to be propelled only by his own strength—and falling into the wringer for it.

"Granted," that displaced copy started. "We could always try—"

"I know what you're thinking," Marco cut in. "And surely if just a normal reconstitute won't work, that one won't either? That's an *enorme* risk."

"I don't see anything less dangerous. If the cracks in time are moving and shifting invisibly, then that's why we're not being pulled and pushed through time right. But, if we do *that*, maybe it'll be fast enough to keep up with the anomalies."

Marco thought on this, noticing that his duplicate had returned to his feet by the motion of that display on the visor. What he was suggesting to himself wasn't just unlikely to work, it was likely to end in serious injury. He'd be exhausted, moving slower through the room with the weight of time on his back. Even if he were able to skip across those rotating portions of the chamber, what would happen if he fell? He'd be protected as long as he remained in that state, but it would be nearly impossible to get back up again inside the tumbling room.

And what if he did make it all the way across? If a standard reconstitute could leave one or even both other Shatterbugs stranded in time, the odds of *this* doing the same were no better.

But that impossible version of him was right; there weren't any safer alternatives. If the odds were no better one way or another, then technically, they were no worse, either. Right?

"I guess we gotta try it." he said to himself. Both of his selves, internal and otherwise. He crouched down in a runner's pose, preparing himself for the sprint of his life. He'd never participated in any sort of track event, but he'd been to enough of Miguel's meets to have a basic understanding of the posture and technique. He thought.

In one fluid motion, the present Shatterbug pushed off with his right foot and brought his left foot out and forward. His arms lifted from the ground and began pumping at his sides. His breath huffed against the domed interior of the helmet, coating the visor in a light fog even in that very first instant of his sprint. And as he performed all of these simultaneous actions, he breathed the voice command into the suit, charged with hesitant hope. "Flicker."

Instantly, he felt supercharged with temporal energy. The prime marconium held in front of his chest warmed, and did not let up. The vibrations all across his body accelerated and kept their pace with his moving limbs. The visor flashed white, and faded. One of the new monitors flashed itself, then faded. Over and over, the sparks of time shone inside the Shatterbug helmet, as the suit carried him in and out of time.

The other Marco was right. The flickers were happening so close to each other—he was shattershocking and reconstituting automatically, so rapidly—that there didn't appear to be any noticeable lags of duplicates left behind or ahead of him in time.

But he'd only just begun.

His first footfall would decide the fate of this experiment.

He dared not look down as the blue boot that wrapped around his toes started to fall. His left foot trailed down through the air, always in the same position no matter what time zone he was in. It inched toward the ground, wherever it might have been, moment by moment, second by excruciating second. Even now, before he'd even properly begun, Marco could feel the weight of eons slowing him and holding him down—and he still had almost two dozen feet to go.

Impact.

As though the temporal anomaly that cursed this castle was somehow on his side, the first sector, rotated by Solace's tendrils behind the scenes, was correct and even for him as the plated sole of his foot reached it.

In just as many seconds as it took for him to reach that first milestone, he pulled his right foot forward and began to take his second step.

He pushed off the ground with his left foot, before that stone sector had time to turn and twist his ankle and make the step impossible. At that moment—that single fraction of a perfect second—he flicked inward, reconstituting. The force of time—of many times—pulling back into whatever instant he was in propelled him. He could see, through all of the flashes of white, through the many frames of minutes that displayed inside the Shatterbug helmet, that he was soaring over the second sector. His right foot was destined to land on the third.

But it was in the wrong position. It was totally diagonal, a whole forty-five degrees from where Marco needed it to be. Then he flashed, and it was thirty degrees in the opposite direction; still not right.

Whether Solace recognized what was happening or not was irrelevant. The inherent erratic motion that the room was already expressing was working against him.

He shifted through time, blinded once again by the flash of his flickers. He opened his eyes. His foot was almost at the lowest point it could be. If he fell much farther and the ground wasn't there to greet him, he would end up shattershocking right into the stone. It wouldn't hurt—not while he was flickering—but it could disrupt his balance enough that he'd begin to actually fall.

Another flash. Another shattershock. In one time, on one of his split monitors, he saw it. The ground was right where it needed to be. A near perfect ninety degrees—flat and even for him. He just needed the suit to be lucky enough to reconstitute him in that frame.

His foot fell another second closer to the ground.

"*Dios ayúdame.*" he whispered. He did not have time to finish in the present, though, before he was pulled through time again with a flash.

Impact.

He felt the wet stone grip against the bottom of his boot. It was slick, he knew that. But it didn't matter.

Marco had landed, and he was shattershocking and reconstituting so quickly that even that sensation couldn't trip him up or slow him down.

He flicked again, pulling his scattered duplicates inward—whether it was across five minutes or fifty, he couldn't tell. Either way, he was being propelled again, pushed forward by the force of some amount of time folding in on itself. Folding through the time scar, even.

In the same second, but also in a different moment altogether, he flew even further across the room. His single footfall, his one running step, carried him over the last sector, and even then he traveled over the wet stone of that stationary platform at the end of the long room.

One foot.

Two feet.

"Fade, fade! *Fade!*" Marco shouted hastily, as his body was pushed through the air, well over his mark. He was going to hit the door, and he would rather have an opportunity to collect himself before barging into another deathtrap.

The suit obeyed. With a final flash inside the Shatterbug helmet, he was reconstituted in some time. Whether it was the same present in which he had begun, or some distance in the past or future, he couldn't yet say.

Shatterbug slammed into the door, his face almost pressed against the reflective blue glass of his domed visor, and his neck definitely caught on the rim of the suit's neck brace, where it met the helmet.

But his feet were on the ground. He made it across.

"It worked!" he celebrated, looking back as though expecting the time-strewn duplicate to be standing on the other side.

He wasn't of course. The other Shatterbug wasn't anywhere. Even his display inside the helmet was gone. Somehow, through some stroke of luck, that Marco had been pulled back into the original, where he belonged.

But that didn't mean it couldn't happen again.

He was going to have to be cautious with his use of the Shatterbug suit moving forward. There was no telling how long his body could stand the flickering, and it seemed that was the only way any extra-temporal Marcos were going to get reconstituted, should they appear again.

Marco let himself sit, his back to the door. His legs slid and stretched against the damp cobbles, with his blue-armored feet dangling safely over the turning sector of the chamber.

"Visor off." he said between breaths, letting the blue helmet fold first into the glass fourths, and then into a collar at the edge of the rest of the suit.

Even through all of this, what was he going to do when he found the others? If he could barely make it through this castle of death—this doomsday machine of rock and steam—how was he going to stop Solace from using it? What could any of them do against that horror?

A force pressed into the small of his back. He flinched, but not in time. The door behind him swung open abruptly, and he was pushed forward and to the side.

His toes turned and caught on the grout of the firm stone bricks, keeping him from losing his balance and sliding back into the rotating gears of the room behind him.

He looked up, expecting a fight.

Instead, Marco saw his face, reflected back at him with an orange hue.

"Visor off." the face said, looking down at him. Its mouth didn't move. Instead, the image parted, giving way to a different face and head. "Marco! There you are; I can't believe it!"

"Miguel!" Shatterbug said, his voice doing nothing to hide his excitement and relief.

He stood quickly, letting his arms guide themselves around his old friend. Shockdrop's did the same, bringing them together in a firm hug, as though they'd been separated for decades.

"Wait, it hasn't been decades, has it?"

"What? No, what do you mean?" Miguel said with one eyebrow raised. "It's been like, a minute and a half."

"That's it?" Marco asked. He expected that the time scar would have put them on different internal clocks, and that coupled with the Shatterbug suit, their experiences since they were separated would have to be wildly different. But for his allies to have just moments ago lost sight of him, while he was searching for many minutes, through nonsensical rooms in impossible configurations? "So R'Bec, and Bahadur? They're still with you?"

"Yeah man, they're right here. Guys?" the athletic Mexican man said, turning his head to call behind him.

Peeking in through the door and around the two bonding heroes, who were still in close quarters after their hug had concluded, were the faces of a Native American woman with slightly dyed-red hair, and an Egyptian man with a curious two-toned crown. They smiled at him in their own ways—her with that alien, 'I guess I should acknowledge that you're safe' sort of way, and him with the compassion of a friend and confidant.

"Alright, let's stick together this time, then." Marco started, his face turning from relaxed to focused. "And find Solace."

"Find me?" a slow, arrhythmic voice sounded from all around, over the churning of the gears and grinding of the stone bricks. "Why, you already have, my dear. Or have you forgotten on your long adventures in my twisting fortress of time?"

"We are coming to stop you, demon!" Ramses declared, holding his ankh as one might hold a microphone. He was proud and determined—they all were.

"Then by all means, come and meet me."

At this, the sector of the room that they all stood in began to move. It grinded against those pieces of stone that continued to rotate. The corners of the room broke away, as the formerly-stationary platform parted from the still wall-and-door that Marco had exhausted himself trying to reach.

They were being carried right to their destination. But somehow, that knowledge did not bring Shatterbug as much confidence as he had been aiming for.

As it was always going to be, the time had come to face Solace and its final progeny.

Issue 19
Delusion Exarch

Their platform was moving, Marco could tell that much. If the walls on either side of them did not give it away as the grout and stone passed by them, the motion—that tugging feeling as his feet strained to hold his body upright—did just as well.

The walls ahead and behind them, though, stayed still. Well, not completely still. They moved at the same pace as their means of transport through the castle of brass and steam. Those two walls acted as barriers, keeping the First Mortal Order in their cage, as Solace pulled them along towards its antechamber.

Not that Shatterbug wanted to escape. Although it would be preferable to reach their arena on their own terms, surprising Solace and Countess Deotce, there just wasn't going to be a way to make that happen. At least this way, the four heroes would be right where they wanted to be. It just so happened that the horrific psychopath wanted them there, too.

As they were carried in a straight line from wherever in the labyrinth of damp stone they had been, the rumbling from beyond the walls grew louder. The gears clanging and grinding against one another were becoming either more numerous or more aggressive. And, just barely audible over that cacophony of industry, Marco swore he could hear the slimy slithering of tendrils, shifting through the cracks of the stone bricks, sliding along and around those huge metal wheels, and indeed, pushing and pulling on the back and front walls of the platform he stood on.

Finally, although the intense sound from all around did not stop, their transport did. With a thud of stone meeting stone, Marco was jerked forward, the momentum of his body trying to continue as his feet worked to hold him still. He landed kneeling on one knee, and with his head angled down, he saw that Miguel and Bahadur had ended up in similar positions of imbalance. R'Bec simply crossed her arms and stared forward, anticipating the dark monster's next step.

Indeed, that front wall that had barred them in began to grind itself against the now-stationary side walls, peeling away slowly to reveal—as much as Shatterbug could recognize it—the throne room.

Even over the ruckus of the clockwork fortress, silence fell on the hero's ears. He got back to his feet and took the first step over the threshold.

They entered from the side of the great hall, between two pillars. The rugs were still gone, but now, so too was the scaffolding. Evidently, the gears and additional pipes that now broke through the walls where those wooden supports had stood did not take too long to install. In fact, Marco was unsure why the scaffolding had been necessary at all, as it was quite obvious by what force the construction had been achieved.

Hovering over the throne, with black tentacles stretching out and reaching around those revealed wheels and tubes—tendrils, that were only visible in the dark due to their absolute perfect blackness which stood out from the simple dearth of light—was the shapeless form of Solace. Those extra wisps curled and undulated around it with conceit and delight, with some arcing down, framing and lending support to the figure beneath it.

Countess Aphelia Deotce did not sit upon her throne. A few feet in front of it, a stone console of sorts had been installed, fitted with apparent levers and gears and ball joints, though even that was difficult to see clearly, only illuminated by the occasional flick of Solace's tentacles behind them. She moved those controls with her arms, while those tendrils that protruded from her otherwise bald head pressed against the sides of the console, as if holding her up and steadying her.

"You have all met my most gracious devotee: Delusion Exarch." the mass of shadow and insanity breathed hoarsely, extending each syllable of its sentence, but none moreso than the name of its female progeny.

"Whatever that monster offered you, Deotce, it is lying!" Marco pleaded with the grey-skinned woman. Shining against her cheeks, he thought he still saw a trace of dried blood, unable to fully smear off with the bloating of her dead skin in the damp air.

"I have only been honest with her, my dear Marco Nieve. I gifted her knowledge, and soon, I will gift her people—her world—wealth and protection."

"Protection from you, you mean. That's not a deal, it's extortion!" R'Bec chimed in from Marco's side.

The voidlike mass hesitated for so small a moment, Shatterbug wasn't sure whether it had truly intended to or not. "Execute the interlopers, Delusion Exarch."

Countess Deotce stepped down from her podium. Her legs moved gracefully beneath the long gown as it dragged around the side of the strange console. Meanwhile, the tentacles that clung to the sides of that brick-like machine hung behind her, flowing like hair in water, but curling at the ends with emotion and thoughtfulness. Interestingly, to Marco's eyes, Delusion's tendrils did not wisp and wave with the same cruel mirth as Solace's own. They were filled with devotion and trust. Not power, but pride.

Yet she slowly moved towards Shatterbug as an enemy.

"Ma'am, please! Don't let this thing corrupt you with its *mierda* and lies!" the time traveler pleaded, his hands held up in deference as he tried to yield to the Countess.

Despite this, Exarch was unwavering. Once she had crossed his arbitrary threshold—once she stood only a few feet from him, and with no intention of slowing her approach—Marco prepared to defend himself.

"Shattershock!" he started.

But at the same moment that he gave the order, Delusion Exarch's dark gift unfurled. The tentacles hanging from her scalp stretched out with impossible speed and strength. Marco felt them latch around the plates of his shins and forearms. He knew the soles of his boots had lost their grip from the ground before his eyes registered that he was being lifted into the air. And then, with the final grunt of his voice command, he was flung across the room, his back hitting a column lining the throne room. He lurched forward—still in the air—and landed on his hands and knees. Although the Shatterbug armor was not pierced, and therefore his skin was uncut, he coughed, spying a few droplets of blood on the very bottom of his visor.

They lightly dotted the two monitors on the sides of his screen. But, on closer inspection, they didn't seem right.

1

In both monitors, he could see a Shatterbug. The face of one, reflected back and forth between two visors.

The two duplicates, who should have been five minutes in the past and future respectively, were looking at each other. Somewhere in time—not where they belonged—two Marco Nieves were together.

"*Oh dio*, this isn't right!" Marco exclaimed.

"She threw us through the time scar, we're all scrambled up!" one of his copies said from whenever they were, as the other worked with them to try and process their shared predicament.

In the present, Shatterbug looked up.

R'Bec had begun her counterattack, assaulting the new progeny of Solace with a barrage of imagined bullets. The two pistols that the Telignen held in her hands were unusual and cartoonish, but their output was unrelenting. "Shouldn't have done that, bitch." she said, her already narrow eyes glaring even more, staring daggers into the grey-skinned Countess.

But for all the piercing that her eyes did to Aphelia Deotce's soul, R'Bec's bullet storm could not do the same.

Although Marco couldn't see every piece of illusory lead hurtling through the air, Delusion Exarch certainly could. Her tendrils, like the graceful fingers of a pianist, danced through the air, jutting forward with speed and calculation. By her lack of reaction, Shatterbug was sure that his presumptions were correct: the Countess was stopping every single incoming projectile with her shadowy extremities. And by the expressions on R'Bec's face, it hurt. A lot.

Finally, the illusionist had to let down. Before the guns even reached the ground—perhaps not even half a moment after she released her grip in exhaustion, pulling her fingers to her temples—the weapons faded into flakes of grey, fluttering to the floor uselessly.

Then Aphelia found her tentacles being pulled and tugged backwards. She was held in place, those extra arms kept at bay by rings of green energy, looping around each of them.

Marco's eyes trailed over to the image of Ramses holding his golden ankh up against the villain.

"You will listen to us!" Bahadur said. Although it was the man who spoke it, Shatterbug felt the confidence of Osiris behind his voice. He was still personally uneasy with the supposed-God's relationship with Al-Malik and with the rest of the heroes, but that didn't matter now. Ramses was a good man, and Marco had faith in that. "Service to this monster will only lead your world to darkness, and your people to suffering. You are betrayed!"

"These invaders would have you deny my blessings." Solace's voice once again howled all around Marco, as though its main form was not in the same room along with them. "They seek to destroy your faith in me, and in doing so, impress their own will on you and your world."

Countess Deotce closed her eyes. Her nose crinkled, and her shoulders tensed beneath the soiled—though still ornate—dress that concealed most of her engorged, dead skin. She breathed in.

And then her eyes opened. The tendrils trapped behind her retracted, pulled back into her head. Delusion Exarch stifled a screech as she freed her unholy hair from their dimensional binds, and then let them back out. In a violent throwing of her head, she sent them all against the Champion of Osiris.

They flicked at and reached for the ankh, shining even in the dim light of the damp fortress. Ramses moved back, his awareness and agility somewhat enhanced by the patron whispering in his mind. Marco could only watch as Bahadur's back inched closer and closer to the wall, and Delusion's movements became more and more cold and precise.

"*Dejalo*, lady!" another Mexican voice shouted from across the room.

With a resounding crash, a shockwave trailed across the room, hurtling over Delusion Exarch and Ramses, then over R'Bec, and finally, above Marco's head as he struggled still to rise to his feet.

Bahadur and R'Bec were thrown slightly, coming to nearly join Shatterbug in his confused, disjointed state against the wall they had entered from. The Countess, however, had sidestepped the attack, somehow dodging it completely. She stood straight and regal, her tendrils already reaching out to latch onto Miguel's wrists, holding them apart.

"How did she—?" R'Bec asked, having apparently recovered from her mental pressure.

"She can see the time scar." Marco said flatly, understanding Solace's true gift to Aphelia Deotce, now. "Or, at least, she knows where it is, and where and how it moves."

Because that was what the psychopathic void really gave its newest progeny. The tentacles were just a byproduct, leakage from the shadows that reached around and inside her brain. The black monster had given her intelligence. Impossible knowledge. An understanding of things that she shouldn't have been able to grasp, and an ability to utilize that otherworldly knowing. She was smarter than any of them, maybe even smarter than Solace, in some aspects. And with the reflexes and tendrils to put that information to work, she was a force to be reckoned with.

She probably had a total understanding of all of their powers. She knew how the Shatterbug suit created and dispersed its doppelgangers, and so hoisted him through the time scar in just the right fashion as to limit his options and minimize their effects. Even if he reconstituted now, it would really only count as the force of five-minutes of time—hardly enough to dent a progeny of Solace, if he even could. Not to mention that without the element of surprise afforded him by time hopping, he was severely outskilled.

Delusion Exarch surely understood that R'Bec's bullets were just illusions, and that although they were real enough so long as the Telignen maintained her focus, they were brittle stones compared to Solace's body—and therefore the tendrils protruding from her head. With seemingly little effort and enough patience, the Countess had to have known that R'Bec's mind would give out.

And then just now, the dead-woman-walking had moved herself through the time scar, not to travel away from the shockwave, but to pass through the spaces between seconds—to avoid it and let it pass over her. Just like Timegaze, and now the Shatterbug suit's flicker ability.

Aphelia Deotce would always have access to understandings that the First Mortal order could never comprehend. She would always know what they were planning and how to interact with it. That was the true extent of Solace's gift to her.

"Aphelia, please listen to us." Marco said, trying to keep his voice composed as the villain held his friend in the air, his arms apart, and his suit useless. Just like Marco's. "We've fought Solace before, on our world. It turned it into a disaster, an apocalypse. It destroyed everything, and now that we scared it off, it wants to do the same thing to every other world—including yours!"

Shatterbug took a step forward as Delusion's head turned back just slightly, so as to see the pleading hero with her left glazed-black eye.

"Stay back, Marco." R'Bec said to his left. With one arm stretched out to her side, as though to keep the time traveler at bay even from several feet away, she held the other to her choker around her neck. Her next words were spoken aloud, but Shatterbug got the sense that the Telignen said them mostly to herself. "We need all our firepower."

In a purple flash, the room was caked and covered in black. But not the same black as Solace's voidlike mass. This darkness had weight. It was just barely reflective, and moreover, it had light behind it. Violet lights, like synapses, danced beneath the surface of the fleshy, furry slime that covered the floor and trailed up the walls. The kept their distance from Marco and Ramses, with clear circles around their feet marking where the ooze dared not cross.

But all the same, the nightmarish material covered and surrounding R'Bec's feet. In fact, it almost seemed as though it grabbed at her eagerly, with the faintest outline of fingers and mouths reaching up from the floor to grip and grab at her ankles. She was held in place.

And so was Exarch. Her feet were in much the same situation as the Telignen's, with Miguel still held in the air. But around her, there were even more hands, even more mouths. And something more.

Shapes stirred beneath the pulsing purple lights on the floor. Figures began to emerge from those covered portions of the damp wall and imposing pillars. Hedgehogs, coyotes, and silverfish leaked out from the corners of the room, all surrounding and closing in on the progeny of Solace.

"Let him go." R'Bec demanded.

Aphelia's face was bare for a moment, held still in thought. "I could pierce your head and banish these demons, Telignen." she hummed.

"You'd be ripped apart before you made it halfway."

A new light glowed on the right of Marco's peripheral vision, signaling that Ramses was powering up as well. A green power hovered around the loop of his ankh, like an aura, threatening the intervention of Osiris' would-be magic.

The Countess pursed her lips, and her tentacles gently set Shockdrop down.

The nightmares vanished. With a sharp sucking-in of air, R'Bec collected them back into herself. The purple choker that had vanished from her neck was now returned, the prison for whatever power she had been holding out on.

The First Mortal Order surrounded Aphelia Deotce, each with their respective abilities at the ready.

"I get what you have now, Deotce." Marco began. "You know what we all can do, and how to fight us. But there's no way you can take us all."

"The creature you swear your allegiance to is a horrific villain." Ramses interjected, trying to reason with the Countess— to turn her. "An insane slayer of humanity, who will discard you without a second thought. We have seen it happen."

"That's right." Miguel said, catching his breath now after landing from his near-stranglehold. "But you're smarter than that *monstruo*, and you have some of its power. Help us stop it!"

"Help us make sure it never does what it did to our world again." Marco finished their group plea.

Through all of this, Delusion Exarch held her ground. She stood firm, preparing to strike with her tendrils, but not quite making a move. Even after the heroes had concluded their shared speech, she was motionless. Her face was still in consideration.

And then her tentacles stopped moving. A new pair seemed to sprout from the sides of her head.

No. They did not come *from* her. *It* passed through her.

The Countess' arms went limp, and then her legs. She dangled in the air, the tendrils hanging from her scalp, her eyes somehow even more lifeless, although their black pools were not any more or less unreflective than before. Her puffy grey skin, which still revealed some features of her old ethnicity, now seemed somehow even more greyed and dead and loose.

Delusion Exarch hung there, her head skewered by the arm of another entity.

Solace had sent one of its own tentacles through her skull. Even now, it undulated in the air, as though sucking out the blackness that it had gifted Countess Aphelia Deotce.

Marco could only stand there in silence, his eyes and mouth agape in shock. His two duplicates, sharing the same time somewhen else, did the same. He did not look, but suspected that even R'Bec would be uneasy at the grisly display of apathy.

"If it serves as any consolation, my dear Marco Nieve," that exaggerated, polysyllabic hum resounded all around them again, coming from every corner of the throne room. Those sounds that would be slurred with a tongue hissed harshly in Shatterbug's ears, and with every click of what would be a throat, his bones shivered. "Her final thoughts were only of loyalty to me. Delusion Exarch had no intention of betraying her God."

"Why?" Marco asked, the sound not even audible to himself inside the blue helmet. He continued, turning to shout at the mass of shadow and psychopathy floating at the end of the room. "Then why? Why would you kill her for absolutely no reason? She was innocent! Tricked by you—she didn't deserve to die!"

If Solace possessed a neck—or indeed, a head—Shatterbug imagined that it would be crooking it, as though in feigned confusion at his questioning tone. "Her purpose, like Jet Wicked and Senility Acolyte, has been fulfilled. I needed her intellect to calculate the optimal path of the marconium through this moving castle. She did so, and now I may bring those schematics to life." it said plainly, although its tone shifted and transformed with each syllable, from condescension, to pain, to confusion, to mirth, and back again.

"And what have you accomplished, then?" Bahadur stepped forward, challenging the dark being, who did not even react at the sudden motion or striking confidence displayed in the Champion's voice. "We can still stop you. We will destroy this castle, and then we will destroy you."

"Why do you even wanna do all this, anyway?" R'Bec asked, taking an equally prepared posture, although her voice projected more a sense of aloofness. "Seems like a lot of work for an omnipotent thing to have all these cronies and machines."

"Because it's insane." Marco answered. "It's evil and malicious, and it just wants people to suffer."

"My dear Marco Nieve, is that all you have learned of me?" the horror asked. Its tentacles wisped with agitation, and the whole castle seemed to stir, though Shatterbug could not place the emotion that such action denoted. "While I do not contest that these things are true of me, they are not my purpose."

Marco did not respond. He would not give Solace the satisfaction of gloating. Of making its case. It said so itself: it was evil and insane. Without reason and without empathy. It would kill and destroy without end, and the time traveler didn't need any justification to turn his thoughts from what he knew was true. Solace had to be stopped.

But Miguel was not so invested. Not yet. He hadn't seen Solace's paradox world, hadn't walked through the streets of New Jackson covered in its tentacles, littered with the bones of its citizens and hazed with the smoke of endless fires. And so Shockdrop did respond. "Then why do all this? What're you trying to do?"

If that incarnation of darkness had a mouth, Shatterbug imagined it would smirk with cruel pleasure at the question, as though the answer were obvious.

"Once all realities are, at last, under my jurisdiction, monotony and logic will fall away. Meaning will become nonsense; reason, replaced with discord. Madness. Destruction. And in the guise of insanity: oppression." At this last word, Solace seemed to flex its many tentacles, even those that stretched from the central mass and into the stone walls of the castle. "This is my dream of the universe—of the multiverse. Perfect, unabated subjugation and control; not of humanity, specifically, but of the laws of reality themselves."

In the corner of Shatterbug's visor, he saw the familiar golden twinkle of Ramses' ankh, held vertically and against the indifferent tangle of darkness floating above. Its loop glowed green as it always did, indicating that the entity inside was expressing its power, through the human Champion and back into the machinery of the ancient tool.

And as the result of that expression, masses of light matching that same bright hue began to latch onto and surround the many arms of Solace that reached into and between the damp brick walls. They flowed down the long stretches of impossible void, closing in on the monster's greater form.

In trying to shake off that assault, the hovering entity swung itself all about, contracting its many extended tentacles in random sequence, in an attempt to jerk itself free.

But beside Marco, his closest friend in the orange-and-purple armor brought his hands together, sending a vertical shockwave hurtling for the now-silent horror. Timed almost perfectly, the attack hit opposite Solace's own movements—it didn't hurt or injure the psychopath, but it did counteract and negate its flailing. The green light of Osiris continued to close in.

Even beneath that glow, though, the time traveler could see those perfectly black tendrils tense once again. Solace exerted as much effort as it could out of its primary shape, willing those extremities to grip and move the castle further. Specifically, it shifted and shook the great hall that the heroes stood on, threatening to move or elevate or altogether crush them.

Still, the heroes persisted. Holding her fingers to her temples in support, R'Bec conjured a glowing yellow platform beneath their feet—Marco assumed this was her doing, anyway, given his past experiences—holding them up off the quaking cobblestones. With another minute flex of its tentacles, Solace sought to throw a column down upon them. The wall behind it broke and fell, and after it, the pillar tumbled straight for the party.

Another clap from Shockdrop, combined with the quick imagination of the Telignen woman, moved the pillar off to the side just enough for it to slide down the simple ramp that had appeared from nowhere. It rolled down harmlessly to the floor, where it continued to roll and shake uselessly with the vibration of the steam-powered castle.

"It is no use, demon!" Bahadur declared, as his magic completely consumed the horror's tendrils, keeping them steady. Only the central mass of intermingling arms remained, though their exact scale and quantity was indeterminable due to Solace's textureless shade.

"Throw everything you got at us, *pendejo*, we've gotchu beat!" an excitable Miguel followed up.

Marco intended to follow up with his own words of victory and self-encouragement—although he was providing little practical support in the moment—but his words became choked in his throat, as Solace took the opportunity first.

"You have accomplished nothing." it hissed. Although Marco thought he placed the tone of some of its words as frustration, he did not get the sense that the voidlike creature was particularly disturbed by its predicament.

"You're trapped, and getting more trapped by the second. You don't have any way to fight us." R'Bec observed. "Time to face facts: you lose."

"Perhaps in this time, I am ensnared. But the marconium is here, and even now, it travels through my stone armor, passing through the temporal scar tissue. Once it reaches the end, its makeup will be forever altered—it will have time traveled. And then I will claim it. All you have done here is ensured that you must stay here to 'restrain' me, rather than disrupt my machinations." The only portion of the horror's body that was not alight with Osiris' power stirred in apparent delight. "In time, you will learn your place, and you will see the true cost of trying to outpace an immortal."

Marco looked inside, deep down and past all of the pride and hatred and fear that clouded his mind and ate away at his heart. He delved inward, and there, he knew that Solace was right. Holding it here was doing nothing; it still had control of the fortress. And they couldn't well go out and stop the walls from moving. Even if there was a way to destroy the building, there was no telling what defenses the shadow monster had at its disposal— if the walls could even be damaged. Titan Black, Jet Wicked—they were all nigh-invulnerable. Flesh wounds did nothing to slow and stop them. And that was organic matter, skin and bone. The stone and metal that made up this palace was far sturdier.

No, whatever they were going to try, it had to be done here. Holding Solace hostage wasn't the answer, but this was the center of the time scar, and the control room for all of the grafted mechanisms. There was an answer here.

The marconium had already arrived. But it would take time for it to be changed. The time scar was moving and shifting, like a morphing bubble. Some places might move faster than others, only to move slower as the rips in time-space passed over again. It was unpredictable—or rather, the only person who could have predicted it was dead.

But, maybe...

There was only one solution. One variable that, if removed, completely shattered Solace's plan. It could even destroy Solace. But doing so was a big ask. There was no evidence to suggest it could be done, and yet, unlike everything else, it wasn't completely out of the question. The question then became, how?

How does one close a tear in the fabric of the universe?

The castle was still moving all around them, still humming and shaking, and occasionally sending whatever pieces of rock and mortar that Solace could spare at the four heroes. There wasn't a clear timetable for the marconium's arrival, so Shatterbug had to assume that it could be at any second. And even if not, if their dark opponent could find a way to wear them down, or to surprise them, then Miguel and R'Bec's defenses might not be able to hold out before the final moment. No matter what way he sliced it, Marco had to act fast.

There was no time to think. No time to ask questions or confer with his comrades. He had promised not to take undue charge anymore, but the situation demanded it of him. He was a hero. And as much as he still had some learning to do in trusting his friends—the fellow heroes of the First Mortal Order—he also needed to learn to have faith in himself, to not second guess himself or put too much trust in the words of his nemeses.

And so, preparing to take a hit from the exertion of his own power, especially so soon after recovering from his flickering not long prior, he planted his feet to the ground and tensed the muscles in his core. Then, with a firm and clear voice, he commanded of his super-suit, "Paradox ambush!"

Marco's visor flashed. Again and again, the inside of his helmet was blasted with light, as the suit parted over and over.

With the moving of the time scar, the hero didn't know in what times all of his duplicates were ending up. But as the effects of his voice command finally settled and resolved, he was left with a crowded display. Strewn across time, in some manner and pattern that the hero knew was not split evenly across five minutes in either the past or future, twenty-one Shatterbugs stood against Solace. Some in groups of several Shatterbugs, some with the other heroes alongside him. But all in the musty throne room at the center of the castle—and he hoped, of the rip in the fabric of time.

"Reconstitute!"

In one brilliant action, the Shatterbug suit strained to reunite all of the scattered duplicates back into one, present time. It was a long-shot, but Marco felt there was no other option. He had to hope that the prime marconium, and the science of his inherited suit of armor, would prove as powerful as his faith in them.

And it was *working*. In that fraction of a moment, when the plates all across his body vibrated ferociously, as the power source and conduit for his superpower warmed and boiled against his sternum, he could *feel* it working.

Although Marco Nieve was not as innately powerful as Solace—he possessed no sixth or any higher senses for the laws of reality and their condition, as the horror evidently did, and he did not have a seemingly endless pool of knowledge and understanding amassed over incalculable human life spans—he felt the pull of the time scar. In that brief frame of time, all of his selves could *feel* the marconium core *tugging* at the edges of the temporal scar tissue, bringing them *inward* and into the present. *Cinching* the frayed ends back together.

Already knowing and understanding the outcome, he looked up at the shuffling figure of Solace, his face smeared with triumph—although recognizing that it was hidden behind the mirrored blue visor.

"How did you..." Solace started, its elongated speech trailing even more with confusion and awe. "I feel it. I—"

The creature's accusations were cut short by a horrific, deafening screech, as though a thousand small and silent creatures suddenly let out a piercing roar of pain. The four heroes all brought their hands to their ears—although Marco and Miguel found themselves struggling even further, their helmets protecting their heads, and so they buckled to the floor inside the armored suits, trying with all of their might to hold consciousness.

"What did you do?!" R'Bec tried to shout over the hideous uproar, already beginning to turn away for the great metal doors at the foot of the room. Despite her best efforts, Marco could only make out her words by reading her lips.

And yet, he still tried to shout back at her through the Shatterbug helmet. "I closed the time scar! Solace can't complete its plan anymore, but it must be having a reaction to the warping reality!"

The Telignen blinked plainly, clearly awaiting a response. Clearly unable to understand him over the tumultuous shrieks, and unable to see Marco's mouth. Not realizing he had answered, she moved on. "Come on!" she ordered, broadly waving her arm— only releasing her hand from the side of her head for a second before the noise became unbearable to her alien ear—and running for the exit.

Marco followed, his chest pounding as his muscles all worked to protect him from the forces of the intense sound flooding the room. He looked back to see Ramses behind him, his ankh sticking up from the side of his head as his hands shielded his ears.

However, he didn't see Miguel.

Looking around frantically, his neck sore from the strain and headache splitting him in two, he spotted his closest friend lying on the ground. Not unconscious, but clearly in unimaginable pain. Shockdrop's legs flailed all about, and he struggled to hold his hands to the sides of his head in any desperate attempt to protect himself from the audio assault. However, his superpower was still on, and even with the lightest tough of his hand against his cheek, a shockwave of some size would knock him about. Worse still, he couldn't seem to work through the torment and bring his hand to the dial on his chest.

"*Miguel!*" Marco screamed futilely. He slowly, and with great ordeal, made his way back—past Bahadur, who offered a supportive pat on his covered shoulder—towards his friend and colleague lying helplessly on the floor.

He crawled and inched over the damp cobblestones, careful to go around the defeated corpse of Aphelia Deotce, whose face now looked sunken and dehydrated. With no blood, and no piece of Solace pumping inside of her, she was empty but for skin and bone. Even her eyes looked to be gone, now. He ducked his head, not wanting to linger too much on his failure as a hero to protect the innocent Countess, and made his way to Miguel.

Shatterbug's ears felt like they were swelling inside his helmet, or more accurately, like they were popping in his head. He was much closer to Solace now, and the intensity of that unbearable racket was far increased. He understood now why

r

Miguel was in so much more distress, and he hoped that he wouldn't succumb to the same convulsions of pain.

He couldn't. He was here to help a friend. To save a hero. He set his hand on Shockdrop's side, easing and alerting the armored man to his presence. Gently and slowly—in no small part due to the beating his body was taking from Solace's immense blaring—Marco brought his hand to Miguel's chest plate, turning the dial around the window of his own suit's marconium core all the way down, and then returning his free hand back to the side of his visor.

Almost immediately, Miguel's hands found their way to his covered ears, and although he wasn't fully recovered, or even protected very much from the horrific cacophony, he found enough strength to look at Shatterbug and bring himself to a sitting position.

Despite this small victory, Marco wasn't sure that his brow could furrow much more, or that his nose could crinkle any harder. There was no doubt about it—the sound was killing them. They needed to get away.

But he couldn't move. And after a moment, he realized in terror that Shockdrop couldn't either.

The constant quaking and vibration in the air, at such high volume and frequency and intensity, had shot their muscles. Their arms could barely support the weight of their torsos as they tried to crawl. Their knees gave away almost as soon as they met the stone floor. The two Mexican heroes were collapsed on the ground of the throne room, under the pressure of Solace's last act of chaos.

In absolute anguish, Shatterbug set the glass dome of his helmet onto the damp bricks. It shook and scraped against the dust and pebbles, as his whole body wracked from wave after

314

wave of sound and pressure expounding from the dark entity above. With jaw fully tensed, ears warm with the faint trickle of blood, and heart beating so hard he thought his neck might pop a vessel, Marco closed his eyes. And as his vision went dark, so too did everything else.

Issue 20
Before the World Ends

"What are you doing?"

R'Bec looked curiously up at Ramses, who had hoisted himself up with a rope materialized from nowhere, and was now dangling from the high struts of the Multiverse Machine. He was investigating some sort of bar and lever on the side of the ring, that much was obvious. Therefore, what R'Bec really wanted to know was why he was doing so.

"I will explain when they wake." he replied distractedly, though with enough volume that the Telignen could hear him from so high up. He nodded vaguely in the direction of the two men lying on the ground in their almost-identical armored suits.

R'Bec and Bahadur had worked quickly to rescue them from the throne room. With a hastily-imagined illusion, the former raked and dragged them across the cobblestone ground to meet them at the door. They each grabbed an unconscious hand of one of the heroes, and then with Osiris' power, the ankh transported the four teammates back to where they had entered this world from.

And now, Shatterbug and Shockdrop were lying face-up in the middle of the metal platform, beneath the still rings of Solace's machine.

"I don't see why you can't just tell me now." she said with a harrumph. She didn't necessarily intend to sound impatient or rude, but she was frustrated—and not unreasonably so, in her eyes—with the intentional obfuscation that Ramses and Osiris were dealing in. There was no real reason why he couldn't just explain himself now, even briefly, and then do so again once the others joined in.

Whether out of equal frustration or just out of having finished, Ramses descended the rope, his feet reaching the Telignen metal gracefully. He tugged the rope slightly with one hand, his ankh in the other, and it dissolved in a flash of green light. The Champion stood face-to-face with the alien woman.

"We do not know how much time we have." he said firmly. He walked over to the control panel—keeping his head turned enough to still look at R'Bec as he spoke to her—and set his fists against the bottom of the console there. "Solace needs to be here for this to work. Hopefully it is not already on its way, but if it is, I do not want us all to be unprepared because I had to explain the plan a second or third time."

"But if it gets here before they wake up, shouldn't I—"

"Osiris agrees with me. We wait." The Egyptian's voice held a gruffness and irritation that was completely foreign to R'Bec's image of the man. Her eyes widened, and she felt the choker around her neck grow tighter with her heat and emotion.

"Wait for... what?" a new voice started, sounding groggy and dazed. "Where... how did we get here?"

R'Bec followed Bahadur's gaze behind her to see a blue figure sitting up off the floor. "Urgh, my head... Visor off." he said. The blue reflective glass parted back, and then the whole helmet folded into a band not unlike the Telignen's nightmare prison,

317

around his neck, to reveal Marco Nieve's face. His eyes were closed, and he immediately brought his fingers up to massage his forehead.

"Good, you are awake." the Champion said, reassurance and politeness returning to his voice, which only angered R'Bec further. "Now we are just waiting on—"

"Miguel!" Shatterbug finished for him. He turned to his side to see his still-sleeping friend, and nudged him in concern. "*Oh dios mio*, please wake up. Please don't do this!"

"Relax, Marco, he's okay." R'Bec said, quickly walking over to kneel on the other side of Shockdrop. She looked to the time traveler, then back down at their faces reflected in the orange visor. "You both took a beating back there, but he got a lot more of it. He might take a little longer to get up."

Marco's fists bunched up on the ground beside Miguel's arm. He let out a long breath, and then relaxed. "You got us out of there."

"We both did." Bahadur's deep voice said as he joined the group in the middle of the Multiverse Machine.

"Well then can't you wake him up?"

"Osiris did not recommend it. His familiarity with the human brain is limited—he did not inspire confidence."

"Same with you." R'Bec clarified. "We had to give you time, we'll have to for Miguel, too."

"How much time do we have?" Marco asked. R'Bec wanted to know the same.

318

A murmuring from below their faces indicated that Shockdrop had started to stir. The two heroes put their hands under the arms of the third, helping to hoist him to a sitting position. Bahadur, however, simply looked down at them, then out at the bright meadow and the sky on the horizon, which had just begun to turn from a brilliant blue to a faint pink over the tree line. "Not enough, now."

Shatterbug looked to the Champion quizzically, before resuming his attendance to his friend. R'Bec made sure he was sitting upright, and once he had retracted his visor, that his head was ok. Satisfied enough, she stood up and glared at Ramses. "Well? Time to fess up, man."

"He has just woken. Can you not be patient?"

"You're the one who just said—"

"*Relajar*, R'Bec..." Miguel mumbled from behind. With Marco's assistance, the orange-clad hero was standing on two feet, and after a moment, he could uneasily do so on his own. "Bahadur, I'm good. Tell 'em your plan."

"Dude, you need to sit for a minute. Do you even know you're okay? Where are we? How many fingers?" Marco asked with three digits held right in his best friend's face, giving no pause between each question.

"I'm fine, man. Just listen, he and Osiris have a good idea, but we have to be fast. Got it?" Shockdrop reassured.

Shatterbug's shoulders slouched, and although R'Bec didn't show it, she agreed with the implied distaste. Bahadur, however, didn't notice.

"As I said, we do not have much time." the Champion started, turning back to face the other three heroes. He had always been the more level-headed one, but his experience in this new world had changed him somewhat. He was different. Not more confident, but more commanding. "We have some understanding of the Multiverse Machine, but we are going to need help. Specifically, we need to wait for Solace to get here."

"Solace is coming *here*?" Marco asked, his voice catching slightly on the last word. His eyes were bulged in disbelief. "Why don't we just leave now, if you know what we're doing? Trap it here and go!"

"That isn't an option, especially knowing that marconium is present in this world. It will build a new machine, far away from us." Bahadur cautioned. "No, it has been thoroughly defeated here. I believe it will try to use this machine and return to our world, to regroup and plan a more sophisticated invasion of another universe.

"The plan is as follows. First, we wait here and allow Solace to direct the machine back home. Second, we ambush it, joining it inside the rings of the machine as before. It will realize that we intend to follow it back, and try to pull the incorrect levers located on these struts," He paused, pointing and drawing the heroes' attention above for a moment. "While also protecting the correct one in sequence."

"Sorry— correct, incorrect; what does that all mean?" R'Bec asked, her brow furrowed in annoyance. If there was one thing Ramses did not do well—and there were many things, in her opinion—it was paraphrase.

"Once the Multiverse Machine is powered on," Miguel started hoarsely, answering her question for the Egyptian. "Those four levers need to be pulled in a random order, one every two minutes. If any one of them is pulled out of order, or one gets missed, it stops the machine."

"Indeed. Now, with Osiris' power, I can redirect Solace's arms away from us *and* from the incorrect levers. It will also try to guard the correct lever, preventing us from pulling it. That is where you three will come in. You will have to get around the creature's defenses to keep the machine operational."

"And then once we're back in our own universe?" Marco held his hand out, as though requesting a gift, to prompt an answer.

As before, R'Bec also wanted to know the answer to the time traveler's question. "Yeah, what's your plan once we're home? Run away and leave it alone? We still can't kill it, or destroy the machine."

The Egyptian was silent, his stoic face unflinching.

"Oh, you don't actually know, do you?" the Telignen accused.

"It's a good plan, guys." Shockdrop tried to affirm.

"How? Think Miguel, we can't just keep following it to universe after universe and stopping whatever scheme it comes up with." reasoned Marco. "This has to end, here and now, and we don't have any way to do that."

"I am open to suggestions, unless you only wanted to criticize me with no alternatives, alien." Bahadur said, challenge in his voice.

"Hey! I don't have to take this shit from you, playing dress-up with your not-even-a-God friend." the Telignen rebutted, pointing her finger directly in Ramses' face. "You didn't come up

r

with a full plan. Why don't you leave that to the people who didn't sign up to be some old guy's submissive?"

"Guys, come on, please." a concerned Miguel chimed in, not assertively enough.

"I don't wanna beat a dead horse, Ramses, but she is right." Marco joined in R'Bec's tirade. "And not just because of our past disagreements. This isn't gonna go where we want it to. We'll have to try something else."

"There is nothing else; we are out of time!" Bahadur barked.

"*Everyone listen!*"

If Ramses had more to say, he bit his tongue at Miguel's tortured command. R'Bec and Marco looked at him, too, unsure of what to say or when to speak.

Shockdrop was huffing, charging through his exhaustion and, R'Bec had to imagine, some degree of anxiety. He was the center of attention, trying to break up a deep seated fight.

"We are the First Mortal Order. We were chosen! And *this* is *why* we were chosen!" he declared proudly, if firmly. "This is a good plan. More than that, it's the best plan we have right now, and it's all we're gonna get. As for killing Solace, we'll have to burn that bridge when we get to it—we didn't take this oath to take the easy way out."

R'Bec glanced over at Ramses, who had tipped his eyes down in shame. She followed suit, accepting some of the blame, herself. If Marco had done so, the Telignen didn't notice.

"So are we gonna do this, *amigos?*"

A thud put R'Bec on alert, and she brought her head up to see that the time traveler had set his hand on Miguel's shoulder, in a pat of camaraderie. "Of course, *hermano.*"

The illusionist held her fingers idly over her purple choker, which pulsed with nightmarish power, but was otherwise back to normal. "Yeah. Sorry, yeah."

They all looked to Bahadur. And he looked to the golden weapon in his hand. R'Bec couldn't tell if he was communicating with Osiris or just avoiding the gaze of his friends, but either way, Miguel spoke up.

"Well?" he said, holding his hand out. In that moment, Shockdrop's arm did not look dissimilar to Corpsegaze's, when it held its open palm out to her in invitation back at Groom Lake. That one motion from a cosmic being had started this journey—even if the first steps had already been taken then, whether she knew it or not—and now that motion from a friend would seek to end it.

After a moment, the Champion looked up. His arm moved, carrying his free hand up to meet the Mexican hero's. They shook, and Ramses nodded to the other three his satisfaction, and behind tired eyes, his apology.

But the festivities were to be cut short. A distant, piercing howl rang through the otherwise silent meadow. They all looked in the direction it had come from—the direction that Shatterbug and the Telignen had walked in pursuit of their enemy.

On the horizon, having just made its way over the canopy of the distant forest, a shadow emerged. It hovered like a cloud, just at the edge where the earth met the sky, which had now turned in greater volume from blue to bright pink, as the sun set behind the approaching form of Solace.

"Look alive, people. We only get one shot at this." Marco said, his voice more raspy than usual. R'Bec imagined it was a product of his masculinity taking control, trying to sound more confident in the face of danger, even if it was only for his own benefit.

The four heroes ducked down behind the machine, leaning their backs against the wiry mesh on its side as their legs crouched on the long, bright grass. And there, they waited for the psychopath to arrive, and begin the fight for the whole of reality.

Issue 21
Second Verse

The journey back took far longer than it should have. Defeated and disoriented, Solace felt like it was wandering aimlessly through the clear sky, its path unclear as it made its way from Co Palluma back to the Multiverse Machine.

A lesser being would count itself foolish, would insist that they should have recognized the volatility of the temporal scar. But Solace knew that none of this was its own fault. How could it have known not only that the insect Marco Nieve could heal that wound in the fabric of reality, but that he would even think to try?

And nevertheless, it was of no consequence. As always, the amalgamation of perfect darkness had contingencies. It would leave this world and return to that which it had come from. It would finish the machine's construction, and from that exhausted universe, it would reach out across all others in a single moment. With total, parallel omnipresence, it would be vulnerable for only a short time, as it searched the whole of reality for a new means of achieving omnitemporality. And, most importantly, that 'First Mortal Order' would be stranded in this primitive world.

The cooled metal felt good on the horror's tendrils, as it wrapped itself around those rings in comfort. The settled machine eased the slimy non-flesh that had been shredded and regenerated in the rippling of time's restitching. Satisfied, Solace let itself hover in the center of the transportation platform, completely independent of its grips on the struts surrounding it. It stretched a single arm over to the console outside of the apparatus, input the commands indicating its home world—where either Jet Wicked or Senility Acolyte would surely be waiting, proudly spouting about their inconsequential victory over the other—and retracted that tentacle back into its main form.

The rings began to rotate slowly. Now, it waited. Eight minutes; that was all it would take.

Movement from the direction of the solitary tree that shared the hill caught Solace's attention. It turned—as though it had a medium of looking that was directional, despite the contrary being the case—to see four human figures standing just inside the rings, which continued their acceleration.

Ah, so this was their plan. Of course Solace would not be so fortunate as to enjoy even a few minutes without the whining of mortals.

"I see you were able to recover from my counterattack well enough, Miguel Jimenez." Solace lied. Its suffering at Delusion Exarch's castle was unplanned. Worse, it was embarrassing. But if there was one thing the psychopath excelled at—and there were many things—it was taking control of less than ideal situations. "Ah, and you intend to follow me back home, is that it? Well, my dear heroes, I regret that I cannot allow any strays on this trip."

The creature let loose two thick, pitch black tentacles, which jabbed down with near-imperceptible speed and force towards Miguel Jimenez and R'Bec of Peplorix.

But they did not connect. At least, not with their targets. Solace's tendrils did not extend through their fragile, plump bodies, did not pierce their meaty insides and come out the other end. Instead, the two tentacles met with each other, both unable to break the other, instead meeting in mid-air, brought together and face-to-face by two glowing green portals.

The shrill, overzealous voice of Bahadur Al-Malik made its way over the rushing of the Multiverse Machine's rotations up to Solace, who lacked any biological audio receptors in the strictest of terms, but heard the man's voice nonetheless. "We did not use Osiris the last time we fought here, demon. You are at a disadvantage, now."

How dare such an impertinent, insignificant human talk down to a void so unknowable and omnipotent as Solace. Solace, the entity that in one lifetime, enslaved the entirety of a universe and the very laws which held it together; who had lived and lied in waiting for the course of a universe—twice—solely out of cleverness and spite; who had sought out and achieved the most impossible feat of breaking down the walls between worlds. Whereas Bahadur Al-Malik, for all of his misplaced confidence, was only a boy, wielding and waving around the science of a long-dead superior—who even then, was nothing compared to that great, black horror—without any comprehension of its intricacies.

"Osiris or no, it is of no consequence. Wherever you face me, it is my domain. So long as this stage remains, I will always hold supremacy over you and your band of infants. You are nothing, to me. You are beneath me. And recognize it or not, the multiverse has already fallen to me."

That all-too-familiar squeal of Marco Nieve blurted out just as Solace finished its gloating session. "Two minutes, get to the lever!"

Solace was already reaching for one of the incorrect levers that was spinning around the arena, knowing that it would shut off the Multiverse Machine and crush all hope of the First Mortal Order's homeward path.

But again, its tendril passed through a hazily defined hole in the world, forcing the entity's arm back against itself. It could not reach the failsafe.

However, that did not mean all was lost. Solace—far more nimble than the mortals, and unbound by the same laws of physics which applied to their feeble walking-cadavers—hovered in defense of the correct switch, keeping them from pulling it. Somehow, they knew how the Multiverse Machine worked, even those parts and mechanisms that it had devised to obfuscate the machine's nature. So why had they waited for the congregation of darkness to arrive?

Ah, that was it. They knew about the failsafes, but they could not decipher how to pilot the craft.

Below and behind the voidlike horror, R'Bec of Peplorix made her way up through the air, on glowing yellow platforms conjured from her mind. Those *j'ops* moved along with the rotating rung, and with Solace.

The monster sent a flurry of tentacles down at her, aiming to swipe her down and keep her at bay until the next mark. She deflected its smaller tendrils with a pair of twin rapiers, also imagined from her mind. Evidently tied into permanence—a skill which Solace recognized as a rare talent among Telignen, especially to such a potent degree—it could not break them so easily.

As R'Bec of Peplorix leapt from her final perch, reaching with open arms to grab onto the lever, Solace had its chance. It pushed a great, swinging tentacle out of itself, bringing it down upon her with almighty force, to knock her from the air.

Impact.

Solace's arm slammed into something. But, there was no follow through. Looking more closely—as though a being of Solace's stature did not see all things within its scope with equal clarity and understanding—the attack was held back. Kept at bay by a wall of green aura; obviously, an extension of Osiris' dimensional weapon.

Regardless of what had stopped it, the job was done. R'Bec of Peplorix reached the switch and pulled down on it as gravity pulled down on her, before she released and landed on the warming metal of the Multiverse Machine.

And the machine continued to spin, the first failsafe avoided.

Like some deranged imbecile, Marco Nieve began running from across the platform, directly for the hovering form of Solace. Indeed, it was deranged, but not without purpose. The time traveler had one hand over his sternum—over the prime marconium. The ruse was not clever; he intended to send the tentacled mass forward in time, to the end of all time, to die.

It would not allow that. Easily and with no great effort, Solace carried itself a little higher, letting its tentacles just slightly graze the top of the spinning enclosure, which had now reached its maximum speed. The Multiverse Machine could carry them to the destination world now, were it not for Solace's needless and nonsensical embellishments.

Following that, the horror let down a few of its larger tentacles, to swipe at the pursuing Marco Nieve and keep him at bay, lest he find some way to propel himself up to it.

But although, Solace sensed, it was *allowed* to remain at an impasse with that human who would call it his nemesis, the interference by Bahadur Al-Malik prevented the voidlike creature from turning the tide in its favor. Portals continued to open, interlocking Solace's stabbing tendrils with one another as they sought to pierce Marco Nieve's head or heart.

And then a new piece was introduced, threatening the careful balance between man and monster. Miguel Jimenez had joined the fray, evidently attempting to use his suit's shockwave-generating capabilities to send his friend flying into the air. He tapped his hand on the metal to throw himself up just as Marco Nieve was standing over him, and then let his other open palm collide with the back of that blue armored suit.

But each time, Solace intercepted. The smallest thread-like tendril crept down from its main form, or from one of the many nearby tentacles, to meet Miguel Jimenez's hand before it impacted with Marco Nieve. That tiny arm was small enough that Bahadur Al-Malik could not see it, but was also too small to bring about any harm to the two humans below. Still, it kept the marconium-powered heroes from gaining an upper hand in that moment.

And now Solace had two targets, two humans to try to kill. It let more tentacles dangle and fall, to swipe and strike at both Marco Nieve and Miguel Jimenez, in the hopes that Osiris' so-called Champion might grow careless, and fail to defend one or the other of the armored heroes.

But the illusionist saw fit to intervene, as well. Walls, blades, disembodied hands, and decoy Shatterbugs and Shockdrops appeared from nowhere, imagined by R'Bec of Peplorix to get in Solace's way. It could see every time; it knew they were only figments of the Telignen's *j'ops*—even the poorly-

330

designed mimics did not distract the perfectly-black horror from its prey—but they were conjured in the very last moments, directly in front of Solace's attacking arms. It pierced them with ease, but its momentum was lost, and they were not so ingrained in the reptilian alien's mind that its eradication of those illusions caused any lasting harm to her.

The tentacled creature once again turned along with the appropriate strut, guarding the next switch in the sequence as it became active. "The next lever is ready!" R'Bec of Peplorix helpfully informed her associates, once Solace was already in position. But that was only half of the battle. It still needed to pull one of the other now-active failsafes.

And it would do one better. Solace stretched out three tentacles at lightning speeds, aiming to release all three of the incorrect switches.

Once again, Bahadur Al-Malik used the computer program's machinations to open opposing portals over two of the levers, sending Solace's tentacles flying into one another. However, the black horror had the upper hand, as the third switch—hurtling all around and, specifically, opposite Solace—was unguarded.

Its tendril reached it and…

Met another of its tendrils.

No. This was not of Solace's body. This blackness was imperfect. Reflective, even if only just. It stood out from the true, impossible tentacle which extended from the creature's greater mass easily to the entity's eyes—if a being with no features at all, of impossible shape, size, and density were to use eyes.

This was a fabrication. A trick.

An illusion.

The Telignen had repelled Solace with a poor approximation of itself. An offense of the highest order. Worse, she was holding onto it, refusing to let the true dark monster destroy its negative image.

And yet, it was causing R'Bec of Peplorix great stress. That was what Solace was hoping for—what it needed. She was holding her temples, holding back screams of pain as she tied and retied the threads inside her Telignen mind, holding her *j'ops* in reality for as long as she could.

Solace reached another arm down, extending out from that one fighting off the false-amalgamation. It stretched out, seeking to wrap itself around the Telignen and constrict her. Crush her.

But a sudden shift in pressure disrupted that.

For a mortal, it would have been difficult for a moving figure to reach down carefully and gently to grip a stationary target. For Solace, though, it was simple calculation and kinetics. As it moved and rotated about R'Bec of Peplorix, following along with and protecting that correct lever, it adjusted itself accordingly, in real time.

So, when the illusionist was abruptly thrown from her still-footing, the horror could not react appropriately. It pulled that tentacle up in alarm, flinching as the wave of pressure passed, carrying R'Bec of Peplorix with it.

Miguel Jimenez.

He had rescued his alien associate, and was now standing proudly at the edge of the arena, beaming behind his reflective orange visor—Solace suspected that the two marconium-powered heroes believed that it could not see their faces, as they made no attempt to hide their emotions.

And on that thought, Solace realized that it had lost track of Marco Nieve. It adjusted its attention behind it, only a moment too late to see the time traveler fall to the ground, a proud smile painting his face.

The heroes had engaged the second failsafe.

The black-tentacled horror looked down on its mortal foes—no, less than foes. They were not worthy of its attention, they did not deserve such active and insistent adversity. They were infants and insects, all of them, and it would not inflate their egos any longer.

"I believe I have humored you for long enough, my dear heroes." Solace hissed, letting a hint of conceit and self-assuredness return to its otherwise inconsistent voice. Always, the voidlike entity sought at least that smallest grip with which to regain a semblance of control. "I recognize that you only seek safe passage back to your home world; but this, I cannot allow."

Solace extended innumerable arms out from itself, wrapping them around the whole of its primary mass, enshrouding and entangling itself. From those tendrils, more still emerged and wrapped around each other and those tentacles which already had done so. Over and over, the pitch-black being engorged itself, each time growing larger and more violent in its movements. To the heroes below, it would certainly appear as though it was only expanding, but the impossible darkness of Solace's form and boundless body concealed the true nature of its shape. Indeed, it was merely extending infinite new arms out from and about itself, continuously. And with each iteration, it took up more space within the rotating boundaries of the Multiverse Machine.

Finally, the inflating entity reached the defenseless bodies of R'Bec of Peplorix, Bahadur Al-Malik, and Miguel Jimenez. It continued its rapid growth, pushing up against them and therefore forcing them backwards. On their knees, lying helpless on their back, or trying with what little might they had to stay standing as they pressed back up to Solace's slimy extremities, they found themselves held only inches away from the dangerously spinning struts at the edge of the arena.

And then Solace pushed harder, grew more.

And they were shoved out of the circle, off the platform, and onto the grass—which now grew dimmer as the sun began to dip beneath the horizon.

Marco Nieve, however. Solace could not risk getting too close to him, even for a moment. The time traveler was avoided, forced to stay on the metal stage. Surrounded by opaque and swallowing blackness, but given a wide berth, to keep that elemental sample away from the otherwise unstoppable entity.

But Marco Nieve, despite his mortality, was no fool. Solace knew this. And although it did not respect or fear the young human, it did give him credit where it might be due. It allotted itself the capacity to be concerned for itself, and for what the man in the Shatterbug suit might try to do—might try to stumble into and succeed, as he so frequently did, by sheer coincidence.

It so happened, therefore, that Solace found the human taking advantage of that afforded space inside the otherwise tumbling tangle of voidlike appendages by beginning to move. To walk. He wandered about the stage, arms held out in front of him like a blind fool, and wherever he stepped, the horror had no choice but to grant him unabated access, lest Marco Nieve cast it through time.

"Ramses, where are you?" a voice rang inside the mess of Solace's tendrils. Evidently, the time traveler was seeking his expelled associates.

"Marco! Marco, where are you?" another person replied. Or rather, they just so happened to call out just after the man inside spoke—those individuals outside could not hear the aimless hero inside, and vice versa.

And yet, Solace felt Marco Nieve's presence inside of it. He continued to move atop the Multiverse Machine—in the confines of the black monster's body. As though he knew where he was going. Or, as though he were being guided.

Osiris!

The long-dead interloper was communicating with Marco Nieve! Solace could see now—it was *looking*, now—Bahadur Al-Malik had his golden implement directed at Solace. No, not at Solace; *through* Solace, at the hero called Shatterbug.

The pseudo-trapped Mexican man found his way to the edges of Solace's expanse, leaving the impossible blackness no choice but to yield to him, letting him once again see the clear sky. And beyond just that, Marco Nieve was now standing in front of his Egyptian companion.

The former hoisted the latter back up and onto the platform.

"Help me." the blue-armored human said calmly. Strategically. "Use Osiris to help me touch this thing with my marconium."

A threatening plan indeed, although predictable.

335

Solace extended an arm between the two, creating a string across the gap it had opened for Marco Nieve's passage. Tendrils reached out from that shadowy tentacle, pushing Bahadur-Al-Malik back.

And then five fingers linked their way around that extremity.

Solace looked. Solace paid attention.

Marco Nieve had one hand on that piece of the horror, and the other on his chest.

He turned his palm.

And Solace shrunk. It scurried back into itself, folding all of those tangled and encompassing arms and tentacles back into themselves and around each other, unfurling and curling itself back into its traditional size and shape. Its tendrils continued to wisp as it hovered high up in the air, still within the spinning rings of the Multiverse Machine, but far from Marco Nieve's reach.

"Number three." Bahadur Al-Malik informed his teammates, as Miguel Jimenez and R'Bec of Peplorix rejoined them in the arena. There was no urgency and concern in his untrembling voice.

It was sickening.

"Shattershock!"

As though echoing Marco Nieve's call to action, R'Bec of Peplorix took a sturdy position in the center of the ring. Solace, as before, planted itself in front of the appropriate lever, turning along with it about the Telignen. With three great tendrils, it reached out for each of the levers once again.

The illusionist, however, single-mindedly protected each of those, with conjured tentacles of imperfect darkness wrestling with Solace's own impossibly black arms. Again, they were so ingrained within her mind that the horror struggled to break them, despite its rivaling power. Still, it could tell that the three-pronged assault was taking a toll on R'Bec of Peplorix, as she clutched the sides of her head more vigorously with each passing moment.

And yet, Solace could not become too complacent. Pulling any of the three incorrect switches would halt the process, but so would preventing the activation of that one which it now hovered before. The voidlike mass shifted the bulk of its attention, therefore, to that lever behind it—if a faceless creature had any side to it at all, frontal or otherwise.

And in good time, too. Bahadur Al-Malik, evidently thinking that the dark entity was distracted by its bout with the Telignen, had used Osiris' power to teleport himself up behind Solace, only inches from the lever.

With violent and ferocious vigor, Solace caught the Champion of Osiris by his leg, pulling him back and away from that guarded switch and letting him dangle helplessly.

"Did you think I would not account for your patron's cunning, my dear?" it hummed and snarled gleefully at the hanging human. It watched him eagerly, waiting to see his face flash from frustration to defeat—to see that failure in the Egyptian's eyes, and it hoped, in the eyes of the artificial consciousness dwelling inside his head.

"Reconstitute!"

Solace recognized the action only a fraction of a moment too late. Propelled by a shockwave that passed over the horror in the same instant, Marco Nieve—charged with the strength of ten

337

a

minutes of time being forced back together into one physical space—leapt into and punched the defenseless Bahadur Al-Malik.

He was knocked loose from Solace's slimy grip, and flung not straight ahead, but at an angle. An angle that just so happened to follow along with the turning of the strut behind. The man with the title of Ramses was thrown into the lever, and as he fell, gravity allowed him to pull on that switch.

And with that, the third failsafe was passed.

But Bahadur Al-Malik was still falling, still tumbling through the air. His loyalty to Osiris was strong, and he gripped the ankh in his hand with unyielding faith.

Faith that was nothing compared to Solace.

The horror reached out at a speed nearly-imperceptible to human eyes, except perhaps for those of someone in great strife and awareness already, such as someone currently hurtling through the air. The Egyptian tried to pull back and protect the darkness' target, but it was no use. Solace's tendril enveloped his whole hand, and with a disgusting slurp and a forceful ripping motion, it stole the golden weapon away.

It hungrily devoured that device, consuming and concealing it in the sea of void that was its formless body. Solace once again reached a pair of arms out to Bahadur Al-Malik, catching him in the air. Protecting him. Entrapping him.

"How useful are you now—how *mortal* are you now—without your precious false God, I wonder?" it teased the supposed-Champion, arming uncountable sharpened tendrils, extending out from each other and Solace's main form, all vying to pierce Bahadur Al-Malik. To skewer and execute him as he hung, once again, in the air.

And then, Solace heard a cry of determination, outside its field of attention.

"Shattershock!" it said, followed shortly by a similar decree. "Reconstitute!"

But the second order... It did not come from the same entity as the first. Not the same iteration of that person.

And then it realized what had happened.

The ankh was gone.

Marco Nieve, no doubt, had sent a version of himself to the past. That past version of the hero called Shatterbug had done something—changed something—such that now, in Solace's present, it had not taken possession of Osiris' machine.

Indeed, not everything was exactly the same as it had been a moment prior. Bahadur Al-Malik was held at a slightly different angle. A different leaf was whistling through the air than the one that had fallen from the nearby tree. Time had changed—it had been altered and repaired, in Marco Nieve's image. And Solace could perceive it, invisible to the forces that resolved the paradox, but unable to do anything about it.

The Champion of Osiris readied his retrieved ankh—the ankh that, as far as he knew, had never left his grip—to fight back against Solace's snare.

The dark horror released, preferring to fight the dimensional tool's abilities rather than defend against them.

"The four of you have grown significantly, even in just one day." applauded the shadowy entity, lettings its excess of tentacles once again wisp ominously as it hovered over the heroes. "Of course, I have watched each of you for far longer. It will be...

difficult... to bring about your unbirth, once every event in time and space are rightfully at my discretion.

"Four of you..." Solace thought aloud. Marco Nieve looked up at the perfect blackness of the horror, furious trepidation on his face—'hidden' behind the reflective Shatterbug helmet—and fists clenched. R'Bec of Peplorix continued to hold one hand to her head, with the other gently tapping at the brace around her neck, which pulsed with the nightmares of a disturbed Telignen, locked away. Bahadur Al-Malik kept the bulk of Solace's shape tightly encircled by the loop of his ankh, held to his eye like some ridiculous spectacle, as though it enhanced his or Osiris' focus of their united power. And Miguel Jimenez...

The voidlike creature expanded its attention. The man in the Shockdrop suit was not with the others. He was elsewhere. Before even the perfect intelligence and comprehension of Solace could react , it saw the orange-armored hero punch into the floor of Telignen metal, shooting himself up through the air just as one of the struts was about to pass by him. He soared high, directly into the lever on the ring, unguarded by the black mass.

It had missed the final two-minute mark. It did not move itself in front of the appropriate switch, it did not try to initiate one of the three other failsafes. But, the sequence was random, and even with only one possible solution left, the targets were moving—rotating about the stage. There was no conceivable way a human, much less Miguel Jimenez, could keep track of the final lever, could be able to maintain an accurate count of time with more attentiveness than Solace.

And yet, the athletic human had been correct.

With the final failsafe lever pulled, and no flash or fanfare, the Multiverse Machine carried the First Mortal Order, and their shadowy opponent, through the space between worlds and to their destination. Back under the glass dome atop the corpse-built compound.

If Solace had eyebrows—or eyes, for that matter—the imperceptible motion it made with its pitch-black tentacles would be accompanied by a harsh, infuriated glare. And it was entirely directed at the blue-armored Marco Nieve.

"This is no victory." Solace's words sent a chill down Marco's spine. He tensed up once again at the slow, arrhythmic speech of that existential monster. "You have only served to delay the inevitable. As I said, you cannot outpace an immortal."

The horror was right, of course. Marco knew that. It was still alive, and the Multiverse Machine was still intact. They hadn't done anything to disrupt its plan. In fact, despite Solace's words, they hadn't even really delayed anything—it was already intending to come back here, to this universe, when they stepped in.

And yet, Shatterbug couldn't help but feel a sense of accomplishment. It *knew* that they wanted to follow along, it *tried* to stop them. But they succeeded. They forced their way back home, fought against that dark psychopath. Even if their goal was only to survive, they had achieved it. That felt like a victory, even if there was still more to do.

"Ramses, the controls!" he barked, trying to restrain the urgency in his voice in exchange for confident suggestion. He wasn't a leader; they were a team. It was time he acted like it.

Still, Bahadur nodded in agreement and took to the time traveler's orders, making his way outside the confines of the slowing rings and to the console at the edge of the platform. Granted, neither he nor Osiris knew how to pilot the craft, but that wasn't the point. They didn't need to go anywhere specific. Silently, within their minds linked briefly by Osiris, they had come up with a simple plan.

"We have to overload the machine." Marco had thought, noticing the God-program's presence in his head back in the other world, while Miguel was making his way into position to pull the final lever. "If you can't make it go to a specific place, we need to confuse it; make it try to travel to a nonexistent one; make it explode!"

"Would that actually work?" Bahadur thought back, their minds shared by the ankh pointing casually from his hand to Marco.

"*It could.*" a more perfect, divine voice said, joining the two humans' conversation. "*If you can set the ankh on the controls, my Champion, I can try to manipulate them enough to shock the system into lockdown. We may be able to collapse the interior as it struggles to bend dimensions appropriately.*

"*But, Shatterbug, it will be dangerous for you three. Ramses will need to stay at the control panel, and you will have to keep pulling the correct levers until it breaks down.*"

And now they were here. For as much as it was a hastily-drawn-together plan, it was all they had. There could be no delays, and no stays of assurance.

"What do you think you are doing, Champion?" Solace teased, letting one of its many pitch-black arms extend, waiting for the rings to fully stop their rotation so it could reach out for the Egyptian hero. "You and I, and Osiris, all know that you cannot pilot the Multiverse Machine."

Although Bahadur ignored the psychopath, Marco didn't. He continued to try for real what he had been threatening in the other world: touch Solace with the prime marconium and cast it through time.

"Shattershock!" he declared, taking a running start in the present and future, as his past self fell to the floor of the enclosure, unsupported by the Multiverse Machine that had yet to arrive.

Solace pulled its tendril away from the rapidly-accelerating edges of the arena, the machine starting up again—although with some difficulty, as evidenced by the grinding and grumbling from the systems beneath the stage. It turned that extremity, looping back and down into the Shatterbug in the present.

Seeing this, that duplicate in the future gave the order, reconstituting all three of his copies into a single person again, in a single moment of time. He used that force to propel him upwards, one arm waving wildly in the air as he clutched his chest with the other. They had to hope that Ramses' and Osiris' work would get the job done, but Marco couldn't rely on it. Solace had to be handled, and this was the one way he knew it could be done. Without great sacrifice, anyway.

Despite the surprise time-jump, however, Solace planned accordingly. Rather than launch a counterattack in what had been Marco's future, it simply moved out of the way, letting the hero fall to the ground, unsuccessful.

He stood back up, now five minutes ahead of schedule. The struts still rotated all around him, and R'Bec and Miguel were still inside along with him, still fighting the shadowy monster. He was glad to know that they had made it this far—two levers would already have been pulled by now, with the third less than a minute away.

"We've gotta get out of here, it's getting unstable!" R'Bec shouted.

"We can't leave, we have to keep it in here!" Shockdrop reasoned. "We're the only thing standing between it and freedom; we go down with the ship."

R'Bec's nose crinkled, and her eyes narrowed slightly. "Wrong. I've got another way."

The Telignen set her fingers deftly on that purple choker around her neck, before bringing both of her hands up to her temples. She closed her eyes, letting herself think more clearly.

Suddenly, as before, the space was filled and caked with that bushy, coarse black material. Beneath the surface of that darkness—which was still, somehow not so deep and voidlike as Solace itself—purple lights flickered and pulsed, moving about like blood through veins. Marco and Miguel were untouched by the substance, a ring around them marked as areas that the nightmarish slime could not impress upon. R'Bec, however, seemed to be trying to fight it off from her feet, as hands and teeth reached up to pitifully bite and grab her ankles.

Solace looked unfazed by the display of dark, alien power. Undisturbed. And its words confirmed it.

"Your abstractions of mental illness are nothing to me." Its voice was slow and exaggerated as ever, taking care to over-pronounce each syllable with a conceited pleasure. "I *am* insanity and nightmare. You cannot frighten me."

R'Bec did not verbally respond. Not to the floating horror, anyway. Instead, she shouted across the platform to Marco, letting her voice carry to Miguel as well some distance away. "Let's go! Get off!"

Her concise orders, though clear, did not fully register to Shatterbug. Why would they want to abandon the machine, and step out of the rings? Shockdrop had said it, and the time traveler agreed: they needed to keep Solace here, even if that meant laying down their own lives to do it.

Unless the illusionist had come up with another way.

Marco was not the leader. They were the First Mortal *Order*. A team; a group. Although he did not fully understand where R'Bec was intending to go with this course of action, he decided to trust her anyway. To have faith in himself as well as his friends.

"You heard her, *hermano*. Let's get outta here!" he said, smiling with pride and camaraderie beneath his helmet, which was reflected back in his friend's orange visor some twelve feet away.

Marco turned on his heel and started to run. His hesitation with stepping on the black-and-violet substance illuminating and concealing the metal floor turned out to be misplaced, for as his foot came down to meet it, the toothy fur parted for him, unwilling or unable to make contact. What limited control R'Bec had of her nightmare illusions was being spent on keeping the two marconium-powered heroes safe.

Solace tried to stop him. Tendrils came down like huge swords, attempting to stab into him from above. But each time, that grimy, glowing mess arced up from below—in the shape of an eagle or a lion or an ibex—blocking the dark entity's attack. The chaotic, violent expressions of the Telignen's imagination were stronger than her normal illusions, and although the impact clearly caused R'Bec some stress, forcing her to let out sharp

1

moans of pain for a moment or two, they held their own well enough against Solace's blunt, if honed, jabs.

Finally, Shatterbug found himself at the edge of the arena, protected from Solace by the horrific animals emerging from the glimmering black puss, but cautious nonetheless. The struts were spinning in front of him incredibly fast—thankfully, this created a barrier between Ramses and their opponent, but Marco was concerned that it would hold him inside, as well. They had entered while the machine was still warming up, but now it was at full speed.

Marco paused.

The machine was at full speed. But surely, a minute had passed since he'd time-jumped. How was the machine still going?

A smirk crept on his face. Their plan was working. The failsafes didn't matter anymore; the Multiverse Machine was confused, acting on its own without full understanding of its orders as directed by Bahadur and Osiris at the controls. If he could just step out, they might really do this.

But the decision was made for him.

As though both of his partners in the arena had thought the same thing, Marco found himself pushed out unprepared—first by a shockwave, and second by the gentle prodding of a fleshy tusk or antler.

In his peripheral vision, Shatterbug saw the next ring approaching from his right. He thought for certain that he would be sliced in two by the artificial speed of the thin metal strut, turning it from a blunt object into a blade. He winced preemptively.

Impact.

Marco's feet hit first. Then his hands, and helmet, until finally, his whole body was resting on the concrete floor, the wind knocked out of him.

He was safely on the ground, outside of the Multiverse Machine.

As he struggled to get up, catching his breath in his hoarse throat, he heard the familiar footsteps of armored boots and of flat, comfortable shoes. Once he gathered the strength to get to his knees, Marco saw the orange form of Miguel, and the leather make-believe clothes of R'Bec joining him.

Shockdrop turned the dial on his chest all the way down, then wrapped his hands beneath Shatterbug's arms to help him to his feet. Marco held his domed head with one hand, holding the other slightly out to steady himself.

But their battle was not over. He could still hear the slimy hiss of Solace inside the machine. And, indeed, the scaly hide of R'Bec's illusions scraping against the Telignen metal.

"Now what do we do?" Marco asked hurriedly, slurring each word into the next as his thoughts moved faster than his lips.

"We hold it in." R'Bec answered harshly, her focus mostly held on the black-and-purple lightshow. Very clearly, to Marco, she was trying to untense herself and keep her shoulders and face relaxed as she manipulated her physical nightmares. They arced up, groping and grabbing at the spinning rings at the edge of the raised platform for support. Strings of sharp saliva traced from one mass to another, pulling and merging them together as the material trailed upwards, off the ground. After a few moments, with the churning of the struts still audible beneath the web of horror, Solace found itself trapped in a dome of Telignen power.

347

A tentacle exploded outward from the enclosure, piercing the nightmare cage. Quickly, though, it was caught on something, and pulled back inside. Although R'Bec yelped in shock, the moment passed, and evidently, the illusion was repaired.

The shadowy psychopath was trapped in the Multiverse Machine.

But they still needed a way to destroy or kill it.

"Ramses, get down here!" Marco said, finally able to get to his feet, given some confidence and strength by the display.

Bahadur grabbed the golden ankh from the console on the stage, and leapt down to join the rest of the First Mortal Order, staring up at the ensnared Solace.

"Do we know this is gonna work?" Miguel asked idly, though still somewhat rushed by the intensity of the events unfolding before them.

After a moment, Bahadur responded, his voice collected, if uneasy. "Osiris is unsure. The failsafes appear to be failing, themselves, but whether the craft will actually travel is unclear."

Another pop of the pulsing violet web sounded, as Solace once again tried to break free from the prison, unsuccessfully. Still, it was enough to make R'Bec breath in harshly, her muscles tightening again in pain. "I can't hold this forever, boys." she said throatily, unable to help herself from gasping for air.

"So we have to make this count. We have to be sure." Marco said. "Can we destroy the machine together?"

"It is Telignen metal." Ramses reminded him. "It will not even yield to her illusions."

"Not her normal illusions," Miguel thought aloud. "But what about this stuff? It's stronger. Maybe she can tear it apart?"

Clearly struggling, R'Bec let just her eyes move to look at Shockdrop. "Not gonna happen. I'm the only thing keeping it from breaking out and killing us on the spot."

"But," Marco started. His mind was moving faster. Maybe it was the adrenaline, or the mortal terror. Maybe it was even a symptom of such frequent time traveling, and having to consider so much at any given moment. Or maybe, it was just the stupidity of a desperate man. Either way, a thought came to him. No; a number of thoughts all uniting into one. "What if we all do it? Together."

"What are you suggesting?" begged Al-Malik with some curiosity, after a brief moment which Marco assumed was spent conferring with Osiris.

Marco brought his hands together, wringing them, his fingers intertwining over each other, as he converted his collective ideas into digestible, communicable words. "If she can do it, then we can all do it. We'll have to work together, more than we've ever done. Bahadur, how big a portal can you make?"

"As great as we need." the Champion replied, holding the golden tool up as though showing it off.

"Okay, then on my signal, R'Bec: I want you to turn your illusions away from Solace and down at the machine. Start trying to rip it apart, just demolish it as best as you can. Ramses: you open up a portal wherever Solace tries to break out, turn it right back inside the rings. And Miguel," Shatterbug paused, holding his fist up in front of him, in solidarity, as he faced his best friend. "Get ready to punch me."

Miguel turned his head slightly, in sure confusion. But after a moment, both he and Bahadur nodded in understanding. Marco couldn't tell if the grunt from the Telignen was her nonverbal agreement, or a reaction to the pitch-black entity once again trying to escape her cage. Either way, it was now or never. Do or die time.

They all took their positions. Marco stood next to R'Bec, facing the Multiverse Machine. Shockdrop, behind him, clocked his suit's dial all the way up. Bahadur stood off to the side, at a good distance to see all the way around and through the domed area of the craft, perfectly centered beneath the glass dome atop the mountain. In the distance, Shatterbug saw a sliver of orange light peak out over the lowest crevice between two neighboring mountains. It was nearly morning again.

"Flicker!" Marco commanded. The Shatterbug suit whirred to life, vibrating constantly across his whole body. Plates shook on his spine, his shins, and his wrists, and the prime marconium burned in front of his chest. Inside his helmet, the visor flashed over and over, as the suit shattershocked and reconstituted continuously, jumping in and out of three different periods across ten minutes of time. At this point, with how much he had exhausted himself throughout the day, there was no doubt that he wouldn't be able to support this state for very long. But they only needed a few moments.

R'Bec, taking the sign, reacted in stride. She dropped her nightmarish substance from the dome, letting it drip and claw and smash down onto the platform of the Multiverse Machine. Her black sludge, dotted and streaked with violet lights beneath the surface, scraped and scratched at the Telignen metal, creating an awful, horrifying noise that reverberated in the round room. Twinkles, like cracking glass, rang in the back of Marco's head, but he ignored it, only intent on ensuring that the woman he was

350

proud to call his ally and friend was okay, as she used her power to rip at the perversion of her people's resources.

Solace, seeing that it was no longer barred egress from the transport, tried to leak out between the still-spinning hoops. However, it only found itself back under the metal struts that it had built, forced to stay and travel along with the machine it had killed for.

"What is this..." it howled, letting each word take a new pitch and tone as it slowly came to realize what was happening. "You cannot destroy the Multiverse Machine; you cannot trap me in here; you cannot stop the Master of All Realities!"

"Evidently Solace, *we* can." Shatterbug said quietly, though proudly. In which time he replied to the cosmic horror, he didn't know. But, it didn't matter—the line had been mostly for his own benefit. "Shockdrop, *now*!"

Somehow—whether by expert planning and timing, or sheer dumb luck—Miguel punched Marco in the back with full force, and despite the flickering, time-jumping invulnerable state that Shatterbug was in, the attack landed. Shockwaves burst from the hero's fist, sending Marco flying across the room. He was moving so quickly, and was on the ground for so little time in each instance of time, that he felt no friction of the concrete against his boots, felt no loss of momentum from the air pushing against him. He just moved, straight ahead, with fist extended towards the Multiverse Machine.

As he hurtled ever closer, he noticed that R'Bec had succeeded. She broke through the outer layer of the Telignen metal, opened a hole in the mesh exterior and, specifically, in the wall that Shatterbug was currently lined up to fly into. He closed his eyes, letting the power of his friend, and the combined strength and efforts of the First Mortal Order, carry him.

Impact.

With a thousand reconstitutions—with the force of ten minutes of time colliding, over and over again—Marco's fist met the internal machinery of Solace's device all across time. In a flash—indeed, in infinite flashes—the whole of the structure was destabilized. Marco felt his body meet with the fuzzy, hardened shape of R'Bec's nightmares, which immediately vanished. Still flickering, he fell to the ground, and along with him, the sharp explosion of millions of sparkles rang out.

"Fade." Marco said, just barely loud enough for the suit to hear him, his energy spent.

The time traveler let himself rest for a moment. Unconcerned with whether they had succeeded, not sure whether he was even safe. He just lied there, on the concrete ground, listening to the crunch of movement around him.

After a few seconds—or perhaps they were minutes—Marco opened his eyes.

Through the blue hue of his visor, he noticed that the floor was shining. There was something on the concrete, like twinkling grains of polished sand.

Oh, that was it. The dome had broken. He was surrounded by sharp, shattered glass.

Carefully, brushing away a spot on the ground, he pushed his weight up on his palms, coming to a push-up position. He tucked his legs under him, coming to sit on his feet, as he looked up and around him.

The cool, thin air felt nice, even through the Shatterbug suit. The sun had come up a little more now, turning the black mountain range into a dark, navy blue. A glimmer of yellow had begun to peek over the horizon, expanding that orange light that was once a sliver to a whole corner of the sky.

More crunches put Marco on alert, the hair on the back of his neck tingling against the meshy undersuit of his armor. Footsteps on broken glass.

He turned his head a little, being careful not to move his body too much over the million tiny daggers that poked up from the floor.

First, he noticed his friends. Miguel, R'Bec, and Bahadur. They stood over him—although like him, R'Bec was clearly exhausted, and both the other two men had an arm not quite around her waist, but nearby and prepared to catch her. They looked down at him, and the Egyptian man let his other hand—still holding Osiris' ankh—come down in offering for Marco to take.

Before he did so, though, he noticed a second thing. The Multiverse Machine was gone. Solace was gone. There were no loose, broken pieces of Telignen metal around, no scraps of machinery or fragments of impossible blackness. Everything was gone. The room—the open-air, mountaintop terrace—was empty, but for those simple machines at the edge of the room, and a small safe along with them.

"We got it, Marco." Miguel said proudly. "Visor off."

"Visor off." Shatterbug echoed, taking the Champion's offered hand and letting him pull him to his feet. "We... we really won."

353

S

"We did. It is over." Bahadur confirmed, smiling with the radiance of a hero, and somehow, of a hidden divinity. He was holding something. A small bag was draped over his shoulder, but Marco didn't look too closely at it, still caught up in the moment.

R'Bec coughed, bringing one hand to her neck—and to the choker that was now restored around it—to catch herself. "We did our job. Solace is gone."

Bahadur took Marco and R'Bec's hands, and she in turn took Miguel's. Although the ankh was caught between two different palms, the Champion of Osiris was still able to call upon his patron's power. A green energy surrounded the First Mortal order as Bahadur prepared to teleport them away from that place of evil.

As the last of Marco's vision turned from the beauty of the Canadian mountain range, a thought crossed through his mind, but just as soon as the idea had come to him, it was forgotten. In a pop, it seemed almost as though it were left behind at the top of the bunker.

Marco blinked.

Epilogue

For some reason, Bahadur felt a subconscious need to bring along the final pieces of Osiris personally, rather than send them off with the ankh's dimensional abilities.

The God's—the ancient human's—brain, head, and throat, stolen by the Sect of the Golden Scepter and abused by the necromancer Jet Wicked, all under the order of Solace, had been sitting atop the mountain, under the now-shattered glass dome. Ramses had sensed them in the safe there, and once he retrieved them, it did not seem right to simply cast them back to the tomb.

No, he needed to carry them there. He needed to present them to the sarcophagus.

Bahadur Al-Malik didn't know what was going to happen. The true nature of Osiris had been steeped in allegory and transformed by the wear of time, and he suspected that this ritual had done, too. Osiris would not be literally resurrected. He would not literally give birth to Horus, a God and Pharaoh. And, he would not literally move on to the afterlife. But the Champion had sworn an oath to serve the artificial intelligence—that approximation of the man once called Osiris—and he would see it through.

However, in acknowledgement of his other oath, he would not do so alone.

Bahadur stood in the tomb of Osiris, kneeling and facing the stone dais and, on the back wall the sarcophagus which contained the assembled pieces of the long-dead Pharaoh, short three. Behind him, the three friends he had made only a day ago.

In full uniform, Shatterbug and Shockdrop, as well as the alien woman R'Bec, were in attendance. They volunteered to see the fruition of Ramses' quest. He assumed that, to a certain extent, they were here to ensure that Osiris was indeed who he claimed to be—that he would not become some new threat for the First Mortal Order to face together, and that he would not kill Bahadur as Senility Acolyte had cautioned—but, the Champion hoped that to at least the same degree, they were here to support a friend. After all, he saw all of them as his friends. How could he not, after all the four of them had been through?

He opened the bag to present the pieces of Osiris. His ankh set in its place on the stone dais, glowing and active for all to hear the digitized human speak.

"*Ramses. Champion of Osiris. Bahadur Al-Malik.*" that perfect, divine voice began. In Bahadur's head, it spoke fluent Arabic—his native language—in a beautiful cadence. However, he knew for a fact that the Mexican-American men, and the otherworldly woman behind him, could understand the God-Pharaoh, too. A convenience of being an incorporeal computer consciousness. "*Relinquish the final body parts, and restore my remains.*"

Ramses removed the two mummified pieces from their canvas bag, carefully setting them on the stone floor. He briefly watched the new shadows dance on the sandstone, cast by the flickering, eternal torches on the walls to either side, before reaching into the bag and carefully gripping the stone urn left within. He set that, too, beside the other parts.

356

"Many Ramses have served me. They gathered what pieces they could. But none have ever recovered so many as you. And now, that legendary line ends, with you." The green aura surrounding the loop of the golden ankh shone brighter, enveloping the three pieces of Osiris with its light. In a flash, they vanished. The urn reappeared beside the sarcophagus, though Bahadur knew that it was now empty. *"With my rotted body whole, once again, I shall read from it the instructions laid out within its structure, and Horus will be born."*

The ankh once again spilled bright green power, which erupted from the cracks of the sarcophagus as well. For the first time to Bahadur's eyes, the orange torches were challenged for their right as bringers of light within the tomb by the overpowering radiance of Osiris' dimensional magic. Because that, in the end, was what all this was. Regardless of the name one gave it, no matter what sciences one could boil it down to, it was astounding—it was magic to Ramses.

And then, something curious began to happen. Something frightening. Bahadur Al-Malik began to glow green. That energy which Osiris wielded through the ankh surrounded and warmed Bahadur. His back grew tense. His head felt protected. His arms became swathed in strength and heat. The Champion found himself carried into the air. And from the sounds of it, his friends behind him were unsure how to react.

"Bahadur, are you okay?" Marco's voice was rushed, and the sound of rustling armor told Bahadur that the time traveler had taken a more active position, likely with his legs spread apart and one fist held out, prepared to strike if necessary.

The shadows of twin swords stretched along the stone bricks of the tomb, informing Al-Malik that R'Bec had conjured weapons preemptively. "He betrayed you, didn't he? Osiris lied!" the Telignen accused.

"No, no. I am alright." Ramses reassured his companions, easing their stress. His voice was relaxed, if uneasy as a result of the floating. "I am safe, I *feel* safe."

After a few moments, the Champion of Osiris was let down. That green power faded away, all across his body. The room was once again lit only by the ceaseless flame of the wall torches. Although that light from the golden ankh remained, it was dimming.

But, after all had cooled, Bahadur still felt different. Warmed. Strong. Gifted.

He looked at his arms. They were covered now, and not by his light-armored attire. Golden braces hugged his forearms, and matching, shining pauldrons covered his shoulders. A black cape extended down from them to his lower back, where it met golden armor that surrounded his abdomen and thighs. Shin guards glimmered in the torchlight, matching the rest of his getup before they became short, gold boots. Finally, on his head, a grandiose helmet. He touched it—his fingers now adorned with six sparkling rings—to find that it was in the shape of a bird, the beak coming down just above his forehead and out some, like a cowl.

"*Bahadur Al-Malik. Your service, your loyalty, and your faith is rewarded. I cannot carry on in this world anymore. I do not need to.*" Osiris' thoughts once again permeated Bahadur's mind, although even that perfect, humbling sound was fading along with the light of the ankh. "*It has always been prophesied that I would birth Horus, to serve as the hero for this world and protect it from darkness. However, it seems that even my people were not so exceptional at interpreting myth and allegory.*

"You *are a hero.* You *have protected this world from darkness, and with this First Mortal Order, I predict that you will continue to strive to do so, and that you will succeed. Although I cannot offer you the power of the ankh any longer, you will find that this world—and all worlds—are not left undefended. You are no longer my Champion, no longer a Ramses. I bestow upon you the name and title of Horus."*

The energy glowed within the ankh's loop for another few moments, before it gave out. And, along with it, Horus felt the presence of the artificial intelligence leave his mind, and those of his friends.

He turned around, to stand before Shatterbug, Shockdrop, and R'Bec, for the first time, as Horus.

The implications were astronomical, and yet at the same time, they were so clear to him in that moment. No longer was he bound by duty to Osiris. No longer was there any question; he was a hero. He was these peoples' friend. And together, they *were* the First Mortal Order.

About the Author

Robert grew up in Phoenix, Arizona, where he began imagining unique stories of superheroes and villains in fantastic tales told orally to his friends and family.

For nearly eight years, these characters remained only in his head before he took to writing down the first adventures of the universe he had crafted, taking extra care in the realism of both the science-fiction aspects as well as in the emotion and psychology of people at their most powerful—and most vulnerable.

Starting with *Shatterbug*, he hopes to tell a wide-reaching story to unite and inspire people, not under one common ideal of what the world should be like, but against the shared understanding of what the world should not be.

Robert currently lives in Phoenix, Arizona, happily back at home in the desert.

Find Robert on Facebook and Twitter: @RobDukeOfficial

www.ingramcontent.com/pod-product-compliance
Lightning Source LLC
Chambersburg PA
CBHW030401180626
46812CB00005B/1876